MELINDA M. SNODGRASS

FINAL CIRCUIT

ACE BOOKS, NEW YORK

This book is an Ace
original edition, and has
never been previously
published.

FINAL CIRCUIT

An Ace Book/published by arrangement with
the author

PRINTING HISTORY
Ace edition/May 1988

ISBN: 0-441-22876-3

Ace Books are published by The Berkley Publishing Group,
200 Madison Avenue, New York, New York 10016.
The name "ACE" and the "A" logo
are trademarks belonging to Charter Communications, Inc.

PRINTED IN THE UNITED STATES OF AMERICA

10 9 8 7 6 5 4 3 2 1

Acknowledgments

A number of people helped me create this book. I'd like to single out for special thanks Laura Mixon, who loaned me all her books on Kenya, and generously shared her experiences of that country. Victor Milán, who patiently listened to me ramble when I'd get stuck, and helped me design the space battles. And Fred Ragsdale, with whom I enjoyed several long conversations concerning the American Revolution and its lessons for the present. Finally I would like to mention a book that greatly influenced the direction of this novel: *Endless Enemies: The Making of an Unfriendly World* by Jonathan Kwitny.

Dedication

This book is for Laura.
With much love and many thanks.

Chapter One

"Allahu Akbar!"

The words, enormously amplified, rumbled across the seared sands of the Riyadh Space Port. Scurrying ground cars froze, and spilled their drivers like raisins tumbling from a box. A few continued running, obviously manned by unbelievers who continued with their work, but throughout most of the enormous complex it was time to render unto God.

There were fourteen people in the lounge in addition to the knot of seven Kenyans huddled near the windows. Mostly Arab and East Indian businessmen, and there was much hacking and rustling as the Arabs and a few of the Indians settled onto the carpeted floor. Two of the Kenyans also faced Mecca, and joined in morning prayer. Wairegi wa Thondu touched forehead to floor, and rocked back on his heels, catching Viriku Amani's look of disapproval. The woman's militant atheism together with her Luo pride and defensiveness made her a difficult companion. But she had skills they needed. And Wairegi found her beautiful: broad shouldered, skin like polished jet, and her hands—strong and capable, all that a woman should be. . . .

He joined raggedly into the traditional response, "Labbaika allahumma labbaika." *I am here, God, at your command,* and castigated himself for being distracted by the carnal.

The ancient phrase flowed easily off the tongue, years of repetition making the foreign words comfortable, even reassuring. His earliest memories were of praying with his father. Feeling safe as much by the presence of that large figure as by the holy words. And now as Wairegi embarked upon a

1

great undertaking he needed the comfort of his God. Let Viriku sneer.

Paul, James, J.K., and Cyril smoked in silence as the two Moslems finished their prayers, but Viriku, with one final disgusted glance, stared out the large picture windows at the Long Range Shuttle. On the horizon shimmers of heat undulated like outriders for the rising sun. The great glowing ball burst over the top of the dunes, striking white marble brilliance from the minaret looming in the west beyond the shuttle. The high-orbit vehicle seated with snub-nosed dignity on its tail seemed to be imitating the slender minaret. *Ancient god versus representative of the new technological deity.* It made a compelling picture, and she wished she had her camera.

Wairegi climbed to his feet, ran a hand across his hair. He was older than his six companions who watched him with serious, unblinking gazes. He was a big man, the sharp planes of his face and the athlete's body becoming blurred under a layer of fat. But it was a compelling face, and his wide-set black eyes held a shadow of grief which drew onlookers, making them want to ask for what he mourned. He was dressed in a well-tailored Western suit, the gray of the cloth picking up the highlights from his silver sprinkled hair. It was unusual to see a Kenyan of his age with graying hair, and it added to his charisma.

Paul, James, Kariuki, J.K., and Cyril watched him with secret, hooded eyes. Whites would have called their faces impassive, but Wairegi read the fear and tension, and gave them a confident nod. Viriku, standing slightly apart from the men, rejected his comfort and reassurance. No trace of fear shadowed her broad, intense face, and her eyes burned with an anger which Wairegi had never seen extinguished. There was something fey (in the traditional definition of the word) about her, and wa Thondu wished again that there had been some other pilot available. But Viriku was the best and the brightest, according to her professors at MIT. All Wairegi could hope was to keep that anger in check, shape her into a weapon to fit the hand, rather than an out of control missile just as likely to blow her friends as her enemies to kingdom come.

"I find it quite incredible that you can grovel toward Mecca when it was our Arab conquerors who sold our black asses into slavery."

"And some of our own tribal leaders," Wairegi responded wearily. "Better add them into your litany of hate. It's ancient history, Viriku. Let's concentrate on the woes of the present."

He dropped heavily into one of the thickly upholstered chairs, and felt his body sag with weariness. He had been three days without rest, and it was starting to tell on him. His hands rubbed nervously across the padded arms of the chair. In any other major space port the decor was all steel and chrome and hard, unyielding plastic, but in Riyadh the Arab fascination with Western comfort still held sway. A land where the ruling family still trundled into the desert in antique ground-driven Cadillacs and Rolls-Royces to go hawking would have Victorian armchairs in their space port, he mused.

The smoke from his companions' cigarettes tickled at his nostrils, and unleashed an explosion of nicotine craving. Doggedly he pulled a packet of gum from his coat pocket, and crammed the sweet stick into his mouth. The sugary taste at five in the morning was faintly nauseating, but it beat another heart attack. One was enough for any man's lifetime. Unfortunately he might live to enjoy a second. There had been no time after his disordered flight from Kenya to have the diseased heart replaced.

Viriku tugged fretfully at the scarf which covered her short-cropped black hair, and finally pulled it off. Wairegi frowned at her.

"We're almost out of Saudi Arabia," she said defensively.

Wairegi glanced at the waiting shuttle. "Not for another hour, and I don't want any trouble. Wear the scarf."

"What a dump," the woman muttered under her breath, viciously knotting back on the scarf. He wondered if she were referring to the space port, the country, or the world in general.

Let her fret, he thought irritably. He had chosen the Riyadh port because of the bribability of most Arab officials, and because he sensed he would find at least understanding and possibly approval for his plans. He only hoped his instincts would prove to be correct.

The door marked "Admin" opened, and a slender, elderly Saudi stepped into the lounge. Wairegi straightened in the chair. The man stared at him from hooded eyes, ran a hand across his perfectly trimmed spade beard, and gave an imperceptible nod. Wa Thondu felt his knees go weak, and his belly turned to water. *It was done!* He pushed out of the chair, and hurried into the men's room.

A few moments later, face dripping with water, he raised his head from the basin, and regarded his image in the mirror. The first step had been achieved. The others would be easier—more dangerous perhaps—but easier.

"The vote of the House being four hundred and thirty-five for versus one hundred and fifteen against, the motion of impeachment is passed. The matter of the impeachment of Justice Cabot Huntington is now passed to the Senate for trial," the clerk of the House of Representatives added unnecessarily for the benefit of the cameras, and the millions of breathless viewers who he imagined lay beyond them.

"Wish the *Post* had never referred to Stanley's winning personality and warmth on camera," grunted Stephen Goggans of Minnesota, heaving up out of his desk. "Now he thinks he's a video personality. Too bad about your nephew," he added as he unclipped his microphone, and dropped the tiny chip into his coat pocket.

"Yes," Anthony Huntington replied in a colorless voice.

"They'll nail him this time. Won't be any providential election to save him."

"Stephen, your commentary on the probable fate of my nephew is of course enthralling, but, I would venture to suggest, a bit premature. The Senate still has to try him, and I hope that the august members of the upper house will have more sense than this three-ring circus."

Goggans shot him a pitying and irritated glance. The famed Huntington arrogance and acid tongue had been clearly in evidence, and most members of the House had learned to fear and resent both.

Anthony frankly didn't give a damn if he'd offended the Congressman from Minnesota. He strode quickly across the floor of the House, a small, somewhat portly figure, and through the door leading to the Majority cloakroom. His brother, Senator Neville Huntington, was waiting for him, ignoring the curious glances being cast in his direction. It was unusual to find a member of the upper house on the House side of the Capitol. But of course with the renewed attempt to impeach Justice Cabot Huntington, it wasn't too surprising.

Neville was a more exotic replica of his younger brother. Where Anthony's thinning hair was an undistinguished shade of brown, Neville's swept back in a series of thick, golden waves from a high, white forehead. He had also kept his figure, something Anthony attributed to his elder's as yet inchoate ambition to be president.

"So you couldn't stem the tide."

"It was hopeless." Anthony pulled his small pocket computer from his breast pocket, and deleted the speech he had prepared in opposition to the impeachment. "I spent hours polishing those elegant periods." He shrugged.

"You were wise not to speak. With emotions in this town running this high it would have looked like blatant favoritism if you'd come to Cabot's defense."

"We're going to have to take a stand somewhere."

"And I'll do it, but it will take several weeks, months maybe, before this thing comes before the Senate. Tempers will cool, and who knows, something remarkable might happen."

"I have it on the best authority that Lis Varllis is in excellent health," said Anthony, holding the outer door for his brother.

"Damn the woman," Neville began, then cut off abruptly when he saw the crowd of reporters clustered like crows on the east stairs.

They dove forward, and Neville slipped a relaxed, welcoming smile onto his lips.

"Morning, fellows, ladies."

"Do you have a reaction to the House's vote this morning, Senator?"

"Well, naturally I'm not delighted by the outcome, but by the same token it will give the Senate a chance to take up this matter, and then the truth will be heard."

"Are you implying that the White House has lied about the events on Mars?"

"No, what I'm *saying* is that you fellows in the fourth estate have a tendency to print and broadcast whatever is given to you, and I think that in such a confused situation the facts can be . . . er, shaded. I'm confident that once the events on Mars are scrutinized under the harsh glare of a Senate trial that my nephew will be completely vindicated." He linked arms with Anthony, and started down the steps.

"Are we witnessing a family war council, Senator?"

"Oh, no, not yet. Meredith still hasn't arrived." Laughter

met this sally. "And here he is," added Neville as a taxi landed neatly beside the steps. "Good day, gentlemen, ladies."

"Hell of a mess," remarked Meredith Huntington as the taxi lifted neatly into the traffic grid.

"I would call that something of an understatement," responded Neville dryly. "What did you learn from State?"

"Well, it's not as easy as it used to be having been banished into the wilderness—so to speak—by the entrance of the opposition into the White House—"

"Finding being a professor of international affairs a bit too limiting in scope?" broke in Anthony.

"Yes, but we'll hope it's a momentary setback. We should be able to regain the White House next time."

"But you were saying," Neville said with a quelling frown to both his brothers.

"Ah, yes. Well, the feeling throughout State and Justice seems to be pretty evenly divided. With perhaps just a hair's weight more support for the administration. And I can't say I blame them. This semi-anarchy which the System seems determined to practice is threatening proper authority. I can't understand what's come over Cab."

"Male menopause," grunted Anthony.

"Whatever, he's still our nephew, and a Huntington, and I'm not going to stand by and see one of our own disgraced and removed from office," snapped Neville with some heat.

"Is that for the family's sake or for Cab's or for your own ambitions?" Meredith asked smoothly, but with a hint of malice in his voice.

"Just because you've never amounted—" Anthony began.

"All of the above," put in Neville before his brothers could get down to serious bickering.

With only a year separating them Neville and Anthony had always been close, but Meredith, nine years younger than Gerard and four years older than Neville, had always been the odd man out. And his career had been something of a disappointment. He had wanted to be an elder statesman, an adviser to presidents, a geopolitical player on a grand scale, and it had never happened. Neville wondered wearily if . . . *if* he became president whether he should select Meredith as NSC director. He forced such thoughts aside, and returned to the aggravating matter of Cabot.

"Now that the impeachment is a reality we'll have to retain an attorney for Cabot, and get him the hell home."

"Hadn't we better leave that to Cabot?" inquired Meredith. "He may want to select his own attorney."

"And what about Gerard?" Anthony asked, bringing Cab's father and their eldest brother into the discussion.

"What about him?" Neville raised a pair of winged eyebrows.

"You know he's out of touch with everything," added Meredith.

"Still, he's our brother."

"Relax, little brother, I've already talked to Cecilia, and she's mustering the international troops."

"Such a waste," Anthony shook his head over the incomprehensible behavior of their eldest. "He could have been a senator by now."

"And Cabot seems to share, at least to some extent, his father's peculiar attitudes."

"He is a federal court judge, Neville."

"Paltry! When he had both Anthony and me, not to mention Mother—who was still governor of Massachusetts—ready to support him in a bid for the House."

"Different strokes for different folks," said Meredith and earned a sour look from the Senator.

"Well, let's just hope his peculiarities don't drive him to ignore our advice. I personally would recommend Saxon for his defense. He has experience in Washington, and he knows which wheels to grease."

"Saxon, hmm, I hadn't considered him."

"Neville, before we warlocks of Endor continue this discussion, could we please decide on a restaurant? I'm starving."

"Anthony," said Meredith. "You have no sense of history."

The subject of all the discussion also had no sense of history. Three months after the calamitous events on Mars, Cabot Huntington, federal court justice of the Fifteenth Circuit Court of the United States, had begun to think that nothing was going to happen. He had left Mars a hunted fugitive, fleeing an arrest warrant on charges of shielding a felon, and later—after the shoot-out at Eagle Port—of inciting rebellion.

And after that . . . nothing. The deep-space squadron had not been ordered in pursuit, but had remained on Mars to "maintain order"; the Earthside press apart from an occasional squeal of outrage had lost interest in him and the

System; and Lis Varllis, the powerful and autocratic White House Chief of Staff, had maintained (at least to Cab's mind) an ominous silence.

For the two months after his and Jenny's arrival in the Belt, he had hung close to Ceres waiting for the other shoe to drop. It had been nervous work, and had laid a strain on his and Jenny's relationship. But as the weeks passed, and still no word came out of Earth, they both began to relax. Cab found the troglodyte existence beneath the surface of the largest asteroid to be depressing and confining, so between hearing cases he had begun tagging along with the Belt's few physicians when they made "rock calls" on the outlying miners.

Cab felt a certain sense of pride over these excursions for it meant he had finally overcome the stomach-wrenching free fall sickness which had held him in its grip during his first weeks in the Belt. There was an experimental grav unit being tested within the colony, but it had a disconcerting habit of cutting out at inconvenient times. It also always took days to repair, and during those times Cab had remained huddled in his bunk puking his guts out. Stinson White, the unacknowledged leader of the Ceres colony, and Joe Reichart, renegade Earth industrialist, had shaken their heads over the judge, and had even murmured about the necessity of returning him to Mars or even Earth if his condition did not improve. With that spur to recovery Cabot found that the sickness began to subside, and for the past month he had been scooting about the tiny fraction of the Belt where men did hold sway. He had learned to space walk, rock crawl, and to pilot one of the tiny craft which served to link the tiny planetoids whirling along between the orbits of Mars and Jupiter carrying in their barren interiors a fragile cargo of human life.

He was at present squeezed, along with a load of medical supplies, bags of clothing, and replacement machine parts, into the back of one of the hospital Curvets. Up front Dr. Cassie Sanchez and her assistant Luther Stokes occupied the only seats, and Stokes maintained a careful lookout while the doctor piloted the tiny craft.

Since Jenny had fallen victim to the flu bug which was presently romping gleefully through the colony Cab had made this excursion alone. He sat with his back against a duffel bag stuffed with clothes, and one of the wall wraps hooked over his shoulders to hold him in place.

"Coming in on Ledawig's rock." Sanchez's voice echoed over his helmet radio. "You should move forward and take a look. The sculptures are best appreciated on approach."

Cab released the wraps and floated off the floor. Aside from the fact that the floor of the craft was littered with boxes and bales making walking difficult, the judge had learned one lesson during his months in the Belt—why walk when you can fly? With a twisting motion he caught one of the ceiling handholds, swam forward, bounced back to the floor, stuck, and peered over the heads of his companions out the curving front window of the tiny Curvet.

The asteroid before them was typical. An irregular hunk of rock perhaps three miles in length, and a mile across. It was shaped rather like a trowel. Cab felt a gentle pressure through the soles of his sticky boots as the braking jets fired.

The rock loomed closer, and dotted among the craters and fissures which pocked the surface they saw the statues. Twisted, mournful shapes, they reached for the icy blackness above them, or huddled in upon themselves, like visions of anguish.

The Curvet closed on the rock, landing jets throwing up a whirlwind of tiny pebbles. Directly before them, blocking the path to the tattered pressure dome, stood a madman's vision of religion. Nearly ten feet high the figure's torso was fashioned from several large plastic packing crates. Enormous pipes formed the legs, and covering all were thousands of carefully trimmed bits of metal creating an illusion of ragged armor. Flexible tubing formed the arms which were held before the statue's breast in an attitude of prayer. Between its fingers looped twisted multicolored wire strung with gaily colored balls, and a large cross fashioned from pieces of some unidentifiable detritus.

"Good God!" Cab exclaimed. "The Colossus of Rhodes disguised as the Pope." Through the curving window of the Curvet the statue's eyes, fashioned from the telescope lenses, peered mournfully at the interlopers.

"Ledawig's got a . . . er, a rather unusual view of reality."

"Ledawig's a nut," Luther said bluntly, showing no patience with the good doctor's delicate turn of phrase.

Sanchez cut the engines, gathered up her medical kit, and headed for the lock. "Oh, don't unseal in the dome. The thing leaks like a sieve, and the air pressure's about equal to what you'd find in the high Andes. Emery's used to it, but you'd go down like a pole-axed ox if you try."

They cycled through the airlock, and dropped lightly to the surface of the asteroid. As on most asteroids, even the relative giant Ceres, there was virtually no sensation of weight, and without sticky boots the three visitors would have bounced like India rubber balls.

They went skimming along in that distinctive style known in the Belt as "rock crawling," past the prayerful statue endlessly telling its beads, and up to the dome entrance. Luther, towing two large tanks of oxygen, headed around the dome, while the others entered. Cab held back slightly as the inner door sighed open. A nut Mr. Ledawig might be, but the judge thought it showed a singular lack of courtesy to not even appraise him of their arrival before entering.

But one glance at the confusion which held sway within the confines of the dome, and Cab reevaluated. A man who could live in this junk dealer's vision of Nirvana wouldn't care if people entered unannounced. Every imaginable type of garbage had been gathered into irregular piles. An ancient space suit hung by its neck seal looking rather like a newly executed corpse hoisted high for the titillation and moral edification of the masses.

Two tables bisected the circle of the dome, one covered with shop tools, the other with mounds of dirty plastic plates all encrusted with unidentifiable bits of dreck. Cab swallowed hard, and wondered how the scarecrow figure huddled on the gray sheets of a cot and seriously regarding them managed to survive. What little air remained within the dome probably had the consistency and odor of rancid wool socks.

Sanchez switched from radio to voice speaker. "Emery, we've brought your supplies, and Stinson tells me you haven't been feeling too well." Cassie lifted Ledawig's emaciated arm, and pressed a pulse and pressure reader against the inside of his elbow.

Cab forced himself to look at the pitiful figure. The fact Ledawig was clad only in dirty undershorts made it somehow worse. The judge shook his head, bewildered but also respectful of Dr. Sanchez's matter-of-fact acceptance of the squalor surrounding her, and her gentle interest in her patient.

Emery Ledawig's overly bright eyes darted between them as he picked up the threads of the spirited conversation he had been holding with himself. Fortunately it seemed to have at least some bearing on Dr. Sanchez's opening remark.

"The body is nothing. It's the mind, ah, yes, the mind."

The words were muffled, filtered as they were by their helmets. "Mine has a mind of its own, you know." This was directed to Cab with that bright, confiding air one often finds in a particularly precocious child.

"Oh?" the judge managed.

"Oh, yes. It watches me, and I sometimes have a devil of a time keeping it in line. It wants to misbehave. The essential elements of the mind are color and contrast."

"He thinks his head is a vid set," Cab muttered, once more back on radio.

Cassie shussed him.

"Emery, you should move back to Earth, or at least to Ceres," she said, continuing her examination.

"Oh, no, I couldn't do that. My work you know. And it"—he tapped his skull significantly, and a few wisps of thinning, stringy gray hair caught on the roughened skin of his finger—"hasn't fulfilled its agenda. When the tableau is completed, all reality will be revealed. The mind knows."

Cassie slid an injection beneath the jaundiced, flaccid skin of his upper arm. "Yes, Emery. I'm leaving you more pills. See to it you take them."

"I will, oh, I will." He unfolded, and tottered away from the cot. "And who is this delightful boy you brought to visit me?"

Cab started. At forty-three he was not accustomed to being classified as a boy. But from Ledawig's perspective maybe he was.

"Justice Cabot Huntington."

"How do you do," Cab said as Ledawig's clawlike hand closed about his glove.

"Charmed." The old lunatic gave him a smile of heartbreaking sweetness. "You must come again soon. We do so enjoy company. How did you find the statues?"

"Remarkable," Cab said gently. "You have an extraordinary talent. It's a shame that people back on Earth are unaware of the work you're doing out here. You should go back, and arrange for a showing."

"Not just yet. The tableau must be complete if the message is to be understood. Good-bye," the sculptor said abruptly, and turning his back on them began pawing through one of the junk mounds.

Sanchez indicated the lock with a jerk of the head, and they left.

"Nice try, Judge."

"I had to say something. That man is dying."

"Yes, malnutrition, radiation, oxygen deprivation. I'd say it's a testament to the power of the soul that he's lived this long." They stood silent watching Luther lope toward them. "And you're still upset."

"Yes."

"Lots of people die out here."

"But not needlessly, in a kind of slow suicide. Back on Earth he'd be committed."

The doctor swung around. "Yes, but this is the Belt, and out here a man is permitted to go to the devil any way he likes as long as it doesn't endanger anyone else."

"Doctor, so far I've found most of you System dwellers to be admirable on a good many levels, but you all share a most annoying habit."

She settled her hands on her hips, and glared belligerently out at him from behind the faceplate. "Which is?"

"Every remark, no matter how innocent, is a signal for you to pull out the soapboxes."

She fell in with his long floating stride. "I sense a core in you that's still of Earth."

He stopped, reached up, and rested a gloved hand against the curving side of the Curvet. Closed his eyes and remembered. The boom and hiss of the surf on the beach beneath his house. The warm scent of horses and alfalfa, the bite of snow on his cheeks as he leaned on his poles and gazed out across Switzerland's peaks.

"I miss a lot from home. Earth holds such beauty."

"And we don't?" Luther asked as he joined them.

"Yes, of course. But it's almost too much, too overwhelming. We're like squeaking ghosts flitting around the skirts of eternity out here." His companions jumped into the lock. "And as you pointed out, it's too damn easy to die out here." He took one final glance back toward the praying statue, then sighed, and climbed aboard.

They made three more stops. Each one was punctuated by a meal and a long sleep period. Cab, like most of the Earthborn, had a Hollywood view of the Asteroid Belt. Swarms of the little planetoids all swirling about the Solar System. In fact the settled rocks were widely separated, and a rock call took several days. At each stop they off-loaded cargo, handled minor first-aid problems, vaccinated children, and gave physical exams. Thankfully they walked into no full-blown emergencies. Cab missed Jenny, and he didn't want to be stuck in the midst of a crisis.

That's why he was piloting as the Curvet boosted toward Ceres' dark, crater-pocked surface. As if his presence at the controls could push the craft to greater speed. The sun was an intensely brilliant point just rising over the curve of the tiny world.

"Without beginning, middle, or end, of infinite power,
Of infinite arms, whose eyes are the moon and the sun,
I see Thee, whose face is flaming fire,
Burning this whole universe with Thy radiance,"

murmured Cab softly.

"Huh?" demanded Luther, hanging behind them.

"It's from the Bhagavad Gita, the manifestation of Krisna in his glory. I always think of it when I see sunrise out here."

"Judge, you are one weird 'hom."

Ceres was the throw point for all ore leaving the Belt so the asteroid did look like a filmmaker's image of an asteroid belt. Or a shark surrounded by pilot fish, Cab thought as he studied the hundreds of chunks of ore set in orbit around the tiny world. Workers swarmed over these bits of vomit from the guts of other worlds, fixing boosters—nuclear bombs really—to their surfaces. Once the trajectories were calculated they would be fired, and the rocks would begin their long looping journeys back to Earth. There they would be snagged by the orbiting stations, smelted, and the processed ore would be sent on to Earth or the Moon or used to build another station, or to complete one of the five new deep-space ships currently under construction by the Air Force.

It was an awesome display of technological genius, and Cabot revised the thought he had had on Ledawig's rock. Maybe man wasn't just flitting about the skirts of eternity, but actually grabbing her hem, and tugging. Despite himself he felt a surge of pride for his species.

The Curvet nosed into one of the three navigation lanes, and Cab settled it softly onto a landing platform. If Ceres had been a standard asteroid it would never have been selected as the primary sight for human colonization in the Belt. It was just too damn big. With the energy to dollars ratio for every liftoff, it made no sense to settle on a rock of its size. But Ceres was not a standard asteroid. Instead, the dark surface was feet thick with hydrocarbons and large amounts of trapped ice, which made for an easy supply of fuel and material. So Ceres had become the hub for business, art, medicine, and schooling for the entire Belt.

The hum of giant hydraulics vibrated through the skin of the ship as the Curvet was lowered into the shuttle bay. A small cart pulled up, hooked onto the drag, and towed the Curvet into its parking space. Cab waved his thanks, and the suited figure on the cart gave him a thumbs up.

"Home again." Doctor Sanchez unsnapped her belts, rose, and stretched. "God it'll be good to get out of this suit."

Cab found himself thinking longingly of Jenny and a hot shower, and not necessarily in that order. He forced himself to stay long enough to thank the doctor for including him on the run, then climbed down the ladder, and headed at a quick trot for the access lock. It felt strange to again be at Earth-normal gravity, but he cynically wondered how long it would last. At least through his shower he hoped. The grav unit had failed during his first week on Ceres, and he had had the dubious pleasure of watching while the spray went in all directions, the water congealing into individual droplets. He had leaped for the door and ended up floating like a lather-covered pinata. Fortunately Jenny had hauled him out, and gotten him strapped into his bunk before he had added drop-lets of his dinner to the water.

The inner door of the lock cycled open, and Cab found himself faced with a welcoming committee when he had been expecting only Jenny. His former partner, now law clerk and lover, was looking pale, her green eyes dark with anxiety, and her fingers plucked nervously at the ends of her long red hair. Stinson White looked grim, and with white scars cutting across the black skin of his face and his black eye patch, that was very grim indeed. Even Joe Reichart seemed unusually grave, the omnipresent half smile missing from his lips.

"Cabot," Joe said without preamble. "You've been impeached."

Chapter Two

"What, again?" He shifted his helmet to his left arm, and ran a hand through his hair, giving himself time to still his jumping heart and quiet the uncomfortable fluttery feeling which had landed in the pit of his stomach. "This is becoming an annual event ranking right up there with the return of the swallows to Capistrano—"

"Is that all you can say?" grated Stinson, his Janus-like face twisting with anger.

But Joe Reichart gave a crack of laughter, and laid a soothing hand on the manager's arm. "Well done, Cabot. Just the right touch of nonchalance. Pity Lis Varllis couldn't be here to appreciate it."

"Thank you. I think I owe my mastery of the art to you, Joe."

"And when you're both finished being so goddamn complimentary, you might pause to consider that this time there isn't going to be a convenient election to save your ass, and keep you on the bench."

"How did you hear?" Cabot asked of Jenny, becoming aware and somewhat alarmed by her silence.

"Your uncle Neville called. Said it might be less of a shock coming from him than reading it over the fax. When he discovered you were gone he went ahead and talked with me because he said I was more . . . intimately involved than others."

And Cab realized that the news of the impeachment was probably bothering her less than this first contact with his blue-blooded family. He knew it rankled that he had never formally introduced her to the Huntington clan. How to tell her that he was only trying to spare her the rough side of his mother's tongue? Cecilia Huntington had never liked any of his lady friends, and he hadn't wanted Jenny to join Christina, and Sophie, and Victoria in Cecilia's catalog of complaints. And now Neville had classified her as a cheri amour. He could foresee some unpleasant moments before this was resolved.

The judge slowly stripped out of his suit, taking his time so he could try to figure out just what to say to Jenny when they had some privacy, and to mull over this latest blow in his ongoing and—to a large extent—unintentional battle with the Earth authorities.

He dumped the suit over the counter at storage, and keeping his voice carefully neutral asked, "What are the grounds this time?"

"Shielding a felon—"

"But I was the object of the felony, if I didn't choose to press charges—"

"Shut up. You asked, so hear me out," reproved Joe. "Inciting to rebellion, and various other high crimes and misdemeanors; to wit, misuse of the high office to which you were appointed."

They walked in silence heading ever deeper into the bowels of the asteroid, Cab's thoughts a jumble of images, memories, and emotions. Nothing very concrete seemed to surface from the maelstrom, and finally just to fill the silence he spoke.

"I think I'll enter a monastery."

"Excuse me, do I have any say in this?" inquired Jenny, and slipped her arm beneath his. Cab was relieved to see the brightness which he thought of as his Jenny banishing the shadows that lingered in her eyes.

"He'll take you into the monastery too. It will be very exciting."

"Joe, I think this situation calls for a bit more seriousness."

"Really, Stinson? It strikes me as farce in the truest sense of the word. DeBaca tries to have Cab impeached in November of last year. Then Long sweeps into the White House, and in his guise as white knight, defender of the right, servant of truth, and instrument of justice returns our young hero to the bench. Unfortunately hero gets uppity again over the blatantly oppressive and illegal acts of the new administration, and hero's dick is once more in the dirt.''

''Joseph!'' Cab blurted, embarrassed by the older man's crudity.

The older man grinned, but continued, but on a more serious note. ''Point is, this time it *will* go to the Senate for trial, and we need to prepare.''

Cab stopped, fists planted on hips, and faced him down. ''I agree. This all needs to be discussed, but I've been suited for much of five days, I haven't shaved, and I think this can be postponed until I've had a shower, and said hello to Jenny.''

''Have fun. What say dinner in my rooms?'' Joe asked, oblivious to the couple's blushes.

''Fine.'' Cab slid his hand into Jenny's, and they headed off for their own apartment. ''Are you feeling better?'' he asked softly. ''I should have asked before now.''

''Yes, much, but that conversation with Neville yesterday almost threw me into a relapse.''

''Yes, I'm . . . uh, sorry.''

''For what?''

''You know. The . . . situation.''

''Cab, your family is I don't know how many million miles away. I can survive their opinions.''

''I should have introduced you earlier. I meant to.''

''But Amadea got in the way.''

He colored at her bland reminder of the lovely Eurasian girl. He had made a fool of himself on Mars, fancying himself in love with her, and her with him, when in fact she had been using him as her ticket back to Earth.

''And by the time we were back together we had to haul ass off Mars just ahead of the troops, and there wasn't much time to go home, and be formally presented,'' Jenny concluded.

He set his hands on her shoulders, bringing her to a stop. ''I'll fix it. I'll make it up to you.''

''Cab.'' She shook her head, and chewed nervously at her lower lip. ''We've got more important things to worry about than my hurt feelings, and my basically ornery nature that makes me throw this in your teeth at the most inconvenient moments.'' She concluded in a rush, and eyed him ruefully.

''You didn't have to say that.''

''I know, but I hate it when I know I'm being a bitch.''

''You never are.''

''Liar.''

"Well, only occasionally." He dropped his head, and kissed her.

She rubbed her cheek, and fended him off with the other hand. "Ow, you are bristly."

"Then let's hurry because it's been five days, and I'm not about to let anything come between us."

But once in the shower, the hot water hammering across his sore back, he found himself lingering. Even the tantalizing scent of Jenny's perfume reminding him of the hours that remained before dinner, and her sultry presence in the bed only feet away, couldn't lure him from the memories. His hand slid across the puckered scar on his left shoulder, massaged at his aching leg, and he suddenly took a look at the events of the past year in terms of the physical. Shot on the EnerSun station, kidnapped and abandoned on Mars, experiencing an ultra-Light crash—and for what? Relations between Earth and her colonies were worse than ever.

The link was still there, forged by Earth's desperate need for the energy and raw materials produced by the System, but the System itself had little affection for the home world. *And who could blame them?* The Fifteenth Circuit had been created to undermine the System's autonomy, and draw at least the American colonists back within the fold. Cab himself had been—in the uncharitable but accurate words of Joe Reichart and Lydia Kim Nu, manager of the EnerSun station—a political hack. Or hatchet. He had at first enthusiastically embraced President Tomas C. deBaca's goals, but then ideals were burned away in the white-hot fire of political expediency. Thirteen people had died in a miserable Soviet mining collective on the Moon. Cab had turned his back on his close friend, handed down a decision based on conscience, justice, and honor, and this . . . he again fingered the scar . . . had been his reward.

Oh, yes, and an impeachment, he added.

Cab's actions during the EnerSun hearings had helped to sweep Tomas from office, and replace him with the charismatic young president, Richard Long. The impeachment proceedings had been dropped, and Cab had returned to his now beloved circuit certain that better days lay ahead. Unfortunately Lis Varllis, the powerful and apparently totally unscrupulous White House Chief of Staff, had indulged in a series of maneuvers against the Martian colonists, and Cab had once more been plunged into a battle with the Earth authorities.

Again blood was spilled, but this time Varllis had decided to lay the blame squarely on the judge. An order had gone out for his arrest, and rather than submit he had taken a leaf from Joe Reichart's book and fled to the asteroids.

And now—impeachment again. But maybe it was better this way. Get it settled one way or the other. But it had been so nice for three months to forget about the crap, and get on with what he loved. Since there'd been no official word from Earth the Fifteenth Circuit had continued to hear cases and (he hoped) dispense justice.

Impeached. He tasted the word feeling anger rise like a choking tide into the back of his throat. There was no cause, but that had meant shit when measured against the juggernaut of Lis Varllis's anger.

Angrily he shut off the flow of water, and padded, still dripping, into the bedroom. Crawled beneath the sheets, and buried his face in Jenny's fragrant hair. Sought, at least for a few hours, the peace that only her body could bring. But even here the past intruded. Amadea's pixieish face floated mockingly before him. He'd been such a damn fool. . . .

Her fingers dug into his cheeks forcing his head up to face her. "Cab, would you stop brooding. The past is just that; past."

"Unfortunately it has repercussions for the future."

"Forgive me, but I don't want a metaphysical or philosophical discussion right now. I want you to make love to me. Convince me—if only for a moment—that I'm the most important thing in your life."

"You are."

"Bullshit," she enunciated lovingly. Then added, precisely in chorus with him,

"Jenny, don't be lewd."

"It's funny, but people always seem to want to look to the past as holding the key to some golden age." Thomas Thondu wa Kamau swung Wairegi into his arms, and held him on his lap, gently brushing a hand across the little boy's hair.

"We're going to regret it," growled Anengo. *"The outsiders don't give a fuck whether we practice female circumcision or not, but lifting the ban on it will bring down the hue and cry. They'll say we're backward, violent and ignorant savages unfit to run a modern nation in the modern world."*

"We won the election by promising a return to traditional

values. I'm not going to prove myself to be a liar within only a few days of becoming president. Poor dears," he said softly, referring to the millions of Kenyans now looking to him for guidance. *"If it means so much to them, their pride, let them have it. And we'll get on with what matters so much to us."*

"The International Monetary Fund is going to scream."

"Let them scream. It'll be nothing compared to the sounds that come out of Teledine. They're going to pay reparations to the Masai, or we'll nationalize the rectenna farms, and we're going to get 15 percent of the power generated. Not that lousy 3 percent that was negotiated by my esteemed predecessor. That was enough when the only concern was adding to his personal fortune, but now we're going to do something for Kenya."

Someone was shaking him—hard. For a long moment Wairegi resisted the insistent pressure, trying to cling to the memory, the comfort of his father's arms. It was no use. His tormentor wasn't going away. He opened his eyes, looked up into Viriku's broad features.

A chill ran through him, and he scrubbed at his face, grateful now that she had awakened him. If she hadn't the dream would have run its course, and even the thought of reliving those final moments made his stomach heave.

"Wha . . . What?"

"Jump-point accelerator coming up."

"Thank you."

She lingered, staring down at him, eyes dark with worry and questions. "Are you certain?" She was speaking Gikuyu. Nonetheless Wairegi took a nervous glance about the shuttle. An enormously fat white man was snoring in the chair across the aisle, and far in the back a tiny brown-haired woman stared intently out the port.

He answered in the same language. "No, only death is certain. But reasonably confident. Security's always been very light out here."

She nodded once, a sharp gesture that set her golden earrings to swaying. They settled back against her neck with exaggerated slowness in the zero gravity.

Kariuki, James, Paul, J.K., and Cyril were stretching, mumbling, gazing out the ports of the long-range shuttle at the gigantic accelerator. Within that immense circle antihydrogen was produced to feed the waiting engines of the few deep-space ships. *Antimatter drive,* it still brought to mind images of science fiction.

J.K. slid into the seat next to him, and pointed. "There's the ship. Nuzzled up against the station."

Wairegi squinted, wishing he had the younger man's eyes. The station, circling endlessly within the confines of the accelerator, was easy to spot, but not the ship. At last he located it.

"Do there seem to be any more? Especially of the military variety?"

There was a hiss like a locomotive venting steam as J.K. sucked loudly on his teeth. "It's not likely. This stupid situation with the Jared colonists has most of the U.S. squadron pinned down on Mars, and only the Russians have enough ships to interfere with us."

"And they won't."

"Most likely not. They'll consider it an American problem."

"Until it's too late."

"You sound bleak. Not having—"

"Second thoughts? No, just regrets."

"They don't merit them. Weep for us, our people rather than for them."

Wairegi's hand shot out, caught J.K. by the wrist. "No, that's what brought me here. I'm done with weeping. When I was younger I was moved by tears, sincere or otherwise. Now I've learned that even an ocean of tears can't wash away the kind of pain we've endured. It's time for something tangible. For generations they've raped and plundered, now they must pay!" His warm, mobile mouth twisted in an expression of disgust. "God, listen to me. I sound like one of those ranting leftists."

"Wairegi, is there *any* political system you respect?"

"Yes, the one I'd create and lead, of course."

A chuckle, rusty at first, shook his big frame. From there it grew until his big, merry laugh filled the shuttle. Died in a series of choking snorts, and he wiped away tears of mirth. Or were they? There was something in Wairegi's face that filled J.K. with unexpressible sorrow.

"You long-suffering people. It's a testament to your strength and patience that you're willing to follow such an unpredictable fellow as myself. But it is said that the fool takes many people with him."

"Mūkūrū, gaya, ūnyonie mūgaire." *(Old man, divide, and*

teach me how to divide.) A small, disgusted sound escaped from Viriku at J.K.'s humble words.

The young man slewed about in the seat, an awkward action in the zero gravity. "It would do you no harm to occasionally shut up and listen. You might learn something."

"Oh, yes, think of all I have to glean from ancient proverbs." She folded her hands primly in her lap, and rolled her eyes heavenward. "Actions for men, words for women, woman cannot keep a secret—"

"Then silence your mouth, Luo woman, and go away!"

"No, I want to hear what Wairegi has to say and my father was a Gikuyu."

The older man winked at J.K., and said lightly, "How wise you both are, to listen." Their bickering was driving him almost to distraction, but he knew it sprang from nerves, and by Allah his own doubts and fears were eating at his soul.

He considered. It would be impossible to impart to these two young ones what twenty years of exile, and a disillusioning homecoming had taught. Also he had no wish to bare his soul to the caustic probings of Viriku Amani.

"After the overthrow of my father's regime I was smuggled to Uganda, then in my early teens on to England. So it was logical I should be first educated at Oxford. I resisted traveling to America because I wanted nothing to do with a country which would set a villain like Mwanyumba over Kenya. Then I realized one should know one's enemy. So I studied political science and international affairs at Georgetown University, and then went on to Harvard to obtain a law degree."

"And what did you learn of this *enemy*, or did they woo you?" Viriku asked.

"I learned that though the Americans have pursued an insane foreign policy, and have displayed an almost unbelievable arrogance, they do possess one of the best and most just political and legal systems in the world. Unfortunately, in their terror of Soviet expansion, they try to deny the benefits of this system to smaller and less powerful nations."

"But your beliefs?" prompted J.K.

"Two things made a strong impression upon me." He cocked his head and considered. "Well, three. One, the American Bill of Rights. Second, Holmes's dissent in the *Abrams* case." He leaned back, closed his eyes, his hands tightening on his knees.

"But when men have realized that time has upset many fighting faiths, they may come to believe even more than they believe the very foundations of their own conduct that the ultimate good desired is better reached by free trade in ideas— that the best test of truth is the power of the thought to get itself accepted in the competition of the market, and that truth is the only ground upon which their wishes safely can be carried out." He opened his eyes, and smiled at the younger man's openmouthed amazement.

"Forgive me. We shysters have a bad habit of spewing out this sort of thing with little or no provocation. It's ironic, too, that Holmes produced this dissent because in *Schenck* and *Debs* he wrote the majority opinion affirming the lower court's decisions convicting under the Espionage Act. But then we get into the 'clear and present danger' morass. . . ." His voice died away, and he buried his chin on his breast.

"You said there was a third," prodded Viriku after the silence had continued for several minutes.

"Ah, yes." Wairegi's dark eyes lit with amusement. "It's interesting how I instinctively placed Holmes before Morgenstern. The perfect lead in from Holmes's competition of the market to Morgenstern's free market economics. What a brilliant teacher I would have made."

"Then you're not left wing."

"Only in so far as I tend to be a champion of individual rights, and I'm afraid the left has no better record in that direction than the right. Certainly not once they get in power. So you see, I really don't have a theory. Just an inchoate sense of what ought to be right and just. Maybe someday I'll find a real platform."

"And how does a little dose of terrorism fit into all this?" mocked Viriku, hanging over the back of his acceleration couch.

Wairegi jerked around, the restraining straps cutting into his chest and belly. "No act of violence will be necessary. The mere threat will be enough."

"And if you believe that you are a great fool!" She dodged his broad hand, and the knuckles whitened with strain as it closed into a fist.

Wairegi stared at his hand as if it belonged to someone else, then carefully forced the clenched fingers open. "It will. It must," he murmured, and J.K. slipped away, dragging Viriku like a recalcitrant foal. Wairegi was speaking to his soul, not to his companions, and neither J.K. nor this useless Luo woman were going to be eavesdroppers to that anguished whisper.

"If someone really wanted to do us a favor they would invent instantaneous radio transmission." Cab glared at the image of Neville's nappy secretary. With the lines of interference running through the picture he looked sadly out of focus. Though to Cab's mind that was entirely appropriate. Michael was an out of focus sort of person.

"They're working on it," grunted Stinson. "Sit down, Cabot. Your pacing around won't affect the laws of physics."

Joe's eyes crinkled, and he exchanged a wink with Jenny, who sat with her feet tucked up beneath her on the large, overstuffed sofa. She tried a smile, but she had a feeling from the sharp glance Reichart gave her that the attempt was not entirely successful. She shaded her eyes briefly with her hand, and wondered why, after all she'd been through during the past year, she was so uneasy about this latest round of insanity out of Washington.

"I suppose I could start talking now. By the time it reaches Earth he ought to be just about picking up the com."

The image of Michael wavered and was replaced by the urbane and smiling Neville.

"Cabot, how are you?"

Minutes later the words came crackling from the speaker.

"Fine," Cab snapped. "Do you realize how long it's taken for us to exchange these inanities?" he fumed to his companions.

"This is your uncle, make nice," grinned Joe. "Besides, he's a politician. He can't help but spout inanities."

"Joe," Huntington said warningly, but there was no real heat in the word.

"Good, glad to see you're not taking this too hard," came back Neville's reply, sounding oddly out of sync with the conversation which had preceded it.

"I'm getting used to it." The judge was also getting used to the time delay.

"I've done a little preliminary vote count, and things don't look too bad. There are a number of undecideds so with a good defense we ought to be able to bring them into line."

"What is the count?"

Cab laid out a hand of solitaire, and studied the cards. He was finding it difficult and confusing to intersperse his conversation with Neville with asides to Jenny and Joe. They seemed to understand, and sat silent.

"Seven who are ready to vote you out right now, but they're diehard Long supporters." The Senator's mobile mouth twisted in disdain. "Or should I say they're toadies of Lis Varllis? But perhaps it isn't politic to be so blunt. I have nine guaranteed to me, ten if you count me in—"

"I presume I can," Cab murmured dryly, but the half-hearted joke fell very flat by the time it traversed the some two hundred million miles from the Belt to Neville's elegant office in the Old Senate Office Building.

"As for a good defense," Neville continued. "I've talked with Bill Saxon, and he's agreeable—"

"Forgive me, Neville, but don't I have any say in this at all?"

The slim brows scaled the Senator's forehead. "You have some objection to Bill Saxon?"

"No, he's a very good lawyer, but I happen to want Kenneth Furakawa."

Neville's teeth closed briefly on his lower lip. "That might not be the wisest choice. He has a rather bad odor. You know . . . the feeling that he's unreliable, a rebel."

"Good Lord! He's been retained by U.S. Steel, Rockwell, IBM, how much more stability do you want?"

"He also represented that Russian during that World Court mess on the EnerSun station."

"Since I was the judge on that case, and it was *my* court sitting as the World Court, I take rather a bit of exception to hearing it referred to as a *mess*."

"Wasn't it?"

"No! We broke Tomas."

"And that is why I don't think having Kenneth Furakawa as your defense attorney is a very wise choice. This is Washington, for God's sake. A town that doesn't take kindly to people who break presidents."

"Yeah, they're afraid it'll be their butts next," remarked Joe, and sucked vigorously at his pipe. It was a measure of his nerves, despite his unflappable expression, that he didn't notice the bowl had gone cold.

"What! What was that?"

"That was Joe."

"Cabot, have you run mad? You've included Joe Reichart in this conversation?"

"Yes."

"You have got to put some distance between yourself and that man."

"And how would you suggest I do that?" Jenny knew that tone; low, flat, dangerous. "Ceres is 1,025 kilometers in diameter. It's a little hard to get away from anyone. Or would you suggest that I stake out an unclaimed rock, and blast out a cave while I wait this out."

"No! I would suggest you get home, and stop acting like a hero in a bad melodrama, or second-rate tragedy!"

"What do you mean by that?"

"This dramatic flight to the Belt. Laying it on a bit thick, wouldn't you say?"

"No, I wouldn't! When you've been shot by thugs sent by the Soviets and your own government, been kidnapped and abandoned in the Martian desert at the instigation of . . . well, I'm not certain who, and had an arrest warrant sworn out against you when you haven't done anything wrong, it makes you leery about trusting anyone."

"Your continued absence will leave an impression of guilt which might be difficult to overcome."

"I'll take that risk. Perhaps close association with Joe has affected my thinking, but I really feel safer out here. I've discovered that people have a great capacity for violence when their power's being threatened, and I am not fond of being a target."

"You're making this very difficult."

"Regretting defending me?"

Neville's lips pinched tightly together, but his voice remained calm, almost affectionate. "You're my brother's only child, a Huntington. I'll not abandon you."

"Thank you," Cab said softly.

A sigh. "Well, if you won't come back, how about Saxon—"

"Furakawa."

"You must have gotten this stubborn streak from your mother."

"I don't think you give Dad enough credit. He stood up to the assembled clan, and refused to run again for Congress."

"You have an odd kick in your gallop, no doubt about

that.'' The Senator rubbed at his forehead. ''Okay, I'll get in touch with Ken, unless you'd prefer to do it?''

''No, you're on the spot, and can better advise him. Time enough for us to talk once he's been retained.''

''How's the exchequer?''

''Adequate for the task. Unless Lis Varllis should find some way to freeze my accounts.''

''Maybe you'd better give me power of attorney.''

''Not a bad idea. This is going to cost a fortune.''

''Just like this call. Take care of yourself, Cabot, I'll be in touch.''

''Well,'' Stinson gusted, flicking on his lighter and sucking his fat cigar, blended of atrocious Belt tobacco and fairly decent Belt marijuana, into malodorous life. ''That was relatively painless.''

''Painless?'' repeated Jenny. ''I thought we were going to see murder.''

Cab joined her on the sofa, and gathered her hand into his. ''No, there's only seven years difference between Neville and I, and we've squabbled since we were kids. He always tries to be condescending, I won't stand for it, and it all ends very amicably.''

''Still, he's an insufferably arrogant son of a bitch. *You're a Huntington after all*,'' Joe mimicked, and gave a snort of disdain.

''And you have no pride of family?'' Cab asked sweetly.

''Of course I do, but I don't think my decaying pedigree should give me the power to make decisions for other people.''

''But you do make decisions for other people. What about your station?''

''Ah, but, Cabot, there are only ten thousand aboard her, and it's a voluntary association.'' He cocked his curly graying head, and the wrinkles about his eyes deepened. ''And if I get too lost in delusions of tin-plated godhood they can always chuck me out an airlock.''

''So what makes the people on Earth such sheep?''

''I didn't say they were.''

''Your attitude implies it.''

''If it did, I'm sorry. That would make me a soulmate with your uncle.''

''It's hard not to start thinking of the governed as rather simple. Command is an isolating condition.''

Stinson's cigar was wafting a truly indescribable odor across the room. Jenny pinched her nostrils, and tried to breath through her mouth. She didn't mind the marijuana so much— for she knew that the explosion which had destroyed the left side of Stinson's face had left bone-deep scars that kept him in constant pain—but the combination! Like breathing dirty socks.

Stinson grinned, the scars stretching and writhing like pale worms against his black skin. "That's one of the advantages of the System. We've got an armed populace, and the nervous-making knowledge that it's a long walk home—especially without a space suit. Sure makes somebody think twice before coming down with a bad case of tin-plated godhood." He shot a grin at Joe.

"Great, so you've got everyone running around brandishing guns—"

"You lived with it on Mars, you're living with it now. And I might add that on EnerSun only the bad guys had guns, and you almost fetched up dead," Joe reminded him softly.

"It still makes me nervous. People get angry . . . there have been some family incidents. I'm trying one of them right now."

"If Jeff hadn't had a gun he'd have taken out after Lucinda with a knife, or a rock, or whatever the hell else was handy," grunted Stinson.

"Cab, we don't have the power to make everyone be good." Joe had lost his perpetual half smile, and his eyes were shadowed. "Maybe it's not in us to bring the kingdom of Heaven to Earth. But whether it is or isn't I'd rather be a wolf living among wolves rather than a lamb shivering among them."

"In other words make it risky for the wrongdoer."

"Yes."

Cab shaded his eyes with one hand. "It's all very alien to me. I'm not saying you won't convince me—you've brought me around to your way of thinking on an appalling number of issues." He sighed. "But this. . . ." His voice trailed away.

"But, you taught Jenny to shoot."

"Yes."

"And you carried a gun on Mars."

"Yes."

"So?"

"So, I'm still uncomfortable with it. I suppose I have an irreconcilable conflict in my view of people. Sometimes I think they're not so bad, other times I think they're . . . we're, animals who need to be strictly controlled." He raised a restraining hand. "I know, I know, why then do I believe that the men and women who get into office in order to exert this control are likely to be any more moral than their brethren in the street."

"Is a puzzlement," Jenny said softly, and brushed his hair back from his forehead. Her green eyes swept the three men. "You know I'm normally ready, willing, and eager to take part in one of these elevated discussions, but it seems like that's all we *ever* talk about."

"Three lawyers in the same room," Joe said. "We keep achieving critical mass."

"Jenny, don't tell me you're losing your taste for legal and political philosophy."

"Maybe just a little, especially when we were invited to dinner, and I'm starving, and all you fellows want to do is talk. Also, I haven't seen *you*"—she dug a slim forefinger into Cab's side—"for a week, and frankly I'd like to get you alone."

"And satisfy another hunger, eh?" asked Joe, and chuckled as both she and Cab blushed.

"All right, we'll postpone saving the world for another day. God knows it's blundered along without any help or guidance from me for several billion years."

"Your modesty does you credit, Joe," Cab said dryly as he rose, and held out his hands to Jenny. "I had begun to think that not a sparrow fell. . . ."

"Yep, tin-plated godhood," Joe agreed as his companions' laughter filled the room.

"You and Lis Varllis, it's going to be the battle of the godheads."

"Jenny, you wound me." Joe tucked her arm beneath his. "I *do* represent the godhead."

"And Lis?" she asked, obligingly playing to his punchline.

"The political pinheads."

Chapter Three ────────────

Andy Throckmorton was intrigued by the little group on the shuttle. The older silver-haired man had seemed tantalizingly familiar, and the way he shot a warning glance at Andy's recumbent form before entering into a spirited conversation with his companion aroused all of Throckmorton's journalistic instincts.

So he had slumped even deeper into the padded acceleration chair, and maintained a steady flow of glass-shattering snores while struggling to overhear the soft-voiced exchange from across the aisle. He did manage to overhear, but it did him a fuck lot of good because it amounted to the most God-awful gabble. Some African language was his best guess. The fact that he had been thwarted in his eavesdropping had no effect on stilling every journalistic sense. His belly was rumbling like a beer keg being rolled over cobblestones, and when his belly rumbled he was on the trail of something interesting.

It wasn't until baggage claim in the station's central hub that one of the pieces fell into place. Andy had been skating along in his magnetic boots noting the way his flab undulated in zero grav, and vowing, yet again, that he would go on a diet when the gray-haired African had paused, head raised like a questing stallion. His arm then raised in a stiff gesture, and Andy had him placed. *Wairegi wa Thondu*, former member of Kenya's ruling elite. He had "resigned" seven months ago, and contrary to most exiled third-world politicos, he had not suddenly reappeared lugging the proverbial suitcase bulging with money and set up expensive housekeeping in Paris.

Wa Thondu's six companions were gathered close about him, and one young man—whose slender height would have made him a welcome addition to any professional basketball team—was clutching at his suitcase as if it contained the crown jewels.

Maybe that's *the suitcase bulging with money,* Andy thought irreverently. *But why the hell come this deep into the System with the graft? Of course that cookie who's with him would make any place a good time,* his thoughts continued as he alternated between watching the one woman in this ill-matched crew, and checking the ramp for his bag.

His ancient, dilapidated grip arrived, and Andy swept it up in one fat, hamlike hand. The Africans had already started out of the baggage claim, and he hustled to keep them in view. He wondered if they would turn off, head for the transport tubes to carry them to the rim of the station, but they startled the hell out of him by continuing around the hub heading for the gate where the *Constellation* lay docked. None of it made any sense. Why was Wairegi wa Thondu—Summa Cum Laude, Oxford; Summa Cum Laude, Georgetown; Summa Cum Laude, Harvard Law School—headed for Mars?

They reached the gate where a bored steward lounged at the desk, doing careful surgery on his hangnails. One of the men asked a low-voiced question, and received a negative head shake in response. Then the Africans settled in a clump of garish plastic chairs, clipped their restraining belts, and sat in abstracted silence. The entire maneuver reminded Andy of pioneers circling their wagons. He decided to go be an Indian.

"Mr. wa Thondu."

The guy was tough. There was the briefest flicker, then a smiling public face was in place, and he replied in a calm, unhurried tone.

"Yes?"

"Andy Throckmorton. Editor, star reporter, ace photographer, and chief bottle washer of *The System Squeak* . . . uh, I mean . . . *Post*."

"Pleased to meet you." They shook.

Andy lowered his bulk into one of the vacant chairs though no one's language, body or otherwise, had indicated he should do so. They sat and regarded each other for several long minutes. It was wa Thondu who blinked first.

"Is there anything I can . . . er, do for you?"

"Yeah, you can tell me why you're headed for Mars."

An almost undetectable shudder ran through the group, and several pairs of brown eyes strained at their leader.

"Why are you so interested?"

"Seven months ago you were secretary of the treasury in Kenya. You resign under a cloud and vanish, only to turn up in this dingy pimple on the face of the universe? Seems a little odd."

"Not really." The tone was still level, pleasant. "My fiancée is a linguist. She and her colleague Mr. Cyril Njonjo are going to study the artifact on Mars. Not wanting to be separated from her I chose to come along." Wairegi laid a proprietary hand on the woman's.

"And these other . . . gentlemen?" Andy asked slowly while eyeing one large mobile mountain disguised as a human being. From the broad, broken-nosed face to the spadelike hands the guy had "goon" written all over him.

"I'm a disgraced African leader, Mr. Throckmorton. We tend to make enemies, intentionally or not. Mr. Mboya is going to see to it those enemies stay at arm's length."

"He looks up to the job." Mboya stared unblinkingly from beneath thick, straight brows, and Andy decided not to challenge him to arm wrestle.

"These other gentlemen are members of my staff. I'm writing my memoirs." A flash of perfect white teeth in that handsome black face. Andy smiled back, but he wanted to tell the man not to be so eager with information. Now Andy really knew something out of the ordinary was occurring.

"The official reason for your resignation was ill health. I trust you've recovered."

Wairegi's smile broadened. "Come, come, Mr. Throckmorton, don't be so coy."

"Okay." He hunched forward, resting his belly on his thighs, hands planted firmly on his knees. "Rumors within the Kenyan administration hinted at large-scale fraud and graft." He held up a restraining hand, but it was a wasted gesture. Wa Thondu made no move to defend himself. Andy sucked in air, and continued. "But more reliable rumors say that the IMF put the squeeze on the President because you were making trouble for the white boys, and you were out."

"You are exceedingly well informed, Mr. Throckmorton." The former cabinet member's tone was decidedly less cordial than it had been only a moment before.

Andy flipped up a palm. "Well, how about it?"

"Let us just say that I'm not a universal favorite within the halls of the IMF."

"Why?"

"You are persistent, Mr. Throckmorton." Andy grunted. "But it seems we must postpone this interesting discussion. We are about to board."

"Can it be resumed?"

Wa Thondu gave him a measuring glance followed by a sharp snort of laughter. "Why not. You may find it shocking."

"I doubt it, I'm a System man."

He watched as the Africans gathered their bags, and clicked awkwardly toward the lock. All except the woman. She was handling the magnetic boots with the ease of an old space hand. Wairegi leaned in, touched her lightly on the arm, and said something in a soft undertone. She shrugged off his hand, and replied with a burst of Gikuyu. She was clearly pissed about something, and Andy would have given a lot to know what about.

"Hiya, Cab."

"Good God, Andy! Put on some clothes."

"What's a'matter, never seen a little flesh before?"

"The operative word in that sentence is *little*. Seeing you nude is not one of the choicer pleasures of life. Jenny!"

"Hi, Andy."

But this was too much for the journalist. Red blossomed like a nova from the centermost point of his enormous belly, and rose like a spreading rash into his chest, throat, and jowly face. He bolted out of range of the comnet, and returned with a towel wound about his waist, looking like an aggrieved caesar.

"That was mean," Cab said, chuckling.

"I know. But fun. Hi, Andy," Jenny repeated.

"Jeez."

"What's the matter? You were the man who wanted to set me up as the madam of your high-priced brothel. A pimp shouldn't suffer from modesty."

Throckmorton scratched at his shaggy, graying hair. "Guess I really didn't think you'd answer the com."

"I didn't."

"So I lost my nerve."

"Andy, why are you calling, and where the hell are you?"

"I'm on the *Constellation* bound for Mars. And then I'm gonna come out and interview the dangerous criminal."

"Andy, stow it."

"Doing an exclusive on us, Andy?" Jenny asked.

"Yeah, actually taking a look at the entire picture. I went to Earth to get the straight poop on this latest impeachment vote. Also witnessed the triumphant homecoming of Lucius Renfrew." The journalist paused, and sucked at his teeth. "Amadea was with him. . . . Looks like she got that job with POW," he added when silence met his first statement.

"Oh?" Cab said, then coughed as the word grated over a sudden obstruction in his throat.

"She's really doing a number on you, Judge old buddy."

"I'm not surprised."

"I should have choked her with that teapot instead of just hitting her with it," Jenny thoughtfully remarked.

"Is she going to be one of the star witnesses against me?"

"Just let her try," Jenny grated. "And I'll tell how she manipulated those kids at Jared to kidnap and abandon Cab, and worked for Gemetics—"

Cab slewed around in the chair to face her. "But we can't bring any of that up. If we did it would implicate Seth."

"And make you a liar," Andy offered. "You've stuck stubbornly to this story that you don't know who the fuck kidnapped you. Better to keep sticking to it. No, what she's doing is massacring you in the press. There's a strangely prudish streak in the citizenry of the United States, and they won't like it that you're coming across like a small satyr, more interested in broads than in the bench."

"Oh, great," Cab groaned, dropping his head into his hands.

Numbing amazement at the woman's gall filled Jenny. "How can she do that? Hasn't she any pride?"

"Honey, if she was willing to put out for Cab she has *no* pride."

"Thank you so very much."

"Uh, sorry. I didn't mean it quite the way it came out. What I meant was that she's a slut by nature—"

"Andy, don't make a bad situation worse."

"I'm not. I'm explaining—"

Jenny swung the screen toward her. "What you're doing is first saying that no woman in her right mind would sleep with Cab unless she had something to gain by it, and then saying that Cab was a boob for not seeing through her. Of course I happen to agree with that—"she gave him a tender smile to remove some of the sting—"but that's not Cab's fault. You come by it naturally. It's part of your sex." She now had two outraged men staring at her, and she tossed back her hair and gave a deep laugh. "There there, fellahs. We'll love you even though you can be putzes."

"So what's the next piece of this big picture, Andy?"

"Talk with Jeanne and Jasper, and Despopolous. And I'm going to try and wrangle an interview with General Saber."

"Think you'll get a straight story from Despopolous about POW's seizure of the ship and the diamonds? After all, he's port administrator, and a federal appointee."

"I can but try. He did open up the arms locker to your band of crazy heroes. By the way, what ever did happen to those diamonds?"

"They're in a safety deposit box in the Ceres bank waiting until we figure out a way to get them to Earth."

"So the Mormons' grand plan to terraform Mars sits on the shelf."

"For the time being. They really couldn't start anyway. Not until this mess on Mars has been completely thrashed out."

"And the man doing the thrashing is General Saber, which is why I want to talk to him."

"Despopolous is at least a System man, but Saber's going to have no love for me or the Jared colonists. We were supposed to take no action until he and the squadron arrived."

"And instead you made like the cavalry, shot up those environmentalists, and blew right past their incoming noses."

"May I remind you that POW shot first," Jenny said stiffly. "And if we hadn't left, Cab would have been arrested, and the diamonds would be impounded. And I somehow doubt the Jared Colony would ever have seen them again."

"Jenny, honey, I'm on your side. I was also there."

"The point is Saber is not likely to be sympathetic. He's an Air Force general, and . . . well, that sort of says it all."

"I don't know, Cab, he might surprise us. He didn't strike me as one of your typical military wool heads when we met him on the shuttle." Jenny's voice faltered slightly under his intent gray-eyed gaze, and she realized that he hadn't forgotten her interest in the handsome Air Force officer. "Well, he might just be . . . he might surprise you," she finished lamely.

"Guess I'll find out when I get to Mars. Oh, an interesting aside. You'll never guess who's on this ship with me."

"Probably not because I'm not going to try."

"Wairegi wa Thondu. The former Kenyan treasury secretary," he prodded.

"Doesn't mean anything to me."

"He's about your age, maybe a little older. Got his law degree at Harvard?"

"Sorry, no . . . wait, I do remember him, or rather knew *of* him. He graduated before I did."

"Well, whatever, it's just kind of strange. Seven Kenyans on a spaceship isn't something you see every day. I'm going to interview him this evening, so I'm getting two stories for the price of one."

"Speaking of price we better stop running up your com bill."

"Not to worry." He lowered a heavy lid over one brown eye, his fat cheeks screwing up into an expression of almost comic secrecy. "I billed it to Joe."

Cab and Jenny gave a shout of laughter. "Andy, you didn't."

"You're a ruffian."

"Now that we know this is Joe's nickel—good-bye, Andy."

"Say hello to Jeanne for me," Jenny instructed as Cab flipped the disconnect switch.

She slid into his lap, twining her arms about his neck. "Andy's coming. That'll be nice."

"That'll be two familiar faces counting Joe."

"There's always Evgeni," Jenny said softly, referring to the brave and stubborn Russian moon miner whose challenge to the superpowers had resulted in the death of most of his mining collective, the fall of an American president, and forced Cabot to abandon his support of the administration which had placed him on the bench.

The fact that Cab's early ruling in support of the administration paved the way for the bombing of the Garmoneya Collective was a sore place on his soul, and he could never hear the Russian mentioned without guilt tightening his gut.

"I don't want to see him. I faced him after my World Court ruling against Tupolev and deBaca. I can't do it again."

"I think you should. He always asks after you, and I think it hurts him that you've never come to visit."

"It would hurt me."

"Okay, I won't push. Shall we get to work?"

"Breach of contract—oh, boy."

"Hey, no one promised a judge's life would be filled with precedent-setting constitutional cases."

"Please, come in." Andy levered his bulk through the narrow doorway. "I took the liberty of reserving the dining room for our little talk," Wairegi continued smoothly, ignoring Viriku's blazing eyes. They had had rather strong words over the wisdom of this interview only moments before the journalist's entrance, and she was still smarting over his preemptory tone.

"Good thinking. Those cabins are like shower stalls. If this is luxury travel I'd hate to be in steerage."

Andy wondered over the presence of *all* seven of the Kenyans. Why hadn't some of them joined the other passengers in the postage stamp-sized lounge? Surely they couldn't all be so enthralled with wa Thondu's words of wisdom? Then Andy pinpointed the emotion which seemed to predominate in the room: not interest, fear; the younger members of this ill-sorted gathering seemed to feel safer when they were gathered together.

Andy pulled his tiny recorder from his coat pocket, and laid it in the center of the table.

"Do I begin at the beginning?" Wairegi asked with a smile.

"Please don't. A man of your age and experience has done a lot of living, and my ass won't take these chairs for that many hours."

"Then what do you want to know?"

"I'm not sure. Let me think about it." A rude sound erupted from Viriku. He didn't miss the sharp look that flew between Wairegi and the woman, and there was nothing loverlike about it at all. "What's the current situation with Teledine's rectenna farm in the Rift Valley?"

Wairegi stiffened, his eyes gone wary. "The situation is as it has always been."

"I seem to remember that forty years ago a somewhat different situation applicd."

"You are very well informed."

"You've told me that before."

"I find it startling in a white journalist. Particularly one who lives off-world."

"The farm was seized."

"A miscalculation, and an injustice since rectified. Teledine has its property back."

"Yeah, because of several platoons of United States Marines. Would you call that a miscalculation, or an injustice?"

"I call it moot."

"Come now, Mr. wa Thondu, that's a pretty moderate reaction. How did Teledine come to be doing business in Kenya?"

"Fifty years ago the company approached the government—"

"That's the single-party government that had ruled Kenya since independence?"

"Yes. They required a vast tract of land which lacked great agricultural possibilities. The Rift was selected."

"Nobody lived there?"

"Very few. It was primarily grazing land for the herds of the Masai tribesmen. The promise was that in exchange for the land Kenya would receive three percent of all power generated to feed and fuel its own growing industrial base." His hand shook slightly as he removed a stick of gum, and crammed it into his mouth. "The outcome was not a . . . happy one for the Masai. They naturally resented the loss of these lands, and there was some resistance."

"What does that mean 'some resistance'?"

"Several thousand people tried to block the construction by squatting on the land with their herds. Teledine told the government to handle it, and they did. Body counts vary depending upon which source you read, but at a minimum two thousand people died," said Kariuki softly.

"Pretty high price to pay for three percent."

"That was the joke, albeit a bitter one." Wairegi abandoned his attempt to keep the interview light and surface. The man was too well informed, and who could tell? Perhaps, years from now, it would help to explain if not exonerate him for his actions. "Sadly, Mr. Throckmorton, the Western exploiters . . . please, don't make a face. What else would you call them?"

"I don't know, but we need a new word. That one has been overused and abused, and the tendency is for most readers or listeners in the West to stop listening to the man who uses it no matter how thoughtful and sincere he might be. But go on.''

"Very well. These *gentlemen entrepreneurs*," he cast Andy an ironic glance, and saw from the answering twinkle in those sleepy brown eyes that he had made a hit. "Usually find a willing participant in the form of our continent's leaders. Personal aggrandizement is usually placed well above national development. Oh, conditions have improved. We no longer starve by the tens of thousands, but Africa still lags decades behind the West, the Orient, even South America. And yet our generals, and presidents and prime ministers are often some of the wealthiest men in the world. But to come to the point.

"Only a trickle of that energy ever reached the Kenyan people. Most was . . . is . . . pirated and sold on the black market. Some say the rectenna farm was the straw. I think it is less easily explained. Whatever the reason there was a popular uprising. The old single-party system was swept away, and for five years there was . . .'' He paused, his dark eyes staring into the distant. "A unique experience in human affairs. But I am biased of course for my father was one of those—dreamers? Revolutionaries? What would you call them?''

"Brave if foolish. But out here we have a soft spot for brave and foolish dreamers.''

"The rest is as you described. There was a growing outcry as Kenya attempted a return to traditional values. It's interesting, is it not, that many so-called revolutionary governments look to the past for their blueprint of the future? Of course it's always a past that never existed outside the confines of our minds, but we're never deterred.

"At first the provisional government only sought to receive a fair rate from the various multinational companies doing business. But there was internal squabbling, and the farm was seized and nationalized, and suddenly every large corporation trembled, wondering how long until they too lost their holdings and investments. The political right squealed that we were godless communists, and that the red flame would soon devour all of Africa, and the left pointed to our bumbling attempts to recreate the past as proof of our savagery. Civilization wears a white face; at least in the minds of most whites.''

"And so the marines.''

"Well, to be fair there were very few American troops actually involved. It was mostly American guns in Kenyan hands." He smiled, trying to hide his pain and heartbreak, but it was a feeble attempt, and must have revealed more than he wished, for Throckmorton's gaze faltered, and he looked away.

"Okay, that's the background. I know from *Who's Who* that you were smuggled into Uganda, remained there until you were sixteen, then went to England and the States for your education. You taught at Mombasa University, served at the UN, and ultimately returned home to serve in the government which had overthrown your father's party. Why?"

"I had hoped to effect change from within."

"And did you?"

"No. Otherwise I wouldn't be here."

"Which is another interesting question. Just what the fuck *are* you doing out here?" There was an uneasy shifting from the younger Kenyans. "But we'll leave that for now." He glanced at his notes which scrolled across the tiny recorder/computer. "According to the economic experts—and God knows I'm not one so I'll have to take this on faith—your policies were improving economic conditions. But then you resigned, and I'd like to know why."

"It was either that or be fired. And that word can have many meanings in Africa."

"But why? You were well thought of by the Mwanyumba government."

"Given my dubious background, I suppose I was." The folds about Wairegi's mouth pulled back in a travesty of a smile, and he scrabbled in his pocket for his cigarettes. Came up with the hated gum, crammed another stick into his mouth. As the fruity taste exploded against the roof of his mouth he reached a decision, decided to throw caution to the winds. He would tell it all, and let God sort it out.

"Are you familiar with the IMF and the World Bank?"

"I've heard of them, I'm no expert."

"Then you will forgive a little lecture?"

"I'd appreciate it."

"What I am about to describe is a neat circle, rather like a dog eating its own tail. Despite Africa's great wealth of natural resources we are still forced to import more than we export, and the balance of trade has shifted even farther to the West because of the flow of raw materials from the System competing with African minerals. The IMF loans money to help us balance our international payments, but the money is actually coming from private banks in the United States, and former colonial countries of Europe. Africa's record for management is not a very good one, so often the IMF demands control over the country's importing and exporting, which can lead to control over the entire economy to insure repayment. This is the situation currently in Kenya. Our IMF minigovernment makes certain that any money received by Kenya for the sale of her resources flows right back out to pay the Western bankers. Often the money only reaches us as a bookkeeping entry. No real cash.

"I am a law-abiding man, Mr. Throckmorton, so I did not lightly reach the decision that what was necessary for Kenya was a repudiation of the foreign debt—oh, not forever, only for a few years. I'm not a thief. My plan was to use the money for internal investments. Investments guided by the principle of the free market rather than by the government's central planners. I am a devoted student of Dr. David Morgenstern." He smiled apologetically. "He enjoys no very good odor among many world economists, but his theories have been proved; in Nicaragua, Rumania, and Syria. I wanted to try for another miracle in Kenya."

"So the pressure came from the IMF, I take it?"

"Yes, with the full support of the Kenyan officials. The IMF allows them to skim off enough in graft to keep them quiet and happy. I would not have been so lenient."

Wairegi stared down at his hands—remembering. The smell of the dust overlayed by the piercingly sweet scent of a coming rainstorm. Women squatting by cook fires feeding in the carefully gathered and hoarded twigs. Woman who was both earth, water, and fire. Only the air belonged to the male. The shrill cries of children. He pressed the tips of his fingers to his eyes. There would be none to carry him into immortality. He had made Kenya his wife, and she had proved to be barren.

"*Cia thūgūri itiyūraga ikūmbi.*"

"Beg pardon?"

"Gikuyu proverb. Bought things do not fill the granary. Meaning that you cannot hope to become rich without cultivating your fields. An appropriate period to our conversation, I think."

Andy didn't argue, just rose, and swept up his recorder.

"Thank you for your time, Mr. wa Thondu. I hope we have an opportunity to talk again."

"I'm certain we will. It is a long journey."

And there was something in the man's face that convinced the journalist that the Kenyan was not talking about time or even distance, but something far more fundamental to the soul of Wairegi wa Thondu.

Chapter Four ─────────────

The hot shower helped, but couldn't completely wash away the gray depression which seemed to be spreading outward from the hard lump in the center of her breast. Aching, soul-deep unhappiness; it lay like a dirty film across skin and hair, and she scrubbed harder, reddening her pale golden skin.

Stepping from the shower Lydia Kim Nu threw back her long silver-gray hair. It hit her bare shoulders with a wet *thwap*, sending droplets running in tiny shivery lines down her back. She slid a terry robe over her dripping body, and padded into the front room of her apartment on the EnerSun station; glad she had had the foresight to mix a shaker of martinis before entering the shower. Now all she had to do was pour, recline, and sip. The ice-cold gin hit the back of her throat like a frozen flame, and seared its way to her stomach.

On the coffee table her own image, looking cool and poised, smiled supercilious out at her from the cover of *Business Week*. She gave a grunt of distaste.

"Keeping the Engine Running in These Stagflationary Times," the headline blazed. "A Portrait of a Remarkable Woman." She picked up the magazine, and stared into her own level black eyes. Water dripped from her hair raising blisters across the glossy cover, blurring her features.

Which seemed appropriate somehow. She was feeling very blurred about the edges, and her life seemed to be decidedly *stagflationary* right now. She needed Joe, ached for him, and he had been gone almost a year. Fleeing the troops sent by

President Tomas C. deBaca to seize the Russian miner Renko and his family. Joe, knowing that Evgeni would stand to his testimony of the missile attack on the Garmoneya Collection if his family was safe, had managed to escape with Irina and Analisa. He had fled to the Belt, and remained there even though the crisis had long been settled.

Wish I'd gone with him.

The magazine sailed across the room, the pages giving an aggrieved flutter as it hit the floor. She lay back sipping at her drink, trying to fathom what her youngest daughter was doing on Earth in the company of a man Lydia despised. She also knew from various friends at Eagle Port that Cab had ''seen a lot'' of Amadea during his time on Mars, yet the judge had never mentioned her child. In fact he studiously tried to avoid any topic which might touch even peripherally on Amadea. Granted they hadn't talked much since Cab and Jenny reached the Belt, but she sensed that something had happened between Cab and Amadea, and it was somehow tied in with POW. How could a child of hers become involved with those lunatics?

Her glass was empty, and she leaned over to pour another. Then with an oath she set aside the glass, and swung off the couch. Becoming drunk and maudlin wasn't going to solve anything.

While the call went through she dried her hair, put on her makeup, and replaced the terry robe with a shimmering caftan. None of it did any good for when Joe's rugged features finally stabilized on the screen the first words out of his mouth were, ''What's wrong?''

''Damn you! I'm looking beautiful and sexy.'' She fumed during the transmission lag.

''Correction. You're looking beautiful and sexy and *very* frayed around the edges.''

''I stand corrected.''

''So what's wrong?''

''Stuff. Tad Bevel's shooting off his mouth about *what the System really wants*.'' She wandered into the kitchen and brewed coffee.

''Good old Tad . . . so nice to know someone has his hand on the pulse of the cosmos. So, *what do we want?* And let me guess, it probably insures lots of goodies for Crater Bay.''

''How well you know him.''

''Tad's good for us. He's a constant reminder that even

System dwellers can be assholes. Keeps us honest. But what else is bothering you, my dear?"

"Oh, things. It's about time for the biannual power down, and satellite shift from the Kenyan farm for maintenance, and that's always such a bitching job. We've had some labor—"

"Lydia," he said softly. "I miss you."

"Joe!"

"And by the way, stop talking bullshit. Tad Bevel and SDS maintenance indeed! Tell me what's really wrong."

It was an uncanny ability, to always say precisely the right thing at the right time. To see through all the subterfuge, and reach the heart of any matter. It was not something you expected to find in the powerful entrepreneur who had built an empire out of the sands of New Mexico, and into the stars which filled her desert nights. Forty years before he had constructed the only totally private space station, and ten years later had helped introduce the hearing boards to bring stability to the chaotic lawlessness of the System. He had then settled back to make money at a fabulous rate, and to drive the Earth authorities stark raving mad.

They had met at a cocktail party "celebrating" her new assignment aboard the EnerSun station. He instantly sensed that this "promotion" was not designed to further her climb up the corporate ladder, and even now she couldn't recall why she had poured out her woes and angers to this total stranger. He had taken her for a ride in his shuttle, letting her get a good look at her new home.

"You're a maverick, just like me. Sooner or later you would have murdered someone with a paperweight if you'd stayed Earthside. This is the best thing for you. In time you'll run this station."

"I'll still be tied to the home office."

"Stick with me, kid, and I'll show you how to beat the system."

She had and he had and they did, and in between all the alarms and joys and crises that make up thirty years of living, they had found time to make a baby. Perdita, all curly brown hair, and dancing slanted eyes. Joe called her imp, and limb of satan, and diablotin, and she had laughed and romped from one scrape to the next. She was a grown woman now, and teaching in the asteroids. Or was she on Earth doing some post-graduate work? It embarrassed Lydia that she couldn't remember.

"Lydia, darling, I'd sit and look at your face for ten or twelve hours, but this must be costing you a fortune."

"Sorry, I was thinking . . . remembering. We had some good times."

"They're not over yet."

"No, but you're so far away, and . . ." She dashed away the tears, surprised and furious by her breakdown.

"I'll come back. There's a liner due at Ceres in three weeks—"

"No! Lis Varllis is worse than any of the others we've faced. She's like a stung bear over this mess with Cabot, and if you were to come anywhere near Earth she'd . . . well, she'd do something stupid. I'm just being maudlin." She forced a smile. "Must be early senility setting in. I turn sixty next week, you know."

"Cry me a river. I'll be sixty-six next birthday."

"No one would put you a day over fifty."

"Lydia, I love you. Why didn't we ever marry?"

"You never asked."

He cocked his head, considering. "True. But I can't picture a little thing like that stopping you. If you had wanted that you would have proposed to me."

For a long moment they sat regarding each other across seven hundred million miles. She suddenly chuckled. "You look like a nervous sixteen-year-old waiting to find out if you really *have* knocked me up. You can relax, I'm not planning to propose. I know I could never take Amparo's place—"

"Lydia, I never knew you possessed this streak of romanticism. Do you really imagine I've been pining over my dead wife for forty years?"

"I didn't know, and I didn't want to ride roughshod over a part of your past."

"It is just that—past. I've never been the type to look back, Lydia, you know that." He paused, tugged at his lower lip. "Shall we get married?"

"No, I don't want the responsibility."

"What do you want?"

She looked surprised. "I think I just answered that. I don't want the responsibility anymore; of the station, the System, my daughters, nothing. And I also don't want to be alone now that I'm getting older. And don't say it, I know I'm being irrational. I can't have it both ways—"

"Yes you can. Quit, and come on out to the Belt."

"You really want me, Joe?"

"Desperately."

She could feel the smile spreading across her face, stretching muscles that seemed stiff from too many hours and days and years of frowns. Joe's lips twisted in that mocking smile that had first attracted her.

"Better?"

"Much." She felt light and effervescent, her mind darting in a thousand directions. She drew breath, and began to arrange her scattered thoughts. "Joe, there is one thing. In my haste to trap you into an invitation, I forgot."

He chuckled. "No trapping was necessary. But go ahead."

"It's about Amadea. Needless to say I'm shocked to find her giving press conferences on Earth blasting Cabot and the Mormon colonists, and working for that scumbag Lucius Renfrew at POW. She hasn't returned any of my calls, and I wondered if you knew whether anything happened on Mars. Something profound enough to turn my daughter into a stranger."

"Lydia, I don't know. Cab and Jenny have been like a pair of mummies whenever I've mentioned Amadea. But there is something there. A man can always tell when one of his sex has been a goat, and Cab has a decidedly goatish feel about him."

"So you're telling me to ask him?"

"Yes, but I don't know if you'll get an answer."

"I'll get an answer," she said flatly, her brows snapping together over her slanted eyes, mouth thinning into a sharp line.

"Poor, Cab," Joe managed after controlling his laughter. "I should take pity and warn him, but I won't. It'll be more fun to watch you roll him up, foot and horse."

"This is *not* very funny."

"Ah, there's my Lydia of old. And don't take Amadea's defection too much to heart. She's young. She'll come around. If it's any comfort you're not alone. Stinson is about ready to kill Musenda, and Carmella confessed to me that she can run a country, but can't fathom her son."

"At least *our* genes are running true."

"Perdita's on that liner I mentioned."

"So she has been on Earth. I'm ashamed to confess I'd forgotten."

"She won't mind, very well adjusted, that girl. And I know she'll be thrilled to know you're joining us."

"She'll probably run screaming from the asteroids, and hide on Charon," was her acid rejoinder. "Mothers and daughters occupying the same space cause explosions."

"There's a few hundred million square miles in the Belt. I think you'll manage."

"I just don't want her to feel pressured by my presence."

"Lydia, stop fretting. I haven't spent all this time on the com coaxing you out of a distempered freak just to have you fall back into one."

"Distempered freak!"

"That's better. See you in three months."

An urgent knocking. Jenny set aside her coffee mug and reader, and opened the door. Musenda White came cannon-balling into the apartment. Her tawny gold eyes were bright with unshed tears, but one look at the girl's flushed face, and Jenny reevaluated—anger, not grief.

"Jenny, I can't stand it!"

"What, Musenda?"

"He's a fossil. No, he's worse than that. He's a damn ice clod from the Oort cloud."

Jenny repressed a smile. "Your father?"

"Yes." The younger woman accepted the proffered cup of coffee, and set to prowling about the tiny apartment. "I want to go home for school. Is that so unreasonable?"

"You are going home for college."

"But that's two whole years away! I want to go now. Sammy Walsh got to go to *high school* on Earth."

"But Sammy's family was one of the first out here, and according to Joe they have beaucoup bucks."

"We're not exactly poverty-stricken."

"Musenda, how did your folks get out here?"

She froze, chagrin and sulkiness struggling for command of her pretty face. And she was pretty. Tall and leggy with cheekbones that would make any modeling agency reach for their contracts. Her skin was burnished ebony like her fa-ther's, but those strange pale gold eyes had to be a legacy from her long-dead mother. Her long hair was cornrowed, and each braid ended in a faceted crystal bead. Jenny had never seen her hair loose, and she wondered how the girl could stand the pressure of all those braids and beads. Then she remembered her own teenage years, and the agonies she had endured in pursuit of beauty.

"Well?" she prodded.

"They were 'dentureds." She flopped onto the sofa, sloshing coffee over her hand. "Okay. I get the point." She wiped the coffee residue onto her brilliantly colored skirt. "But I still think men shouldn't be allowed to sire children past the age of forty. It makes them too damn old to understand us once we're grown."

"Better not let Cab hear you say that."

Musenda bounced around to face Jenny, more coffee adding to the stain on her skirt. "Oh, shit! You're not . . . I mean, are you pregnant?"

"Good God, no!"

"You poor white girls, you can't hide a thing." Jenny pressed her hands to her burning cheeks.

"I'm really not pregnant."

"But you'd like to be."

"I'm also old-fashioned, I'd like to be married first."

"Oh, pooh!" Musenda was up prowling about the apartment again. "So you think I should wait?"

"I don't see that you have a lot of choice. And believe me, it wouldn't be much fun to have to work while you're in high school."

The straight little nose wrinkled. "Boys aren't everything."

Jenny threw back her head and laughed. "And this from the girl who's the despair of every man under the age of twenty-five on Ceres."

"I don't try."

"You don't have to, darling."

"Where's Cab?"

"Playing racket ball with Joe. I told him he was getting fat, and he flew off in a huff to the gym."

"Is he going to be impeached?"

"He's been impeached, the question is whether the Senate will remove him from office."

"Oh. That's confusing. So what do you do?"

"Hire a good lawyer, argue that Cab hasn't committed treason, bribery, or any other high crimes and misdemeanors, and hope that Cab's uncle Neville has enough clout to sway the Senate. Fortunately he's on the Judiciary committee which should help."

"It must be awful to be so far away from the action, and not able to *do* anything."

"It also has some compensations; at least we're beyond Lis Varllis's reach. The worst problem is that she can try Cab in the press, and there's nothing we can do to retaliate. No way to get our side before the public and the Senate. All those shenanigans she pulled on Mars—"

"What, what is it?"

"My God, I can't believe Cab and I missed it."

"Missed what, missed what?"

A slow smile touched Jenny's lips. "We probably couldn't present evidence about the agency harassment of the Jared colonists during the Senate trial. Some toady of Varllis's would try to have it ruled immaterial, but if we . . . ." She darted to the com.

"Jenny, you're driving me crazy! What?"

"Shhh. Could you please page Justice Huntington," she requested of the Com-Op. "Tell him to please return to his apartment immediately."

"Paging," came the flat, mechanical response.

"Now, will you explain?"

"On Mars there was a pattern of systematic harassment of the colonists. OSHA shut down their diamond mine for safety violations, while SPACECOM banned the exportation of diamonds which were to buy the mining equipment which would have removed the safety problems, and further banned the importation of the equipment until the environmental suit was settled."

"I remember Dad talking about that. They didn't want the colonists to begin terraforming Mars." Musenda frowned. "But how does that relate to mining equipment?"

"Because with the equipment Jared could have dug diamonds out of the ground at a tremendous rate, and those diamonds were going to provide the capital to begin the project. It was rather a stretch, what we call bootstrapping in the law, but you can see how the machinery was peripherally involved with POW's objections to the terraforming."

"You lawyers think like this all the time?"

"All the time."

"You're crazy."

The door flew open. "Jenny, what's wrong? Are you all right?" His hair was sweat-matted, and plastered across his forehead, and a sweat stain darkened the front of his warm-ups.

"I'm fine."

"You're—"

"I've had a brainstorm."

He dropped heavily into a chair, and eyed her with both revulsion and fascination. "Joe's coming too, but he said it wasn't anything serious so he's taking a shower."

"That's nice. You can take a shower too, but after I tell you." She pressed a kiss onto the corner of his mouth. "Cab, the Jared suit under the Administrative Procedures Act requesting judicial review of the agency actions is still pending."

"My God," he said blankly, and pushed back his unruly forelock.

"I'm still lost," Musenda announced.

"I can hear the case, and then the public as well as the Senate will be aware of the administration's activities on Mars. And then my actions won't look so completely lunatic."

"Was it a brainstorm?"

"It was more than that. It was brilliant." He cupped her face in his hands, and gave her a hard kiss. "Jenny, I love you."

"Excuse me." They turned to Musenda. "I thought you'd been impeached."

"But not removed."

"There's that illusive difference again."

"Musenda, you're a federal judge until you're removed, and only the Senate can do that. In the 1980s there was the case of Justice Clayborne who continued to draw his salary while serving time in a federal penitentiary. The situation continued for over two years until the Senate finally got around to removing him. If Neville can draw out these hearings for a month or so we'll give Ms. High and Mighty Lis Varllis something to whine about."

Jenny knuckled her chin. "Andy's a stringer for UPI. He can wire—or whatever you call it when you're in the middle of the Asteroid Belt—the evidence presented during the hearing. We should call him, and tell him to skip Mars, and get out here as soon as he can."

Musenda eyed them, her lips narrowing into a thin line. "I thought you two were different, but you're not. You're just as bad as Joe and my father! You're going to cause so much trouble that I'll *never* be accepted in a school Earthside!" Her voice caught on a sob, and she whirled, and ran from the apartment.

"What was that all about?"

"Cab, sometimes I think you live on another planet."

"Jenny, that was an incredibly hen-witted thing to say. *Of course* I live on another planet. I'm stuck on this freezing ball of rock, I can't go home because of that power-mad bitch in the White House, I've been impeached—for the second time in less than a year—"

"But you don't notice the people around you."

"That's not true, I . . ." He tugged ruefully at a sideburn. "You're right. I don't. So, what was that all about?"

"Musenda and Stinson have been bickering ever since we arrived. She's got stars in her eyes about Earth—"

"There you go again."

"All right!" She gave an exasperated toss of her long red hair. "She's got her eye on Earth, and has turned it into some kind of wonderful fairyland. She's also at the age to rebel, and what with her dreams of home, and her father's staunch pro-System stand, she's making Stinson's life a misery." Jenny gazed at the door, sighed. "She's been fascinated with us since we actually come from that magical place."

"And because you're a good and sympathetic listener?"

"Yes, that too. I remember being that age, and it was damn hard. Fortunately I was too busy and too tired because of ballet to get up to much mischief, but Musenda is ripe for it. And today we've just become part of the enemy."

"Foolishness! I don't have time to worry over the emotional agonies of an adolescent."

"What are you going to do when you have some of your own?"

"Lock them in a closet until they're twenty-one."

"That's not an answer."

"Why are we having this conversation?" His eyes widened in dismay, and a deep red suffused his pale cheeks. "Good God! You can't be . . . you're not—"

"No," she snapped, averting her head. "Though why you should act so surprised . . . We haven't precisely been— Oh, never mind. Let's call Andy."

"Wait." His hand closed softly about her wrist. "You're not happy?"

"I'm very happy. But—"

"But what?"

"No, you're obviously satisfied with things as they are."

"Jenny, don't be angry with me. Especially when I don't know what I've done." His long lashes veiled his dark gray eyes.

"You haven't done anything."

"Is that the problem? Well, is it?"

"I don't know what you mean."

"And I don't know how to make it any clearer."

"No, you don't want to make it any clearer."

"Jenny, I hate it when you women get vague and meaningful and intuitive." But he didn't ask for any further clarification, as if fearing what she might say or demand if the conversation should continue.

The door to the office closed sharply behind his erect back. Jenny grabbed a reader, and called up the pleadings in their latest case. The pages scrolled by, and she registered not a word.

She was feeling very battered, and angry enough to turn this from a spat into a full-blown fight, but she had vowed on Mars that if she could only find him alive she would never fight with him again. Which was really stupid because that vow had lasted about two hours as she recalled. But she continued to give power to the promise. Possibly as a means to keep from looking at her real fears. Or fear really, centered in the person of one tiny, incredibly beautiful Eurasian woman who had mesmerized Cab. And if Cab could be so affected by Amadea, might it not happen again? Which put her in doubt of the strength of his love for her, and she was damned if she would blackmail him into marriage. She had to be certain. The proposal had to come from him, freely, and without any coercion. But if it didn't come soon . . .

"Jenny, I can't reach the ship. There's no response, and Phobos station has lost all contact."

She jerked up, stared at him with deepening horror as the full import reached her. "Dear God . . . Andy."

Chapter Five

It wasn't every night he awoke from a deep sleep to find two soft and decidedly female hands gripping his shoulders. Andy came up out of the bunk like a broaching whale, and flailed about in the dark.

"Ow!" came a cry as his hand connected with something. "Andy, for God's sake."

The voice was hauntingly familiar, but at weird o'clock in the morning with his head full of dreams and his eyes gritty with sleep, he couldn't place it.

"Listen."

He waited for her to amplify as to *what* he was supposed to listen to.

"To what?" he slurred after an appropriate interval of time had elapsed.

The pleasantly warm feminine thigh which had been pressed against the bulge of his belly was removed. He peered about, and reached for the overhead light, and a glass of cold water took him full in the face. Spluttering, gasping, wiping away moisture, he opened his mouth to bellow and was stopped by a hand across his lips.

"Andy, it's Dita. Are you awake enough to absorb that?"

"Dita. How the hell did I miss you?"

"So much for journalistic observation skills. I boarded this ship at the jump point same as you did. You've just been too busy pursuing your big story to notice."

"You have *not* been at dinner where I might—would— have noticed you."

"That's true. To tell you the truth I caught a bug just

before leaving Paris, and I stuck to my cabin trying to shake it. But none of that matters.''

"Oh, yeah, you wanted me to listen. So I'm listening.''

"Not to me, idiot, to the . . .''

"Engines,'' they finished together, as Andy finally focused on the niggling sense of something not quite right which had been licking at the edges of his consciousness.

"We're not due for burn for another two days. Something's happening.''

"Avert your virgin eyes. I gotta get dressed.'' He snapped on the light, and Joe Reichart and Lydia Kim Nu's daughter stood revealed. She was studiously studying the metal seam above the cabin door.

"You don't suppose it's some sort of technical problem?'' he asked as he rolled out of the tiny bunk, and cracked his shins on the stationary table.

Though the three antimatter ships were touted as "luxury,'' they were in fact exceedingly cramped. It had been expensive to build the giant accelerator, so to recover the cost and make a profit for Earthside shareholders, the precious antihydrogen was priced very high. And since the bigger the ship the more fuel it burned . . . hence these tiny cabins. Andy had heard it was even worse on the military vessels.

"There would have been an announcement. Something soothing to keep the passengers happy, or some instructions if the situation were critical.''

"You're right.'' He grunted as he bent over, and pulled on his socks.

"I think we should start at the control room.''

"Would you stop trying to manage everything. You're just like your mother.''

"Most people would say it's my father in me.'' She turned and faced him, hands resting lightly on her hips. "Okay, what do you think we ought to do?''

"Check out the control room.''

Perdita Kim Nu slipped through the door into the narrow corridor. Andy was right behind her, but he almost left a piece of his slacks behind as the emergency lock-down warning bleated through the ship shutting and sealing all the doors.

"Shit! Now what?''

"We go on. That isn't the collision signal. So the inner doors ought to be open.''

"Just locking the twitty grounders into their cabins so they can't get in the way of the crew."

Dita paused. "So maybe it is something legitimate."

"Do you believe that?"

"No."

"Neither do I, we go."

So far everything had gone like clockwork. Which made Wairegi nervous. You plan for foul-ups, and when they don't come you're always left with the superstitious sense that now something *really* bad is going to happen.

Their timing had been dictated by the laws of physics and astrogation, and their need to take the ship during its night cycle when only the crew would be abroad. According to Viriku they were cutting it incredibly fine, but if they could manage to secure the controls within their twenty-minute window she would be able to reprogram the computer, pull them out of Mars trajectory, and send them on toward the asteroids.

They had done it in fifteen, and so Wairegi worried.

Viriku huddled over the computer, her shotgun leaned up against the panel close to hand. It looked odd. The old-style weapon on the bridge of the most technologically advanced machine yet built by men. But there was a sound reason for their choice of weaponry. The dispersal of shot from a shotgun blast would tear a man apart, but not pierce the delicate skin of the spaceship. They were also carrying null-gee pistols. Large bulky things, their size was dictated by the size of the booster shells. If they should have to fight in space or on the surface of an asteroid, they were prepared.

His eyes roved the bridge. Kariuki, James, and J.K. were cradling shotguns. They seemed relaxed, but the dart of their eyes betrayed their nervousness. Paul and Cyril had marched away the four on-duty crew members; one gesticulating and arguing, the other three looking stunned. At their signal Viriku had locked down the cabins, and the ship was theirs. Paul and Cyril were taking a final swing through the ship just to be sure no one had slipped past the closing net, but Wairegi wasn't anticipating any problems.

And that was a mistake too. Complacency would be as deadly as miscalculation. He would have to watch himself.

Viriku shifted uncomfortably, reached into the pocket of her jumpsuit, and pulled out a grenade. The click of the metal on the console was loud in the quietly humming room, and drew Wairegi's attention from the stars holding steady beyond the wide ports.

"What the devil do you mean by carrying one of those things. My orders were explicit—shotguns only!"

She swiveled slowly around in the chair, head thrown back, eyeing him from beneath slitted lids. "And it was a stupid order." Kariuku sucked in a quick breath as Wairegi's hand tightened into a fist. Wa Thondu took a stiff step forward. "Sooner or later someone is going to have to die. One hopes it's one of theirs rather than one of ours—"

"No! That is not the purpose of this undertaking."

"Oh, of course, how could I have been so stupid." She snatched up the shotgun. "We're carrying these as walking sticks."

Wairegi snatched the weapon from her hand, and flung it across the room. J.K., with admirable presence of mind, leaped for it and managed to catch it before it struck the floor, but the glance he exchanged with Kariuki was one of wide-eyed terror.

"I will not have killing! A bluff is all that's needed. We saw that this night. Face a man with a gun, and he'll instantly surrender."

"And what if they hadn't? What if they'd told you to go to hell, and fought us? Were you going to apologize in your best British cricket-field accent, beg pardon, and offer to return to your cabin until we could all have another go at it? This isn't a *game*, wa Thondu, no fair play, no sportsmen all, this is a war, and people die in wars!" Viriku was on her feet, screaming into Wairegi's expressionless face.

"And what would you have done with that little grenade? If they hadn't surrendered?" asked Wairegi.

"Fought, and if that failed, blown us all to hell. Better that than a jail cell in Nairobi."

"We're in shit," whispered Andy. He and Perdita were huddled at the base of the ladder leading to the control room, and the voices were floating down with painful clarity. "What do we do?"

"Head for the arms locker."

"Is there one?"

"Who knows? But it's worth a try."

"Dita, I'm afraid I'm one of those fellows like wa Thondu

described. Point a gun at me, and I start thinking about my skin.''

"So maybe they'll feel the same when *we* point guns at them.''

"I had a feeling she wasn't going to let me off the hook,'' he remarked to the cosmos. "You're not going to let me off the hook?''

"No.''

"That fire-eater upstairs isn't going to surrender.''

"Then I'll shoot her first.''

"Just make sure she hasn't primed her little toy, okay?''

"Andy, we're the only people still free. We have a duty to the other passengers and the crew.''

He caught her by the shoulders, held her in place. "But maybe we can best serve them by not engaging in beau geste. It's two against seven, Dita.''

Her exotic slanted eyes were bright with unshed tears. She dashed away the moisture with the back of a hand. "Damn you for being rational. I want to fight. This is an outrage. Let's at least *see* if there's an arms locker.''

"Okay. It's not a very big ship to play hide and seek in, but maybe we can keep out of their way.''

They turned, stared down the double barrels of a pump shotgun. "So much for guerrilla warfare, pardner.'' The journalist dropped an arm over her shoulders. "We didn't even hear 'em a sneakin' up on us.'' Perdita just sighed, and pressed her curly head against his chest.

"They were hiding down below.''

"We weren't hiding, we were lurking, or skulking, something romantic and ballsy like that, but not hiding.''

Wairegi ran a hand across his face, tried to ignore the bands of pain that were tightening about his temples. "Mr. Throckmorton, you are most troublesome. You should be serenely sleeping in your cabin, unaware of events.''

"Yeah, well, sorry to disappoint you, but not all of us are groundhogs. We can tell when a ship enters premature engine burn.'' The Kenyan noticed the rueful, apologetic glance he shot at his companion.

She was small and fine-boned with wide-set eyes whose epicanthic fold gave testimony to her mixed heritage. Tumbled brown curls just touched her collar, and she had the look of a pugnacious tomboy.

"And you are?"

"Perdita Kim Nu."

She announced the name as one who is used to it commanding instant respect and recognition, but it meant nothing to Wairegi.

"So what happens now?" Andy asked.

"You will be locked in your cabins."

"I take it we're being hijacked. You object to the word?" the journalist asked, seeing Wairegi's frown.

"We are temporarily taking command of this vessel."

"I hate euphemisms," Kim Nu muttered. "They seem designed to soothe someone's elastic conscience."

"Take them to their cabins," he snapped at Paul.

"Just a point of interest," Andy called as he was prodded toward the ladder. "How did you get all the heavy armament aboard?"

"I bribed an official at Riyadh. They are sympathetic to our cause. Now you make a face, Mr. Throckmorton."

"It's so melodramatic. But at the jump point?"

"Even easier. There is no baggage or passenger check. I suppose they assume any would be . . ." He paused groping for a word.

"Terrorists?" Kim Nu suggested sweetly. "Or if you prefer a euphemism there's freedom fighter, or liberation—"

Viriku darted from her chair, and struck the smaller woman. The slap cracked through the room, and jerked Dita's head around. She lightly touched her lip where it had split on a tooth. "If you weren't armed I'd beat the holy snot out of you, but there's one thing my father did teach me—never, ever, fuck with a gun."

Wairegi roared with fury, his hands closing about Viriku's neck. He shook her like a rat in a terrier's jaws, and flung her aside. Then stared, horrified at his hands.

Viriku struggled up onto an elbow, one hand rubbing at her bruised throat. "So, there is some passion in you." She coughed, trying to ease the pain. "And if you have to learn to be ruthless on me, so be it."

"Be quiet! My God, how could I have—"

"Because you're a man, not a plaster saint! I am so *sick* of your peaceful righteousness! You'll lead us all to hell because you don't know your own soul. Are you the wise elder statesman, or a violent revolutionary? Well, you better make up your mind before we get to Ceres because then the hard decisions begin.''

"And your decision would always be to kill, and kill and kill!''

"Yes! They were never backward about killing us. And we should start here. Jettison the prisoners. It's safer than guarding them.''

"My God, you're a monster.''

"Maybe, but at least I know myself. You know nothing.'' She turned her wide, compelling eyes on the other men. "We need someone else to lead us, but you won't heed me. You'll follow blindly because he's a man, and I'm only a woman, and a Luo woman at that. Well, be damned to you all!''

"Will you continue to pilot this ship?''

"Yes. Because I do believe in what we're doing, and I can hope that these fools will realize how useless you are, and replace you before we reach Ceres.'' She knelt panting on the floor at his feet, but there was nothing about her to suggest defeat. She was like a wild animal ready to spring.

A whisper of movement from the door reminded him that the two whites had been interested spectators. He turned with grave dignity. "I can assure you that no harm will come to you while you are aboard this ship.''

Andy nodded, but Perdita, swinging onto the ladder, said acidly, "I'll be sure to remember that when we all go space walking together—without our suits.''

Lieutenant-General Ingvar Saber was not a happy man. He did not like being in an office. More to the point he did not like being in an office on Mars. He had a feeling that the order of martial law which had been laid across the planet had nothing to do with societal unrest and an awful lot to do with massaging some politico's bruised ego. But that was any field officer's dilemma: trying to keep a fighting force at peak while wrestling with contradictory and sometimes downright idiotic orders from home.

He was a handsome man in his mid-forties with eyes like slivers of blue arctic ice, and tightly curled platinum blond hair. It made an odd contrast with his deeply tanned skin, and despite rumors through the squadron it was entirely natural.

He tossed his pen onto the desk, and it sank beneath a litter of papers. *Ah, military efficiency*, he thought, pushing back his chair and pacing over to a narrow window. *Orders are all handled electronically now, but we still have to have a welter of paper with my elegant signature on it to make it official. Stupid waste of time.*

The view from the tiny fortresslike slit was uninspiring. Red sand, seared by the landing jets of hundreds of ships over the years. A jumble of warehouses like children's blocks, the reactor cooling towers of Eagle Port. The tops had been neatly blown off them, and tiny suited figures jetted about the jagged stumps like swarming gnats. The repairs didn't seem to be progressing with much speed.

Their hearts probably aren't in it, he thought with a sigh. Though Eagle Port was a government colony, and though the squadron had been received with perfect courtesy by the residents, Ingvar still sensed an undercurrent of resentment. They were colonists first, and civil servants second.

He spun away from the window with its view of the damaged cooling towers. They were symbols of the troubles which had brought him here, and kept him chained to this desk.

Four months ago the radical environmental group POW had seized a Belt freighter. It had been loaded with diamonds from the Jared colony—a Mormon enclave some 700 kilometers from Eagle Port—payment for a load of heavy mining and milling machinery. The colonists had armed themselves, and the squadron had been ordered in to restore order. Actually the squadron had been ordered in before the full-blown crisis developed, and it was this timing which still disturbed Saber. He had a feeling that certain individuals groundside had known *well before the fact* that trouble was about to erupt on Mars.

In addition to restoring order he'd had orders to arrest Justice Cabot Huntington. Saber was no ship's lawyer, but to his mind the grounds for arrest had seemed flimsy at best, and trumped up at worst. But he was a soldier, so he did what he was told by the civilians. Unfortunately (or fortunately, depending upon a person's point of view), Huntington and his gorgeous law clerk had boarded the freighter, and flown Mars right under the noses of the incoming squadron.

He had arrived to find the shivering survivors of the POW takeover, and a gang of very angry colonists. They hadn't waited for help from Earth, they had shot it out with the environmentalists, and recovered their property. All except the diamonds. Those troublesome chips of carbon had been aboard the *Gray Goose* when she lifted.

The real shock had been to find that the Jared colonists were using Eagle Port's military-issue weaponry. Specially sighted and designed for Martian conditions, supposedly kept under the sole authority of Mike Despopolous, Port Administrator. Mike and his assistants had been found locked in their own arms locker, but Saber sensed it was a ruse. Despopolous was as much on the side of the Jared people as . . . well, as anyone could be.

Which brought him around to his original point. He and his squadron were tolerated interlopers, and he was being used as a patsy for someone Earthside, and he hated it, and . . . and the paperwork wouldn't wait.

With a groan he dropped back into his chair, and tried to concentrate. He also had that journalist coming to interview him, and it would look odd if he didn't—

A sharp chime, and his aide, Major John Adams, entered.

"What now?"

Adams, his teeth very white in his black face, grinned at his superior's wretched tone. "How did you know I was bringing you bad news?"

"Instinct. It comes with command. S-so, give me the worst."

"Phobos station has lost contact with the liner *Constellation*."

"Details?"

"Not many. Suddenly its beacon cut out, and they lost all radio contact."

Saber knuckled his eyes. "This is of course very upsetting, but why tell us?"

"Do you want the official word, or my theory?"

"Both."

"Okay, officially we've been ordered to check it out. Unofficially what I think is that Trans-United having misplaced this very expensive piece of hardware screamed to their Congressmen, who in turn screamed to the White House, who in turn screamed to Defense—"

"Who are now s-screaming at us. And just what is it they think we're s-supposed to or can do?"

"Find the ship, or what's left of it if something did go catastrophically wrong."

"Morons! Do they know how fucking enormous s-space is?" Major Adams knew a rhetorical question when he heard one, and remained silent. "Like looking for a s-single s-snowflake in an arctic s-snow field. It's a waste of fuel and man hours, though God knows we're not accomplishing a damn thing here. In fact, if it wouldn't cause an uproar, I'd go . . . but no. I'll s-stay here and file papers like a good boy. Detail a s-ship, and let's get on with this exercise in futility."

"Yes, sir." Saber bent over the papers once more, but quickly became aware that his aide had not yet left the office. He looked up, one pale eyebrow quirking inquiringly. "Sir, permission to ask a question."

"Granted."

"Just what *are* we doing here, sir?"

"Maintaining order."

"Excuse me, sir, but I think all we're doing is creating a shitload of ill will."

"Major, you know I can't agree with that s-statement."

"Can you comment?"

"I'd rather not. It might incriminate—" An urgent knocking caught him midsentence.

Adams opened the door, and was almost bowled over by the entrance of a small plump woman in a rumpled blue flight suit. "Lieutenant Kim Nu, sir!" Her salute was textbook crisp, and made Saber's response seem all the more lackadaisical by comparison.

He didn't know her well, in fact hardly at all, since she was aboard Tracy Belmanor's ship, but he did know she had some of the quickest response times in the squadron, and was generally thought to be a brain. She was also a member of that odd and elite breed—the entry fighter pilot. From the 1990s fighter planes had become increasingly more sophisticated. Computer and structural advances had insured that they could fight at higher and higher speeds. Unfortunately, even the invention of gee suits had not been able to completely block the effects of high-gee stress on the one weak link in the complex chain—the humans who flew the machines. Tests indicated that the perfect pilot for these super planes were short overweight women with high blood pressure. Congress and the Pentagon had tried to resist the evidence, but after one disastrous year in which twenty-two planes had crashed because of pilot blackout, they had bowed to the pressure of economics. Women now flew the fighter jets.

"Lieutenant, what can I do for you?"

"I heard about the *Constellation*, sir." Saber and Adams exchanged glances, but it was pointless to protest or deny. Within the small, close-knit space squadron even the most secret of orders were common knowledge within a few hours. "And I came to request assignment to whichever ship you send out. My sister was—is on that ship, sir," she continued breathlessly.

"Your devotion to your s-sister does you credit, Lieutenant, but you know how hopeless this probably is."

"Yes, sir, but I'd still like to try. We might get lucky."

"Denied."

"Sir!"

"It's been my experience, Lieutenant, that people with a personal s-stake tend to make dangerous decisions."

Her brow furrowed, intensifying the slant of her dark eyes. "I'm hardly in *command*, sir."

"Nonetheless your request is s-still denied." He picked up his pen, then relented and added, "Personally, Lieutenant, I think it likely that the *Constellation* has had mechanical difficulties, and that we'll hear from her before too much more time has passed. Therefore I'm going to wait eight hours before s-sending out a s-ship."

"And if you're wrong, sir. If she's even now bleeding her air into the vacuum?"

"Then leaving now won't make a damn bit of difference. Dismissed."

"Yes, sir." She spun on her heel, and left.

"And now I'm in trouble with both Earth and S-System."

"How's that, sir?"

"Because that woman is Lydia Kim Nu's daughter, ergo it is also Lydia Kim Nu's daughter who is aboard the *Constellation*, and last but by no means least, Lydia Kim Nu is one of the most powerful figures in the S-System." He held up a hand, forestalling any comment. "And, last, but not least, there are my s-superiors groundside who are going to have my butt for delaying eight hours before s-sending out a s-ship. God, it's great to be a general."

"Yes, sir," agreed Adams with a wide grin, and closed the door behind him.

"Ms. Varllis, there's still no report on that missing spaceship. . . ." Trigg Williams recoiled at her expression, the words dying in his throat.

She moved in on him, leaned in over the desk, palms flat on the clear plastic surface. "I am sick to death of hearing about space." Her voice was low, each word enunciated with careful clarity. "I suggest you not mention the word in my hearing for at least three days."

She started into her office, her cap of silver-blond hair brushing at her jawline.

"But, ma'am, Senator Roth is demanding an update. He's called three times."

She turned back, rested a hand against the door jamb. "Trigg, you're the first male secretary I've ever hired, and you're starting to make me regret it."

"Yes, ma'am. Excuse me, ma'am," he muttered, staring into his computer screen.

She knew inwardly he was writhing. A small bug on a pin. Trapped between his boss—alternately described as the toughest White House Chief of Staff since Regan, and the Mona Lisa of politics—and the powerful senior Senator from Connecticut. The knowledge brought no answering wave of pity for his predicament.

The cool lilac and white atmosphere of her office closed about her. Usually it exercised a beneficial effect on her nerves, but today it would have taken a Valium to quiet her jumping thoughts.

She propped her elbows on the peach-colored blotter, and dug her nails deep into her scalp. Dictatorships were the best. No need to consult, to listen to boobs, to give careful consideration to moronic suggestions. Just one or two people at the top making the decisions. Whoever had invented a White House staff meeting . . .

"I feel I must bring up the situation of our squadron on Mars."

Jack McConnell's high-pitched nasal voice cut through the silence that had fallen over the meeting. With his long bitter face, and the heavy tangle of brow, like a thicket from which his eyes peered like small woodland animals, the Secretary of the Air Force had the look of an Old Testament prophet.

"What's to bring up?" asked small, tubby Rachael Weiss of HEW.

"General Abrams and General Saber are concerned over the squadron's continued presence on the planet. It's costing a fortune in taxpayers' dollars, and it's also costing us the good will of the Martian colonists. General Saber feels that nothing is to be gained by continuing the occupation.''

"That's for the President to decide,'' Lis snapped.

"Which is why I bring it up.'' The Secretary of the Air Force stared down his bony nose, but Lis refused to drop her eyes.

The men and women seated at the long table looked to President Richard Long. He was a youthful-looking man with cinnamon-colored hair, and clear brown eyes. Today those eyes were troubled, however, and he stared unseeing down the length of the table.

"Sir?'' pressed McConnell.

Long stirred. "I confess I'm not too well informed about the situation on Mars.'' He pointedly avoided looking at his Chief of Staff.

"Our sources indicate that the unrest is continuing.''

"General Saber?'' McConnell inquired just a shade too politely.

"*Other* sources.'' Lis forced herself to relax her jaw.

The Secretary of Defense shook himself like a large dog rising from a nap. "I confess,'' he drawled in his soft South Carolina accent, "that I'm none too happy about havin' all but one of them ships out around Mars. Might give that Tupolev fellow notions.''

"Surely several thousand warheads both here and in orbit should be enough to nip any 'notions' in the bud. The presence or lack of six more antimatter ships are not likely to tip the balance.'' Lis's scorn was obvious.

"No sayin'. Mr. Tupolev is a mighty dangerous man.''

"Who hasn't let out a peep since that mess over the mining collective.'' Attorney General Christina Holland seemed to realize she had committed a major gaffe, and busied herself by searching through her handbag.

The cabinet again looked to the President for guidance. The silence seemed to come seeping from the walls.

"Why are we on Mars?'' McConnell wheezed.

"To maintain order,'' Lis gritted.

"Does it need maintaining? Lucius Renfrew and his people left two months ago.''

Long at last spoke. "Jack, it's critical that we reestablish control over the System.'' He lapsed back into silence.

"We're using the squadron to send a message,'' Lis continued. "That this kind of lawlessness and anarchy will not be tolerated."

"Thank you, Mr. President, Ms. Varllis. I was beginning to think there was no rational reason behind our continued presence on Mars. I would like to go on record, however, as being in opposition to this policy. I don't think the full ramifications of this action have been examined, nor do I think that alternatives have been considered."

"Thank you, Jack, your objections have been noted."

Holland had emerged from her examination of the depths of her purse. "Which brings me to a related topic." The Attorney General's usual expression was one of sweet vacuity, a useful blind which had caused more than one legal opponent to underestimate her. The A.G.'s next words brought home to Lis that she had made the same mistake. "All this agency action on Mars . . . may I assume that these rulings by SPACECOM and OSHA were in the nature of another of these *messages*?"

"You may not!"

"Then they were justified?"

"Naturally."

"I hope so," Holland murmured beneath her breath.

"Why?"

But Lis had never received an answer for news had arrived of the loss or at least the loss of contact with the *Constellation*, and the cabinet meeting had adjourned shortly after that disquieting bit of news.

Space! Space! Space!

And what had Christina Holland been driving at? The Jared colonists had filed suit under the Administrative Procedures Act challenging the agency action, but that case had fallen into limbo with the flight of Cabot Huntington. So she had nothing to worry about. No one would ever know that there had been no grounds for the various agency actions on Mars.

She wished now she hadn't been quite so heavy-handed in her harassment of the Jared colonists. For if it should come out, Rich would take the blame. He wouldn't even be able to claim ignorance because the public was notoriously unforgiving of presidents who lost control of their White Houses.

She could bury the trail in a bureaucratic whirlwind, replace agency heads who'd been closely involved in the Martian rulings, discredit the Jared colonists, but that still left

Huntington as a free and troublesome agent. And he might pull some legal prestidigitation before he could be removed. And hurt Rich. And hurt her.

She lifted her face from her hands, and keyed up the computer. *Marshals, Federal. Locations.*

Somehow she had to rope Huntington back to Earth. *Abilene, Anchorage.* Once groundside she would find a way to keep him safely muzzled until his trial was concluded, and he had been removed from office. *Baltimore, Boston.* But in order to accomplish this she needed a ship, a *fast* ship, to pluck him from the asteroids, and return him home. And the *Constellation* had vanished—*Carson City*—and six of the Air Force's expensive toys were in orbit around Mars, which left her with one to be ordered out, preferably before McConnell or Saber could object.

Her mind darted about grasping at facts like a goldfish thrashing after crumbs. She felt hemmed in by problems, and it only added to her anger and bitterness to know that many of them had been self-made. But not the basic problem. That had been created by those damned colonists demanding more autonomy, more rights, ignoring Earth's rights to their production and loyalty. *Ceres!*

She jabbed, stopped the endless scroll of names and cities across the screen. *Irving Pizer.*

A sharp burning, and she realized that she was clasping her hands so tightly that the blood was receding from the fingers. Carefully she unlaced her fingers, and shook back the circulation.

The final piece was in place. A ship and a marshal. It was all she needed, and this time they would break, bend to the government's ultimate authority.

She pushed aside the terrifying thought that the last time it had been tried a president had fallen. Speed and daring, that was all that was required. And grit enough to withstand the public outcry (should any arise). They also had the good fortune to be three years from an election. It was timing which had defeated deBaca, and the fact he'd tried half measures.

She would not make the same mistakes.

Chapter Six _____

"Judge?" whispered Irving Pizer, sliding into the vacant seat next to Cab.

"Yes?"

"We need to talk."

Several members of the audience were shifting, and eyeing them with hostility.

"Jenny, will you excuse me?"

She leaned over him to Irving. "Is it trouble?"

"Depends on how you define trouble," he hedged.

"I'm coming."

"So go!" a man in the row behind hissed.

They slithered out of the row of theater seats, Cab casting reluctant glances toward the tiny stage. Not that this amateur production of *The Taming of the Shrew* was so good, but it was a welcome change from canned entertainment. It had the vibrancy that only a live production could hold. Nor was it that unusual. The citizens of this tiny outpost had a bewildering array of musical, theatrical, and sporting events from which to choose.

In the lobby Irving ran a hand over his bald pate. Liver spots mottled the tan skin, and were echoed on the back of his knobbed and veined hands. Irving had run the Ceres police force such as it was (he had once described it as three men, a boy, and a dog) for the better part of forty-five years.

Cab had a good deal of affection for the little man. Jenny said it was because he had finally met a person of the male persuasion who was actually shorter than he was. There had been some stiff words over that as he recalled. But that wasn't the reason. In all of his life Cab had never met a man who bubbled with more good humor than Irving Pizer. In four months he had never heard a sharp or angry word escape the man's withered lips, and his continual stream of amusing remarks kept everyone chuckling. They were never funny after the fact. Onc of those "you had to be there situations," but God he was a delight in person.

He was also the oldest living colonist anywhere in the System. Joe guessed him to be ninety-six, though Irving would only admit to eighty-one.

"So, where do we conduct this conversation?"

"In a bar," Irving said firmly. "Only place for it, a bar."

Ceres didn't possess an elegant watering hole like the White Owl on the EnerSun station. Instead three utilitarian bars vied for customers, and all did a very good business. Which perhaps said something about the type of people who settled in the Belt, though Cab hadn't quite been able to figure out what.

Ike's was the closest so after a quick ride through several tunnels on the people-mover they plunged into the dimly lit, smoky interior. Jenny staked out a secluded booth, and switched on the fresher.

"There, now I can see you."

Ike, his ever-ready antenna for gossip up and operating at the entrance of this interesting trio, slouched over.

"Hi, what can I getcha?"

"Beer," Jenny said quickly.

"Beer," Cab echoed firmly. It was the only alcohol that could be depended upon to taste even remotely like its Earthly counterpart. Unless you ordered import which cost the Earth.

"Martini. With an onion."

"No onions. We're all out. None till next shipment."

"Hell of a situation. No onions. I'd like to know why we don't grow pearl onions. Something shady going on here. We should appoint a government commission." He dropped one lid in an elaborate wink. "Think of the benefits to flow from such an action. Unlimited, state-subsidized pearl onions, and work for the indigent."

Irving continued to babble on in this vein until Ike, defeated at last by rapid-fire nonsense, gave up on learning anything interesting, and slouched away.

"Nosy busybody. 'Course if I wasn't so busy with important matters like drinking, and trying to keep on living, I might be a nosy busybody too.'' He grinned, and rubbed at his jutting blade of a nose.

The drinks were served with a lack of ambience that only Ike's could achieve. The owner/bartender then turned large, sad accusing eyes on Irving and drooped back to the bar.

Cab mopped at spilled beer with a handkerchief. ''Shall we get down to business?'' Jenny took a long drink of beer as if fortifying herself, and tried to lick the white foam mustache. Cab leaned in, and carefully dabbed it away.

''Thank you. I suppose cocktail napkins would be a level of decadence unknown at Ike's. Here.'' She pushed her glass to Cab.

''You don't want it?''

''The sip was enough.''

Irving was glaring at the green olive floating in the gin. ''Cabot, I need your advice,'' he said abruptly, still not removing his gaze from the offending olive.

He pulled his attention from Jenny. ''It's yours to have. Provided I have any to give.''

''I've been ordered to arrest you.'' Cab choked, beer going up his nose. Jenny pounded, and he coughed and mopped at his streaming eyes with the already damp handkerchief.

''What's he been up to, Irving?'' she asked, still slapping Cab on the back. ''Indecent exposure? Extortion? Bribery?'' Her voice faltered and died away at the serious expression in the old man's eyes.

''Not a local matter, Jennifer. You may not know—hell, I'd almost forgotten—but I'm a federal marshal.''

''Oh, God,'' Cab groaned. ''Lis Varllis.''

''I've been ordered to arrest you, and hold you until a ship arrives from Earth. Put you on that ship, and ship you out.''

''So what's the advice you needed?''

''What should I do, Cabot?''

''Arrest me. What else can you do?''

''And I'll be on that ship back to Earth with you.''

''I don't understand.''

''I don't think Stinson and Joe, not to mention my friends and associates, and less-than-respectful descendants are going to love me much if I do my duty. They'll run me out on the proverbial rail.''

''Irving, what do you want me to say?'' He clasped his hands at his breast. ''Please, Marshal Pizer, don't arrest me! And then you'll be in trouble. No.'' He shook his head.

"What are they going to do to me? I'm a zillion miles away."

Cab folded his arms on the table, and rested his head on the back of his hands. "This is such a mess. I should have been a law professor. Then I wouldn't be in this uncomfortable situation."

"Greatness is, however, too often anything but happiness. It is often a tumult in which the heavens are at war with each other."

"That isn't much comfort, Jennifer. And I'm not great. I don't covet greatness."

"Joe says you've grown up to it, however," mused Irving. "Not quite sure what he means by that, but it sounds like a quote, or part of one."

"I'm charmed to know Joe is discussing me behind my back."

"Oh, stop being unreasonable. I hate it when you get touchy. As if you've never discussed people." Jenny shook back her hair, and glared at him.

"We're off the subject." He looked back to Irving.

"I'm not going to arrest you, Cabot."

"Then why pull me out of the play?"

"Because I want to know if there's some legal way we can get around it."

"No, there isn't. The United States obviously views the Belt as American territory."

"Lot of people out here who aren't American."

"That's nothing new. When we bought Louisiana, expanded into the Southwest, took Hawaii, we absorbed the populations already present whether they were Spanish, French, Polynesian, or whatever."

Irving tugged at his chin. "So you're not going to help me out on this? Give me an easy way to avoid this order?"

"I can't. None exists. You either do your duty, or you refuse, and we deal with the problems that that will create."

"Well, it's too much for an old guy like me." The little man slid out of the booth.

"Where are you going?"

"I'm going to do what every cop does when he's faced with something the laws don't cover."

"Which is?"

"I'm going to pass the buck."

"That would be to me."

"Nope. Sorry, didn't mean to be rude. That means Stinson. Besides, I tried to pass the buck to you, and you didn't want it."

"That's because there's nothing legally I can do."

"You just don't have any imagination, Judge, that's the problem." But one withered eyelid dropped pulling the sting from the words.

For a few moments Stinson blinked at the ill-assorted trio in the hall. "Nine-thirty on a Friday night. Must be trouble." He limped back into the apartment leaving them to follow or not as they chose.

"This is a night for trouble," he continued as he lit a cigarette. "Kids and carters, jurists and cops."

"Are you drunk?" Irving asked bluntly.

"No, I'm at the pleasant buzz stage on my way to total drunkenness."

"You don't sound very pleasant," Jenny remarked as she walked into the tiny kitchen and began preparing coffee.

"My dear, I'm the soul of amiability." Since he was presenting his ravaged left side to her the remark seemed singularly inappropriate.

"So what's this about kids?"

"Musenda. We had another fight."

"And carters?" asked Cab, settling himself in a chair.

"It'll be in your bailiwick in a day or so. Johnson Whitson claims he arranged for the B. & M. Carters to tow his ore on the tenth. They didn't show, and the delay has cost him money because he missed this week's throw."

"Breach of contract." He made a face.

"I keep reminding you life does not consist of constitutional problems," Jenny sang out. "Besides, what are you complaining about? Irving brought you a constitutional problem if ever I've heard one, and you don't want it."

Stinson's gaze shifted from one to the other. "Now it's my turn. Why cops and jurists?"

Irving explained in a few quick, well-chosen words. The administrator fiddled with his eye patch, and nervously touched his twisted scars.

"Joe needs to hear this."

Cab threw up his hands. Jenny's glance kept the words bottled up, but it was a struggle. The colonial passion for discussing everything with ten or twelve other people ran directly counter to his own private nature.

Also, he possessed a guilty secret, and he didn't want to reveal it before all these people. He wanted to go home. And now he could with no loss of face or honor because he had been forced to it. Had to go in order to protect Irving. He had tried to ignore the pangs of homesickness by throwing himself into an exploration of his new world, but it had been self-delusion. He didn't like it out here. It was cold, harsh, ugly, and dangerous. He wanted to go home.

Joe arrived, perpetual smile in place, and heard the story. By the end the tiny half smile had become a broad grin. He rose, and paced away, rubbing gleefully at his hands.

"This is it, isn't it?" Stinson asked cryptically. "I was right to call you."

"Yes, this is it."

"*It* what?" snapped Cab.

"You're a hero to the System, Cab. They're not about to let you be taken."

"That's very flattering I'm sure, but—"

"You're one of the things we're willing to risk a confrontation over. And of course Varllis has played right into our hands by a direct interference with our rights on Mars. The Jared colonists may be keeping silent because they still haven't totally realized that Earth is their enemy, but the people watching are getting the message. Who will be next? How long until the military closes in, and removes their rights."

"Joe, stop speeching at me and get to the point."

"Sooner or later the System has got to be recognized as an autonomous unit, but because I'm a pragmatist I prefer to start the challenge well beyond Earth's reach. We will politely inform the authorities Earthside that we cannot comply with their order for your arrest and removal because we are not a territory of the United States. In short—independence."

Stinson and Irving stared at Reichart as if witnessing an epiphany.

Cab sprang to his feet. "Now hold on! You're going way too fast."

Joe turned to face Cab. "In what way?" He had lost his smile.

"There's more to independence than just running up the flag, saluting three times, and saying we're independent." He stared up into the older man's face. "There are close to one hundred thousand people in the Belt. Some of those people aren't going to want independence, maybe a majority of them. I'm not very comfortable about sitting in an apartment on Ceres, and making so monumental a decision without some kind of debate and consideration of the issues.''

"What's to consider?'' broke in Stinson. "There's been ample interference from Earth. The big companies who sent out the majority of the colonists have been careful to limit our imports, hampering our effort to build a solid industrial base. We've been forced to buy expensive finished products from Earth which keeps most of the 'dentureds deeply in debt. They're not satisfied with having us give up twenty years of our life to repay them for the passage out, and a few necessities to start mining. No, they've got to grind us down, and down, and down!'' The manager jammed his heel in the carpet and twisted, then paused, panting, swept a hand across his brow, and continued in a quieter tone. "Most of the 'dentureds would jump at a chance to be free from that.''

"So you're going to repudiate all obligations? That's a terrible idea. You do this, and the Belt is going to have to do all future business strictly on a cash basis. Our word, our credit, won't be worth a damn. Repudiation is a short-term solution. Corporations are considered persons, but unlike people they don't die. Companies and banks have a hell of a long memory, and they won't forget that they lost several billion dollars at the moment of our glorious independence. We won't be able to borrow a dime, and it's tough to build a new nation without credit.''

"Are you afraid?''

Blood rushed to Cabot's face. "How dare you!''

"I've been building for this for forty years. I'm not about to see the initiative lost because of one man's timidity.''

Joe laid a restraining hand on the manager's shoulder. "Stinson, he's right.''

Cab's forefinger jabbed out at Joe. "And economics aren't the only issue to be considered. There has to be some moral imperative also.''

Stinson frowned. "What moral imperative?''

"There must be a debate among the citizens. Why should four men, and one woman—and by the way you can jump in any time—'' he challenged Jenny.

"I will, don't rush me.''

"Make so momentous a decision for an entire society?''

"And you would be willing to be arrested and returned to Earth in order to avoid this premature separation, is that correct?" Joe asked.

"Yes."

"But Irving says he won't arrest you."

"And I won't either."

"So are you going to arrest yourself?"

The judge threw his hands into the air. "All right, if you're determined upon this course, at least approach it in small steps. Rather than declare independence let's send a polite, carefully worded message back to Earth that we cannot comply in returning the person of Justice Cabot Huntington because the Belt does not have an extradition treaty with the United States."

"Isn't that saying the same thing?"

"It's less of a red flag. It may give us time for the debate that I believe we so urgently need."

"And a time for *you* to write a little declaration." Joe's smile was back in place.

"Me!" Cab yelped.

"Certainly."

"But what would it accomplish?"

"It would place before mankind the common sense of the subject in terms so plain and firm as to command their assent."

"Don't quote Jefferson to me!"

"What's wrong, Cab? *Are* you afraid, or are you reverting to type, and have decided that the people of the System shouldn't be allowed to govern themselves?"

Cab dropped into a chair, elbows resting on knees, and stared at the floor between his feet. *Memory.* The scent of burning leaves as he rode across a frost-touched meadow, the horse's breath forming long streamers in the cold autumn air. Storm-driven waves beating against the foot of the cliff beneath his California home. Set against that the stunning view of Saturn from Iapetus, crimson dust devils like living creatures playing tag across a Martian plateau. It wasn't ugly. It was beautiful. And the danger? Species like individuals couldn't stand still. They either advanced or died, and advancement entailed danger and risk. The people of the System were willing to take those risks. Didn't they deserve the chance to do it on their terms?

"I don't have the skill for such an undertaking."

"You're a man of words. That's your calling. You're a scholar, a constitutionalist, a jurist. Who better?"

"Any number of people." Jenny's hand closed convulsively on his shoulder. He looked up into her delicate heart-shaped face. "What do *you* think I ought to do?"

"Write the piece."

"Fine time for you to jump in," Cab muttered.

She ignored him, and leveled her green eyes on Joe. "But I also think Cab's right. There must be debate and discussion."

"All right." Joe then added pugnaciously, "But I'm going to see to it that Earth gets the message loud and clear. It will put heart into the rest of the System."

"In what way?" she asked.

"Once we've shown them that Earth can be faced down they'll follow our lead." He rubbed his hands again. "System independence is almost here."

Cab raised his head. "I think you delude yourself."

"Why?"

"If it were anyone else but Lis Varllis you might be able to bluff them down, but she's a dangerous, prideful woman. She will view this move by the Belt as a direct challenge to her authority, never mind to that of the United States. I'm afraid if we give her this kind of challenge she will respond, and the outcome could be tragic for all of us."

"I was right, you are afraid," said Stinson scornfully.

"You bet I am. They have a deep-space squadron."

"Now *you're* indulging in delusions," snapped Joe. "Lis maneuvered the President into sending the squadron to Mars, and the result has been a crisis for the White House. The press had pointed out that while what happened on Mars was regrettable and an example of frontier lawlessness, the response was far too extreme. Varllis may hate us, but she has to have Long before that squadron flies, and he won't send in the military again."

"One could easily argue that this is secession, and as you may remember we had a little altercation over the issue of secession. It was called the Civil War. Why not this time?"

Jenny reentered the debate. "It would be far too expensive. The Belt is not that vital, and Earth has to know that they'll continue to receive the ore. Who else are we going to sell to?"

"I think Jenny's right. Long's not going to order in the troops without a clear crisis or threat. Your small person, whether it's on Earth or in the Belt, does not rank as a crisis."

Cab stiffened, then slowly expelled a pent-up breath. "Call it premonition, but I think we're about to make a mistake."

"I don't. You've been using *we're* rather than *you're* all along," Joe said smugly. "You're with us."

"God help me, I am. But that doesn't mean I'm going to agree quietly. I'm going to fight you on the method, and I *still* think—"

"Okay, Cab, we'll go with a politely worded refusal because of the lack of an extradition treaty."

"Thank you."

"And what do we do about this warship that's on its way?" asked Irving.

"Hope they call it back after they receive our politely worded refusal," Joe replied.

"And if they don't?"

"Offer to buy them a drink," suggested Stinson.

"Ah, yes, the Belter's solution to everything." And though he smiled, Cab couldn't shake the feeling that all hell was about to break loose, and he was going to be at the center of it.

Chapter Seven ———————————

Cassie, 2:00. Clinic.

It was snooping. It made him feel guilty as hell. But after a cautious glance over his shoulder, just to be certain Jenny didn't reenter the apartment, Cab continued to leaf through her appointment book.

He paused at a date two weeks before. Another appointment. He stroked thoughtfully at his sideburns. Over the years he was the one who was always coming down with whatever exotically named flu was popular. Jenny enjoyed, frankly, disgustingly good health. So why all these doctor appointments? He knew she was friendly with the plump doctor, but if these were social get togethers why meet at the clinic?

He was conscious of fear. If Jenny were sick . . . if anything were to happen to her. He pushed aside the thought groping for rational explanations. Routine checkups. Meeting at the clinic because it was centrally located, then going off to do something fun. Not sickness. No problem. Not to worry.

He continued to worry.

An incoming call pulled him from his frowning contemplation of the date book. The image coalesced, and he found himself looking into the slightly vague, humorous gray eyes of Christina Holland. She was now Attorney General, appointed in April to replace an ailing Casper Wentworth, but he hadn't had a chance to congratulate her. At the time he had been too busy fleeing Mars to avoid arrest and an ignominious return to Earth.

But when he saw her all of this passed in a second, and left behind earlier memories. When they had both been on the ABA's Young Lawyers Committee, doing whatever it was that young lawyers did. Saving the world, or at least contemplating it. Christ! It all seemed so long ago.

"Cabot, I know this isn't going to be the most satisfying of conversations what with the transmission delays, so I'll just plunge right in and get the amenities out of the way. Yes, thank you, I'm fine. Yes, the appointment did come as a surprise. Wish I hadn't taken it now. I won't ask how you are, I know you're fine. You're sitting in the asteroids launching bombshells at Washington."

She held up two message disks, one in each hand. "The disk on my left contains a very polite, embarrassed message from Mr. Irving Pizer, explaining how—golly, gosh, gee—he just can't comply with our request to have you arrested and returned to Earth because the Belt, slash, System doesn't have an extradition treaty with the United States, slash, Earth. What are you doing out there, Cab?"

"And *this* disk—" she waved it for emphasis—"contains your message—duplicated to Mars—for the parties in Jared versus OSHA, and Jared versus SPACECOM to hold themselves in readiness to try this case beginning Monday. It's Wednesday now, Cab. The remaining two drive ships aren't flying, Cab, because we've lost the *Constellation*, and until they figure out what happened, Trans-United is being cautious, and the squadron's on Mars—"

"Whose fault is that," he broke in though he knew his interruption wouldn't reach her for minutes.

"And I have no way to send out an attorney to represent us in this matter—"

"Why don't you use the Air Force ship you were sending to collect us?" he suggested acidly.

"I repeat Cabot, what are you doing out there?"

She laid down the disks, and busied herself at her terminal. He knew she was filling the time while he spoke, and his message crawled back to Earth.

"The colonists have decided that this arrest order was as good a time as any to try to define the exact relationship between Earth and the Belt. Maybe even for the entire System. That's the major reason for the quibble over extradition." He chewed at his lower lip debating whether his next remark would sound too pompous, then decided to go ahead. "Also, a small part of this—a very small part—is the fact that I'm something of a hero out here. It would not make the colonists happy if I get hauled back to Earth like a common felon. Wouldn't make me very happy, either, because I haven't done anything wrong.

"As for the Administrative Procedure hearing. You don't have to send one of your bright young things. I intend for this to be argued on the briefs alone. So I suggest you use the next four days, and ruin somebody's weekend, and send a brief out to me. That is if you can think of anything to justify the outrageous abuses that took place on Mars."

He sat back to wait.

"Cab, Lis Varllis is going to go into orbit. She and the President will have to be informed of these latest developments. And she's not the most . . . stable—no scratch that, might be scandalous—unemotional person in the administration. She's going to nail your dick to the wall."

He flushed. "What do you think of the agency actions?"

Minutes later she frowned, rubbed at the bridge of her nose with a forefinger. "Honestly, I think we're going to have to be very, very creative to come up with much, and you're not going to be sympathetic. Actually I probably ought to ask that you be removed because of bias."

"But who would hear the case? The Fifteenth Circuit has sole jurisdiction, and it's currently sitting in the Belt, and by your own admission you can't send out a replacement for me because nothing is flying."

"I'll call back that Air Force ship," she threatened, but he could tell she wasn't serious. Any more than she had been about asking for his removal.

"Christina, dear, for old times' sake, for good times shared, for any love you might still harbor for me, do me a favor. Don't tell the White House about the upcoming hearing. I know Justice doesn't keep the President informed about every case they're prosecuting or defending. Let us get in one or two good licks before they clamp down. We've been getting clobbered in the press. Give us a chance to get our side out."

The minutes crept by. Cab nervously drummed his fingers on his knees, went into the kitchen for a glass of water, fidgited.

"It will mean my job."

"Tell them you were flustered by this declaration of independence by the Belt."

"I *am* flustered. You'll never get away with it. You have no grounds."

"Yes we do. The grounds which have spoken with authority for three hundred years. The fundamental right of law for a people to make their own rules, and be governed by them."

"My God, are you trying to be the Thomas Jefferson of outer space?"

"I hope not, but if it comes to it I will do my poor best. We've been manipulated, exploited, lied to, and finally murdered by the benevolent governments groundside. Perhaps it is time that we demanded a redefinition of roles from the parent countries, and if that fails, then separation. World wide, System wide, people are better fed, better clothed, housed, and educated than at any time in human history. They're not helpless children needing the guidance of benevolent overseers—"

"Cab, Cab, whoa!" She grinned, then sighed, and wearily rubbed at her eyes. "Remember all those late-night discussions over a plate of pot stickers in that hole in the wall Chinese joint in San Francisco? We were both so idealistic. And now I find you still are. I seem to have lost it somewhere along the line." She regarded the backs of her hands, then continued. "I don't know if what you're doing is correct, but it does deserve to be discussed. So I'll keep your little secret about the hearing. Is it something intrinsic in the American character to cheer for the underdog?" The warm smile faded, and the hard-headed attorney was back. "But this extradition matter is quite another thing. You're talking about tearing apart the Union. And you better think it through because it may be a choice between backing down, or losing more lives."

She didn't wait for his reply. The transmission ended, the screen dimming from the warm pastels of Christina's office to a dull cold gray. It echoed the winter in his soul.

Muhammid Ali Elija launched into his attack before the door to Lydia's apartment had closed fully behind him. "Lydia, you've got to reconsider."

He was a big rugged man who used his rather terrifying appearance to intimidate. Lydia had known him far too long to be intimidated.

"Well, I'm not. We've been over this at least a thousand times, and—"

"You can't get to the Belt unless you sign on to one of those outgoing colony sail ships, and then it will take you years, so why don't you just tell them you've decided to stay on until the drive ships are running again."

"No, I want to be ready to go the minute the ships are back in operation, and this way I can have my successor trained and in place—"

"And your successor is a goddamn Earthside goon!" roared Muhammid.

Lydia sank wearily onto the couch. "You know I wanted you to take over as manager, but they wouldn't listen." She gestured vaguely toward the outer wall of the space station, and the distant Earth where the board of directors of EnerSun Inc. had suddenly become very recalcitrant, and refused to consider her recommendation for the successor.

"Lydia, you had no right to give them this opportunity to fuck with us. You owe it to the System to stay on. Especially now."

"I owe! I have no right! Why the hell don't I have the right to find some happiness in the time remaining to me? I've given my life to this station, in System. After twenty-five years of fighting I'm tired, and I want a little peace."

"With Joe Reichart? What, he's ready to retire too? You know wherever Joe is there's a crisis. Peace? Joe don't know the meaning of the word."

Lydia smiled, a soft reminiscent expression in her black eyes. "That's true, but at least I won't be separated by millions of miles. I'll be able to sit back, and watch him perform. I'll be supportive rather than a comrade."

"Oh, puke!" The woman bridled. "One of the finest minds in the System, and you're going to be supportive. I'd like to kick you around the Moon and back." He stopped, cutting off the flow of words, and a look of contrition filled his brown eyes. "I'm sorry, that was a really crappy thing to say." He smiled crookedly. "And I sure am doing a lousy job of making you reconsider, ranting at you this way."

She rose, took his elbow, and urged him toward the door. "Muhammid, even if you had taken the most dulcet of tones with me it wouldn't have worked. My mind's made up. I'm retiring. I'm joining Joe. It's going to be up to you to retrain and woo the new manager. He'll learn. You can't live out here without learning." The big black man made a rude noise. "We did it with Cab," she reminded him, giving his arm a gentle shake.

"Tha' jus' because he be a unique honkey," he replied, slipping into the ghetto patois of his youth. "He also had a bunch of manipulating women around to get his mind right."

"Well, you'll just have to get Mr. Townsend laid by an appropriately patriotic System lady."

He hesitated, then plunged on. "Speaking of patriotic System ladies." Lydia's expression tightened, and he hurried on. "What about Dita?"

"What about her?"

"Shouldn't you stay . . . for her sake?"

Lydia rested her shoulders against the door jamb, and eyed him with astonishment. "What are you saying? That you think my daughter's dead, and I ought to stay on as a memorial to her?" He made a negating gesture unable to meet her eyes. "Or is this some new form of superstition? If Mama's a big honcho the universe won't fuck with her little girl. I don't know what's happened to my daughter, and it's tearing at my soul, and now you dare to throw this up—"

"I didn't mean it that way."

"Well, I hope not. Good day, Muhammid."

He stood in the hall for several minutes regarding the closed door. Wondered if insanity was catching. He must have been crazy to even think that the tragic news about Dita would somehow effect a change in Lydia. Once she'd made up her mind about something, nothing could change it. But she was nuts for quitting. He considered the other signs of insanity; the stuff that had happened on Mars, and the stuff groundside. *Stuff* seemed to sum it up. It defied any clearer description. Which brought him back to his original thesis; madness could somehow infect an entire station, or a planet, or a system. Sure seemed to be something to the theory because things were crazy everywhere.

"Once upon a time, in fact so long ago that none but the wise now remember, Ngai sent the chameleon to earth with the good news that humans were to live forever."

His father's voice was velvet in the darkness. Outside, the rain hammered down, slashing the leaves from the trees surrounding the house. Every few minutes a great sheet of lightning forced through the shutters and illuminated the room. Then thunder, almost drowning out his father's voice. Wairegi was scared of the lightning and thunder, but not when his father was with him.

"But the chameleon is very slow. He crept down from Mount Kenya, and journeyed toward the Gikuyu people. But by the time he got there Ngai had changed his mind. He sent a swift bird to reverse the message. And so death came to the Gikuyu people."

The bed shifted as Thomas Thondu started to rise. Wairegi gripped at his sleeve, holding him in place. "Is there anyone who has never died?"

"Little weaverbird, you know there is."

"I've forgotten."

With a sigh Thomas Thondu settled back. "There were—"

Once upon a time."

Once upon a time there were two young orphans. The clansmen who looked after them were tolerant, but there was little love. One night they saw the moon sailing across the cloudless sky in her fullness. After some minutes of intense looking the moon seemed to be smiling at them, and she smiled even more as the minutes went by. The children put forth their arms to reach her. The wind came, and blew great gusts all over the place, and in a whirl of wind the children were carried up through the sky and the clouds and finally to the moon. And they found their mother there! And now these children with their mother appear whenever the moon is full. Meanwhile their clansmen below look up in envy at the mother and her children sailing blithely in the sky, for such peace and such quiet can never be attained by mortals. These people did not taste death, which is a thing everyone wants to escape."

"Silly. There are no mother and children on the moon. There are only white men."

"So clever, where did you learn so much?"

"In school."

"There are black men there too."

"Gikuyu men?"

Not yet. But there will be when your father has finished. I will give you the stars as playthings. . . ." His voice seemed to be coming from a great distance, and Wairegi drifted into sleep, safe in the cocoon of his father's voice, the lingering scent of roasted bananas, and his mother singing.

The thunder was close by, entering the house. Wairegi sat up, crammed the thin edge of his blanket into his mouth to *hold back his cries. But it wasn't thunder for the deep booms were overlaid with splintering cracks. Thomas Thondu's voice raised in anger, his mother's sweet bell-like tones sharp with fear and pleading.*

Wairegi crept from bed, dragging the blanket for security, and a reminder to be silent. There were men in the front room. Their military fatigues made them inhumanly bulky. Thomas Thondu, a shotgun cradled in his arms, faced the intruders. He was using that voice, *the one that left Wairegi feeling sicker and more afraid than any spanking. But the men weren't scared. They shouted back. It was strange, but he couldn't understand the words. There was just a barrage of sound. He huddled between wall and sofa.*

Suddenly there was more sound. Fire and smoke belched from one of the shotgun's barrels. One uniformed figure blew back, falling like a thrown sack of beans. Sound assaulted his ears, and his father danced like a maddened puppet. Flowers of blood blossomed on his shirt and pants. Mother, struggling in the arms of one of the killers, screaming. Perhaps his ears were numbed by the barrage of gunfire, but to Wairegi it seemed that only her mouth was working. No sound emerged. She broke free, flung herself onto Thondu. One man lifted his rifle, brought down the butt onto her head. Over and over again. Like a man crushing a scorpion. That sound he re-membered. Like a ripe melon falling from a truck.

Wairegi awoke. His scream of anguish only a rawness in the throat. Slowly he lay back, and let the sweat cool to a clammy dampness on skin and pajamas.

The dream.

It came when he was under great stress.

Or when he felt guilty.

He pushed aside the unwelcome thought, but it refused to remain banished. It was like a disciplinary voice from the grave. Thondu's admonishings to a son who was still six years old.

But they had killed him, and beaten his mother to death with their rifle butts, and what he did now was in retaliation for those murders. He couldn't say that to his followers. For them it was all God and country, the redress of four hundred years of oppression, but deep within himself he knew the truth. He would hold the world to ransom, perhaps even kill to avenge his parents. Then at least there would be release—for them, for him. He failed to consider that perhaps neither

Thomas Thondu wa Kamau nor Ruth wa Thondu would have welcomed this act of blood payment.

"I still fail to understand why Justice Huntington refuses to return to Earth, and answer our questions in person," mourned Senator Melissa Smith of Washington in that high, breathy, faintly complaining tone she always had. "This working through sworn depositions with a man a million miles away is very unsatisfactory."

"Actually more like two hundred million," Kenneth Furakawa corrected with a dry little cough. He didn't like Senator Smith, and he made the remark because he knew it would fluster her.

"Then, perhaps, given the difficulties of this trial, we ought to simply recommend conviction, and see Justice Huntington removed," she retorted spitefully.

"Such a return to Star Chamber tactics might be very welcome to certain factions within the present administration . . . and their staunch supporters in Congress, but it has no place in American jurisprudence which for three hundred years has been a model for justice worldwide.

"Furthermore," he continued, his voice hardening. "One would like to see some presentation of evidence of wrongdoing on the part of Justice Huntington before one should even breathe a word about conviction or removal."

Senator Hank Stratton, another fervent supporter of Richard Long, added his bit. Unfortunately he was well versed in legal history, and cut the ground from beneath Furakawa. "No evidence of wrongdoing is required for conviction, at least not as that term is known to criminal jurisprudence. We do bear the responsibility of hearing proven facts, the reasonable and probable consequences of which are to cause people to doubt the integrity of the respondent presiding as a judge."

It sounded like a quote, but Furakawa couldn't for the life of him remember from where. It was also correct, and he smoothly left the subject, wishing that Stratton hadn't been appointed to the ad hoc committee which would prepare the records of Cab's case, and pass them on to the full Senate.

"As you have mentioned, the facts must be proven, and thus far all that this committee has heard are a series of shrill and unsupported allegations of misbehavior." He shot a look at the three House managers. Two stared back defiantly, but Julian Whitney dropped his eyes, and fidgited with his reader.

The three representatives were the prosecutors appointed from the House, and they were another example of Lis Varllis's political acumen. Juli Forbis and Bob Farns were staunch Longites while Whitney's eclectic sexual tastes were the best-known secret on the Hill. So the possibility of blackmail overrode what Furakawa knew to be Whitney's basic fairness.

The elderly Japanese-American gathered his scattered thoughts, and continued. "I think the problem is not that Justice Huntington's integrity has been called into question, but that the integrity of the executive branch is under serious question." There was a stir from the phalanx of reporters lining the walls of the hearing room. "No one in Washington would be so naive as to suggest that impeachment is anything but a political weapon. It has been a political tool since its inception in 1386. And the fact that rascals are caught within the net of impeachment should not blind us to the fact that many impeachments have had no basis in merit, most notably the impeachment of President Andrew Johnson. But that trial served one purpose. It established for all time that the removal of public servants does not rest upon the passions of the legislative branch. It gave the men and women of America who serve this nation the courage to act from principle without fear of retaliation, without the blackmail of impeachment.

"The Johnson trial set this precedent for presidents, and I submit that this trial of Justice Huntington will free the judiciary from the revenge of an outraged executive. I further submit that Justice Huntington's only crime was to attempt to throw the clean light of justice and fair play into the murky corners of executive and agency capriciousness."

Smith and Stratton exchanged uneasy glances with the prosecutors, and Furakawa hid a smile. His use of the word capricious had nothing to do with chance. He was reminding people of Cab's ongoing hearing under the Administrative Procedures Act section 706A of alleged agency misconduct in regard to the Martian colonists.

"I trust that you're going to be able to back these incredible statements with some evidence," Stratton said.

"I expect with better evidence than the esteemed prosecutors from the House have to offer with respect to my client's supported misconduct."

Bessie Mixon, senior Senator from Maine and chairman of the ad hoc committee, spoke up. "Since it is now eleven-thirty, and in a probably hopeless attempt to keep the proceedings civil if not polite, I'm going to recess until two P.M. so people can have lunch, and get their blood sugar up.'' There was a wave of quiet laughter from the spectators punctuated by the fall of the gavel.

Neville Huntington sighed, pushed out of his chair, and wished that his nephew weren't such a troublesome man. As chairman of the powerful Appropriations committee Neville was allowing work to stack up while he darted in and out of the impeachment hearings.

Not to mention the after hours family powwows. He glanced at his watch. He was already late for yet another one. Meredith, who had been presenting a lecture in Edinburgh, wanted an update on the hearings so Neville had arranged for both his brothers to join Kenneth Furakawa for lunch in the Senate dining room.

He left the Caucus Room with its marble walls and Corinthian pillars and stepped into a hallway filled with scurrying aides, all of them serving senators from the Gulf states, and from this frenzied activity he presumed that Red Beaty had finally come to the end of his oratorical fireworks, and there was going to be a vote on the fisheries question. This was one vote Neville felt no qualms in missing. Instead he forced intense, white-faced young professionals to dodge past him while he continued to brood.

It couldn't be denied that there was a good deal of family loyalty present in the Huntington clan, but Neville had to admit that this level of togetherness was beginning to drive him mad. The clan met, talked incessantly, and parted feeling bloated and gritty-eyed, for these meetings usually took place over meals, went far too late, and ended with the lowering realization that they had solved nothing. *Once more dear friends into the breach.* He steeled himself, and entered the private dining room, giving a nod to Rex, the maitre d'.

''Table in the corner, Senator, like you like.''

His eyes swept across his assembled guests, at first not registering that there were two too many people. And that one of them was a woman where there should be only men. A pair of piercing blue eyes set beneath upswept black brows were turned on him, and he groaned for his two uninvited and unexpected guests were Gerard and Cecilia Huntington, Cabot's parents.

Gerard was a washed-out version of his younger and more

flamboyant siblings. The famous Huntington gold hair had faded to a pale gray, and his comfortable tweeds bagged about his slender, stooped frame.

Cecilia, however, bloomed like an exotic orchid in the midst of the small, dark dining room, and completed the task of totally overshadowing poor old Gerard. Her long black hair was swept high onto her head, and held in place with a series of pearl and diamond combs, and the heather tweed of her perfectly fitted suit intensified the blue of her eyes.

She presented a smooth, powdered cheek to Neville, and he gave it a chaste salute. Years before things hadn't been so chaste. He had been fascinated by Gerard's dramatic, dynamic wife who seemed to pack into her tiny five foot frame more drive and energy than ten men. When Gerard unaccountably flew in the face of family tradition, and refused to run for a second term in the House, Cecilia, in a frenzy of rage, had turned to Neville for comfort. Their brief affair had ended abruptly when Cecilia decided to run in her husband's place, and politics had become her only passion. Neville was now glad that things had turned out as they had, and he had ended up with Patricia. Think of the scandal if he had taken his brother's wife, and they would have killed each other before a year was out. Two such powerful personalities would not have been conducive to marital bliss. So she had stayed with Gerard, and served in a variety of official positions, and had ended up as Ambassador to Great Britain.

"So, what brings you back from old foggy?" Neville asked jovially as he settled into his chair.

"Don't be obtuse," snapped Cecilia, summoning a waiter with an ease that left most of the men at the table feeling decidedly inferior. "What do you think brought us back? A glass of white wine."

The others placed their drink orders and waited until the waiter was safely on his way before resuming the conversation.

"I don't see why you bothered to come. You can't do a damn thing," grumbled Anthony, poking at the sculptured butter pat with his knife. There was no love lost between the youngest Huntington brother, and the elder's wife.

"I'm quite sure that's true in your case, Anthony," Cecilia responded with biting sweetness. "But I can foresee several avenues to pursue."

"Actually, I'd like to see you take on Lis Varllis," put in Meredith, his eternal cynical smile in place. "It would be the match up of the century. You're both cut from the same cloth.''

"Ah, but I have the edge in experience.'' She smiled, Meredith always had a beneficial effect on her temper. A sudden frown washed across her delicate face. "But it can't be denied that Cab's made a balls up of the situation.''

"Thank you for saying it for me,'' Neville said. "I didn't want to hurt your feelings, but my nephew—''

"Oh, I can't agree at all,'' said Gerard, stunning his brothers into frozen immobility. "I think he's acted with honor and bravery.''

"Well, perhaps, but you must admit it's not very politic.''

"I believe that's what I said.''

Soft gray eyes met blue, and Neville reminded himself that though his brother might be incomprehensible to him, he was nonetheless a major brain. It didn't do to underestimate him.

Anthony broke in brightly. "So how does it feel to be back on the Hill, Gerard? Bring up any memories . . . or regrets?''

"No, Tony. I still agree with Twain that there is no distinctly American criminal class except Congress. I'm just as happy to be out of it.'' He nodded toward a large round table in the center of the room where four women and six men were interspersing vigorous chewing with equally vigorous talking. "Take Texas over there . . . oh, excuse me, Midland, Lone Star, Texacola, Alamo, and Texas. What was served by the state splitting except to gain a voting block in Congress?''

"Don't be so critical, that's one block that I think I've about got wooed over to our side.''

"Forget Texas.''

"Sometimes we'd like to.'' Cecilia shot Neville a sparkling glance.

"The point is Cab should be here.'' Her forefinger jabbed the table for emphasis. "Not hiding in the asteroids acting like a criminal.''

"Oh, I don't think he is doing that,'' came a new voice from behind her. Cecilia slewed around, and looked up into Furakawa's dark eyes like tiny brilliant points buried among the wrinkles. "Gentlemen.'' He inclined his head to the Huntington brood, and took a seat. "If Cabot were not in the asteroids how would he sit as Justice of the Fifteenth Circuit, and hear Jared versus OSHA, and Jared versus SPACECOM and Jared versus Department of Commerce? In fact, because

I've been reading the pleadings in the case I'm going to call a surprise witness that I think will set Messieurs Whitney and Farns, and Madam Forbis on their ears.'' He shook out his napkin, dropped it onto his lap, and gave them all a sweet and inscrutable smile.

"Well, who is it?'' demanded Anthony.

"The Attorney General, of course, Christina Holland.''

The reaction was everything he had hoped for. The men, Gerard included, fell back speechless. Cecilia frowned, caught her lower lip between her teeth.

"Christina Holland. Cab went out with her for a long time. Never came to anything.''

Gerard gazed at his wife, a peculiar expression on his lined face. ''As I recall, you didn't like her, my dear.''

"What's her testimony going to accomplish?'' inquired Meredith, sipping at his scotch and soda.

"One of the allegations is that Cabot took a personal and biased interest in cases to be brought before the bench. That he advised the Jared colonists to bring suit under the Administrative Procedures Act. He did, of course, as is indicated in Amadea Kim Nu's deposition, so we won't deny the act, but we will use the really damning evidence coming out of Cab's hearings to show *why* he took this somewhat irregular action. That in fact justice was served by his interference.

"For those of us who are not shysters could you be a little more specific?'' asked Meredith with a humorous glance to Gerard.

"Do you mind a little lecture?''

"Could we order first?'' Anthony moaned. ''I can stand it better on a full stomach.''

They talked of trivialities—the Skins' chances for the upcoming season (no worse than usual), the latest hit musical from Brazil, the increasing unrest in Africa and South and Central America—until their meal arrived. Anthony cut into his chicken cordon bleu, paused fork halfway to his mouth.

"All right, now I'm ready.''

"Agency—administrative—law is perhaps the most massive and complex area of American jurisprudence. Second only to the income tax code, I think. It has been rather picturesquely referred to as the 'headless fourth branch,' and I think there is much justification. Who oversees this massive regulatory sea? The President? Hardly likely. It would take a staff of thousands to regulate the regulators. So to all intents and purposes we have a sub-strata of politics formed by the agencies with a virtual free hand.

"The only limit on their power is the courts with their power of judicial review. From the beginning the courts have been very reluctant to substitute their judgment for that of an agency with its presumed expertise, and in recent years the trend has become even more hands off. Now I think Cabot is going to redefine that traditional role." He paused, and slowly opened his soft-boiled egg. Four methodical bites, and he was finished, daintily blotting his lips with his napkin.

"Are you sure that's all you want?" Neville asked, feeling gauche about interrupting the old gentleman, but also feeling that his duties as host required it.

"Quite sure. You find that many appetites decrease when you reach my age," he twinkled.

"Please go on."

"If you're certain you wish me to." There was laughter in the dark eyes. "I think Mr. Meredith is looking rather stunned."

"No, no, go ahead. I'd like to try and understand just what the devil Cab is up to."

"Cabot apparently encouraged the Martian colonists to bring suit under sections 702 and 706 of the code—702 guarantees a right of judicial review by any person suffering legal wrong because of agency action, or adversely affected or aggrieved by agency action. The Jared colonists might certainly feel aggrieved at having their diamond mines closed, and an embargo placed on certain selected items all of which impacted on them most adversely. Cabot's task is to determine if that is merely the opinion of disgruntled laymen or if real abuses exist.

"After reading the briefs and the press reports, it appears to me that Cabot is seeking to find grounds to hold unlawful and set aside the agency actions using a shotgun technique. He is investigating whether the agency actions were arbitrary, capricious, an abuse of discretion, or otherwise not in accordance with law. Whether they were in excess of statutory jurisdiction or authority; without observance of procedure required by law; unsupported by substantial evidence; or unwarranted by the facts."

Meredith let out a long grating moan.

"Have I lost you, Mr. Meredith?"

"No, no, just a bit of commentary on the legal profession."

Furakawa smiled, and resumed. "Thus far Cabot's task has

been an easy one. There seems to have been virtually no fact finding by the agencies in question. Just rule making in a vacuum, and perhaps dictated by less than honorable motives.''

''Such as?'' asked Gerard.

''The Jared colonists believe that the agency harassment they endured was a clumsy attempt to keep them from competing with a powerful Earth-based corporation.''

''Proof?''

''Unfortunately very little, but that isn't strictly necessary. The point is there are no grounds to justify the agency actions on Mars, so Cabot can set them aside.''

''More importantly it will set people to wondering *why* these actions were undertaken, and by whom,'' said Neville softly.

Anthony leaned over, and gave his shoulder a cuff. ''Stop humming 'Hail to the Chief,' brother dear, it might be just a tad premature.''

''But Lis Varllis is taking an inordinate amount of interest in Cab's impeachment. Perhaps because his actions on Mars spiked some fondly held plan? No wonder she wanted him back on Earth! She was trying to keep certain damaging facts from becoming public. And if it weren't for Bessie Mixon—bless her little pointed ears and her sense of fair play—Forbis and Farns would have rushed this out of committee and onto the Senate floor, and Cab would have been removed by now.''

Everyone was staring at him with varying degrees of interest, outrage, abstraction, and inscrutability. He gave a crack of laughter.

''Ceci, I may live to be grateful to that son of yours yet. Here I was cursing him for causing all this trouble in the first place, and then for ignoring my advice and staying in the asteroids, but now . . .'' He grinned broadly.

''So glad Cab could be of use,'' murmured Gerard, and the gentleness of his voice couldn't completely mask the irony.

Chapter Eight

"Cassie." The doctor, looking more shapeless than ever in her white lab coat, looked up from her portable reader. "I've caught you at a bad time," Cab added, seeing her frown.

She gestured at the reader with her free hand. "I'm on rounds."

"May I walk along? This won't take long."

"I don't give medical advice in hospital corridors."

It didn't look much like a hospital. The founder of the facility, Dr. Mathias Shephard, had firmly believed that people didn't heal well in the harsh confines of a Belt colony. His pet theory was that Earth was utterly unique in all the universe. (He would have been almighty pissed if he'd lived to hear of the discovery of the inscription rock on Mars. God shouldn't have had the bad taste to make aliens.) Shephard postulated that man's internal rhythms echoed the tides and winds and seasons of his home world. Unable to take all of his patients to Earth he attempted to recreate Earth within the bowels of Ceres by using a series of holographic images superimposed on the walls.

Seashores, alpine vistas, sylvan pathways. Even the corridors were decorated. Cab and Cassie were currently walking through a stand of mighty trees, their leaves touched with autumn fire. They marched in perfectly regular rows into the distance. It was a shame that normal forests were never so obliging or artistically arranged.

The doctor shot a sideways glance at Cab's rigid profile. "So talk, I'm short on time."

"I'm trying to figure out how to put this." He rubbed at a sideburn. "Is Jenny . . . ill?"

"Why do you ask?"

The judge stopped, grabbed her by the shoulders, and forced her to a halt. "Then something is wrong. When I saw she'd had three appointments with you in the past two months I just knew it."

"Oh, Cab, stop babbling! Jenny is not sick."

"Then why all the appointments?"

"Did Jenny tell you about this?"

"Well . . . no. I just happened to be flipping through her appointment book," he began casually, and ended up sounding defensive.

"Snooping, huh?" He flushed. Her level brown eyes met his gray ones. "Cab, my word of honor. Jenny is not sick. But it's not my place to talk to you about her private dealings with her physician. You want answers, ask Jenny."

"I understand your position, but I still wish you could see your way clear to tell me. I'm responsible for Jenny—"

"The hell you are! She's a grown woman."

"We are involved," he challenged. "And sooner or later we'll marry."

"So? The state of holy matrimony doesn't confer ownership. Your *involvement* makes Jenny just as responsible for *you* as you are for her." She waved him away in disgust. "You're an anachronism, Cab."

"Damn you!"

"Cab, beat it. I'm busy."

He stormed away, muttering, then spotted Luther Stokes at the nurses station busily making time with the lady behind the desk.

"Luther!"

"Oh, hi, Judge."

"Luther, you handle all Dr. Garcia's record keeping."

"Yeah, I'm her med-tech, that's part of my job."

"Then you'd know why Jenny came in to see the doctor?"

"Yeeeah." He drew out the word cautiously.

"Will you tell me?"

"No."

"Damn you man! Why not?"

He rolled an eye expressively toward Cassie's retreating figure. "You ever try crossin' her? My life wouldn't be worth a damn. No sir, you couldn't find enough money to make it worth my while. Throw in a trip to Earth—still wouldn't do it. Half interest in Reichart Industries—''

"I get the picture, thank you," said Cab with savage sarcasm.

"Nice talkin' with you, Judge. Gonna be comin' out with us again soon?"

"It will be a cold day—"

An unholy whooping filled the corridor. Nurses, doctors, and patients froze, staring white-faced at the speakers which continued to emit the awful sound.

"What the devil is that?" yelled Cab.

"Alarm."

There was a flurry of movement, and Cassie, Luther, and Cab intersected in the center of the hall.

"What does it mean?"

"I don't know. I haven't heard that thing in over twenty years. Could be anything."

"Cabot Huntington, report to Ceres central. Cabot Huntington, report to Ceres central. The voice quavered nervously so this was a living person issuing a page, not the ubiquitous computer with its synthetically generated voice.

"Jenny," he whispered, and pelted for the exit.

"That doesn't necessarily follow," Cassie bellowed after him. "Don't be an idiot, and always assume the worst," she concluded in a normal tone as the doors of the elevator sighed closed behind him.

Jenny was fine. Or so he thought until he got a good look at her white face. She and Irving were huddled in the center of the central computer complex. From this technological fish bowl trajectories were plotted, thrust calculated, burns programmed, weights calculated, and profits entered in the accounts of the multitude of miners scattered throughout the Belt. It usually hummed with quiet efficiency. Now it looked like a disturbed ant hill.

"What is it?"

Irving silently handed him a set of headphones, and keyed for a playback.

"People of Ceres. This is Wairegi wa Thondu. I currently control the antimatter drive ship *Constellation* in orbit about Ceres. You have one hour to send up to me a representative to hear our demands. Should you ignore this order, or attempt to approach or damage this ship, I will detonate the engines. I have hostages, and my pilot tells me that this catastrophic mixing of matter and antimatter will kill all personnel in the upper levels of the asteroid. Please do not force me to this step. I would prefer to harm no one.''

Irving punched in another command.

"We also intercepted this."

"To the governments of Earth. For too long Africa and the other developing nations have squabbled over the crumbs falling from the tables of Western plenty. We have given over our land, our resources, and our bodies to fuel this miraculous advancement, and have received nothing. We were promised a portion of this wealth, but these promises have been as empty as the treaties and guarantees issued during the colonial era. When complaints have been made they have been savagely suppressed, and tame governments, acceptable to the great powers, have been erected in our countries. Colonialism still exists, it just wears a different face.

"But no longer. Within forty-eight hours from the time this message reaches Earth a United Nations commission will be formed with power to examine these abuses. Companies and nations will agree to be bound by the findings of this commission, and to repay to Africa the wealth so wantonly stolen from her. The United States and the Soviet Union will withdraw support from their puppet governments, and Africans will be allowed to choose for themselves their own rulers.

"If these demands are not met we shall send a rain of destruction onto the Earth. It will take years for the first of these rocks to reach Earth, but the one thing we Africans have learned is patience. You may be able to destroy or deflect some of them, but sooner or later one or three or five of these rocks will get through. I need not describe the devastation which will ensue. We hold the Ceres colony. This is no idle threat."

Cab laid aside the slender headphone, dug the heels of his hands into his temples, then squinted up through the clear shimmering dome trying to distinguish the *Constellation* from a hundred other bright spots which littered space around Ceres. He also for the first time fully appreciated the complaints about the main control center. Why in the hell had it been built on the surface when they had a perfectly good asteroid right below their boot soles? Of course they had only been concerned with meteor strikes. No one had ever contemplated a lunatic detonating an antimatter engine over their heads.

"Where's Stinson . . . or Joe?"

"Out canvassing the Belt. Talking about independence, getting feedback from the people. The way *you* wanted," accused Irving.

"So now this is my fault? You're the chief of police, do something."

"I'm too damn old for this." And he did sound old, old and querulous.

Jenny pulled Cab aside. "He's right. This kind of emergency is beyond him." She gazed up at him, and what he read there made his heart turn over.

"It's beyond me too."

"No, it's not. You have the stature, the presence to speak for all of us. Somebody's got to go up there, and negotiate with this man, and with Joe and Stinson out playing hookey there's no one but you." Her hands wove nervous patterns in the air between them.

He gripped them, clinging to her in a frenzy of anxiety and indecision. Then straightened, put her gently aside, and stepped to the radio operator. "How much time do we have left?"

"About forty-two minutes."

"Right. Prepare a Curvet. And tell this wa Thondu character that I'm coming. Jenny?"

"What?"

"Aren't you . . . I mean, well . . . will you come with me?" He stumbled, his voice failing at her dismayed expression.

She pressed a palm against her stomach, repeated his words beneath her breath, suddenly turning on Irving. "What will happen if they carry out their threat, to Ceres, I mean?"

A young engineer looked up from her console. "Who knows?"

"But you have to! E equals MC squared and all that stuff!"

"Sure, I could figure it out if I knew how much antimatter was on that ship, but I don't. There's an FAA ruling that civilian vessels can only carry three times the necessary fuel for their complete run, but some captains ignore it, and stockpile. They probably figure a matter-anti-matter explosion is preferable to being stranded out by Saturn."

"But that's stupid! There are other ships that could bring them fuel—"

"Jen. Jenny. Jennifer!" Cab wrapped his arms about her, gripped hard trying to still her shivering.

"I'm sorry," she whispered into his coat.

"No apology necessary," he murmured back. Turning to the engineer, "So what are you saying? Worst case."

"Worst case is that that puppy is loaded with a couple of extra snowballs of antihydrogen. If it is, it will crack Ceres like an egg. If not, it might only blow the top layers off the rock."

"So if we pull people deep into the rock—"

"They might survive."

Cabot pulled Irving aside. The old man was looking every day of his ninety odd years. "Irving, we can't be a party to this."

"I know."

"You've lived out here for fifty years. You know these people. Where do they . . . how do they . . . will they stand on this?"

"You don't have time to take a poll, Cabot. It's up to you." He shuffled toward the door, then paused and looked back. "I'll see what I can do about forting up, but there's no way I can squeeze seven thousand people into the lower levels."

"I understand, just do the best you can." He dropped an arm over the old man's shoulders, and propelled him toward the door. "Use the old Anglo-Saxon drill—children first, et cetera, and use the Curvets. We can at least get a few people away."

Irving paused just over the threshold. "This is all going to take time."

"I'll keep them talking," Cabot promised.

Jenny touched him lightly on the arm. "I'll go see to our suits, and meet you at the hangar."

He gave her a desperate, grateful hug, then raised his voice to include everyone in the room.

"You've all heard these messages. What's your impression of this man?"

"It's a real crack-brained idea," spoke up one of the computer techs. "How is some UN commission going to undo all of the abuses?" She shrugged. "It's an impossible task."

Cab touched her shoulder. "Pull up everything you can find on this wa Thondu." She opened her mouth, and he forstalled her. "I know it won't be much. Groundside affairs aren't a big item with us, but get me what you can."

He paced nervously back to his engineer, peered at the strings of numbers on the screen. "How does it look?"

"How should I know? Just the same as it looked five minutes ago!"

Huntington paced away, hands clasped tightly behind his back. "So it's a real crapshoot," he muttered. "And I *hate* to gamble."

"Sir." It was his bright-faced young tech. "I pulled a bio, and printed it out just like you like." It touched and embarrassed him that his affectation was so widely known.

"Also," she paused and chewed at her lip.

"Go ahead."

"Well, for what it's worth, sir, I don't think this guy's real comfortable with his threats."

"That's my impression too. I just hope we're right."

"I wonder if Andy's safe?" Jenny murmured as the hydraulic platform carrying the Curvet whined toward the surface.

"If he is I'd say he got a hell of a lot bigger scoop than he bargained for." A flick of a gloved thumb, and the engines came to life sending a heavy vibration through the soles of his boots, seat, and hands where they gripped the stick. "Read me that bio."

She smoothed the page on her knee, clumsy in her thick gloves, suddenly swung her helmeted head to face him. "Cab, do you know what you're going to do?"

He paused, then resumed entering the *Constellation's* orbit into the navigational computer. "Not precisely," he hedged. "Maybe that—he jerked a thumb at the reader—"will give me some help."

"Sorry."

He leaned over, squeezed her hand. "Nothing to be sorry about. Jenny, I'm glad you're here."

And he meant it. Too often during their time in the System they had been apart during times of crisis. He had been on Earth when the residents of the EnerSun station challenged the presence of the Soviet and American troops; he had been bleeding his life away while Jenny and Peter Traub and Lydia Kim Nu had been pursuing his attempted killer through the orbiting junk heap around the station. On Mars they had tried to keep him in the sick bay while Jenny and the colonists stormed the hijacked freighter. He had managed to get into that action, but Jenny had been on the far side of the ship. This time—for the first time—they were in it together. And for some reason it had a calming effect upon him. He wasn't wracked with worry for her safety. Because if the unthinkable happened they would at least have been together at the end.

Two grim-faced men with guns met them at the airlock. As they marched through the ship Cab considered his opening move. Wa Thondu would be expecting them to come as supplicants. Better to throw him off stride initially. It probably wouldn't work for long—a man who had read at Oxford, and graduated summa cum laude from Georgetown University, and third in his class from Harvard law school was not likely to stay rattled for long.

Still, it would enable him to work by a series of degrees to his final position, and then (with luck) the situation would provide him with an opportunity to offer a compromise. *And if it turned out that compromise was impossible?* He groped for Jenny's hand, and clasped it hard.

Four men and one woman waited on the bridge. By age alone Cab would have picked wa Thondu, but he also had incredible presence. He was a man who would draw the eye in any company. The Kenyan had a voice to match, deep and mellifluous as he asked, "You are?"

Cab lifted his chin, and stared down his nose. It was not an easy effect to achieve when he was only five feet five and wa Thondu cleared six feet by several inches. "I demand to know the condition of the crew and passengers of this vessel," he rapped out.

The Kenyan blinked, and was startled into an answer. "They're quite safe."

"I would like to ascertain that for myself, and then we can get down to business."

"You are very demanding Mr.—"

"Justice. Cabot Huntington. My assistant Jennifer McBride."

Wa Thondu spared her scarcely a glance, but the black woman, huddled at one of the consoles, turned a curious, yet hate-filled glance upon Jenny. That expression swept away the momentary burst of elation Cab had felt. They weren't negotiating over wages and benefits here. If he failed . . . He jerked his mind from that thought.

"As I was saying, Justice Huntington. You are, I think, in no position to be demanding anything." Wa Thondu's expression was thunderous.

Cabot arched his brow. "Oh?"

The Kenyan gestured toward the woman. "Viriku Amani is a very fine engineer. It is she who has rigged the device to detonate the engines. All it will take is one touch, and this colony will die."

Bluff, or did they really have sufficient antimatter?

"That may be, but you'll die with us."

"Yes, but we are desperate people, Judge. We came expecting death. We have nothing to lose."

"A stupid and silly statement!" Cab flared. "A human life is worth substantially more than nothing! And you're making no sense. If you blow this ship you will have lost any hope of making the changes you desire. The Earth will breathe a collective sigh of relief, write off a few more nuts and kooks, spare a momentary flicker of regret for the colonists, and get on with life."

Cab's mouth was horribly dry, and he would have given almost anything for a drink of water. He bit at his cheek and tongue trying to get the saliva flowing.

"Justice Huntington, I did not send for you so we could debate the relative merits of the course I have chosen. You are here to listen to my *demands*, and to RETURN TO THE INTERIOR OF CERES AND MEET THEM!" A shudder ran through the large frame, and when wa Thondu resumed it was in a more moderate tone.

"I require the instant surrender of the colony. And there will be no attempt at a double cross, for at the smallest sign of trouble Viriku will carry out my threat. Our technicians will then plot trajectories for fifty large Earth cities, and will prepare appropriate rocks for their journey to Earth. We will boost one—the governments of Earth should have no difficulty deflecting one—but it will indicate to them our sincerity. We will then wait for them to agree to our demands, and if they refuse . . ." An eloquent shrug. He rocked back on his heels, folded his arms across his massive chest, stared down at Cab.

Waited.

Long minutes passed. Nervous rustlings from the subordinates. Another long silence. And falling into it, a single word.

"No."

Chapter Nine ─────────────

It was a scene of orderly panic. Aides huddled over computer terminals. Small knots of cabinet officers forming and breaking apart like eddies in a tidal pool. The President standing in the center of the control center plaintively asking for the fourth time "but can they really *do* that?" Jack McConnell, who in addition to being Secretary of the Air Force, was a damn fine astrophysicist, finally whirling and snapping out, "Yes!"

And rather than rattling him this straight, unadorned answer seemed to focus Richard Long. Looking grim but calm the President by sheer force of personality pulled his dithering advisers to the big circular conference table, and brought them to order.

The large grids of fluorescent lights threw a yellow pallor across the pale faces which were lifted expectantly up to him, and Long frowned. He hated this place, like a noisy tomb, and he tried to recall how he had been hustled down here. Oh, yes, an overzealous aide operating under the mistaken belief that large rocks were going to start falling out of the sky at literally any moment.

He shoved back his chair, rose. "I'm going back upstairs."

The shame-faced aide, whose friends had been busily and gleefully explaining to him that it was "going to be *fucking years*" before those rocks arrived, stepped forward, perhaps contemplating an apology, met the President's gaze, slunk back. Long entered the elevator, rested his shoulders against the wall. No one but Lis tried to join him, and her he froze with a glance. There was a small choked sound from his normally silent and invisible secret service agent, and Long realized that Jennifer was right—Lis was not liked. He banished the disruptive and trivial thought, tried to concentrate. But all he could focus on was his campaign promise that unlike his predecessor he would defuse situations before they became crises. *What a joke.*

Long took a circuitous route, and they had all reassembled when he arrived. His eyes roved about the table. Sixteen men and two women representing the most powerful nation on Earth. One black face among the whites—General Rager, Chairman of the Joint Chiefs. He nodded to Lis, and with the barest minimum of glances to her hand-held reader, the Chief of Staff began to detail the situation.

"James Wairegi wa Thondu, son of the legendary Thomas Thondu wa Kamau—" .

"Why legendary?" asked the Secretary of Defense.

"He was the man who led the revolt which ousted the single-party government which had ruled Kenya since independence in 1963. His group claimed to want a return to traditional values and attitudes, and did in fact bring back certain of the outlawed customs such as female circumcision. They also claimed to favor free enterprise, but records from the Gartin administration indicate a strong socialist to communist bias. The new regime began a policy of 'Kenyanization' which was a thinly disguised attempt at nationalization. The United States and several other Western European countries protested these actions, and withdrew support. Wa Kamau's government turned to the Eastern bloc for aid. During the late twentieth and early twenty-first century the Soviets had made large inroads on the African continent. If Kenya, one of the most powerful and economically stable countries in Africa, had fallen into the Soviet block, it would have been a major black eye both politically and strategically for the United States.

"President Gartin pledged support and advisers to the freedom fighters of Mwanyumba wa Makeri—"

"He's still President of Kenya, yes?" piped up Treasury, always anxious to show off his grasp of foreign affairs.

"Yes," replied Ashley Cummings, the Secretary of State. A strange expression flickered across his usually impassive face.

"And what?" asked Christina Holland. The Attorney General's calm gray eyes coolly met the Chief of Staff's, blazing blue ones as Lis turned on her.

Three days ago Christina had endured a difficult hour with Lis screaming at her over her failure to keep the White House informed about the Fifteenth Circuit's review of agency actions on Mars, and Christina's unexpected and very damaging appearance before the ad hoc impeachment committee. The Attorney General's testimony had been very forthright about the lack of hearings or a coherent record to support any of the agency actions. Though the hearings had been closed, Cab's repellent gaggle of uncles had made certain that each damning revelation reached the press. The result had been some rather searching questions in the *Post* and the *Times* suggesting that perhaps the agency orders had their origins in the White House.

So Lis was on the rampage. Finally after one swear word too many, and the accusation that Christina herself had been the source of leaks, Holland had snapped. In a voice quivering with rage she cried, "I'm being asked to defend the indefensible, and like Milan at the *Post* I want to know who was behind these scandalous actions! And as for not testifying—baloney! Cab is being railroaded, and I'm not going to be a part of the smear job that's being done on him."

"Maybe you don't want to serve this administration any longer?"

"Maybe a little house cleaning would be in order. There are several heads that I think should roll before the public loses all faith in this administration!"

The dull, flat whine of a disconnect signal had been her only reply. And shortly thereafter the freeze-out had begun. Christina was fairly confident that her days with the Long administration were numbered, but since she wasn't out yet she decided to continue to pursue a question that Lis obviously didn't want asked. She repeated, "And what?"

Cummings stroked at his perfectly trimmed beard. "Well, he really is the most thoroughgoing rogue."

"That doesn't tell them much." It was the first time the Chairman of the Joint Chiefs had spoken, and several people tensed. Army General Rager's outspoken qualities were well known, and none knew that better than Lis Varllis who had endured a most unpleasant run in with him back in April.

Lis's eyes were boring into the Secretary of State's bland

face. "Well, it's just the usual." He gave a dismissive little shrug.

"The fact that atrocities are commonplace doesn't necessarily make them right," murmured the General with gentle irony.

Cummings glanced again to Lis, then gave another shrug. This one fatalistic. "He murders his political opponents despite some gentle hints from us and the British that that's really not very good form." He shot a tight little smile about the table. "There are vicious reprisals against any form of dissent, and graft at a mind-boggling level. Mwanyumba's reported to be the fifth wealthiest man in the world.

Lis was looking less and less pleased with this recitation.

"And we're of course fully supportive of this man?" asked Christina.

"Well, yes." Cummings gave an apologetic little cough. "You see, there's no one to take his place."

"One wonders why that's our problem rather than Kenya's," mused the General.

"Kenya has certain vital mineral deposits as well as the largest rectenna farm in the world. If those receivers were to fall into the wrong hands it could disrupt economies worldwide." Lis's voice ripped stridently across the silence like a file on metal.

"But to bring this back to this Wairegi fellow," interposed the President.

Lis scrolled forward. "Wa Thondu was educated primarily in the West, and returned to Kenya four years ago. Colleagues suggested that he wanted to achieve reform from within."

"Which is pretty sporting of him considering that he witnessed the murder of his parents by Mwanyumba's troops." The General paused, his eyes glittering dangerously in his black face. "Armed and trained, I might add, by the United States."

"That's just a story," snapped Lis.

"What? That we trained them or that they murdered wa Kamau and his wife?"

"The point is he joined Mwanyumba's government, serving as finance minister. Then six months ago he was fired, and disappeared from sight."

"Considering Mwanyumba's technique for dealing with out of favor subordinates one can hardly blame him," said

Christina dryly, and raised a nervous titter from the assembled officers.

Long held up a finger quieting the laughter. "During his tenure in office was there any hint of this extreme and militant position toward the West which he is now espousing?"

"Some. At a meeting of the IMF in Paris last year he accused the World Bank, private bankers, and the IMF of strangling the Kenyan economy in order to serve only the interests of themselves and certain large multinational companies. He later told the press that economic aid as it was currently applied was the greatest lie of the age. That there was no consideration of the best interests of the Kenyan people."

"Hmmm."

Frowns flickered about the table as they considered this.

"One can only presume that he became frustrated trying to effect change from within, and decided to take a more direct approach—like dropping rocks on our punkin' heads," said Rager, lapsing back into a soft southern drawl of his childhood.

"What about those colonists on Ceres?" spoke up Admiral Parker, the National Security Adviser. "I mean, they're in danger too. Any chance they might take this guy out?"

Lis snorted, an oddly vulgar sound, and very much at odds with her delicate beauty. "Hardly! They're more likely to throw in with him, and help him chuck rocks."

"Lis, we don't need that kind of wild talk," reproved the President.

"They're talking about independence. How much loyalty can they have? Especially when Joe Reichart and Ca—" She cut off. "When Joe Reichart is in charge out there."

"So what do we do?" came the faint moan from HEW.

Rager frowned grimly down at the table. "Go out there, and take them out. You don't bargain with terrorists."

"Most of the deep-space squadron is already on Mars, which puts them a quarter of the way there," added Jack McConnell, then paused and scratched his head. "Shit, that may not be right, depends upon where Ceres and Mars are in their respective orbits."

Long waved down the Air Force Secretary. "Whatever." He sighed and rubbed at his eyes. "This is more than just an American matter. The calls have been coming in from all over, and since the safety and security of the entire world is at stake, I think we must involve the other countries with deep-space capacity.''

''But not the Saudis,'' snapped Lis.

''No, not them,'' the President agreed.

''Why not?'' Christina asked.

''Wa Thondu and his little band of galloping goons departed from the Riyadh port. Their weaponry had to be smuggled through there, so fuck the Saudis.''

Rager made a face. ''Which leaves us cuddling up with Tupolev.''

''Crises tend to make strange bedfellows,'' the President replied.

''Nonetheless, I'd be careful. The American public's memory is not *that* short, and it's been less than a year since your predecessor and Tupolev joined forces to murder thirteen people on the Moon.''

''DeBaca wasn't directly responsible,'' protested Long.

''No, he just turned a blind eye so the Soviets could pull the actual trigger—so to speak. I'm not all that comfortable drawing a distinction between sins of commission and sins of omission.''

''You're an inspiration to us all, General,'' Lis purred.

''Glad to hear *you* say so, ma'am,'' he purred back.

''Like it or not the Soviets have almost double our number of antimatter drive ships, and I think they have to be included.''

''Bets on how many of them are currently operational?'' murmured McConnell sotto voce to Rager.

''So, what's the plan?'' asked Parker.

The President held up a finger. ''First, I talk to Tupolev. Second''—another finger was raised—''we make soothing seminegotiating sounds at the terrorists, stall them until the squadrons can reach Ceres. Xing Tao of the UN can handle that.''

''And if they don't stall? If they send off a few thousand tons of joy toward Earth?''

Long's face went gray. ''Then we do whatever it takes to destroy or deflect them.''

''And what do we tell the press . . . and the people, of course,'' Fred Downs, the Press Secretary, added hurriedly.

''That the situation is under control, and it should be resolved within a few days. Then find something else to draw the attention of those vultures in the media, and let this thing fade in the minds of the public.''

"It'll have to be something pretty big to supersede this."

Long cocked an inquiring eyebrow in Christina's direction. "Anyone we can throw to the wolves?"

"Other than Cabot Huntington?" she inquired sweetly, and smiled with satisfaction as the shot went home. "There's your Transportation Secretary. He's currently under investigation by a grand jury."

"Is an indictment likely?"

"Probably."

"Then hurry along that indictment."

"I'll see what I can do, but I don't think it's going to draw much attention from a menace from space."

"That will be all. I just need you, General, Jack, Lis, and Parker to remain."

The others mumbled and grumbled to their feet, and Christina, despite the strain of the past hours, found herself smiling as two of the junior aides preceded her out the door speculating as to why it was *always* transportation.

Rager settled deeper into his chair. "And now you call Tupolev."

"Yes."

"He'll try to manipulate you, so keep it short and sweet. You get into a long drawn-out talk, and he'll steal your testicles."

"You think we're wrong for including him?"

"No. His ships will come in handy because we've got to crush this thing fast and hard. I'm just warning you that he'll try to turn this to his advantage. The Soviets have had very little representation in the outer System—a research base, a handful of colonists—he'll try to use the presence of the Soviet fleet as a way to gain influence in the Belt. Don't let him. Make it clear he's entering United States territory on your sufferance, and that our man . . ."

"Saber," McConnell supplied.

"Saber is in overall command of the operation."

Lis was seething. She had always been Rich's chief adviser. Gathering information from the cabinet officers, forcing them to send their reports through the filter of her office. But Rager disliked and distrusted her, and he had given her nothing. Now she was left standing like a secretary waiting to dial the com or bring coffee while the men set policy and made decisions.

"It isn't general knowledge," the President continued with

a reproving glance at Lis. "But the Belt is currently making noises about moving toward independence, and this is just the kind of confused situation that the Soviets like to exploit. They may offer their support to Belt colonists, and get themselves invited to stay after the crisis has been resolved. We could find ourselves out in the cold.

"I don't think that's likely. The one generalization you can make about the System dwellers is their fierce independence and distrust of authority. I can't picture them turning to one of the more repressive regimes on Earth for support and aid."

"They'd do anything to give us a black eye," gritted Lis.

"Joe Reichart's not that petty. He's fought hard for thirty years to establish the System as a separate entity. He wouldn't risk it all now just for one final act of spite." Rager's dark eyes were leveled uncomfortably upon the Chief of Staff.

"Well, personally I hope the squadron arrives to find the Ceres colony in full support of the terrorists. Then Saber can bomb them all, and that should silence Joe Reichart and Cabot Huntington once and for all."

"Lis!"

"Oh, Rich, just joking."

The effect of that simple negative was electric. Viriku's hand jerked toward a switch, wa Thondu stopped her with a slashing gesture, and Cab's stomach climbed back down out of the back of his throat. The men exchanged dismayed glances, and Jenny, taking two quick steps toward Cab, reached for him, then regained control and stood silent at his side.

"You must be mad!" It was a penetrating scream of fury and confusion.

"No, sir, that we're not. But we are utterly convinced of *your* derangement. You would kill millions of innocent people to reach a handful of the guilty, and you want us to be a party to that crime. Well . . . we won't, not even to save our lives, or the lives of the crew and passengers."

Viriku, her voice high and thin with anger, burst out, "So kill them, and send their bodies back. That will make them think again."

"Viriku Amani, shut up!" Wairegi screamed in Gikuyu. They were all looking at him—Kariuki, James, Paul, J.K., Cyril—and he had no idea what to do. "Take them." His arm swung in a wide aimless arc. "And lock them up."

"Where? We're out of cabins."

"Put them with that journalist and the woman. Now go, I must think."

"Wairegi, what *do* we do?" J.K. asked softly.

"Why ask him?" Viriku demanded shrilly, advancing on wa Thondu. "He's a fool, and a coward."

"Gītoī kīraragia kīūī njīra," Wairegi intoned.

"Always a little quote, some quaint bit of Gikuyu wisdom that will be apt to every situation. Well, in this case you have chosen rightly . . . I *am* a fool to have gone with a fool. But now having gotten us into this position, O Mighty Leader, what will you do to lead us out?"

"I don't know—"

She turned on the other men triumphantly. "You see!"

"Yet! But I will think of something."

"Better think fast. Our deadline is far past, and we sit here dithering. Those people below are no doubt sniggering into their sleeves at the spectacle of brave terrorists afraid to act."

"To be laughed at by men is not to be wept by hyenas."

"You too? You'll imitate him to your grave, won't you, J.K."

"Stop it, Viriku. You're not helping."

Her head swung from one to the other. All she saw was despair and confusion. With a snort she stalked back to her console, hand outstretched. "Well, I am *not* afraid to die. So I'll do what the rest of you fear."

The five men erupted into a frenzy of action. It was James, the silent one, who reached her, jerked her back just before she reached the switch. For a moment she struggled wildly, fingers straining, then collapsed.

Her dark eyes were glittering with a fey light when she raised her head. "You see," she whispered. "You are afraid. That white man speaks, and you're afraid. Better to just surrender now. Maybe this white man will be merciful as well as commanding to us poor little misguided kafirs."

"We have come so far," Kariuki murmured. "Do we give up now having achieved nothing?"

"We have frightened them. Some will be curious. They will investigate Mwanyumba. . . ." Wairegi's voice trailed away.

"You don't believe that any more than we do," said Cyril. "That man was right. Once we were taken they will forget about us. We haven't done enough, we must do more."

"What? How?" Wairegi spun away, and brought his fists down on the back of one of the chairs. "I can't kill—"

"Which means we did come out here for nothing," Viriku said. "Because if he can't kill a few thousand here, he could never have killed the millions who would have died if Earth had failed to meet our demands." She focused on Kariuki knowing that leadership would fall to him if Wairegi were to be discredited. "We are at war," she pleaded. "People must die in a war."

Kariuki stared at his feet, then back at Wairegi. His expression was one of mingled fear, confusion, frustration, and disappointment.

"I must think. Give me a little time," pleaded Wairegi. "Perhaps we can salvage something."

And Viriku cursed for Kariuki's expression turned to one of compassion for his tortured leader.

"Sweet Jesus! Cab, Jenny!"

Andy came rolling toward them, his round face split by a smile. But there were deep lines carved about his mouth and his eyes were sunken and haunted. A curly-headed woman bounced from beneath the bed covers, and stared with pugnacious curiosity at the couple. There was something tantalizingly familiar about the small, slim figure, but it eluded Jenny before she could fully grasp it. Andy chugged toward her, arms outstretched. Jenny hugged him close, and he clung to her like a child frightened by a nightmare.

"Thank God you're here. We've been going crazy. What's happening?"

Cab's eyes remained on the silent, motionless woman. "I'm Cabot Huntington and this is Jennifer McBride."

"Pleased to meet you. I've heard a lot about you from my father and mother. I'm Perdita Kim Nu."

Jenny chivied Andy toward the bed, and he dropped heavily as if their arrival had drained the last of his strength.

"To repeat Andy's question. What's happening? Is my father here?"

"No, I'm afraid he and Stinson White are out rock hopping." Cab's mouth twisted. "At my insistence I might add."

"So we're doing our poor best to stand in for them," spoke up Jenny, while still continuing to smooth Andy's thinning dishwater blond hair.

"What exactly are these people up to? When Andy and I

tried to save the day we learned that we were heading for Ceres, but nothing more.''

In a few brief words—punctuated by occasional amplification from Jenny—Cab gave them the story.

"Well," gusted Andy, rubbing at his belly. "We're still alive so I guess it was only a bluff."

"Maybe, but *my* refusal was certainly not a bluff. So at the moment we've achieved stalemate and I'm blundering around in the dark. Do I stand arrogantly by our refusal? Do I offer them the chance for negotiation—"

"No!" broke in Dita. "Never negotiate with terrorists."

"Now whoa there! That's a little too dogmatic for me." Andy was recovering some of his old sparkle. "Wa Thondu's not an evil man—"

Cab's forefinger shot out. "And that's the kind of thing I need. I've read a brief biography of the man, but I have no feel for him, no feel at all." He clasped his hands before his face.

"Wa Thondu's an intelligent, thoughtful man, but currently he ain't rowin' with all his oars in the water."

"He's crazy?"

"No, no, not in the literal sense, but he's certainly bats on the subject of the Third World's—and more particularly Kenya's—mistreatment by the great powers. I'd say he's a man driven to desperation, and being forced by that same desperation into a desperate and crazy act. I mean, face it. This idea is really cheese-headed."

Cab held out his hands palms up, and waggled his fingers encouragingly. "Background, Andy. All I know is where he went to school, and his majors."

"Right. Father led the revolution against the one-party system. Father was killed by counterrevolutionaries armed and trained by the United States. Wa Thondu returns to Kenya at Mwanyumba's invitation—"

"Who's Mwanyumba?" put in Jenny.

"The thug who's run Kenya for the past forty years."

"He wasn't . . ."

"The man who ordered the deaths of wa Thondu's parents? Yep, he was."

"How could Wairegi work for him then?"

"An overblown sense of self-sacrifice and forgiveness, coupled with a sense of destiny. Wairegi's a Moslem, and he seems to have an almost mystic sense of balance and history.

He probably saw something metaphysical in his father's greatest enemy sending for the enemy's son as he, Mwanyumba, nears the end of his life. Full circle. See?''

"Not really.''

"Cab, you're a pragmatist.''

"Yes!''

"Anyway, Wairegi returns to Kenya determined to effect change from within. But old Mwanyumba isn't ready to embrace the will of the cosmos, and make peace. He begins to suspect his finance minister of plotting against him, (rightly so), and more worrisome, plotting against the West who's been propping up Mwanyumba for the past forty years. He sends orders to have Wairegi killed—that's the way he deals with political opponents, great guy huh—Wairegi runs, and—'' Andy paused for breath.

"And somewhere along the line cooks up this nutty idea, and now here he is, and here we are, and what are we going to do?'' Dita concluded having little taste for all this speculation, and armchair psychology.

"What exactly does he want?'' put in Jenny. "The ultimatum he sent to Earth is very vague and fuzzy.''

"I think his thoughts on this are pretty vague and fuzzy. He wants democracy returned to Kenya, he wants the Third World to have a fair share in the economic boom that is hitting the rest of the planet. But more than that I think he wants truth, beauty, and justice and indoor plumbing to hold sway over all the world.''

"And to achieve this great goal he's going to drop rocks on people's heads until they get their minds right,'' muttered Jenny, dropping her chin into her hands, and staring with frowning abstraction at the far wall.

A long silence lay over the room after that.

Cab shook himself, and asked, "But he's not a killer?''

"No. Not by nature, no.''

"So what do we do?'' repeated Dita.

"We wait.''

Chapter Ten

General Saber strode down the hall issuing orders in a rapid-fire staccato to the two harried aides scurrying after him.

"Cancel all s-shore leaves. I want flight checks run by twenty hundred."

"Sir," Captain Taguci ventured. "A number of our crews are under strength because they've gone to Elysium to see the alien artifact."

"Damn!" A whisper under the breath. "Well, get them back!" he roared.

"S . . . sir."

"And hurry Despopolous on those s-supplies." A plump, small figure hurtled past, heading in the opposite direction. "Lieutenant Kim Nu."

"Sir?" She slid to a stop, and looked back inquiringly. Two spots of bright color burned in her round cheeks.

"Good news about your s-sister."

"Yes, sir."

"And I hope you don't think too harshly of me for refusing permission for you to s-search."

A number of the General's peers thought he showed too much familiarity with his staff and subordinates, but his staff and subordinates wouldn't have agreed. Tasya knew that any one of the seven hundred men and women who served in the deep-space squadron would have cheerfully laid down their lives for him.

"No, sir. I was out of line." She raised her chin slightly. "But I'm glad we're going. She's in a crack, that's for sure, and I want to make sure we pull her out."

117

The General cocked an eye down at her. "You s-sound like this is a common occurrence."

"Dita is very much her father's child. Her life consists of tumbling from one scrap into another."

Saber laughed. "Well, carry on, Lieutenant, and we'll try to get you out to the Belt in record time." His face fell back into grim lines as soon as she was out of sight. "S-Stanley, check out the refueling." The young officer waited expectantly, fingers posed over the keypad of the portable computer. "S-So go!"

"Y . . . yes, sir."

Major John Adams, his handsome black face impassive, said, "You are, in the words of the poet, grumped."

Saber stopped, looked back at him with a puzzled frown. "Which poet?"

"Me."

"Oh." They entered the office, and the General dropped into his chair. "And yes, I'm grumped."

"Care to talk?" His commander made an irritated gesture toward the littered desk. "Busy work, sir. You can't do anything for at least five hours. Until we get our crews back."

"I can talk to the Russians. Oh, boy!" he added sarcastically.

Adams settled onto the edge of the desk, dug into his shirt pocket, and pulled out a pack of cigarettes. He then froze in the act of putting one to his lips, and looked questioningly at his commander. Saber waved permission. "What's he like? Your counterpart on the other side, I mean."

"Brilliant, ruthless, an international playboy, s-something of a gadfly to the Kremlin, and s-something of a mystery to us. Years ago, when he was just a captain he won s-several distinguished flying medals during the Uzbek war."

"Sounds impressive, but we shouldn't lose sight of the fact that they did lose."

Saber propped his feet on the desk, and folded his hands behind his head. "I s-suppose, but it s-sure as hell wasn't much of a victory for the Uzbeks. Three million dead, their agriculture destroyed, what industry existed demolished. They're technically independent, but . . ." He shrugged expressively. "Anyway, that's Admiral Casimir Verchenko."

"That doesn't tell me much."

"I don't know much. I'm just repeating department and intelligence s-scuttlebutt."

"But you'll be in overall command."

Saber held out a hand, and wobbled it back and forth. "That's what *our* s-side thinks." He sighed, and ran a hand across his face. "I just don't like the idea of a Russian armada s-steaming toward an American holding." He met his aide's humorous look, and smiled wanly back. "S-Steaming. Archaic term to describe a technological wonder, isn't it?"

"We'll have to come up with a new one."

"Yeah, in our copious s-spare time."

Adams had been with Saber long enough to know dismissal when he heard it. He slid off the corner of the desk, and headed for the door. It hadn't closed enough to cut off Saber's murmured remark.

"I only hope we can trust them."

It didn't tend to build confidence.

Admiral Casimir Verchenko sat with one knee negligently crossed over the other, and blew smoke rings toward the ceiling. The Soviet Premier, Yuri Tupolev, frowned, but bit back the sharp reprimand which had risen to his lips. Verchenko's amused contempt for civilians was well known, in fact he was damned contemptuous of any authority, preferring to trust to his own brilliance and dash. So far it had payed off.

Admiral Bulatoff, Supreme Commander of the Soviet Space Fleet, was less controlled. Shifting his heavy body in the chair he growled at his junior, "Show a little respect, Verchenko."

Casimir unfolded his long slim length, and crushed out the cigarette. "Oh, so sorry. I thought I was. I find it so hard to judge these things, being just a simple sailor." Since this was delivered in his most ironic most arrogant, most slap-in-the-face manner, it did little to mollify Bulatoff.

The grizzled admiral began to puff like an outraged pouter pigeon, but Tupolev waved him back into his seat. "My dear, Casimir. I do wish you hadn't had those three years at Oxford. Despite the fact it was twenty years ago you can't seem to shake the effects."

Verchenko threw back his head and laughed, displaying a set of perfect teeth. Tupolev felt a momentary surge of jealousy. Not only was he brilliant and dashing he was also movie-star handsome. His slender height and exotic coloring—

rich auburn hair, and elongated green eyes—made his two companions seem like squat gray barrels.

The Premier realigned his pen set, bringing it into a perfect intersection with his letter opener, contemplating the rectangle formed by the green blotter as if seeking oracular wisdom.

"So, orders." Casimir straightened slightly. "You are to be under the nominal command of Lieutenant-General Saber—"

"A good man."

"But orders must flow through you to our other vessels. Keep our crews away from the Americans, and out of their colonies."

Verchenko began to whistle. A tune which was unfamiliar to Bulatoff, but known to Tupolev—"How You Gonna Keep Them Down on the Farm." "And once we're out there?"

"Deal with these niggers."

"Yes, sir."

Tupolev paused for a sip of tea. "There is another matter. We have learned that the Ceres colony refused to arrest and return Cabot Huntington Earthside, claiming that there exists no extradition treaty between the Belt and the U.S."

Bulatoff frowned down at his hands where they gripped his knees. It was obvious he was out of his depth, and Tupolev momentarily regretted that loyalty was the usual standard by which command and promotion were measured.

"The first salvo in a bid for independence?" asked Verchenko.

"We think so."

"And you want me to help it along once we have freed the colonists from their brutal black captors?"

"Yes."

"From navy flier to space cadet to diplomat. I wonder where it will all end?"

"In a work camp if you fuck this up!"

"Oh, yes sir!" A textbook salute. "So I am to somehow manage to remain behind, and engage in talks with the Belters, and offer our support to their brave little revolution while General Saber flies serenely home."

"Yes."

"Saber's no fool. He—"

"No, but Long is."

"Might not go serenely along with this."

"He will obey orders, and I will see to it that Long orders him home."

"And how will you do that?"

Tupolev pulled thoughtfully at his upper lip. "I'm not certain whether Long's devotion to peace is based upon a touchingly naive faith, or whether it springs from fear. Whatever the source he is a man who relishes a confrontation. He will back down rather than offend us and appear an oppressor to the world at large."

"So we are to portray the colonists as brave freedom fighters flinging off the yoke of capitalist oppression?"

"Yes."

"And what if they don't agree to our stage managing their baby revolution?"

"It's your job to see that they do."

"I hope they haven't noticed that once we support a revolution we always stay."

"You disapprove?" grunted Bulatoff.

He laid a hand dramatically against his chest. "I? Question policy? Never." He dropped the flamboyant pose as quickly as he had assumed it. "But the Belters might. The System dwellers, both ours and theirs, have shown a distressing tendency toward independence and free thought."

This direct reminder of the challenge by the miner Renko, and the Garmoneya Collective, infuriated Tupolev. The disastrous outcome—a public censure by that bastard Huntington in his capacity as a World Court Justice—had led to a revolt within the Politburo which had almost toppled Tupolev, and a massive loss of face worldwide. Poland and Hungary were still busy churning out jokes about his discomfiture.

"You have your orders. Now get out! And remember," he held up a warning finger. "You fail and you can just kiss your Western travel pass, and Italian car, and little French lover, and penthouse apartment good-bye."

Verchenko's green eyes widened slightly at the reference to the Frenchman, and Tupolev smiled with satisfaction. *Yes, you arrogant bastard, we know!*

"Yes, sir!" Verchenko snapped off another salute, whirled on his heel, and marched from the office.

"It was perhaps not wise to preface so delicate a mission with a threat."

"What, you think he'll betray me?"

And Bulatoff, seeing a way to at last discredit and destroy his hated bird-of-paradise rival, pursed his lips thoughtfully, and carefully considered his words. Having come to maturity in the rough and dangerous world of Kremlin politics, he decided it wouldn't hurt to plant the suspicion as firmly as possible.

Then if Verchenko failed *(please God let him fail)* Tupolev would make the only logical conclusion—logical by the paranoid standards of the Kremlin—that Verchenko's fascination with Western lifestyles went far deeper than mere hedonism.

"He has been much in the West, and often in the System. Perhaps after this crisis is resolved he should stay a bit closer to home, and once more acquaint himself with Russian values."

"Thank you, Admiral. I will consider what you've said."

Bulatoff nodded, and withdrew, smiling faintly as he looked back to see Tupolev once more staring with frowning concentration at the blank green expanse of his blotter. He would have been distressed to know that all that concentration was focused upon him. The Premier had about decided that a man with so little subtlety and so obviously uninformed about his subordinates was perhaps past due for retirement.

It seemed as if hours had passed, but a fourth check of his watch in as many minutes confirmed it; only forty minutes had elapsed. Jenny, Andy, and Dita sat in a line on the narrow bunk, but Cab was unable to relax. He remained standing, rethinking every action since the crisis had begun. Trying to see if there was anything he could have done differently, trying to come up with some other alternative.

The door sighed open, and the bed sitters bounded to their feet. Cab forced himself to finish lighting his pipe. When it was burning to his satisfaction, he slowly turned and regarded Wairegi.

"Justice Huntington, you are playing a dangerous game with your people's lives."

Dita opened her mouth, and Jenny gave her a hard pinch. She subsided. Cab sucked thoughtfully at the pipe stem.

"In the first place they're not *my people*. I don't own them, I live with them. And secondly this is not my decision alone. I speak for all of us."

"Apparently not *all*. Several small vessels have left the asteroid."

"We're evacuating the children, but the rest know there aren't enough Curvets to go around. They're digging in, hoping to survive, but they're with us."

"Does your little colonial paradise always enjoy such unanimity of purpose?"

"No," said Cab serenely, ignoring the sneer. "But we've never before been ordered to be a party to mass murder. That does tend to put all our petty squabbles in perspective."

Wa Thondu gripped the judge by the shoulders, and began frenziedly shaking the smaller man. The pipe was wrenched from between Cab's teeth, and fell clattering to the floor. "You *must* agree. You *must* surrender."

Andy, Jenny, and Dita advanced, froze again as Wairegi's companion thrust the barrel of the shotgun in their direction.

"NO!" The judge yelled, and Wairegi threw him aside. Cab came up hard against the edge of the bunk, rubbed at his thigh, drew a deep breath, continued in a quieter tone. "But if you stop holding a gun to our heads we would be willing to talk."

"Talk, what good is talk? We've talked for two hundred years, and been answered with bullets."

"Very dramatic," Cab replied with fine Bostonian dryness. "But hardly meaningful. Talk is the means by which civilized people solve their differences."

"And when talk fails?"

"Why talk of failure when we haven't even *tried* it yet?"

"They're trying to trick us, Wairegi."

Jenny stepped forward. "Look, you haven't exactly endeared yourselves to us, what with the threats and all, but we *are* willing to listen. I'm a white woman, and a very privileged one, so I can't fully understand your experiences. But that doesn't mean I won't *try*. If you have legitimate grievances—and it sounds like you do—we might be able to help."

"How?"

Jenny faltered a bit under Wairegi's flat stare.

Andy picked up for her. "You told me that despite the torrent of energy and raw materials flowing from the System to Earth many of the developing nations never get a piece. Well, hell, that would concern us, us System folks, I mean." He mopped at his round, gleaming face with a handkerchief.

"Who are your enemies, Mr. wa Thondu?" asked Cab softly. "The people of Earth? Or a few select and powerful people?"

"It's hopeless. The governments of the West and their powerful multinational jackals want to keep us in bondage.

We are a source of cheap labor and unending consumers. They will never allow us to develop our own industrial base. Then we might compete with them, both politically and economically.''

Cab briefly closed his eyes, and winced at the overly dramatic delivery. ''Mr. wa Thondu. About a year ago the then President of the United States, Tomas C. deBaca, told me that without the flow of energy and raw materials from the System, society would grind to a halt. He then added that *we're scared of them.* Now, I can't promise that the System will take an interest in your cause. That would have to be decided in debate by the stations, Mars, the Moon, and the Belt. *But we might.* And we have the clout to force at least a discussion of your problems. That's the sensible course. This—'' he made a wide sweep with his arm—''is madness. Your threats alone are enough to turn possibly sympathetic allies against you. And, I repeat, we will *not* be a party to your madness. So either do your worst, blow this ship, kill as people as you can, or lay down your weapons and try talking to us.''

''Your colonists would really help?''

Cab stretched out a hand. ''You have my personal guarantee that I will put the question before the System. I can't promise the outcome, but you will at least have a forum. You will be heard.''

Cab noted that wa Thondu did not look to his companion for guidance, he stood, chin sunk on breast, chewing on his lower lip. And in that moment Cab had more respect for the Kenyan than at any time since the crisis had begun. His motives might be confused, his plan untenable, but he was a man who would make his own decisions, and take the responsibility for the decisions.

Cab did risk a glance to his friends. Andy was still sweating, great beads of perspiration gathering on his brow and matting in his sideburns; Dita stared glumly at her hands which lay tangled in her lap; and finally Jenny. Her courtroom poker face was firmly in place, her stance relaxed yet commanding. Which made her break down in control on Ceres all the stranger. It was puzzling—

''I can't do it,'' said Wairegi heavily. ''I am not a murderer. But may Allah forgive me if I have chosen wrongly.'' The young Kenyan behind him bowed his head and lowered the shotgun. "You will keep your word?" Wairegi's eyes were haunted.

"I will keep my word." Cab closed his hand firmly over the Kenyan's.

"So, Judge, what must we do?"

"Lay down your arms, free the crew, and uh . . . I guess come down to Ceres with us."

"And we better let Earth know that the party's over. God alone knows what mischief they've gotten up to since Mr. wa Thondu's little ultimatum."

"You know, you sound a lot like your father when you say that."

"Cussedness and cynicism must breed true," Dita offered with a faint smile. She walked quickly to the young Kenyan, and took the shotgun from his limp grasp. "I'm going to hang onto this until that crazy bitch up top is safely in custody," she explained as Cab's eyebrows lifted.

"You didn't see her juggling her little grenade," Andy added.

"No, we just saw her perched like a vulture over that toggle switch. One touch and *boom*." Jenny's hands arced expressively.

"Viriku will obey my orders," Wairegi said, then added in Gikuyu, "*I hope*."

"Wairegi, perhaps we should get her away from the control room," offered J.K. nervously, also speaking Gikuyu.

"English, please," Cab said, feeling like a hero in a third-rate adventure show.

"Will you trust me to go alone to the control room, and bring down Viriku?"

"You don't trust her either?"

"Let's just say I would prefer not to tempt fate."

"All right."

"We'll be waiting at the foot of the ladder," put in Dita.

Her voice carried clearly down to them as she descended the ladder. "I knew it would come to this." Wairegi's response was an indistinguishable rumble. "You're too squeamish. Kill one of them, and send their body back, and—"

"Surprise," said Dita softly, her lips skinning back in an unpleasant grin. The expression further narrowed her already slanted eyes, and gave her an amazingly feral look.

Viriku didn't respond to the shotgun poking her in the

back. She remained frozen, pulled up to her full height, and stared at Wairegi.

"So now you add betrayal to cowardice." A glob of spittle hit the floor between his feet, and he flinched.

"Come on, move." Dita prodded her again with the barrels.

"With pleasure so long as you take me away from this *kinyonga*."

Head held regally high she paced away, with Dita trotting to keep up with her long swinging strides. Wairegi had gone gray, and Cab stared at him.

"What did she call you?"

"A chameleon."

"Oh." He glanced at Jenny and shrugged.

"The most despised creature in Gikuyu culture."

"Oh," Cab repeated, much softer this time.

"It is responsible for the presence of death among mankind." The big man turned, and climbed swiftly up the ladder to the control room.

Chapter Eleven _____

The banks of machines filling Ceres Control hummed, a self-satisfied chorus of stubby dwarfs. Set against this constant drone was the low murmur of voices, the delicate click of keyboards. Andy, one hand groping in a box of chocolates, the other still continuing to type, glanced up as Jenny laid a hand on his shoulder.

"A fuckin' Pulitzer is on its way," he mumbled around a mouthful of chocolate and caramel. "I can feel it coming." He gestured toward the neat lines glowing on the screen.

"No hard feelings, I take it, Andy."

"Nah, all's well that ends—"

"With a Pulitzer Prize."

"Jenny." His face folded like a baby about to cry.

"There, there, Andy. I'll stop being mean. You were saying?"

"Just that my story, together with his—" he jerked a thumb toward a nearby chair where Wairegi wa Thondu alternated between huddling and periodically erupting into a frenzy of typing—"his exposé and statement of conditions and problems in Kenya and Africa should get some action."

"In the System," she held out a hand, palm down, and waggled it. "Maybe. On Earth, I doubt it."

"Jenny." He slewed about to face her. "What's happened? You used to be our number one cheerleader, drum beater, always ready to stand up and be counted, take a stand, make a difference." The tone was bantering raillery, but his brown eyes were concerned as he stared up at her.

"Like Candide I'm becoming increasingly attracted to the notion of tilling my own garden." She began to drift away.

"It never works, darlin', vandals always come through, and kick the shit out of it."

"Now who's being cynical."

She continued her circuit of the control room heading for Cab. All of their various activities—Andy writing his story, wa Thondu preparing his plea to the System, Cab informing the authorities Earthside—could have just as easily taken place from their rooms, but they had all ended up back in the bowl to report to Irving, and it had just seemed simpler to stay. Probably because none of them were quite ready to come down from the emotional high produced by fear and excitement.

She reached Cab just as his call finally went through.

"This is Cabot Huntington calling from Ceres Control. I'm calling to inform the President that the crisis has ended. The Kenyans have surrendered. The threat's over."

"The President?"

He shrugged. "I didn't know who else to call. And I think we've had enough dramatic worldwide announcements for one day."

She wrapped her arms around his neck, rested her cheek on the top of his head. "Cab, you're too modest. Here you have a chance for glory—*Judge Saves World; Proof There Is Justice*—and you pass it by."

His fingers laced through hers. "No, I'm not modest. I know the depths of my arrogance far too well. Sometimes it frightens me because it's all so very alluring, and I could become so addicted so easily."

"Pooh!"

"Not pooh, true. There's a lot about me, Jenny, you still don't know."

"Ditto."

A sudden frown creased his forehead, and he swung around to face her. "Which reminds me. Why have you been seeing Cassie? Professionally I mean."

"Who says I am?"

"Your appointment book."

"Who said you could snoop?"

He stiffened. "I think I have a right."

"Why?"

"I live with you, Jennifer."

"That doesn't mean you own me."

"We're not talking about ownership here, we're talking about concern!"

"Cab, if we were married. Relax! I just said *if*. Hypothetical question here. *If* we were married, do you think that would give you more rights in me and toward me than you have now?"

"I'm not sure I understand the question," he hedged. Jenny made a rude noise. "All right, yes, I suppose so. I'm a traditionalist, you know that."

"How traditional is traditionalist? We need some definitions here."

"Jenny," he exploded. "This is really irritating me. I hate these guessing games. If I say the wrong thing *boom*, you get mad and I get resentful. So what are you really asking—"

"This is a joke, right? Who is this?" The young man whose features suddenly settled on the comscreen had a youthful tenor voice, and the air of a person who took his position far too seriously.

"No! This is not a joke! This is Justice Cabot Huntington, and I *demand* to speak to the President!"

Cab sat fuming, and drumming his fingers on the edge of the console as the message, and the reply, made their slow way through the Solar System.

"Look, some clown just can't call up the White House on the public com, and expect to speak to the President—"

"Look, you moron—"

"And the crank calls have been coming in by the hundreds over the Belt emergency, and—"

"Forget it!"

The smirk seemed to take a long time to fade.

"What now?"

"We'll make a public announcement."

"Once more into the limelight, dear friends," sighed Jenny.

"The announcement has been verified by Senator Neville Huntington. Apparently Justice Huntington actually succeeded in talking down the terrorists, and obtaining their surrender," concluded the President, his eyes sweeping the length of the table, and his assembled cabinet officers.

"They're in custody now?" asked Cummings.

"Yes, all except wa Thondu who is busy drafting manifestos."

"What?"

Lis threw a printout of Wairegi's essay, Andy's story, and Cab's brief and terse message to the various System settlements into the center of the table. "*This* just hit the news services. Included with it is a request from Huntington to the System to discuss this terrorist's demands, to decide whether there are legitimate grievances."

"So?" asked Defense, and McConnell carefully explained for an ability to grasp the ramifications was not one of Defense's strong suits.

"The System is feeling threatened by Earth, and therefore hostile toward us right now. They might view wa Thondu and the Kenyans as fellow sufferers, and decide to help them."

"How?"

"A boycott sounds like a safe bet." There was a strangled sound from Commerce.

The President waved a dismissing hand. "That's just grandstanding. It's not going to happen."

Lis rounded on him. "You can't know that. And more importantly, who does Cabot Huntington think he is to involve himself in foreign policy?"

"Lis, you're overreacting. Neville explained that the judge was trying to find some face saving way for wa Thondu to surrender. This kind of discussion hurts no one, and God knows there have been abuses. Besides, I'm going to forestall any System action by calling for the UN investigation myself."

"Mwanyumba isn't going to like that," put in Ashley Cummings.

"Mwanyumba is old and sick, and this country has had a bad habit of clinging to aging dictators long after they can serve any useful purpose. This will allow us to look like . . . well, like what we should be, champions of freedom worldwide."

"So we pull back the squadron?" asked Jack McConnell.

"I think yes."

"Is this open to discussion, Mr. President?"

"Of course, Lis."

"I see several problems with that. First, just because we pull back our ships, what's to say the Russians will too? They have virtually no holdings in the asteroids. This would offer them the perfect opportunity to cruise out and offer support to the Belt. Remember, we not only have this gang of terrorists out there, we have an ongoing and underhanded bid for independence on the part of our territory.

"Which brings me to my second point. If we allow the Belt to flout us on this matter of Cabot Huntington, if we allow them to simply drift quietly into independence, how long before we lose the rest of them? Near-Earth stations, the Moon, Mars, all of them?"

"So what is it, exactly, that you're advocating?" drawled Christina Holland.

Lis kept her eyes locked on the President's. "Let's allow the squadron to continue to Ceres. Take custody of the Kenyans, and return them to Earth for trial." The President shifted uncomfortably. "That isn't going to undermine our position. We can still support reform in Africa without condoning acts of terrorism. It will simply show that we're evenhanded and that we won't tolerate these kinds of incidents. And finally let's round up Cabot Huntington, Jennifer McBride, Joe Reichart, and Stinson White."

"On what grounds?" demanded Christina.

"We have already established grounds for arresting Huntington—"

"Isn't that going to look kind of shitty when the whole world knows that Cab's the one that kept the sky from falling—literally—onto their little pointed heads?" Contempt hung heavy in her voice.

"Never underestimate the ability of the public to be distracted."

"By what?" snapped Christina.

"By anything! It doesn't matter. And as for Reichart and White, well, they're inciting to rebellion."

"Same as Cab, huh?"

"It is not legal to secede from the Union. *That* was laid to rest in the 1860s. I shouldn't have to tell you this, you're the Attorney General."

Christina turned her fine gray eyes onto the President. "Sir, it's very difficult to maintain a sense of unity with people who are hundreds of millions of miles away. We stood in exactly the same position with England three hundred years ago, and it was distance that defeated them too."

The President's thumbs were rasping through his sideburns. It was a nervous, uncertain gesture that drove Lis crazy. But this time, to her surprise, it did not lead to more dithering. Instead he reached a decision.

"No, I think Lis is right. If we allow one part of the System to secede the rest will follow. We can't risk that. It will send the wrong message, and before long we may see the same problems arising in our groundside spheres of interest. South America has been bubbling for years, a show of weakness at this time could be disastrous. Draft an order for General Saber. And for God's sake let's keep this in this room. I don't want to read about it in the afternoon issues. Also, we want to catch them this time. Joe Reichart slipped past deBaca last year. We lost Huntington on Mars. We can't afford to lose them again."

They all rose as the President left the room. Lis then favored them with a cold stare.

"Just a final little warning. If word that the squadron is proceeding on to Ceres gets out, and we lose these people, I will personally head the internal investigation to find the leak. And when I find it . . ." Her pale blue eyes raked the room. "I'll squash it. Understood?"

Tasya Kim Nu pressed herself against the side of the narrow corridor to make room for a couple of crewmen heading for the cockpit. Despite its insulating wrap one of the pipes was uncomfortably hot against her back. She resumed walking, longing for her bunk, and a few hours of uninterrupted sleep.

One writer and commentator on modern American society had compared the men and women who crewed the antimatter ships to submariners. Which had of course caused a howl from the Air Force. The rivalry between the Navy and the Air Force had caused more than a few barroom brawls over the years, and a whole series of silly designations. Cockpit instead of bridge, the troops carried aboard a deep-space ship weren't marines, they were Emergency Response Force airmen (affectionately referred to as ERFS). But the Navy had had the final and most ironic laugh for the ships were called . . . well, ships. The Air Force's official designation was "excursion capsule," so it was no wonder it was never used. The only time Tasya had heard it outside of lecture halls was in a very naughty ready-room song about the ERFS who flew on ECs.

But all of this aside, the original premise was an accurate one, thought Tasya as she slipped through the hatch into the women's bunk. The ships were small, cramped, and claustrophobic. Only in science fiction movies did you see wide corridors, and spacious rooms.

Iwa Ichiko was hunkered on one of the top bunks carefully painting her toenails. The total complement of the *Intrepid* was eighty officers, ERFS, and enlisteds. Of that eighty only seven were women. So of necessity they were close. Their primary function was to fly the MRV fighters, but they also had assignments aboard the ship proper.

Theirs was a strange and amorphous position. Logic and economics would have indicated a ship crewed totally or at least primarily by women. A woman's metabolic rate was eleven calories per pound per day while her male counterpart required twelve. But Congress and a large and vocal segment of the American population opposed women in combat positions. Unfortunately the new breed of interactive fighter plane required their presence.

And as always when philosophy and reality came face-to-face an accommodation was reached. Congress, being staffed by several hundred lawyers, turned to convoluted legal reasoning for the solution. Taking a leaf from free speech cases of the early twentieth century—(when is speech not protected by the First Amendment? Why when it isn't speech of course!) —they redefined combat, gave the women a safely neutral designation, and *violà*, legal gymnastics triumphed yet again.

It was Iwa with her quick wit who had put the final stamp on the lunacy by remarking dryly that there sure were a hell of a lot of "clerk/typists" dying in "air disasters." For the women had seen combat in any number of little brushfire wars that seemed to pop up around the world with such distressing regularity.

Tasya flopped onto her bunk, and folded her arms beneath her head. "Who are you primping for?"

"Hey, who knows what fleshly delights await me on scenic Ceres. Maybe my white knight will be waiting." Tasya made a rude noise, and Iwa launched a pillow at her.

"What's the scuttlebutt?"

"Pretty scutty. Word is the crisis is over," she held up a restraining hand, then cursed as a drop of polish fell from the brush onto her bare thigh. "But don't dance in the street because we're not headed home or even back to lovely"—her nose wrinkled in disgust—"Mars."

"How come not?"

"Well," she said, drawing out the word. "I just happened to overhear Colonel Belmanor—"

"Snooping as usual."

"Hey," she spread her arms in an embracing gesture. "A girl's got to get ahead in this man's Air Force. Anyway, he was on the horn to the General, and it seems our esteemed Commander in Chief, Richard Malcom Long, wants the troublemakers back on Earth where he can keep an eye on them."

"Makes sense. Personally I'd just space them after a stunt like that." She cocked her head to one side considering. "Which is why it's probably a good thing I'm in the military, and not on the civilian side of things. I'm too bloodthirsty."

"As I was saying!"

"Sorry."

"That's not the most interesting part."

"Oh?" Tasya sat up, and crossed her legs beneath her.

"Our beloved Colonel Tracy was having a pretty spirited argument with the old man."

"No kidding? What about?"

"If you'd stop interrupting I'd tell you. It seems that the Great White Father groundside wants us to bring back more than just the terrorists. He wants several big wheels from the Belt who've been making trouble. The Colonel said that if we do that the entire System may go up in flames."

"He's right."

"Oh, yeah, you're a raggedy assed colonist too, aren't you?"

"Born and bred, just like Belmanor."

"Well, it ended with the General asking in that oh so soft, oh so dangerous voice just *how* Colonel Belmanor proposed that he disobey orders coming directly from the President."

"Who are they after?"

"I don't know."

"It's a sure bet Joe is one of them," mused Tasya.

"Hey, where are you going?"

"Now that the crisis is over I can finally get in touch with my sister. She was on that liner that got hijacked you know."

"Right. And that's what I'll tell them when they come to gather information for your court-martial."

"You're too bright, Iwa."

"Yeah, that's what my dad always used to say."

•   •   •

Szablewski and Tasya shared a shallow, but friendly relationship. But his rather protuberant blue eyes swiveled toward her making him look like a terror-stricken frog after she voiced her request.

"No dice . . . uh. Only . . . uh, ship to ship, or ship to Earth . . . uh, communication."

"This is ship to ship. She's aboard the *Constellation*."

"So why did you say Ceres before?"

"Slip of the tongue."

"My . . . er, ass! You're . . . uh, picking at nits."

"Look, I thought she was dead, that was bad enough. Then I find out she was hijacked, I want to see if she's all right. You can understand."

He stubbornly shook his head, and Tasya glared down at him.

"Problems, Lieutenant?"

She gasped, whirled, and wished, like every junior officer on board, that Colonel Belmanor wasn't quite so light on his feet.

"No, sir." She sucked in a deep breath, and plunged on because she knew if she didn't Szablewski would, and it would sound better coming from her. "Just hoping to get in touch with my sister. Make sure she's all right."

Colonel Belmanor's velvet brown eyes locked on hers. He usually maintained an icily aloof manner toward his juniors though more than one young female officer had sighed over his dark, if somewhat portly, good looks, and wondered if she could warm those eyes. Now something was passing between them, and Tasya didn't think it was because he'd suddenly discovered her manifold charms.

"It seems a reasonable enough request. Just keep it brief, Lieutenant."

"Yes, sir, and you can tell the General, sir, that I'm—"

"Thank you, Lieutenant, but *I'm* responsible for what occurs on my ship."

"Yes, sir, of course, but—"

"That will be all, Lieutenant." He drifted away.

Five minutes later Szablewski had to swallow his stomach for the second time. Belmanor was back, hands locked behind his back, rocking slightly on the balls of his feet.

"Lieutenant Kim Nu make her call?"

"Yes . . . uh, sir."

"How is her sister?"

"Uh . . . fine, I . . . uh, guess. They were speaking some crazy Chink language, so I couldn't understand.

"Excellent. Carry on, Airman."

"Uh . . . yes, sir." He bent over his console, shaking his head over the mysterious ways of the brass.

Chapter Twelve   ————————

A guided missile that slowly resolved itself into the form of his daughter shot past Joe as he stood in the doorway of his apartment.

"What the devil is going on?" he announced in a loud, aggrieved voice. "I rush back to save the day only to find the crisis is over, I've missed all the excitement, Cabot is a hero, and now you're tearing up my apartment. And how did you get here anyway?"

"Oh, hi, Dad." A quick, distracted peck to the cheek. "Glad you're back, but don't get too comfortable. We're leaving."

He dropped into a chair, pulled out his pipe, and began to tamp in tobacco. His brown eyes were twinkling as he watched Dita's energetic perambulations. "Oh, we are are we? Why?"

"Tasya called to warn us that the fleet isn't turning back, and they've orders to—"

"Dita, my love, you share the most irritating habit with your mother. You never explain anything. You just take charge, and produce a flurry of activity which, while it may have meaning for you, engenders a sense of breathless confusion in your victims."

"I'm sorry." She perched on the arm of the chair, and snaked an arm around his neck. "I was heading back—"

"You finished your Masters?"

"Yes. Now who's delaying matters? Ship got hijacked, but you know about that."

"I heard the ultimatum."

"Things were tense for a day until Cab managed to talk down Wairegi . . . you know, he's a hell of a fellow."

"Who? Cabot or this Wai . . . Wai . . ."

"Wairegi. No, Cabot. I suppose Wairegi may be a hell of a fellow too, but I'm still not disposed to look very kindly upon him. I don't like being hijacked, kidnapped, locked in a cabin with Andy—"

"Oh, Lord."

"Threatened." She paused for breath.

"I get the picture." He sucked at his pipe, and mused aloud. "So Cabot saved the day. And by the way he *is* a hell of a fellow. He just needed time to shed some of his more aggravating and arrogant attitudes." Straightening, he prodded her with the stem of his pipe. "But what's this about Tasya?"

"Earth, threatened with death from the skies, ordered out the deep-space squadron together with the Russian fleet."

"Good God!"

"I knew that would please you. 'Course you could hardly blame them. I wouldn't sit by, and let people drop rocks on me. Anyway, Cab reported that the crisis was over, but that didn't deter our fearless leaders. They saw a chance to stop the independence movement out here—oh, yes, I've heard about that, you have been busy, Dad—so the squadron is coming on with orders to arrest the Kenyans and the Belt ringleaders." She cocked her head to one side, considering. "It probably didn't help that Cab honored his promise to Wairegi to have the System discuss the Kenyans' grievances with an eye to a possible embargo."

"Oh, Lord." Joe dropped his head into his hands. "And he talks about *me* setting him up on a mountain of dynamite, and not telling him."

"Well, I think it showed courage and a sense of honor."

"Oh, undoubtedly, but perhaps not a great deal of caution. What our dear Cabot has done is finally make the inchoate fears of the groundside powers a reality. A boycott from space."

"We're just *talking* about the possibility."

"Sweetheart, in the mind of a politician words are as dangerous as actions." Joe lit his pipe, and took a few thoughtful pulls. "And what about the Russians?"

"Oh, they're coming too. Nobody wants to miss this party."

"Hmmph." Joe grunted. "They must be up to something

devious which they will no doubt screw up. They have only a fingernail hold out here so—"

"Dad, their motives should be of less concern to us than the fact that they're on their way. It's time to decamp, depart, abandon, leave, in short vamoose. You can analyze their motives later."

"Yes, dear," he said meekly, and Dita punched him on the shoulder. "Well," he pushed up out of the chair. "Since you've packed for me, shall we go see our conquering hero?"

Cab threw open the door and was faced with Joe Reichart playing "Hail to the Chief" on a plastic kazoo. He was not amused. Jenny, however, collapsed chuckling onto the sofa.

"Joe, for Christ's sake."

"How does it feel to be a hero, Cab?"

"Did Dita bring you up to date?" he asked, pointedly ignoring the sally.

"Yes. I feel rather like the Founding Fathers decamping from Philadelphia with the British nipping at their heels."

"And which Founding Father are you, Joe?" asked Jenny, giving him a hug.

"Oh, Franklin, of course. Witty, urbane, lewd, irreverent."

Cab eyed Joe with suspicion. "I suppose you're saving Adams for me."

"Well, you are a Bostonian."

The judge was not fooled by the innocent delivery. He knew Adam's reputation: a rabblerouser, a troublemaker, and obnoxious and disliked even by his fellow patriots.

"I'm glad some of you are finding this so amusing. I'm afraid I can't, the situation is too serious."

"Really? I think of it as more high farce."

"Joe, things could get out of hand very easily."

Reichart shot a glance to Jenny. "Is he always this way?"

"Cab tends to be a pessimist."

The judge's lips tightened perceptibly. "Since entering the System somewhat less than one year ago I've been shot, assaulted, kidnapped, survived a Martian sandstorm, found myself threatened with a gun by someone I had trusted—" He broke off, and flushed deeply.

"And had to charge a killer laser," he concluded in a rush while Joe laughed and asked at the same time,

"What, Jenny get frustrated . . ." His voice trailed away as he looked from one embarrassed face to the other.

"Amadea." The good humor leached from the older man, and he sank into a chair.

"And just how did you arrive at that?" demanded Cab, tension raising his voice several tones. "I never said a word about Amadea."

"Yes, that's right, but you've had a guilty, hangdog air about you, and both Lydia and I suspected it had something to do with Amadea. We just never dreamed how bad things were." He raised his hand, and pinned Cab. "Are you going to tell me about it?"

"No."

"Jenny?"

"You heard the man."

"The ever-loyal Jenny—"

"God damn it! Why does everyone assume I'm just an appendage of Cab?"

The closing of the bedroom door cut sharply through the uncomfortable silence.

"What did I say?"

All at once their differences were forgotten. They were two men faced with that eternal dilemma—a woman.

"I don't know. She's been behaving very strangely recently."

Cab tensed, expecting Joe to return to the topic of Amadea, but apparently forty years in business had taught the older men when something was a losing proposition.

"I take it you're organizing this evacuation?"

Cab hurried into speech. "It seemed the prudent course, and you weren't around—"

"Oh, I'm not blaming you, or resenting your usurpation of my position." Brown eyes gleamed. "But have you considered where we're to go?"

"I hadn't gotten that far," Cab confessed.

"We need a good-sized rock to hide the ships. It will take at least three Curvets depending upon who's coming."

"You, me, Jenny, Stinson—"

"Dita."

"Stinson's daughter?"

"I doubt it."

"Andy?"

"Possibly." Joe tugged at his chin. "Yeah, three ships because we'll have to carry our own food. We can't expect some poor Belt family to put up this herd. We'll want something reasonably close to Ceres so we can monitor the situation.''

"You know such a rock?''

"Yes, I think Evgeni Renko's stake will do very nicely for us.''

"Oh, God, no!''

"Have to face him sooner or later, Cab.''

"I faced him on EnerSun, that was enough.''

"Cab, you're on the same side now.''

"That ought to really weigh with him considering that I almost got him and his family killed, and did manage to destroy his companions in that collective.''

"Cabot, there's a difference between accepting responsibility for your actions, and positively wallowing in guilt and self-pity. That's better,'' said Joe approvingly when the younger man's head snapped up, his features pinched and white with outrage. "You didn't order the missile strike that plastered that collective, and you weren't the American President who turned a blind eye to the Russians' murderous shenanigans.''

"Is there no other rock?''

"Oh, probably thousands of them, but I think you should face Evgeni.''

"So now you're my spiritual counselor as well as my political tutor?''

"It's one of the perks of old age. You can be a pompous old fart.'' He clapped his hands onto his knees, and pushed himself to his feet. "Well, I've got to go, and call Lydia, let her know what's going on.''

"Is that wise?''

Reichart gave a snort of laughter, scratched in his mane of graying hair. "And lo, the student becomes the master. No, it's not wise. I'll have to figure out some other way to get word to her.'' He paused at the door, and looked back. And found Cabot hunched over, face in hands. He crossed to him, and laid a hand gently on one bowed shoulder. "What's the matter, son?''

"My life was so safe, controlled, comfortable. I knew who I was, and where I belonged. I never asked for all this. I'm scared, Joe.''

There was no answer for that. Reichart just tightened his fingers on Huntington's shoulder. Sighed. Walked to the door.

"I'm glad you're back, Joe. Now you can take over."

The older man felt a flicker of disappointment mingled with relief. And knew that his own motives, hopes, fears, and desires were none too clear.

"Jennifer, you're taking a big risk. You should stay here."

"I can't, Cassie. There's a warrant for my arrest too."

"Have you told him yet?"

"No."

"Good God, woman, he has some rights. You didn't do this all by yourself."

She scraped hands, grown clawlike with tension, through her long red hair. "Look, I don't have time to go into it all. Explain all the reasons why I haven't told him—"

"Jenny, your problems, real or imagined, with Cabot don't concern me. Cosmic rays do. You spend too much time putting around in that tin can"—she gestured toward the Curvet—"and you're going to end up with severely damaged embryos."

"It's only three days to the Renkos'."

"Thank God for that, but you stay suited the entire time— the shielding's pretty good on those suits—and the minute you arrive you crawl down in the middle of that rock, and you stay there!" She stumped away, a blocky, unlovely figure whose short hair had been agitated into an erect brush by her nervous fingers. "And for God's sake tell Cab!" she yelled, whirling and backing out of the hangar.

Jenny glared after the doctor. Furious with her for trying to force the issue, bitterly grateful that Cab had been out of earshot so Cassie's last heavy-handed attempt had failed. She knew that Cassie considered her silence to be foolish, childish, stubborn, stupid, and incomprehensible.

But Cassie's opinion notwithstanding, Jenny had very good reasons for what she was doing. Foremost among them being Amadea, and all that had passed between the beautiful Eurasian and Cabot on Mars.

After the events on EnerSun her and Cab's relationship had shifted from friends and colleagues to lovers. They had returned to Earth to fight Cab's impeachment, and she had moved in with him. There had never been any talk of the future, it was just something they shared, sufficient to the moment. But Jenny had assumed he loved her.

Then had come Amadea. Beautiful and seductive the young

Eurasian had swept Cab away in a maelstrom of passion. It had been all act on her part. A way to ingratiate herself with the judge come to hear the environmental battle over the fate of Mars, a way to sway and influence him, and when that failed she arranged to have him murdered.

After their flight from Mars Cab had begged Jenny's pardon, and she had forgiven him. But the damage had been done. A thorn of distrust had been driven deep into her soul, and she couldn't seem to dislodge it. Only once in all the months had Cab ever said he loved her—that dreadful day on the Martian desert with a sandstorm screaming past their mangled Light.

"I love you, Jenny, but I love her too, and I don't know if I can make a choice."

Unfortunately the words had been seared into her memory.

So if she told him now that she was carrying his child—*children*, twins for Christ's sake—he would instantly marry her, and she would never know. If he had married her for her self or because she was the receptacle of his immortality.

"So, this is farewell. I've enjoyed our discussions, brief though they've been, Mr. wa Thondu."

"Though you think I am horribly misguided on my points, Mr. Reichart."

"On a few."

"How charming," muttered Viriku. "Eat a little more shit for the nice white people, Wairegi."

Kariuki seized her by the shoulders, and forced her into a chair. "Shut up."

"Oh, I forgot, I'm supposed to be grateful. Wishing them well while they scamper away leaving us to face the jackboots. Lovely."

Stinson's lips tightened at the scorn in the young Luo woman's voice. Joe maintained his usual Cheshire cat smile, Irving shifted uncomfortably, and Cab stared in deep abstraction at the far wall.

She hadn't even noticed when he beckoned to her.

He thought Jenny would want to be a part of this final meeting with the Kenyans, but she hadn't even noticed. Cassie had yelled something to her, something that had outraged his law clerk. Every nuance of her body was familiar to him now, and he had read fury in every taut line.

But time was passing, and the ice-thin barrier that had

sprung up between them kept him from making another, more obvious approach. He had followed meekly in Joe and Stinson and Irving's wake, and wondered . . . wondered.

"What did you expect after the shit you've pulled? We've treated you a hell of a lot better than you—"

"Deserved, Mr. White?" suggested Wairegi with a sad little smile. "No, we can expect no more, and frankly I am not sorry to be returning with the American military."

"Milking it for all the PR possible?" suggested Joe.

"Hoping that by remaining in American custody we will be tried under American jurisdiction and by American jurisprudence. That way we will at least receive a trial. Mwanyumba would most likely have us driven into the hills and shot." Raising a fist to his mouth he gave a self-deprecating little cough. "And of course I'm not overlooking the PR value of a Western-style trial. One additional forum in which to be heard."

"All this talk of trials. Why can't we just stay out here. We've made our point," piped up Cyril.

"Frankly because we don't want you," Stinson said bluntly.

Eyes closed, Wairegi sucked in a deep breath, and shook his head. "No, we must face the consequences of our actions. We must not be like the fool who hides beneath the eaves of a hut, and thinks no one will see him."

A grimace twisted Viriku's mouth. "So we go meekly back to Earth, and into some jail somewhere to rot, and have accomplished nothing."

"And what would have constituted accomplishment for you, Ms. Amani?" inquired Joe softly. "Several million dead?"

"You broke faith with us!"

They brought Cab out of his brown study, and surging to his feet. "No! That we have not! I kept my bargain with you though many would argue that I owed no loyalty to a gang of terrorists. I allowed you to communicate your grievances to Earth and the System. And you've been treated with fairness and courtesy since being taken into custody." He slid a cold gray-eyed glance at Viriku. "You came out here prepared to die for your cause. Well, fine, we won't stop you, but your immolation on the altar of Lost Causes and Grand Gestures is going to have to be a solo performance. You have no right to involve others in your private Götterdämmerung."

"You're a coward as well as a sophist. There are some

things worth killing . . . dying,'' she amended quickly. ''For, Justice Huntington.'' She laid a heavy emphasis on the honorific making it a mockery. ''I hope you are forced to indulge in it before the end.''

''Joe, I've had about as much of this company as I can stand.'' Revulsion thickened his voice. ''I'll meet you back at the bay.''

Wairegi seemed hurt by his curt dismissal, but Cab was too immersed in his own private worries and problems to spare much thought. He had had enough of playing front and center on the world's stage. He longed for privacy, and Jenny, and an end to the inexplicable problems which had sprung up between them like a patch of thorns.

Chapter Thirteen

"Ms. Kim Nu, I see no reason why you can't proceed as planned on to the asteroids."

Reginald Townsend had a rich, fruity voice, and smugness seemed to drip from every well-rounded vowel. Lydia took a rein on her temper, and tried to adjust to standing before her desk while a stranger occupied her chair.

"In the first place there is no ship available. It will take the *Constellation* at least two weeks to return to the jump point, and I seriously doubt that Trans-United is going to send out a passenger liner when there's a chance of war breaking out."

"War?" His brows climbed toward his balding pate. "Ms. Kim Nu, surely you exaggerate."

She released a pent-up breath, and quelled the urge to remonstrate with him. After three days in his company she knew it was useless. He assumed he knew everything, about everything, and anything he might not know wasn't worth knowing. His prejudices had the strength of Holy Writ. And she did not envy him the coming months. Even a man as subliminally arrogant and unaware as Townsend would be beaten to a pulp by the pigheadedness of the average System dweller. But until that happened there was going to be a good deal of discontent, and she cringed as she pictured the dislocations that would ensue in her perfectly running station.

Only it wasn't her station anymore.

The thought was a bleak one, and not for the first time, she found herself regretting her impetuous decision to chuck it all and join Joe.

"Then go to Earth, and have a little holiday until the liners are running again.'' He picked up· as if there had been no disquieting remark about something as vulgar as a possible war. ''Visit your daughter.''

''Frankly, Reginald, the last thing I want to see is my daughter since she's chosen to ally herself against her family and friends, and take up with a bunch of nuts.''

''That's very cold-hearted of you, Lydia. You should be more forgiving and understanding.''

''Then please forgive *me*, Reginald, when I tell you that not everyone shares your brand of religion.''

''Oh, I'm aware of it.'' But his thin smile indicated his distaste for the admission.

To be right with Reginald's God one had to be born again. Lydia's problems with her replacement had begun the first day out when he felt compelled to ask if she had experienced this epiphany. Raised a Buddhist, and still occasionally making a nod toward the religion of her childhood, she had lifted hackles by replying that she had done it some four or five thousand times, but still felt Nirvana was far beyond her.

''Reginald, thank you for your concern over my well-being, but I think you could use a bit more orientation. I'll stay until this crisis in the Belt is resolved.''

She left, fuming, trying to comprehend *why* EnerSun, usually so savvy and knowledgeable, sent this prating, posturing buffoon as her successor. Elija would have been perfect. He had lived on the station for fifteen years, was an excellent administrator and businessman, and he understood and was sympathetic to System problems. Of course, after her bitter and sarcastic conversation with Alex Sullivan, President of EnerSun Inc., over the occupation of the station by American troops, they didn't want a System patriot. The fact that a riot had broken out against the occupying troops demonstrated to the board just how tenuous groundside control of the station was.

So they sent Reggie, dear Reggie who (to borrow a phrase of Joe's) was dumb as a box of rocks, and therefore couldn't be lured . . . or—*grasp, naughty word*—even seduced by the free-thinking, free-living spacers. Though God knew the colonists weren't completely united. Tad Bevel had been swearing undying loyalty to Earth, and deploring the Belt actions. Of course, Tad had always been a toady.

Back at her apartment she swallowed a handful of antacids. Her stomach had been giving her hell for several days, and she knew what that meant—trouble, big trouble on its way. Over the years she had developed a superstitious faith in her gut's ability to forecast the future.

Seating herself at her small desk she pulled the politely worded message from Trans United from a cubbyhole.

We regret to inform you that until the current situation in the Belt is resolved Trans-United will be dropping their service to the asteroids. Thank you for your interest in traveling Trans-United, and we will inform you as soon as regular service is resumed.

So that was that. No chance of joining Joe now. But it wasn't the only reason. Duty and responsibility, her twin gods, once more held her in thrall. With relations tenser than they had ever been between Earth and the System, there was no way she could go haring off to the Belt in pursuit of her own pleasure, and leave her people in the care of a moron like Reggie.

She had tried to reach Joe last night to inform him of her decision, but he had already left, vanishing like a will o' the wisp into the labyrinth of the Belt. While applauding his caution and foresight she had nonetheless experienced an almost heart-stopping panic when she realized that she would not talk with him again until the crisis was over.

At least Dita was with him. Funny, aggressive, tomboyish Dita who had always seemed to live life in a state of high *alt*. Dear Dita, the favorite child, though Lydia had tried to hide it from the others. Lydia bowed her head inspecting her nails. She hadn't been perhaps the best mother, being too taken up with her work and the System. Perhaps it had been selfish to have them. But something bright and beautiful and special might have been lost from the universe if her five girls had not graced it. And following hard on the heels of that arrogant little thought came a wry smile. For there was always Amadea to keep her humble.

And she realized that she never had pinned down Cabot about his dealings with her youngest on Mars. Now he was gone too, and Jenny with him. Even Andy had joined the general exodus from Ceres. Lydia hoped that this didn't indicate the fat journalist's belief that there was a story to be had by sticking with the . . . Her mind shied violently from the harsh implacable reality of *rebel*, but after some reflection she realized that it was the only appellation which fit. Fear coiled through her mind, and she was disgusted with her cowardice. Had she spent twenty-five years fighting for System's rights only to falter now?

She had counted on negotiation, and distance, and the inertia of dinosaurlike bureaucracies to eventually lead to the independence of the System. The inevitable separation of parent and child; painful, perhaps, but not violent.

Only now there was an armada cruising toward the Belt.

The station had been genteel, Mars had been quaint, Ceres rustic, but this was positively primitive.

Cab eyed the rock walls, the uneven floor which threatened to turn an ankle with each step, the jumble of cots bolted into the walls of the cavelike room, bare power lines festooned across the rock, naked bulbs sending a harsh glare across the whole unappetizing scene.

Evgeni Renko's rock was a large one by Belt standards. Joe had done well by the Russian, keeping his end of the bargain, and staking Renko to one of the best pieces of floating real estate in the Reichart asteroid holdings.

But, God, to have to live here for who could tell how long.

If Cab was dismayed by the accommodations, he could tell that Evgeni was equally dismayed by the mob which had descended upon his home. The living quarters had been designed for three—no four—people; Irina was expecting, and by the look of her very soon—so the refugees from Ceres had to settle in the Renko's den/dining/living room.

The very real awkwardness which had existed when Cab and the miner shook hands had faded as Evgeni realized that with the Russian navy in orbit around Ceres he probably wasn't going to be able to take Irina to the hospital to deliver. Whether one of the doctors could make a rock call was equally problematical, so Stinson called up a map of the settled Belt, and tried to recall every midwife or doctor living off Ceres and how soon one of them could reach the Renkos.

Cab was sorry for the man beset with this very real worry, but he was also cravenly grateful for the distraction. To face the Russian brought back all of his guilt over the destruction of the Garmoneya Collective. His stomach gave a heave. Jesus, he thought, he hadn't had trouble with null-gee nausea for months; must be nerves over facing Renko, not to mention the devilish predicament in which he currently found himself.

Joe, of course, was enjoying every moment of the adventure. Cab eyed Reichart and Dita with disfavor as they bustled about directing the placement of supplies. Cab, flushing with embarrassment, suddenly heaved off the cot, settled slowly to the floor, and hurried over to help. *What the hell was the matter with him?* Lying sulking on his cot while others worked.

Irina, made awkward by the swell of her belly, struggled with a canister. Cab lifted it quickly from her hands, and brushing back a hanging strand of blond hair she gave him a wan smile.

"We haven't met yet. I'm Cab Huntington.

"So very kind. Thank you, Your Honor."

"Cabot, please." She just gave a mute shake of the head. "It's very good of you and your husband to take us in like this."

"It is the least we could do. We owe Mr. Reichart so much. So much." She glanced about. "I must see about . . ." But her voice trailed away before he learned what.

Cab watched her shuffle carefully away, her sticky boots making an odd rasping sound as they pulled loose from the rock floor. He felt rage and pity for the woman trapped into such a bleak and forbidding life. And what of her child? His eyes shifted to Analisa carefully hooking the straps of a sleeping bag beneath a cot. How old could she be—six, seven? And already hard at work. And what about a child born under these conditions? Would they ever be able to return to Earth? And if it went on long enough what evolutionary mutations might result?

A sense of panic and alienation washed over him, and snagging Jenny by the wrist he pulled her into one of the bore holes which radiated off the main room.

"What's up?" She brushed back his hair with gentle fingertips, but her smile seemed tired and rather sad.

"I need a hug."

"Okay." She obliged, then with her head still resting on his shoulder added, "Any particular reason why?"

"I don't know." He rubbed at his forehead trying to banish the bands which seemed to be tightening about his skull. "It's hard to express. Here, in this . . . place I guess I finally realized how far from home I really am. It makes me unhappy and homesick, and then I feel guilty for feeling homesick. Everybody else seems to be enjoying this so much. Except Renko, of course. Aside from the inconvenience of our presence he has to be worried, wondering if they'll come looking for us. What they'll do to him and his family for sheltering us. And Irina. I get the most horrible sense of hopelessness when I look at that poor woman. What kind of a life can this be?'' His arms swept out, fingertips almost brushing the sides of the bore hole.

''A hard one, but she's with Evgeni and it's what he wants so it's what she wants.''

''We've done this to you for generations, haven't we? Go blazing out to conquer new worlds without a thought for our spouses and children.''

Jenny took an abrupt step back out of the circle of his arms. ''Now don't start thinking we're too fragile to cope. Granted, biology probably makes it a little harder on women than on men, but frankly we're just as tough if not tougher than you *Lords of Creation*.'' There was a brittle edge to her voice, and her green eyes were glittering.

''Jenny?''

She gave him her shoulder. ''We should get back and help. That way you won't feel so guilty.''

''Redheads. Redheaded women,'' he muttered to himself. ''What did I say this time?'' he yelled, plunging after her.

''It's just your whole attitude.'' She bit off the words in a low whisper.

''About what?''

She whirled to face him. ''Women, and relationships, and children, and marriage.'' She seemed to be chewing on something else, but then ended with only a disgusted gesture.

''How did we end up on this subject?''

''Heaven only knows. Lord knows you usually avoid it like the plague.''

They were in identical poses. Arms akimbo, small frames bristling with anger, faces only inches apart.

''I *hate* it when you start fights, and won't tell me what we're fighting about!''

''Maybe the fact that you *don't* know is the problem. Oh, forget it! Just forget it!'' He stared in horror as she dashed away tears.

''Jenny.''

''Damn! I hate tears, they're such a damn manipulative tool. And I'm *not* crying because we're fighting. I'm crying because I'm overly emotional right now. *You* can't make me cry.''

''This makes no sense at all.''

"It does to me," she said with dignity, and reentered the room.

And he wondered, as he fumed after her, why when they were under warrants of arrest, faced with the total dissolution of Earth/System relations, a possibility of war in the Belt, why, *why* was he in more of a funk over this personal spat than with anything else?

"Probably because human beings are such irritatingly irrational creatures. And the female of the species is the worst of all," he added, but he kept his voice low. His bragadocio did not extend to allowing either Dita or Jenny to overhear him.

Chapter Fourteen

"Welcome to Ceres, General. I'm Irving Pizer, Chief of Police."

"And S-Stinson White?"

"Unfortunately away, at present."

"And Mr. Joseph Reichart?"

"Also regretfully away."

"I s-see, and I suppose Justice Huntington and Jennifer McBride are also unfortunately and regretfully away?"

Pizer's laughter wheezed out like an ancient pipe organ at Saber's wry expression. "Yes, sir, that's about the size of it. But I don't expect you to take my word for it. I presume you'll want to search."

Saber's comscreen on the bridge of the *Victory* was split offering him not only a view of the ebullient ancient on the asteroid, but also Admiral Casimir Verchenko's lean features.

"I think you should, General."

The thin cigar twitched from one side of the American's mouth to the other, and Adams watched the jaw muscles clench as his commander bit down hard. "Admiral, when I need advice from you I'll ask for it. This is an American outpost, and I think I'm the best judge as to the Chief's veracity."

"As you wish, but you will certainly look very silly if we go cruising blithely home again with our terrorists only to discover that your renegades were hiding here all along."

"Admiral, if I were in the middle of the Asteroid Belt, and wanted to elude someone, I certainly wouldn't hide on Ceres.

Not when I've got a ready-made maze extending in all directions for s-several hundred million miles.''

Verchenko smiled. ''Speaking of our terrorists, hadn't we better establish if they're present, or if they too have fled into your maze?''

Dull red suffused Saber's cheeks, but he switched back to Ceres. ''Mr. Pizer, I presume the Kenyans are s-still in custody?''

''Oh, yes. They'll be ready when you want them.''

''Then I'll s-send down a s-squad to take control of the prisoners. Our . . . allies will also be s-sending down a contingent.''

''I understand.''

Saber considered. He personally resented the hell out of being sent to arrest Huntington, and that lovely woman, but he was still in the military, and it would look bad if he didn't make every effort to locate the fugitives. He was pretty damn sure they had enough brains to head into the Belt so there could be no harm in searching.

''I'll also take you up on that offer of a s-search. We'll try to inconvenience your people as little as possible.''

''Thanks, we appreciate it. But I'll pass the word so one of your boys doesn't get met with an iron skillet.''

''You're fired!''

''May I know why?'' Blazing anger, and a sick sense of failure combined to form nausea, but Christina Holland was careful to school her face into an expression of disdain.

She was standing before Lis's desk like an errant schoolgirl while the Chief of Staff eyed her with equal parts loathing and satisfaction.

''The President wants no traitors on his cabinet.''

''In the first place I resent the hell out of that, secondly I want to hear it from the President, and thirdly I want to know just what it is I'm supposed to have done.''

''Huntington, Reichart, and all the rest are gone. We received word from General Saber.''

''Working fast, aren't you? And with no proof. I'm not to be given a chance to defend myself against this charge?''

''We have all we need.''

Christina leaned in, resting her hands on the desk. ''Lis, you are the most simplistic bitch. Just because I screwed Cab twenty years ago doesn't mean I'd go all soft and warm and puddly now, and betray a presidential order. Now, do I get to see the President?''

"No." She dropped her eyes to the reader, a clear dismissal. "Be out of your office by this afternoon."

Christina paused at the door, glanced back. "You know, I didn't warn Cab, but you're making me wish I had. And I wish you luck in my replacement. Maybe you'll find the kind of yes-man you're looking for, but sooner or later, Lis, you're going to realize that the purpose of a cabinet is to advise, not merely echo. I'm just afraid it's going to be too late for the President, and by the time you wake up this administration will have been totally discredited. Which is a shame because Richard Long is a fine man. It's sad that he's going to be ruined because of you."

"OUT! GET OUT!"

"Just going. Good luck, Lis. Oh, and I hope you find a man to replace me. That will leave you less competition." She shook her head, and gave a sad cluck. "You really do take this Mona Lisa thing far too seriously."

They had all gathered in a bedroom of their small apartment/prison. J.K. reading, Paul watching the bunch and leap of muscles in a powerful bicep, Kariuki studying his palms as if trying to read the future, and the youngsters James and Cyril just sitting. Wairegi was lying on the bed pondering the bone-deep, soul-devouring weariness which had clamped down upon body and mind. Was it fear of the future, or had Viriku's constant harpings about his "failure" finally convinced him that in fact he had? Or was it really something physical?

His gaze swept the room, pausing to rest on each of the young faces, so proud and strong and fine. Suddenly he became aware of the missing face. Straightened abruptly and demanded, "Where's Viriku?"

J.K. looked up from the reader. "I'm not sure. She was here a minute"—he glanced at his watch—"well, more like fifteen minutes ago."

Wairegi surged to his feet, checked the neighboring bedrooms. Hurried to the bathroom. *Empty*. The others had begun to trickle out after him. Living room, kitchen. *Nothing*. Back to the living room where Wairegi pivoted, and stared about as if expecting her to materialize from beneath the sofa, or out of the video screen.

Kariuki stepped to the door. Gave it a push with the tips of his fingers. It swung quietly open. Six pairs of eyes all mirroring one thing—dismay. Giving way quickly to fear when they realized that the military had arrived.

"How did she " began Paul.

A slash of Wairegi's arm brought silence. "Who knows, who cares. That's not important now. She must be found." There was a concentrated rush for the door. "NO!" They recoiled as if before the lash of a whip. "Kariuki, call Mr. Pizer and inform him. Tell him I have gone to search." His face was bleak. "She is my responsibility."

Kariuki sensed what lay beneath the words. "Surely she won't . . . I mean she seemed less bitter. Perhaps she only intends to hide."

Wairegi gripped him by the shoulder and the forearm. "I pray you're right. Call Pizer, stay here."

"If you're not back in thirty minutes I'm coming to help you," said Paul.

"No, no, that would soon have all of us wandering off one by one in search of each other. All it will accomplish is to make our captors—both old and new—nervous."

"Knowing that Viriku is loose should be enough to do that. God knows it makes *me* nervous," added James bleakly.

"I'm getting really tired of having a picture shoved under my nose, and then being sent onto some station, or down to some asteroid, and told to find somebody. Especially since they never tell us *why* we're supposed to find them. And usually after we've caught them, and I find out *why* we've caught them, I'm sorry I ever caught them in the first place."

"Pruden, when did anyone ever tell you orders made sense? This is the Air Force, boy, and we're ERFs, ours is not to wonder why . . ."

"Gnota, you're an insensitive slob. Not a deep, sensitive, philosophical type like me." Pruden touched the com panel by a door.

"Yes?"

"Excuse me, ma'am, Airmen Rob Pruden, we have orders to—"

"Oh, yeah." The door swung open. "Come on in." She was a short dumpy woman with curly brown hair, brown eyes, and brown skin. A bathrobe was clutched about her, and she had the irritable look of a person recently awakened.

"You'd think they'd have something better to do with my tax dollars than send grunts out to disturb me after I've spent seven hours in surgery."

"Not grunts, ma'am," corrected Pruden as he and Gnota checked quickly through the small apartment. "We're Air Force, a much more elevated service than our counterparts on land or sea."

"Excuse me. Have you seen any of these people." Gnota fanned out the photos of Cab, Jenny, and Joe.

"Yes. I ran a pregnancy test for her, and I treated him." A blunt forefinger jabbed down at Cab. "When he was puking up his boots from null-gee sickness—"

"I mean recently." His chin thrust out pugnaciously only to be matched by an equally pugnacious thrust from her.

"Well, be more specific. Yeah, I saw them two days ago before they all decamped. Which is probably a good thing because they sure weren't going to get any sleep if they had stayed—"

Pruden chuckled, and swept up the pictures. "Thanks, ma'am. Sorry to have disturbed you."

"Bitch!" grumbled Gnota as the door shut behind them.

"Now, now. Temper, temper. Hearts and minds, Gnota, remember? Hearts and minds."

"Fuck!"

They continued their search. Pruden reflected back on the occupation of the EnerSun station. It was during the riot on that station when he had suddenly decided that he hadn't joined the Air Force to stand by while Soviet goons abused American citizens whom *he* had sworn to defend. He had thrown down his shotgun, and walked away, and fully expected a dishonorable discharge. But the brass seemed to realize they had put an intolerable burden on their soldiers, and he hadn't even received a reprimand.

A transfer from the ODS platform and onto one of the deep-space ships had seemed a safe move. But then *wham*, déjà vu time, working in concert with the Soviets. Not that he minded coming after those terrorist goons, but the terrorists were under wraps, and here he was once more fucking around with Americans. Of course the Lieutenant had said they were traitors, but Huntington was the guy who'd slapped the Soviet Premier on the snout, and that didn't sound much like a traitor to—

His rambling thoughts cut off with the suddenness of a

shattering glass. Peripheral vision had caught an anomaly. Something that didn't belong. Reaching over his shoulder he pulled free his shotgun, and called to Gnota, "Cover me."

"Huh?"

"Cover me!"

Moving fast he came up against the wall next to the storage closet, held for a heartbeat, then spun around the corner, shotgun at the ready. He didn't know the airman on the floor; huddled like a child exhausted from weeping who had finally fallen asleep. But he wasn't asleep. The garrote had left a vicious red weal about his throat, and Pruden could just see the blackened tongue protruding from between slack lips.

"Shit!" muttered Gnota, and gagged slightly at the smell of released bowels.

"Inform the Lieutenant." Pruden knelt, and ran his hands quickly across the body. "Whoever did it stripped him."

Gnota wasn't paying any attention. Hand to throat mike he was busy reporting. He glanced down at Pruden. "He wants to know who did it."

A sharp exhalation of exasperation. "If I knew that would I still be sitting here?" Gnota spread his hands apologetically. Pruden chinned on his mike. "Lieutenant, whoever did it now has five grenades, a shotgun, a Baretta, and enough ammo to do some real damage." He listened. "Yes, sir."

"What's the scoop?"

"Regroup at control, start on a new grid search. Some fun, huh."

Gnota pulled the photos out of his coat, and stared down at the four faces. "Think any of these guys did it?"

And though Pruden didn't much like the thought it did seem to be a possibility.

Better to have a handful of might than a sack of justice.

Slim hands slid down the length of the barrel; exploring, caressing polished steel, hand closing on the grip with such violence that the grooves dug deep into her palm. Muscles tensing as she yanked back, opening the breech. The smooth satisfying slide which carried the shell into the chamber.

In quieter or perhaps more knowledgeable company the sound of a pump shotgun being cocked might have given warning. But Viriku wasn't worried. Partly because she was past fear, partly because the main concourse was a scene of bustling activity. People drifted in and out of the handful of shops which ringed the central mall. Forming a triangle in the center of the brick floor, three spindly trees in square planters thrust hopefully toward the light panels.

From her vantage point on the upper concourse Viriku could see the occasional uniform, both Russian and American, among the shoppers. Her position was a good one. A concrete bench set near the railing protected her back, and a shrub in a concrete planter offered cover to her left. Sooner or later they would rush her from both directions, but by then it wouldn't matter, the killing would have begun.

She had been very young when she realized how useless was protest as a means of change. You protested and the people with power—people with *guns*—came and killed you. Not that she had ever experienced it firsthand. Her father's family was comfortably middle class, trading with the white West, grateful and arrogant by turns at having such a good relationship with their overlords. They had been careful never to rock the boat. Then had come the divorce and life had been less comfortable. Bitter over the disruption of her world . . . she had joined the militant and violent African League, and had first tasted the pleasure and the sense of accomplishment which accompanied killing. People were sheep when faced with a gun. They shivered and cried and begged and died, and fear spread. And it was fear which effected change.

Her throat tightened as she contemplated the fear which Wairegi could have unleashed upon the world if he had any balls in his pants at all. She had come into the Belt knowing she would die, but thinking she would at least see the beginning of the death of the white world. Wairegi had come praying for change, and for peace. Willing to use fear, but only so far. Unable to see that spilled blood was the greatest driving force in human history.

Earth was beyond her vengeance now, but she could at least exact a toll from the smug, smiling, self-satisfied white colonists (and the epithet applied equally to Stinson White, who though his face was as black as hers was indeed well named. His soul was white) who had reduced Wairegi to a "boy," a "nigger." She would die, but at least she would not return home to face the jibes and laughter of the black world.

She sighted down the barrel, targeting the exact center of a Russian sailor's chest. Viriku was a Black Marxist, and while her group acknowledged a debt to the Soviet revolution they despised its accommodation with capitalism—increased use of a private sector, private farm plots, the profit incentive—which had begun in the last years of the twentieth century. Viriku's goal had always been to kill whites, and she didn't care if they were philosophical brothers under the skin or not. It had been a brushfire war in Uganda which had taught her the primary weakness of the Russian military. *Overreaction.* Let one Russian sailor fall, his chest a bloody hole, and his companions wouldn't stop to think . . .

As she watched the milling throng below she thought briefly and regretfully of her machine pistol. It would have created such an effect. She nuzzled her cheek against the butt of the shotgun, rested the barrel on the railing, sighted, inhaled slowly and . . .

"Jesus Christ! What was that?"

Gnota made the mistake of thinking the Lieutenant was asking a real rather than a rhetorical question. "Gunfire, sir."

"I'm *aware* of that, Airman. Come on."

He was a young man with a carefully clipped blond mustache, and a number of irritating affectations. Like the overly dramatic sweep he made with his arm as if ordering a cavalry charge. It was an unnecessary order for Pruden. He was already in motion, shotgun cradled against his stomach, running with a long, low stride. The tunnel debouched into a large central mall area. Pruden caught only a glimpse of running people as he swung his back against the tunnel wall allowing the lintel of the archway to shield him. The chatter of gunfire, screams, and cries, and finally the dull *crump* of a grenade filled his ears, and he swallowed bile. The mall wasn't that big, and he could picture the carnage which remained after the grenade had exploded.

Lieutenant Westin went pelting past waving his sidearm. Like Custer at Little Big Horn, the Texas Rangers at the Alamo, the Legionnaires at Camerone Mexico, the charge of the Light Brigade.

"Lieutenant, for God's sake, NO!" bellowed Pruden, but it was hopeless; glory called, and brains had vanished in that white-hot glow. Westin plunged past into the chaos of the mall, and was blown back with half his face gone—a worthy successor to other more memorable historical incompetents.

• • •

The deep-throated *boom* of a shotgun told the story. Wairegi began to run. But with each laboring step the floor seemed to move farther away. The strike of shoe against vitrified stone jarred through the length of his body, but it seemed somehow distant and far removed.

He skidded into madness. A mall filled with thrashing figures. The sharp chatter of a machine pistol sounded nearby, and flakes of stone left a stinging pattern across his cheek. He flinched, saw the curving staircase, headed up. A numbing pain had closed about his left side, and he could hear his blood rushing through veins with sound like the angry surge of waves.

The stairs came floating up to meet him, but he caught himself on his palms. He seemed to have lost all sense of his legs so he dragged himself forward. His eyes just cleared the final step, and through the frame formed by a bench he saw her. Prone, she was firing with methodical care. Not like the soldier below who had simply sprayed bullets across the crowded mall. Viriku was picking her targets. Only her profile was offered to him. It was beautiful. Expressionless. Deadly.

Wairegi pushed, managed to lift his torso a few inches above the step. Called to her. Only a hoarse croak emerged, easily lost in the tumult of screams and gunfire. He tried again, screaming out her name, its passage through his throat leaving a burning trail. Viriku looked over her shoulder, eyes flat, reptilian black. Her lips drew back in an expression that was somewhere between a smile and a snarl. Then slowly, deliberately she turned away, and resumed firing.

He was on his feet, staggering forward, then pain exploded in his chest. Lying on his back he stared up at the light panels set into the rock high overhead, and wondered how he'd gotten there. The agony continued. He plucked and groped at his chest with fingers gone stiff and cold, but found no wound, no blood. A darkness which seemed to be closing in from all sides. His last thought was of failure.

I'm sorry . . . sorry. . . .

"Sir." It was Major Adams. Saber laid aside his pen and looked up. "A disturbance on Ceres, sir. We're getting garbled accounts from several sources." He was addressing his superior's back. The General was already on his way to the bridge.

Irving Pizer was glaring out of the screen. "Saber, your

people are killing my people down here. And when my officers tried to restore order those crazy Russians shot *them*. Now you better get it fixed because it's open season down here on anything in a uniform.''

"I'll s-send down —"

"NO! Recall your men—"

"Sir!"

It was an urgent breathless squeak. Saber slewed around, his glance resting briefly on the young airman's white, drawn face and fixed eyes. He followed her mesmerized stare to the graphic computer display. *Zeus descending in a golden shower, beautiful silver-tipped spears*—the designers of the graphics were nothing if not imaginative—unfortunately their poetry could not disguise the deadly intent of those gold and silver slivers.

Anguish raked his chest along with a burning rage.

"Verchenko!"

"Gnota!"

But he was gone, buried beneath an avalanche of falling masonry. Pruden gagged, and spat out a mouthful of vomit as he realized that two feet farther to the right, and he would have been a grease spot too. After Westin's disastrous entrance into the mall he and Gnota had shown more caution. Darting from shop to planter to garbage can they had grabbed fleeing citizens, and forced them into cover. All the time Pruden was trying to make sense of what was essentially an insane situation.

The Russians with their automatic weapons were cleaning up on the unarmed citizens. But not all the citizenry were unarmed because several shopkeepers appeared with an assortment of handguns and shotguns, and began shooting back at the Russians. As for the two airmen in the mall, they seemed as confused as Pruden felt.

Something small and dark and deadly came arcing down from the upper concourse.

"Rpahata!"

Which Pruden took to mean grenade since one was rolling lazily back and forth in the center of the mall. It detonated, and something moist and ragged landed with a splat nearby. Pruden didn't look too closely. Ignoring the tangle of bodies he measured the distance to the upper level, and concluded that it would have to be a record-setting throw to hit. And if he missed the few people remaining below would be shit out of luck.

But the Soviets didn't have to rely on muscle. One man carried a grenade launcher and he used it. Everyone held silent for a long moment after the final thunderclap died away, but nothing else unpleasant came tumbling down. Unless a person counted the rivulet of blood that welled over the edge of the concourse, left a dark smear on the white brick, and shed a few drops onto the floor thirty feet below.

That's when he and Gnota moved, trying to find out who had been lobbing grenades off the upper level, sensing perhaps that they would find their comrade's killer. But then had come a deep soul-jarring rumble that set the ground to heaving beneath their feet, and brought down the concourse on top of poor old Gnota, and Pruden's rad reader had given its high-pitched whine, and turned from its usual silver to an attractive shade of pink.

For a long moment he simply gaped. He had never heard the sound outside of basic training, and he sure as hell didn't much like hearing it now. The only bright point in what had become a pot of shit was the pastel color of the patch. Still, to be on the safe side he decided to head for the colony's lower levels.

He joined a shopkeeper who was trying to support a young black woman. Her leg looked like it had been through a meat grinder, and Pruden found it amazing that she was still conscious. A lone Soviet sailor stood before the nearest tunnel mouth, waving his machine pistol in a hostile if somewhat confused manner.

"Oh, cut it the fuck out!" bellowed Pruden. "And help with the wounded. Some asshole is dropping missiles on our heads, and I'll bet the asshole is red."

The young Russian reared back. "Is inconceivable. It is *you* who are dropping bombs."

"Who gives a fuck who's doing it." The girl's voice was ragged with pain, but she still had enough spirit to stare down both the soldiers. "Let's just get out of here."

"Yeah," added the shopkeeper sourly. "We can assign blame when the war is over."

Chapter Fifteen

Pizer was gone. And with him the control center. *Stupid to have put it on the surface,* thought Saber, then realized that the builders of the colony probably hadn't expected to have a nuclear missile detonated on the surface of their worldlet. Two to be exact.

"Admiral Ver—" began the radioman.

"What in the fuck are you doing?" Saber realized he was screaming, and controlled himself.

"I did not authorize the launchings. One of my captains overreacted when he received word that our marines were under attack. He will be dealt with."

"I'm s-so glad." Sarcasm lay heavy on the words. "That's going to make *s-such* a difference."

"There was provocation. Our troops were attacked."

"How do you know this?"

"A report from one of my ground commanders."

"Great. We get one trigger-happy colonist if . . . I repeat, *if* it indeed happened the way your man reports, and *you* respond with a missile s-strike."

"I will not take this tone from you, General. I am an officer in the Soviet Space Fleet."

"Your objection is noted."

"I demand an apology."

"You can't demand one goddamn thing! By all rights we're at war." Saber plunged on even as Verchenko stiffened. "But I'm not going to make a bad s-situation worse. You back off from this *American* colony, and—"

"And what? You will pillory us in the press—"

"Sounds good to me," murmured Adams sotto voce, and received a blazing look from his general for his pains.

"Lay all—"

"Admiral! I'm not interested in assigning blame, or making brownie points with the press or the brass back home. I'm interested in preventing a war. If it isn't already too late. *Now will you back off?*"

"Very well. But we get the Kenyans."

"Fine!"

"You shouldn't have let him take those Africans."

Saber swung slowly away from the com. "Major, I'm not particularly worried about my image right now. If Verchenko wants the Kenyans s-so he can look like a big hero back home that's fine by me just as long as he gets the hell away from Ceres. Now call—"

"Sir, Admiral Fujasaki, the captains of the ESF ships, the Brazilian—"

"I don't have time to talk to them right now. I'll give them a full briefing after I return from Ceres. I've got to get down there, and assess the s-situation. Then I can s-see about reassuring our nervous allies."

And our equally nervous civilian governments, added Adams to himself.

The Soviet fleet, accompanied by the two ships of the European alliance and the Brazilian Sun, swung majestically out of orbit observed and monitored by many wary and vengeful eyes and ears. Red Suttcr and other members of the High Stakes colony met in an inter-family meeting which lasted all of ten minutes—the shortest on record, and soon Red's Curvet, towing a small pod barge, slipped out on an intercept course with the Soviet fleet. While Dietrich, towing the same cargo, went cruising toward Ceres.

"Casualties s-stand at fourteen hundred and twelve. The little s-shooting s-spree in the mall claimed twenty-three, the bulk were killed when the Russians got trigger-happy and lobbed those two missiles. Fortunately the bulk of the colony is buried deep, otherwise it would have been worse than it is. I lost s-seven men. Two in the mall, and the other five from unrelated violence elsewhere in the rock. Apparently the colonists assumed—and one can hardly blame them—that they were under attack s-so a few declared open s-season on anything in a uniform. I have no information on S-Soviet casualties.

"Rescue crews found a young black woman, and Wairegi wa Thondu in the wreckage of the mall. S-She's been positively identified as a member of the Kenyan terrorist group, and wa Thondu . . . well, you know about wa Thondu," fumbled Saber. He gave his scalp a hard rub, and continued.

"S-She was armed with U.S. Air Force s-standard issue, and that combined with the garroted airman found earlier would indicate that s-she and wa Thondu were the igniting s-spark, not the colonists. The s-settlers were overall incredibly forebearing as we s-searched their homes for Reichart, Huntington, White, and McBride. I think this is just another example of how a s-single incident can erupt into full-scale violence. A tragic event all around."

Saber muted the microphone, and sat back to wait for his message to reach Earth. Adams set a cup of steaming coffee before him, then unlimbered a hip flask, and splashed a liberal dollop into the coffee.

"Trying to get me drunk?"

"Trying to get you to relax. You've been up for over thirty-six hours."

"Had things to do."

"Shoveling shit."

Saber blew across the top of the cup, then took a cautious sip. "Never reported to a president before."

"Which is some of the shit I'm talking about."

"Major," Saber reproved.

"Well, it's true. You made your report to General Abrams. Why involve the civilians?"

"He is Commander in Chief, and he might want to hear it firsthand, not filtered through Abrams and McConnell, and Parker, and God alone knows who else."

Adams grunted.

They continued drinking in silence for several moments, each engrossed in his own thoughts. The General sighed and stretched, revolving his neck in an effort to relieve the dragging tiredness which gripped him.

"It's funny how many wars throughout history have been s-started almost by accident. Couple of countries rattling s-sabers, and breathing fire, and then some incident s-sparks it, and s-suddenly the generals and politicos are looking at each other, and wondering *how* the hell they got here."

"You think we're at war?"

"I think we're on the verge of one. If this isn't handled with tact and consideration we will have just taken part in the opening s-salvo of the first inter-system war."

The com chimed indicating an incoming call. Saber leaned forward, and boosted the audio as the lean, handsome features of the President of the United States steadied on the screen.

"General Saber, I've discussed your hypothesis with several of my advisers, and we frankly feel you're being naive. You claim the colonists did not open fire on our troops, and you seem to be indicating that it was wa Thondu and this Kenyan woman working alone. But who's to say she was not working with the colonists? She was free, which could not have happened without aid from the Ceres colonists." Long's face hardened.

"If the colonists want a fight we can by God give them one. I am not going to allow this kind of lawless behavior in one of America's territories. You are to leave one ship to hold Ceres. You will then take the remainder of the squadron and begin a sweep for the ringleaders of this rebellion. I want a show of force on this. If you are attacked, you will respond quickly and fully. Good luck, General."

The picture flickered, wavered, and the screen went dark. Saber fell back in his chair gulping for air.

"Jesus Christ."

Adams, his face like an ebony mask, fiddled among the coffee service. Finally, after a suitable interval, he asked, "Is it a war yet?"

"No! The s-shots have only been coming from one direction. If the colonists keep cool. If they don't resist our s-search. If we can convince Reichart and Huntington and all the rest to turn themselves in in the interest of peace. Then . . ." His voice trailed away, and he stared up at his aide. "That's a lot of 'ifs' isn't it?"

"Yes, sir."

There are a lot of rocks in the Asteroid Belt. There's also a lot of space between those rocks. So when you come as a hunter there's not much cover. On the other hand, in trying to produce a road map of the belt, the tendency had been to use the ten major asteroids as reference points. The radio chatter Red had intercepted indicated a future rendezvous between the Russian fleet and the American squadron so it was a pretty safe bet they would select one of the big rocks as the meet point. And sure enough the Soviets had cruised serenely off to Camilla. Which meant Red had some cover. Assuming of course his quarry had not taken up a position around the little rock.

They had, so Red rejected plan one, and moved on to fall back on plan two. He would boost past, leaving as much tail as possible in the hope he could lure out one of the lumbering antimatter ships, and then—

He cut off the thought before it made him cocky. First play fox and hounds. *Then* see if things could progress.

He was a big man whose rich coloring, both hair and face, had dictated the nickname. A luxuriant mustache drooped at either side of his mouth, and his lips writhed busily, pulling first one side and then the other into his mouth for a nervous chew.

As he darted past he opened his radio to a general band call, and announced, "Fuck you!"

There was a babble of interrogatory in some kind of monkey talk, then a sharp voice said in English, "Identify yourself."

"I'm the Red Avenger, and I'm going to kick your butts from here to Earth and back again."

It drew their attention. Two ships fired maneuvering jets, and came looping out after him.

"Oh, shit, Mama, your boy's in trouble now," Red muttered to the empty cabin, but a kind of manic excitement had seized him, and he followed the snivel with a wild laugh.

The big antimatter ships had a lot more thrust than his little Curvet, but lacked agility. He was going to count on that to see him clear.

The Captain of the lead vessel made some grandiose statement about this being the the deep-space vessel *Potemkin*, and to heave-to. Red threw the speaker a bird, then followed with a long rude raspberry.

"Hey, here's a little present for you," he bellowed. A vein was pulsing in his temple, and his brick-red face had become almost purple in his excitement.

A thick forefinger shot out, and flipped a switch. The signal flickered down the hitch, and the pod barge began to blossom like a flower responding to the first touch of the morning sun.

The dolly panel pushed out the cargo, and a small charge dispersed it. Rocks, hundreds of them, floating serenely out in all directions, directly in the path of the oncoming warship. It wasn't very spectacular when ship met rocks. No retina-searing explosion, just a big metal tube heeling over as its navigational computers were minced. Trails of crystallized oxygen streaming from myriad small holes in the hull. That was kind of pretty, like a Fourth of July pinwheel but formed of ice not flame.

Red's war whoop filled the Curvet, but died quickly as the sensors began their shrill warning—oncoming object. He tried evasive maneuvers, but the object which was closing with him was no mindless hunk of rock. Its brain, though pigmy in size, was designed and guided by humans to hunt and seek and kill. Command guided, it was not fooled when Red cut his engines, and tried to coast away from his own signature.

Red hoped to survive. He was suited, and even if it trashed his engines his little ship would continue along its present course. With luck he could call for help, and obtain a pickup. But his luck proved to be bad. The missile slammed through the front of the Curvet, turning instrument panel and man into scrap metal and ground meat.

"Then it's war," declared Dita.

"Why? Why does it have to be war?"

"Doubts, Judge?"

"Yes, hundreds of them."

"I thought you were on our side," grumbled Stinson.

"I *am*, but this is—" He ran distracted hands through his hair. "It's a fucking mess."

Dita's voice was sharp with scorn. "Scared?"

"You're damn right I am."

She turned her shoulder to Cab, and looked at her father. "He's a coward."

"And you're displaying the maturity and responsibility of a thirteen-year-old," snapped Jenny.

"You'd take his side no matter what!"

"That's not true! I didn't take his side on EnerSun."

"Ladies!" shouted Cab.

"Shouting, and making jingoistic speeches isn't going to solve anything," bellowed Andy.

"We're supposed to be having a discussion," yelled Stinson.

"We've got to get organized," wailed Joe.

"Take some kind of stand."

"Figure out what the fuck we're doing," added Andy.

"How can we when we've got cowards along."

Jenny bristled, and Cab began coming out of his chair. "Now just a damn minute! I took it once—"

"Ladies, gentlemen," said Irina in soft, distressed tones. "Please don't wake Analisa." She covered her ears with her hands, shook her head. "You are all shouting so much."

An embarrassed silence fell over the room. Evgeni Renko, who had remained mute throughout the squabble, ran a hand over his long, sad face.

"Everyone is upset. Is no wonder." He pushed back his chair. "I will get vodka. Then we will try again."

"Without any nasty cracks about people's courage," muttered Jenny. Her cheeks were still as red as her hair.

Dita opened her mouth, then subsided as her father laid a restraining hand over hers.

"Is it war?" asked Irina, huddling in on herself.

"No! Let's not start there," demurred Cab. "Look how far we got last time."

"So where do we start?" demanded Stinson.

"I think that's the problem." The plastic vodka bottle crashed onto the table, and Joe paused to take a pull at the nipple. "We're like an anthill that's been poked with a stick. Everybody running in all directions, and some of us just standing and gawking, and wondering how in the hell we ended up in this mess."

"Which means it's not yet a war. It's a series of escalating incidents which could certainly end up in a war unless we do something."

"So, got any brilliant suggestions, Judge?"

"Dita."

"Dad! You're the leader of the System. Have been for thirty years."

"I'm a spokesman—one of many. Don't try to give me a crown, Dita, I don't want it."

Andy waved his hands in the air. "Okay, okay. What have we got? Something sparks a rumpus and riot on Ceres. Saber thinks it was Wairegi and that crazy Kenyan bitch—"

"But we'll never know now," interrupted Jenny. "Since the Kenyans were aboard the Russian ship and they weren't suited." She waved away the vodka when Andy offered it to her.

"And Earth isn't buying that explanation anyway. They want to cast us as a bunch of crazed anarchist killers."

Stinson's face was thunderous, tightening the scars almost into a monster's grimace.

"Next we get some crazed—" Cab broke off at Dita's expression, and amended the word. "Some hotheaded colonial deciding to revenge Ceres by attacking a Russian ship, and managing to kill some of the crew and the remaining Kenyans."

"Hey, they got to croak him," threw in Andy. "Everybody's even, right?" His face collapsed into sagging folds like a disconsolate baby. "Now all we have to do is convince them of that."

Joe faced him. "So you think we should talk?"

"Hell, why not. You can always start shooting later." Andy tried a smile, but it was a thin, sickly attempt. "And I'm not too wild about the idea. Martha's on the Moon. Lotta missiles on the Moon."

"I know," Renko said heavily.

Cab reached for the bottle, took a long pull. Jenny laid a hand on his thigh, alternately squeezing and massaging. The bottle made another complete circuit of the table before anyone spoke again.

"Richard Long is in a tough spot," Cab began slowly. "He's got to appear in control; responding quickly and firmly to this challenge to U.S. authority. That's going to predispose him toward Lis Varllis. And she's . . ." He shook his head, searching for an adequate explanation. "Well, my uncle says she's one of those people who can't separate political challenges from personal attacks. This has become a private fight with her. Against Joe and I . . . and, well, everyone out here. She's going to want the President to stand firm and offer no compromise—"

"Which gets us where?" asked Stinson.

Cabot steepled his fingers before his mouth, and Jenny looked down, sensing what was coming. "She's not going to back off this thing unless we give her a bone, a big one. She's ordered the squadron out to search for us. If they're attacked by another of these cowboy heroes they'll strike back. Maybe at Curvets, maybe at—"

"Would you get to the point!"

Jenny leaned across Cab, and enunciated succinctly into Dita's face, "Shut up!"

"I think we should offer ourselves in exchange for a cease-fire and the withdrawal of the Earth ships."

There was an eruption of confused conversation. Cab sat silently in the midst of the maelstrom, Jenny's head resting lightly on his shoulder.

"Do you go along with this craziness?" Stinson demanded of the silent woman.

"Yes." She shook back her mane of red hair. "I don't like it, but I also don't like finding ourselves in a war that seems to have started by accident. I don't think any of us—here or on Earth—have really considered the kind of devastation that could result from an all-out break between Earth and System. I think it's a small price to pay to prevent wholesale slaughter."

"Wonderful! All for the greater good! So you'd sacrifice my father, and I suppose my mother too, and anyone else you could think of. Peace at any price."

"I'm asking, not coercing. Your father can make up his own mind about this."

"Big of you. My father—"

"Is right here, and really hates being discussed as if he were a piece of furniture. There's a lot of merit in what you're saying, Cab, but you're making a very large assumption."

"Which is?"

"That you can trust Lis Varllis. What's to stop her from hustling us home on a fast ship, and then sending back out the squadron to thump on the colonists?" Huntington frowned. "Didn't consider that, did you?"

"I just can't believe . . ." He shook his head helplessly.

"You didn't believe she could trump up all those charges against you on Mars either."

"*Et tu*, Jenny? I thought you were with me on this."

"Cab, I'm not here to be your Greek chorus—"

"All these classical allusions," murmured Andy.

"Once the decision is made I'll stick with you, but we aren't to that stage yet. We're still discussing. And frankly Joe's made a good point."

"Yes, he has, damn him." He gave a rueful smile. "And I was going to be so noble."

"Don't. Nobility sucks if you're dead. Even sucks if you're just in prison." Stinson rubbed irritably at his empty eye socket.

"There might still be a way to pull this off. We'd need General Saber on our side." Cab nodded at Jenny. "We met him once, and he seemed—and I'll admit this is a snap judgment based on short acquaintance—but he seemed like an honorable man. From the transmissions we've intercepted it's clear he's not very happy about this situation. If we returned with him, and he guaranteed that we would receive a fair—" Cab's hands crossed back and forth negatingly before his face. "Yaaagh. Stupid idea. Forget it."

"Yes, I was about to point out that last I looked we still had civilian rule back home," Jenny said. "And I can't picture Saber leading a military coup just for us."

"Are we right back where we started from?" asked Evgeni, shaking the bottle by his ear. He set it down with a mournful expression.

"Yes," answered Cab disgustedly.

"Not quite." Reichart pinched thoughtfully at the tip of his nose. "Despite what you may believe," he glanced quickly at the judge. "I'm not hot to have a war start. Let's try talking. Long and Varllis will of course assume we have the power to speak for the entire System—which we don't—but what they don't know and can't comprehend won't hurt them, and maybe we can get a cooling off period. A time to find some answers, and maybe prove to everybody's satisfaction that this does seem to be based on a series of misunderstandings."

"It's going to be uncommon difficult to characterize Amani and wa Thondu blowing away that Russian soldier—"

"And I still have a hard time believing Wairegi did that," sighed Andy.

Stinson glared. "It's going to be hard to call it a 'misunderstanding.' "

"Viriku wanted some big-time killing. She sure as hell got it," murmured Jenny.

"The real irony," added Joe softly. "Is that her name, Amani, means peace."

Cab picked up the vodka. "Well, here's to it."

But the bottle was empty.

Verchenko's copper-colored eyebrows made a determined climb for his hairline. "Please repeat that, Admiral."

Long minutes passed before the gravel-gargling tones of Admiral Bulatoff ripped from the speaker. "Repeat? What do you mean repeat? You have your orders, obey them. And the Premier indicated that if the target you select happens to be the home of Evgeni Renko, he would shed no tears."

The young Admiral fell forward onto the desk, and buried

his head in his arms, not caring how the action might be construed by his superior. He wondered if his superiors, those old gray men in the Kremlin, had any idea what the asteroids were like. For a moment he contemplated the mental image of a bumpy rock like a video cartoon with a *big* sign stuck in it that said *The Renkos*.

He exhaled sharply, the explosion of air ruffling his bangs, straightened, tried again to communicate.

"I thought the idea was to win hearts and minds."

"What?"

Verchenko briefly closed his eyes. "An American military expression. Make the locals love you. They're not going to love us very much if we start bombing their settlements. You should also be prepared for us to lose a number of ships. General Saber will not stand quietly by while we attack an American territory."

Let them chew on that, he thought as the message made its slow journey. Surely they would reconsider, but then he reflected how logic often had very little to do with political or military decisions. Immediately after the thought he recalled several incidents in Kazakh and Uzbek, and wondered if he were quite so immune to power blindness as he liked to think.

"The United States government realizes that this revolt by the Belt represents a grave threat to the home world. From space there are no boundaries. An attack from the System could fall on the Americans or on us. It is better we work together to halt this threat. The American President knows this, and will order General Saber accordingly."

Verchenko listened openmouthed to the grandiose and noble periods rolling sonorously off Bulatoff's lips. *Who in the hell was he quoting?* The American President? *Impossible.* Tupolev? *Possible.* Had these two powerful men really agreed to something as stupid as a retaliatory strike? Or was Tupolev merely going to present the Americans with a fait accompli, and then dare them to make trouble? Either way it left Verchenko feeling as if icy fingers were digging into his belly.

"What about the Moon and the stations?"

"They will be dealt with."

"I don't think it's a very good idea to fight a space-based power."

"They have no military."

"They have solar-power satellites, and big chunks of refined ore, and rocks, let's not forget the rocks. I lost a ship to those rocks.''

"Are you questioning orders?''

Yes, say yes.

"No, sir, merely discussing them.''

"You have no right to discuss anything! You have your orders, obey them! Or else we will think you are maybe a coward and a dissenter. And a work camp would ruin your pretty boy looks, wouldn't it?''

"Yes, sir,'' Verchenko mumbled, and Bulatoff minutes later broke the connection having received his junior's capitulation.

Verchenko hoped that Bulatoff took his affirmative as acknowledgment of his orders, not agreement with that ''pretty boy'' crack. He then decided he had bigger things to worry about than whether his obnoxious superior had managed to take a slap at his masculinity and sexuality.

Like finding a target for a retaliatory strike, and worrying about all those rocks.

Captain Vladimir Goncharenko made his report. He was a thin dyspeptic man with thinning hair, and cold flat black eyes.

"We had the good fortune to locate a surface colony, and in an effort to comply with your orders we used a single nuclear warhead—though convention C/G missiles would have been sufficient.''

He busied himself with paperwork until his message reached Earth, and a reply returned. The burly form of Admiral Bulatoff swung around in his chair.

"Identity of the colonists?''

"I'm almost completely confident that I located the home of the traitor Renko.''

"Excellent.''

"There is one other matter, sir. I feel it is only my duty to inform you that Admiral Verchenko issued an unusual order to his captains.'' He paused. It wasn't politic to look too eager to blacken the name of your commanding officer. Best to wait for signals from even higher up.

"Yes?''

"He instructed us to radio warnings for three hours before the bombings were undertaken, and to allow any colonists to evacuate.''

"And did you obey this order, Captain?"

"I hope I know my duty, sir." He cast his eyes modestly down, then added, "Unfortunately, Renko's radio appeared to be malfunctioning."

"Yes, unfortunate."

Bulatoff cut transmission without the usual exchange of civilities. Goncharenko smiled grimly at the empty screen, then keyed up a recon photo of the asteroid's surface. Infrared clearly showed the outlines of the glowing crater. The camera continued to slide around the irregular rock, and came to rest on a titanic figure buried to the waist in the surface of the asteroid. The great head was thrown back staring with sightless eyes into space, arms raised beseechingly toward the stars.

Verchenko got the word off the fax. With an explosion of wrath he stormed to the bridge, and ordered them to raise Goncharenko.

"What the devil do you mean by reporting directly to Moscow?"

"I thought it was my duty—"

"Well, you can rethink—no, scratch that—you get your butt back to Ceres, and don't you have *another* thought without clearing it first with me!"

"Sir . . ."

"What?" He rounded on the radioman and the boy blanched.

"Message from Ceres, sir. They've received a bulletin which they think we will find interesting."

"Put it on."

The long features of Evgeni Renko settled on the tiny com screen.

"Sorry to disappoint you, but I ain't dead yet."

Verchenko threw back his head, and laughed until tears came. "Hear that, Goncharenko? Want to make another quick call to Moscow?"

A blank screen gave back static. It was the kind of insubordination Verchenko could enjoy.

Tina Duvall and Muhammid Ali Elija were at her door. The young woman with the weight lifter's body and tiger eyes was chewing nervously at her full lower lip. Muhammid just looked grim, and on his wide, broken-nosed face that was a lot of grim.

"Lydia, can we bother you?" asked Tina.

"You always manage to." Her sally drew no smiles, and she stepped back indicating the apartment. "Come on in."

"We've got a problem," said Tina as she settled onto the couch.

"Personal or professional?"

"Professional."

"Then it's out of my hands. I'm not the Chief Administrator of EnerSun One, Reginald Townsend is."

"Yeah, and he's the biggest fanny with ears both on the face of the Earth and off."

Lydia touched her fingertips to her forehead. A tiny frown wrinkled her broad brow.

"Are we giving you a headache?"

She smiled at the younger woman. "Adding to the one I already have. But go ahead."

"We're due for power down, and satellite shift today."

"I know."

"Well, I went to Mister Bozo Brains, and told him I want to delay for a few weeks—"

"Smart."

"Which considering that I'm grid manager is certainly within my rights. But he's refused."

That brought Kim Nu upright in her chair. Three pairs of dark eyes met and mirrored fear. "Oh, my God."

"I tried to explain, but he wouldn't listen. I thought maybe it would carry more weight if he heard it from a man so I called in Muhammid."

"And I tried—as if speaking to a retarded child—to explain that since the Russians squashed that poor old crank in the Belt there's been a lot of hotheaded talk flying around the System that has the grounders shitting in their pants. Those crazy Kenyans got Earth thinking about how vulnerable it is way down in the gravity well, and now everybody's in a tizzy about killer rocks and purple death rays from space."

"Then I pointed out," continued Tina. "That an SDS satellite could fry a city, and that we've got five grids of the suckers. And if we started shifting them . . ." She spread her hands expressively.

Lydia sighed. "I'll talk to him."

"Lydia, what can I do for you?" Forced jocularity.

"Reg, we can't move those satellites."

His lower lip pooched out. "Not you too."

"Yes, me too. You've only been here a few weeks. Listen to those of us with more experience."

"It will put us horribly behind schedule, and without maintenance our output will drop."

She rested her knuckles on the desk and leaned in on him. "Forget the goddamn bottom line. I don't know whether you've noticed or not, but we're on the verge of a war between Earth and the System, and those satellites are weapons."

"Oh, come now." Sweat was beginning to bead his brow and upper lip.

"Such a concept may not have occurred to you, but you better believe it's on the minds of the leaders—both military and civilian—down below."

"But everyone *knows* SDS satellites have to be maintained," he wailed.

"No! Engineers know."

"I'll have the board put out a statement."

"Oh, great," she said bitterly. "And what if some missile crew on one of the military platforms fails to read your little statement?"

Townsend came to his feet. "You know the trouble with you people out here? You're paranoid. That's your whole trouble. There wouldn't be any problem between Earth and the colonies if you people would just relax and stop reading significance into every little move or statement from below."

"Oh, you're right! How could I have been so foolish? Silly little me. *Of course*, the government should be allowed to tamper with our individual liberties, and treat us as second-class citizens—"

"You'd like an incident, wouldn't you? A chance to point your fingers and say, 'See, see, how terrible all our leaders are.' "

"I'm trying to *prevent* an incident, you moron! Everybody's on a hair trigger because of events in the Belt."

"And there wouldn't be any trouble if your *boyfriend* and that judge would have just turned themselves in. They've got no right—"

"Let me guess; to make trouble, right? But back to the subject. You must not move those satellites."

Stubby fingers beat at his chest. "*I'm* in charge here now, and I say we stick to the schedule."

"Tina will refuse."

"Then I'll fire Tina's butt, and find someone who will. It's time you people learned that it's a whole new ballgame now. You're going to learn responsibility, and stop—"

"Making trouble. All right, Reg, and I honestly hope that you're right. Because if you're not . . ."

She didn't finish the sentence. The possibilities were simply too horrible to contemplate, much less vocalize. She slammed from the office, bile clawing at the back of her throat.

Chapter Sixteen

The servo whispered across the deep carpet. There was enough movement of the tiny machine to set the glasses to chiming softly as they rocked against each other. Patricia eyed the squat little device with disfavor, and quickly snatched a glass.

"I hate that thing," she confided to Cecilia. "But Neville doesn't think it looks good to have human servants in demeaning positions. A chef is all right. . . ." Her voice trailed away under her sister-in-law's ironic gaze.

"Ah, Neville's constant pursuit of the Presidency."

Patricia blinked, trying to determine if Cecilia was being sarcastic or not. "Neville would make a wonderful president."

"I'm not saying he wouldn't. And you'd be a perfect first lady." Amused malice laced the words.

Neville circled the room, serving his brothers and their various wives. Sunny, Anthony's blonde and breathless beauty, held out her glass for a refill. Neville grimaced. He was something of a wine snob, and always enjoyed finding something obscure for people's enjoyment. To have Sunny gulping it down was an offense. To cover his irritation he launched into a dissertation on this night's offering.

"I found this in a tiny winery near Karlsruhe. No more than ten acres of vines clinging precariously to those monstrous hills on either side of the river. I doubt they bottle more than two thousand bottles a year."

"Fascinating," drawled Meredith. Neville flushed.

"I think we're about to get this mess resolved," the Senator continued with an abrupt change of topic. "Cabot has contacted the President."

Gerard started, sloshing wine across his thigh. "How do you know that? We haven't heard a word out of Cab."

"I don't think he wants to involve the family, which is good of him."

"So how do you know?" asked Cecilia, her voice sharp with irritation. Her frown deepened as her brother-in-law merely tapped the side of his nose, and gave her a smug, knowing look.

"Neville's being mysterious again."

"Meredith, you can be a real ass when you want to."

"I hate to interrupt this exchange of brotherly civilities," snapped Gerard. "But I'd like to hear about my son." Glances were exchanged over this unusual show of spirit from the eldest of the Huntingtons.

"Apparently Cabot and Joe Reichart, and those other people, whose names I can never remember—"

"Jennifer McBride and Stinson White."

"Oh, yes, thank you, Gerard.—Have decided that whatever their differences with Earth they're not worth precipitating a war over them. They've offered to return to Earth if the President will withdraw the squadron."

"Did this call come *before* or *after* the Russian destruction of that harmless old sculptor? A retaliatory strike on a madman. Lovely!"

"We don't know if any of that is true. It might be Belt propaganda."

"And our claiming that it wasn't might be propaganda too."

"One thing's sure. We know it wasn't Evgeni Renko," piped up Meredith brightly.

"That's right, laugh your way to hell."

"Gerard," warned Cecilia.

The oldest of the Huntingtons swept a cold gray glance across his siblings and wife. "Yes, I know old Gerard is terribly out of character, but sometimes I do notice things beyond my books and my planes. And now I want some answers."

"Answers to what?"

"Like why you're acting like an unpaid member of the Long cabinet, Neville. They're not even our party."

Anthony hid a smile. However apolitical Gerard might claim to be, he still had the Huntington family abhorrence of the opposition.

"Like you, Gerard, I believe we are in a deadly crisis, and such being the case it's time to set aside petty party politics and work together for a peaceful solution. I think Cabot has made a positive step in that direction by swallowing pride—" He flashed a rueful smile about the room. "A difficult thing, God knows, for a Huntington to do—and offering to return."

"And I still say that the wanton attack on that settlement may have changed Cabot's mind. And while we're on the subject, why isn't the President raising hell about Russian aggression in an American territory? Or has he accepted the colonists' arguments of independence and is going to leave the fight up to them?"

"You know the Soviets. There had to be retaliation for the destruction of their ship, and my source indicated that they presented the President with an accomplished fact and then challenged him to make trouble."

"And since trouble is the last thing Long can contemplate." Meredith shook his head. "I've never seen such a spineless man in the White House."

"I don't think that's fair. If he had responded to the Soviet action it would have brought the Russian fleet and our squadron into direct confrontation. And such a confrontation might very well have sparked hostilities on Earth."

"And right now we've got enough trouble with the threat from the System," put in Anthony. "We've simply got to show a united front. And who knows, something good might grow from this situation. It'll be the first time since the Second World War that America and the Soviet Union have worked in unison. Maybe this time we can maintain the good feeling."

"So we just wink, and shrug at the fourteen hundred deaths on Ceres, and the old man on that asteroid?"

"Gerard, no one is saying that these deaths aren't regrettable, they are." Cecilia slewed around to face her husband. "But there have been losses on our side too. Several young airmen, and the Soviets have lost over ninety counting that ship and their marines on Ceres."

"Not to mention the unfortunate Kenyans. I'd say their karma was decidedly bad," said Anthony with a half-apologetic smile over his ironic enjoyment of their deaths.

"I'll shed no tears," responded Cecilia, her blue gaze steely.

Neville waggled a hand, demanding attention. "Recounting

the death toll is pointless. As horrible, as tragic, and as upsetting as it was, we have to put it behind us. Cabot's brave offer has shown us how to work for the future. It's time we buried our dead, and resolved our differences with the System. They've got to realize that there can be no separation of Earth and space. Our interests are the same.''

''Are they? I wonder.'' Gerard rested his chin on his hand, and gazed off with that dreamy-eyed expression that was normal for their elder.

Meredith sipped his drink, primly crossed his legs at the knee, and fixed Neville with a stare. ''The chatter coming out of the system has been rather warlike. Their contention is that they've been exploited by the Earth for fifty years without adequate representation or consideration for their needs and goals.''

''Gibberish! Utter nonsense and gibberish. There have been far too many intemperate remarks on both sides, but that will die down now that we've got control of the situation. Yes, what?'' he snapped.

The tiny robot having magically been transformed from bartender to com operator warbled out, ''Call for you, sir.''

Neville ran a hand across the waves of his gray-blond hair, and exchanged a sheepish glance with his wife. ''You're right, dear, I _don't_ like that thing. I know the Japanese have used them for years,'' he called over his shoulder as he left the room. ''But it gives me the creeps, and—'' The closing of the study door cut off the rest.

He didn't bother to seat himself at the big cherry-wood desk, just leaned over and keyed the release. The frozen features of Rose Marie Beaty, his tiny and efficient administrative assistant, trembled as the call came off hold. It was then that the Senator noticed that she still hadn't lost the frozen, stricken expression.

''My God, what is it? The President,'' he gasped as the most horrible nightmare available to Washingtonians leaped to mind.

''No. The EnerSun orbital station has just been destroyed.''

The great leather swivel chair caught him in the back of the knees as he collapsed bonelessly into its enfolding, fragrant depths.

''Say again.''

''The EnerSun station.''

''Who? How?''

"There's an absolute pilgrimage heading to the White House, and they're staying mum. What I've got I've gleaned from State and the Pentagon. Apparently a missile crew on a weapons platform spotted the station shifting their solar satellites. They queried, but got no reply—or so they claim—and suddenly this young captain was the man on the spot. Did he wait and see if they really meant to fry Dubuque, or did he act? He acted."

"Survivors?"

"None. or that's the current situation. Maybe they'll find a few, but a hit from a thermonuclear device doesn't tend to leave too many—"

"Ten thousand people." His voice sounded like it belonged to a stranger. He tried to regain control of his whirling thoughts.

"Do you want me to issue a statement?"

"No, let's wait for the White House."

"The press is milling in the hall, wanting answers about your nephew. Trying to tie this in."

"Hold them at bay, I'm on my way."

"Neville?" Patricia's voice was a dove's coo, hurt, questioning as he charged through the living room.

He dropped a distracted kiss onto her lips. "I've got to get to the Hill."

"But dinner?" She gestured helplessly toward the kitchen, then toward the dining room.

Cecilia was on her feet, blocking his way. "What's happened?"

His eyes rolled helplessly about the room. To Meredith looking bland, Anthony his plump face avid, Gerard sitting with unnatural stillness as if sensing the horrible nature of his news, Patricia her eyes darkening with despair as she contemplated her ruined evening. Sunny patting her arm, but dividing her attention between Anthony and himself. And Cecilia, the iron and velvet maiden. No way to put her off.

Oh, God, and after he'd made such an ass of himself with all those pompous little speeches about mending fences, and putting the past behind them, and—

He sucked in a breath, and told them. Simply, plainly, baldly.

"It changes nothing." Cecilia stood with hands clenched at her sides, frowning down at the floor. "If anything it only makes Cabot's return all the more imperative."

"No, my dear." Gerard rose slowly to his feet. "I would say that it changes everything."

"What the hell do you know about it?"

"Nothing—about all the political ramifications. But about my son . . ." He tilted back his head, and thoughtfully regarded the ceiling. "I think I know him better than you."

Cecilia gave him her shoulder. "Neville, I'm coming with you."

"And I better get back to the Hill too," added Anthony.

"Tony," wailed Sunny.

"Stay with Patricia."

"And what about you?" demanded Cecilia, turning on her husband. "Are you going to stay here too?"

"No, I thought I'd go to church."

Six pairs of eyes stared at him blankly.

"To pray for the dead," he explained softly. "I know they don't enter into the calculations of the mighty, except as a factor. But I thought it would be nice if one of us did honor to their memory."

"Even though they may have been planning to kill thousands on the ground?"

"Somehow I don't think so." Husband's and wife's eyes met in a duel. "I can't picture Cabot admiring a person who could contemplate such an act. And I know Cabot admired Lydia Kim Nu."

Irina was just emerging from the bedroom. Cab and Jenny glanced from the untouched tray to Irina's liquid brown eyes. She gave a tiny almost imperceptible shake of the head and walked on. Jenny's fingers were chill as they slipped into Cab's hand. He gave them a hard squeeze.

For a moment longer he hesitated, then squared his shoulders and entered the alcove which served as the Renkos' bedroom. But for two days they hadn't been using it. For two days they had been sleeping on cots in the main room. For two days Joe Reichart had been sitting in silent anguish in that darkened chamber. Two days since the word of the destruction of the EnerSun station had reached the Belt.

Joe was sitting as he had been the day before. Cab felt a flicker of annoyance, quickly and guiltily quashed. If it had been Jenny . . . His hand tightened convulsively about hers. Reichart was in profile, staring sightlessly at the rough stone wall of the alcove. The dim light threw his hands where they lay upon his knees into relief, and Cab noticed, as if for the first time, how aged they had become. The blue veins writhed like knotted bruises beneath the tan skin.

At the rasp of their sticky boots he lifted his head, and quietly regarded them. And what he saw shattered Cab, for Joe Reichart had become an old man. Jenny's shoulder, resting lightly against his upper arm, telegraphed her shock. The judge slid an arm around her offering support and accepting the comfort of her touch.

"Cab, Jenny."

Jennifer slipped from his grasp, and knelt on the floor before Reichart. Gathered the limp hands into hers. "Joe, you've got to eat something."

Pulling a hand free he brushed back the fringe of her bangs with a forefinger. "Ah, the ladies. The ever-practical ladies. Dita tells me the same thing. Irina tells me the same thing. Lydia would tell me the same too; if she were here."

Jenny dropped her head.

"Joe, don't." Cab paused, realizing that the coldness of the words might be construed as criticism of Joe's grief. He tried again. "Jenny and I didn't want to impose on you. You and Dita had to share your grief, and that's tough to do with an audience. We do want you to know how deeply sorry we both are."

"And how inadequate we know the words are. I only wish there was something I could *do*." A vehement shake of the head set the red hair flying.

"I know." Joe's eyes slid to the Judge. "You and my Lydia had your differences, but you grew to admire her."

"Joe, more than that I liked her."

"She had a great deal of respect for you. She believed that if you once came to see our side you should be a great force for change and good within the System."

Panic fluttered like a captured animal somewhere deep within Cabot's soul. For two days he had watched his companions watching *him*. Looking to him. Waiting on him. Now Joe.

"That's very flattering, but a little too mystic for me. I just blunder along, doing my poor best, and trying to learn." Joe had returned to his contemplation of the rock wall.

"Joe, you can't go on like this," said Jenny softly, giving his hands a small shake. "Lydia wouldn't want to see you this way. She'd pin you with a look out of those hawk eyes." Her voice was growing thick with unshed tears. "And tell you to get cracking."

"She was tired the last time we talked. Bone and soul weary. She wanted a little time to herself and for herself. She was going to join me, and then some asshole killed her."

"Then get mad about it! Let's do something about it!" Cab blazed.

"What? And how?" He shook his head, a sad little gesture.

"That's what you do best. Tweaking the nose of the groundside authorities. Running circles around their stupid regulations."

"This is war, Cab. People are dying, or haven't you noticed? Maybe because of my tweaking and maneuvering and cutesy and cunning little tricks. Well, it's out of hand, and I can't cope anymore. I'm tired too, Cab, and maybe more than a little guilty."

"Great! That's just great! There's an armada out there finding and killing our people. And now you want us to surrender to these people?"

"You were the one who suggested it."

"That was then, this is now."

"So what's different?"

"Everything!" His voice cracked, and he coughed to clear it. "They don't want an amicable settlement. If they had they would never have allowed the Russians to go cruising for a target. If they did they wouldn't be publishing *shit* like this." He yanked a news fax printout from his coat pocket and flung it onto the floor.

"They created the climate, Joe." Jenny took up the argument, giving Cab time to regulate his ragged breaths. "They did nothing to placate or reassure the System. They painted us as crazed killers ready to destroy the home world. I don't believe for a minute that the station was moving those satellites. Someone saw something, or thought they saw something, and as we've been portrayed as bloodthirsty animals, it wasn't hard to decide to press the big one. Mom, apple pie, and America were riding on this kid."

"According to this," Cab shoved a paper disdainfully with a toe, and it went floating several inches above the floor toward the door. "He's a goddamn hero."

The old man just shook his head, and leaned back in the chair. Jenny rose, pushed back her hair.

"I'm going to bring back that tray, and this time you're going to eat something. Even if Dita and I have to sit here and poke it down you."

The rasp of her footfalls faded. Silence hung in the room, but not the uncomfortable silence of two people caught in a pause in an argument. Reichart had simply disengaged. He didn't care. Cab crossed to him in a swift stride. Laid his hand on the back of the chair, gripped as if it were Joe's shoulder, as if he could somehow transfer his passion.

"Joe, don't do this to me." *Nothing.* "You're a natural leader. You must have planned for this. Dreaded it perhaps, hoped it would never come, but planned for it. They're looking to *me*, Joe. To *me*. I never wanted this. That's why I stayed a lawyer, became a judge. They had it all planned out—Mother and Neville. A state senatorship. Maybe governor. A politically appropriate marriage. Then on to Congress. But I resisted. I'm not sure how."

"Cabot." Reichart, moving with painful slowness, cranked around in the chair. "I frankly don't give a damn." Huntington jerked as if he'd been slapped. "A part of me is dead. Just leave me the fuck alone."

They were all gathered about the big table. The microwave humming as Irina reheated the meal. For a long time they didn't notice him standing silently in the archway. Bits of conversation pursued each other about the table like nervous ferrets chasing each other's tails.

"At least Rohana and Jamila are safe. The other stations have submitted to military takeover to avoid EnerSun's fate. Same with the Moon bases."

"Yes, they have a glowing crater where the Garmoneya Collective used to be to remind them if they should forget," put in Evgeni wryly.

"So that leaves us," grunted Stinson.

"To do what?" asked Andy.

"Something," produced Dita. "We have to do something."

Stinson rubbed irritably at his eye patch. "Yeah, if we just throw in the towel I bet they relocate a lot of the Belt settlers. Send out 'safe' colonists. Set up a military outpost."

"Is that so bad? They're killin' us now. What's to be gained by going on?"

Cab pushed off from the wall, missing its support the minute he did. His knees felt very weak.

" 'They that give up essential liberty to obtain a little temporary safety deserve neither liberty nor safety.' Written over three hundred years ago. I think it still has meaning for today." Andy's eyes dropped beneath Cab's cool gray-eyed gaze. The judge reached out, and pressed his shoulder. "I know, Andy, I understand. Martha's on the Moon. You're worried. Scared. We all are." He swept the table daring anyone, particularly Dita, to disagree.

"Four days ago I was willing to return to Earth if that would have halted hostilities. Not anymore. Washington gave Ledawi to the Russians, like a nervous owner appeasing a surly dog. They destroyed the EnerSun station—ten thousand people—for no reason at all. Personally I think they were after Lydia, and didn't care how many died in an effort to get at her. It was a calculated act of terror, *and it worked!* The near-Earth orbitals and the Moon bases are knuckling under. They don't have any choice. There are weapons platforms, and military bases littering space and the lunar landscape. *But not out here.*"

"No, out here we've got a fucking armada."

"But it can be handled. Our first macho cowboy proved that."

"And got blasted for his trouble."

"I never said it would be safe or easy," he flared at Andy, then rubbed a hand wearily across his eyes. "That man's mistake was taking on the Russians in a lump. We know from the orders we've intercepted that they've broken up the fleet and the squadron into hunter/killer teams of two and three. Two or three Curvets and a load of fist-sized rocks can handle that. But this time we'll hold back a reserve of pebbles to cover the retreat. Any missile passing through a halo of small stones is going—"

"To be Swiss cheese," offered Dita.

"Precisely. We can also use cover more effectively. Time our attacks when the enemy ships are near rocks. Use the rocks to mask radar."

"And we know they'll be near rocks because they're searching for us, damn them to hell," said Stinson.

Evgeni spoke up. "I assume when you talk of *we* you mean more than just the seven people in this room."

"Of course. This will have to be a Belt-wide resistance."

"With what as our final goal? The ultimate destruction of

Earth?'' Stinson was gray beneath the black skin, and his smile more sick than predatory.

"No, that's the thing we must avoid at all costs. That's why we have organized an effective defense so that our people won't feel trapped and helpless. It's that kind of thinking that leads to desperate acts. Like an assault on the home world. But fighting the antimatter ships in the Belt will give us hope, and drive home a lesson to the leaders on Earth.''

"What lesson?''

"The lesson that it's taken me a year to absorb. That Earth can't control the System. And more to the point that they can't win against the System. Without the home world our existence would be pretty damn bleak, but we could survive. The reverse might not be true.'' He paused, head bowed as he considered. "We're going to need to split up, coordinate the effort from several different points within the Belt. Stinson, can you show me an image of the settled areas?''

"Sure, nothing easier.'' He crossed to the Renkos' computer terminal, and punched up a revolving three-dimensional image of the Belt. "This is programmed into every new colonist's computer, both on a rock and in their ships. Gives you a chance to find help if you need it.''

"Are the bad guys likely to have this map?'' asked Andy.

"Probably not. When they hit Ceres Control they wiped the master. I hope our people had the sense to erase their own private maps, but maybe it won't occur to the military to look for such a thing.''

"Looks rather like an octopus,'' remarked Jenny, leaning in over Stinson's shoulder.

Cab rubbed at his face. "All those little fingers. We're going to have to split up to have any hope of coordinating this thing.''

"And how do we talk? If we can intercept them they can sure as hell intercept us,'' Andy pointed out.

"So we don't talk except in person.'' Cab indicated the four main tentacles. "Each separate area is going to be functionally on their own. Guerrilla warfare rather than textbook battle plans.''

"Probably better that way. Guerrillas tend to knock the snot out of regular armies,'' Dita said.

"But within the fingers we've got to communicate.''

"Andy, you're starting to irritate me." Dita's dark eyes were stormy.

"No, he's right to point out potential problems. If we don't solve them now we may end up solving them by dying, and letting our replacements learn from our mistakes. Which doesn't appeal to me as a solution." It was a weak sally on Cab's part, but it drew a few smiles.

"After thirty years out here people have begun to develop a kind of oral shorthand. Saves on cost if you can get the message across in the least number of words. It'll take the enemy some time to figure out the rock talk." Stinson shrugged. "By then maybe we'll have come up with something better."

"By then maybe we won't need something better. We can hope that Earth gets the message, and this nonsense has stopped." Jenny's green eyes glittered in the harsh light.

"Amen," said Renko, laying a hand on her shoulder.

"There is one other thing," the redhead continued. "These little outposts stand out like a candle in a dark room. The energy signature makes them absurdly easy to locate. I think we should evacuate as many of the children, and enough men and women to care for them, as is possible."

"And take them where?"

"Iapetus. It's an international and neutral scientific enclave."

"Won't they view this as trying to draw them in on our side?"

"No, I don't think so. I think, they'll view it as a humanitarian action."

"Who's going to run this evacuation? I'm sure as hell not. I want to kill a few of those fuckers." Tendons and muscles tightened as Dita set her jaw.

"I will."

"Jenny!"

"Someone has to go, Cab."

"Is good idea," put in Renko. "If I know Analisa and Irina, and new baby are safe, I will fight harder."

It was a good idea. Cab knew it. But the thought of facing the coming conflict without Jenny made it all the more horrible, and his self-doubts again leaped up to gnaw at him. He stared down at his hands where they gripped the back of Stinson's chair.

The former leader of the Ceres colony flung himself back in the chair pinching Cabot's fingers. "So, we're agreed. Anybody have any profound and final words of wisdom?"

"I tell you now, gentlemen . . . and ladies. We must all hang together, or assuredly we shall all hang separately."

"Very nice, Andy," murmured Cab dryly. "But don't you think Franklin would like to have credit for it?"

"Damn shysters. Heads like lumber rooms, just stuffed full of quotable quotes to amaze and overawe the simple folk. And I was gonna look so fuckin' intelligent and erudite."

The room exploded in nervous laughter. Everyone but Cab. He was watching Jenny, a frown between his upswept brows.

Chapter Seventeen _____

Colonel Belmanor stood stiffly while his general occupied his desk chair. Major Adams, Saber's ever faithful shadow, lurked against one bulkhead, arms folded across his chest.

". . . because of these unwarranted attacks upon innocent civilians, and because of the continued illegal presence of warships within the System, the citizens of the Belt have no choice but to fight for the defense of their homes, their families, and their basic freedoms. We do not reach this decision lightly, and even now we pray God that the leaders groundside will show their wisdom by averting this conflict.'' The speaker's voice hardened.

"But if not, if they choose to continue this arrogant and unlawful attack upon us, be assured that force will be met with force. This is the only warning you will receive. If by twelve noon Greenwich standard time tomorrow the assembled forces of the United States, the Soviet Union, Europe, Brazil, and Japan are not withdrawn from the Belt, they will be treated as hostile combatants and attacked.''

Saber snapped off the recording, and leaned back, arms folded behind his head. "I s-suppose I don't have to tell you the groundside response?''

"No, sir. We'll fight.'' Belmanor's voice was heavy.

"We've always been a s-small, close-knit s-service, Colonel. S-Sprinkled throughout my s-squadron are over s-seventy S-System-born men and women—''

"Are you questioning our loyalty?'' There was a harsh edge to the young colonel's normally soft tones.

Saber rapped out, "No, I'm trying to avoid putting too

great a s-strain upon that loyalty.'' Belmanor flushed. ''I trust that whatever is s-said within the confines of this office will go no further?''

''Yes, sir.''

''Very well. I'm not any more comfortable with this s-situation than you are, Tracy. Less maybe because I'm responsible for the entire s-squadron, and I don't think this is going to be quite the pushover the civilians back home are expecting. I have a hunch that pride and pigheadedness in Washington have pushed us to this crisis. But whatever the reasons we have our orders, and I'll do my best to carry out those orders until I'm told otherwise.

''Now, I don't want to relieve from duty every S-System-born s-serviceperson, s-so I've reached a compromise. My earlier orders were to leave one s-ship to hold Ceres. I'm going to do s-so, and that s-ship will be the *Intrepid*. I'm going to reassign those S-System-born people who s-so choose to the *Intrepid*. Now, how does that s-sound?''

''We'll be undermanned.''

''Not s-severely.''

Belmanor considered. ''Okay.'' Saber stretched, rose, and pulled the recording. ''By the way, who was that?'' Belmanor indicated the tiny tape chip.

''Cabot Huntington.'' The young captain's mouth formed a surprised ''o.''

''Which is just another example of what a fucking mess the grounders have made out of all this,'' Saber grunted to his aide upon their return to the flagship. ''It takes a lot to alienate a man like Cabot Huntington.''

''Maybe he's a black sheep—''

''He undoubtedly is now.''

''A rebel.''

Stanley poked his head in the door. ''Admiral Fujasaki to see you, sir.''

''S-Send him in.''

The Japanese admiral was a round and dapper little figure as he strutted in, and snapped off a salute.

''Admiral.''

''General.''

They exchanged bows.

''I am come to tell you that I must regretfully leave you and return to Earth. Orders have come from Tokyo.''

"I don't blame you or your government one bit."

The Japanese seemed surprised by the response, but plowed ahead with his explanation. "It was proper that the Japanese Space Service should offer her one ship in defense of the Earth against a common foe, but now it has become an American matter, and would be improper for us to interfere."

"I quite understand, and personally, Admiral, I wish the Russians s-saw it the s-same way. Unfortunately my government s-seems—" He pressed his lips together. "A drink with me, Admiral?"

The drinks were served, brief toasts were exchanged, Fujasaki tossed back the brandy, and left. He was decidedly in a hurry to put as much distance between his ship and the Belt as was humanly and mechanically possible.

"Wimp out," remarked Adams, seating himself on the corner of the desk.

"No, good s-sense. Why s-should the Japanese risk the pride of their nation on a fight that isn't theirs? Wish I could be recalled to Tokyo, or Toulouse, or Tashkent."

The com chimed, and Saber's brows rose in a comic expression of "what next?" It was Verchenko.

"So we are to go cruising together, General."

"S-So it would s-seem, Admiral."

"I should tell you that we have lost our brave European and Brazilian allies."

"I just got the s-same message from the Japanese. And while we're on the s-subject of allies, Admiral, there are s-several things that we have to get s-straight before we do go cruising."

"Such as?"

"How many nuclear missiles do you have left?"

"Why?"

"Because I damn well want them off your s-ships!"

"They weren't all that effective against that settlement."

"You'd do well not to remind me of that incident."

"We all have our orders."

"S-some of them more barbarous than others."

"You can afford to be noble and forgiving. None of your ships were destroyed."

"No, fortunately the colonist panicked, and released the load too early. Avoiding the rocks was easy."

"And he got away?"

"He got away. But their s-strategy got me to thinking. One

good hit could cripple a s-ship. It could even conceivably be captured. And the last thing we need is for the Belters to have the bomb." One hand placed the words in the air like a banner headline. "You can imagine the panic that would cause Earthside."

"So I leave my few remaining nukes?"

"You leave them."

"All right, we only have three left anyway. So what are our plans for cruising?"

"I'd s-suggest s-seven groups of two, and one group of three."

"I presume those groups will consist of one Soviet and one American ship?"

"Yes."

"And what are they to do, these groups?"

"Locate s-settlements, demand s-surrender, and ascertain whether any of the fugitives are present."

"And just how are we supposed to do that? These Belters have had the foresight to dig themselves deep into the skins of these asteroids. It makes it a little difficult to overawe them with just conventional missiles."

"We land, and go in after them."

"Oh, lovely."

"S-Still time to head back to Moscow, Admiral."

"I wouldn't want to deprive you of my help, General."

"Kind of you."

"And what of us? Do we separate to cover different quadrants?"

"Would it hurt your feelings, Admiral, if I told you that I would prefer to keep you under my eye?"

Casimir threw back his head, and roared with laughter. "Ah, Saber, what a pity we're on different sides."

"At the moment we don't s-seem to be."

"And it bothers you, eh?"

"Yes." They studied each other. "Verchenko, what's your government's interest in all this, anyway?"

"I haven't a clue." Saber grunted. Casimir laughed again. "General, perhaps some night when we are both too drunk for our own good I will tell you stories of Moscow's confusion and irrationality."

"S-Sounds like heady s-stuff. I can't wait. Why don't you and I form up the team of three?"

"Fine. Will the third ship be one of yours or one of mine?"

"Let's toss for it."

"What with? A plastic card?"

"My 1928 s-silver dollar." Saber fished in the desk drawer. "Came down from my great-grandfather. Family folklore s-says it s-stopped a German bullet during the S-Spanish Civil War back in the 1930s."

"Charming these folktales."

Saber held it up to the screen. There was a deep dent slightly to one side of the eagle. "Call it."

"Tails."

It came up tails.

"S-So I'm outnumbered."

"But not outclassed."

"Is that a comment on your s-skill, Admiral?"

"No, upon the equipment. Ours is dreadful stuff."

Saber leaned back, and shook his head. "Your reputation doesn't do you justice, Admiral."

"Thank you."

"Why assume that's a compliment?"

"I always hope for the best."

"Hold onto that optimism. I think you're going to need it in the coming days."

Goncharenko staggered about the bridge. Emergency lights were all that were running, throwing a murky red light across a scene of confusion and panic. The ship was bleeding air like a punctured bladder, and Goncharenko reluctantly admitted that the American captain had been right to insist upon space-suits whenever the searching pair approached a rock. He was gone now, limping from the scene of another disastrous encounter with the Belt defenders. Goncharenko slammed his fist into the back of a chair. The damned Americans had given a better account of themselves than his crew. More missiles fired, more Curvets destroyed; now all he had to do was revive the sagging spirits of his crew, and begin repairs—

A soft thud translated itself through the skin of the ship. Heads jerked up like coursing hounds on the scent. Several more followed.

Minutes passed. Suddenly a shrill young voice screamed over the intercom. "They're cutting through the hatches. *They're cutting through the hatches!*"

"Get to the arms locker! Issue shotguns! Prepare to repel boarders!"

Prepare to repel boarders, his mind repeated in disbelief.

"They're *capturing* our ships?" Disbelief sent the President's voice up several octaves.

"No, sir," Jack McConnell, the Air Force Secretary, chuckled. "They're capturing *Russian* ships."

"Our turn will come," grunted General Rager, Chairman of the Joint Chiefs.

Brandon Childes, the Secretary of Defense, slewed around in his chair. "That's pretty damn pessimistic!"

"Realistic. Unlike in the movies, there's no burn in space."

Abrams, the Air Force Chief, took up the tale. "Which means you can end up with a disabled ship which functionally isn't very badly damaged. It can easily be repaired, and put back into space."

"Against us," McConnell concluded glumly.

"They're just a bunch of ignorant miners," objected Lis Varllis.

"Who've had to make do with very little, and learned to be pretty good jacks-of-all-trades. They'll have the people out there to make the repairs. It may not be pretty, or pass a government inspection, but they'll fly."

"Cruise," corrected Abrams.

"So what are you telling me?" asked the President. "That these people are going to *win*?"

The various military men exchanged glances. It wouldn't have been politic to say yes. Abrams settled for a more neutral response.

"What we're saying is that it isn't going to be the pushover the people and the press are expecting."

"Then there's going to be hell to pay in Congress," put in Childes. "There's already a very vocal faction who's accusing us of violating the War Powers Act. They're going to force us to negotiate if this thing drags on for too long."

"And Senator Huntington is leading the baying pack, I'm sure."

"No, he seems to be trying to walk the tightrope; remaining supportive but neutral."

"He has Presidential aspirations," remarked the President. "And I sure as hell don't want to give him an issue that he can use against me in three years. This thing is turning into a nightmare.''

He glanced at his White House Chief of Staff, and several people wondered if they had really read dissatisfaction in the look. Unfortunately, it was gone too soon to be sure.

"Well, at least we'll get Huntington removed," Lis said spitefully.

"Petty, petty." But the remark had been made in a very low undertone, and she couldn't ascertain who had said it.

Fred Downs, the Press Secretary, spoke up in a different tone. "I am having a little trouble about how exactly to present the Russian presence out there. I think a lot of the country is wondering why in the hell we're letting Russians shoot at Americans.''

"Because with seven ships we don't have a hope in hell of catching Reichart and Huntington, and all the rest," spat Lis.

"Play up the 'there are no boundaries from space' aspect," suggested the President. "That if the colonists decide to bring the fight home to us it could hurt the Russians just as much as us. Brotherhood of man, and all that." He sent a weak smile around the table. "And who knows, maybe something good will come out of this. We have shown that as a planet we can pull together against a common threat.''

"So you want us to keep fighting?" asked Abrams, cutting through all the politics and the philosophy.

"For the time being, yes. They can't keep this up forever. The supply problem is bound to get to them sooner or later.''

The assembled brass exchanged another significant glance.

"Here it is, fellas. The garden spot of the asteroids. The playground of the Belt. Hot and cold running water, a tasteful and very extensive tape library. Now shuck those suits, and settle right into this hydroponic paradise.''

Andy Throckmorton's humor seemed to be wasted on this audience. He could only assume it was a language problem. The captain of the captured ship had turned out to be an English speaker. He frowned and asked, "And if something breaks the integrity of this habitat? Without suits we will die.''

"Hey, life's tough. You didn't join the Space Cadets to be safe. And it's going to take a mucking big something to bust through fifty feet of rock." Andy's expression hardened. "Like the something you guys used on poor old Emery

Ledawig. And since we don't have the bomb, and are also the good guys, we don't bomb defenseless people. . . .''

The Captain's face turned several interesting shades.

Evgeni Renko barked out something in Russian, the seven other colonists gestured with their weapons, and fifty-two surly and confused Soviets climbed out of their suits.

"We take the suits in an effort to keep you content and happy," said Evgeni. "With suits you might be tempted to reach the reactor, and use it to signal a crude SOS. And if you did that we would have to come back to kill you."

"And we don't want to do that," put in Andy in the unctuous tones of a children's show host. "So you just get comfortable, and wait for the end of this little war." He pulled down several of the tapes at random. "You can learn Spanish, or gourmet cooking on a budget, or read the collected works of Dostoyevski. You'll like that."

For a moment Andy contemplated the people who had lived and worked on this asteroid. Their personalities could only be gleaned from the personal effects they had left behind. And they didn't fit the standard view of dirt-ball miners. It would make an interesting story if he could locate them. Some were undoubtedly on Iapetus, the others scattered through the Belt, either fighting or evacuating other rocks and other families.

He had wired several stories to AP. Good stories. But he wondered what the protocol would be. Could they give a Pulitzer Prize to a journalist who was also fighting in an armed rebellion? Surely they wouldn't be so narrow-minded. Or worse yet—assume he was *biased*. Why, nothing could be further from the truth.

Inwardly laughing at his own sarcasm, he helped gather up the discarded suits, and ferried them back to the waiting Curvets. They weren't of the best manufacture, but extra suits were always welcome. Suits were the one thing they were going to have trouble replacing.

"S-so, are you going to get drunk, and tell me all about Moscow's confusion and irrationality?" Saber looked curiously about the Admiral's cabin aboard the Soviet flagship.

It wasn't unlike his own quarters aboard the *Victory*. Small, cramped, conduits snaking overhead. The only real difference was that the tiny room seemed to be filled with furniture. Apparently Verchenko couldn't fold his bunk into the wall. Saber decided his design was superior. Verchenko was also a man who revealed more of his personality through his possessions. Where Saber's quarters were austere almost to the point of monasticism, Verchenko's was filled with paintings and knick-knacks.

There were two very nice bronzes done in a rough primitive style placed at each corner of the desk. One was a fighting stallion, neck arched to the breaking point, nostrils flaring, mane lifting from the force of its fury. The other was a nude. A woman, caught in the act of lifting her long hair, breasts upthrust, an expression of hedonistic pleasure on her strong face.

"Only if you agree to reveal all about Washington."

"They're more pigheaded than—" He folded his lips together.

"Say it, Saber, don't be so unfailingly loyal." The green eyes glittered.

The General changed the subject instead. "Those are nice." A gesture toward the bronzes.

Verchenko looked up from where he was pouring out two brandies. "Thank you, they're mine."

"Are you one of those irritating—thank you." Saber settled onto the edge of the bunk. "People who are just filled with talents, hidden or otherwise?"

The Russian smiled over the rim of his snifter. "Yes."

"Not overly afflicted with modesty, are you?"

"Not in the least. I don't believe in it. Modesty's one of those foolish notions developed by the ignorant and untalented to make themselves feel better. Cheers."

"S-Skol."

Verchenko savored the brandy, rolling it about in his mouth before swallowing. "You know," he said in tones of melancholy reflection, "they seem to have an unlimited supply of rocks."

"They do at that. Maybe we s-should take a few of those barges, and turn the tables on them."

"It would be a wiring nightmare."

"True." Saber took another sip of the brandy. It was very fine. French he would guess. "We're doing well with command guided missiles, but we're burning up the heat s-seekers at a fabulous rate."

"Ditto. No one seemed to take this into account when they built these ships, heh? Bad enough to run supply lines across several thousand miles. When it runs into the millions." He shrugged, and the arched brows climbed the high white forehead.

"That's because they were never really designed for s-space combat. Or at least that's my theory."

Verchenko handed across the bottle, then settled more comfortably into his chair. "Oh, tell me your theory. I love theories."

Saber eyed the elegant figure sprawled in the chair; one knee hooked languidly over the arm, the foot swinging with a hypnotic rhythm. For an instant he had an uncomfortable feeling about the Russian, then reminded himself not to be narrow-minded and bigoted.

"I wonder if this constitutes treason?" mused Saber, rotating his snifter, and watching the amber liquid roll about the sides of the glass.

"Too strong a word. A little minor disloyalty. A bit of bitching about the politicians." The light tenor voice deepened and he added drolly, "Get them damn windbags out of our hair. Let us get on with what we do best. Fightin' and killin' and winnin'."

"My God, I didn't know you knew S-Skip Hudson. That's his favorite drone when he's holding down s-space in the bar of the officers' club."

"Actually that was my modest imitation of General Dobrinin."

They laughed.

"The fact is," Saber said, returning to the original topic. "I think my esteemed s-service and the Defense Department has to s-share the blame. We were in s-such a s-sweat to have a deep-s-space s-squadron—to one up the Navy, to keep our s-share of the gravy train—that they told any number of absolute whoppers to Congress to get the appropriations. The threat from s-space aliens." Verchenko laughed and Saber pulled a face. "Matching and countering the S-Soviet menace."

"That's right, we did deploy our first antimatter vessel before you did. So you don't think we are the cutting edge of terror technology?"

"No. If we're only another platform for launching missiles, why bother? We've already got an abundance of platforms."

"Ah, but only around Earth. Maybe our superiors were wonderfully foresighted, and saw that sooner or later we would have to drop missiles on planets without platforms."

"Then how about s-ship on s-ship? Do you think we've thought that through?"

"Alas, no. You know, it's damn hard to fight in space."

"Yeah, especially when they s-seem to have just hundreds of those little s-ships, and can use pack s-strategy on us."

"My crews are becoming unbelievably skittish about asteroids. They are undertaking amazing maneuvers to avoid them, assuming that one of those little Curvets is lurking behind each and every rock."

"Can you blame them? We're getting our clocks cleaned."

"I wouldn't say that. What is the score? We've destroyed seven of their ships, and searched eleven settlements."

"And they've captured two of yours, demolished one, and really fucked over one of mine. And we're running out of missiles." The neck of the bottle clinked aggressively against the snifter as the General refilled his glass.

"Then you don't think we can win?"

"Frankly, no. Not unless we s-send home for a s-shitload of nukes, then s-stand off, and plaster every s-settlement we find. And if we begin s-such terror tactics what's to keep the Belters from using the s-same tactics against Earth?"

He swung out of his chair, and began to pace the confines of the tiny room. "Why are we s-still out here anyway?"

"Presumably because your territory is attempting to secede from the Union."

"Then what the fuck are *you* doing here? I'm a good s-soldier. I love my s-service, my country. I've never questioned my orders before—" He broke off, and stared down into his glass. "I'm drunk."

"Not so you'd notice."

"I s-shouldn't be . . . I've never s-said things like this before." He rolled an eye at Verchenko. "And you're s-sober as a judge. Damn you!"

"Saber, I'm not trying to trick you or put something over on you. Really." Verchenko seized the bottle, placed it to his lips, and threw back his head. His adam's apple worked as he drained the remaining brandy in one long swallow. He coughed and patted himself on the chest. "I like you," he concluded in a thin, breathy voice. "You can trust me."

"Yeah." The glass crashed onto the desk. "I'm going back to my s-ship."

"Saber." The Russian's arm was about his shoulders, and the earlier feeling became a certainty. "Don't go away angry. I too am very upset about this situation. Talk to me."

"Why? And about what? We just fight the wars, we can't s-stop them."

Verchenko's green eyes were fixed and very distant. "I like to fight. Battle has always thrilled me."

"Bully."

"But it should be like a game. Over quickly, and back to reality. Art, music, fine food, elegant and witty company. You are right, Ingvar. Too much is at stake here."

The American stepped away from the encircling arm. "I s-see. We talk for an hour, and s-suddenly you're convinced. The war is a bad idea. Credit me with a little intelligence, Verchenko."

"I do, but please credit *me* with a little intelligence also. You're in agony because you are battling countrymen with whom you secretly agree. I don't care a rat's ass for these Belters. I do care about you, what you're going through." Saber made a rejecting motion, and Verchenko smiled cynically and a little sadly. "Oh, not to worry." He flung himself down in his chair. "You see, quite safe."

"I'm worried," he resumed, "but my concerns are purely selfish. Life back home would be damned uncomfortable without the power and materials from space. And life on Earth after several thousand tons of granite and basalt has been dumped on it doesn't bear contemplating. I'm *not* a patriot. At least not in the modern sense. I think my government is a collection of fools and criminals. I love my country, but Russia, icy, snow-covered, flower-filled, rich and beautiful Russia has nothing to do with the party."

"What are you saying?"

Casimir threw his hands into the air. "I don't know. Now *I'm* drunk."

Saber fidgeted, shifting from foot to foot, thrust his hands into his pockets, removed them, brushed nervously across the top of his hair. "Well." The clearing of his throat raked across the silence. "Thank you for having me. Good brandy, and interesting talk." This taking of refuge in the banalities of social amenities seemed to steady him.

"My pleasure."

"Next time you'll have to accept my hospitality."

"If there's time. Who knows, tomorrow we may catch your rebels."

Late in the night cycle Saber sat at his desk reading over the letter he had just completed. Blues guitar filled the room, a soft wail drowning out the constant ship-board noises.

Colonel,
I've just had the strangest encounter with Verchenko.

Saber eyed the screen, wiped it clear, and tried again.

Belmanor,
I've just concluded a meeting with Verchenko which contained a number of interesting undercurrents. Verchenko seems to have the same doubts about our presence in the Belt which have been tormenting me. I've spent the past three hours wondering if this was merely an act, but instinct tells me no.

Our conversation had another effect; it set me to won- dering just what in the hell is our duty and responsibility? Only to obey orders? We saw the results of that mentality in Germany in the last century. When do we have to make a choice between the wishes and orders of our leaders, and what we feel is required of us as ethical human beings? And what if some other military commander decided that ethically he had to spark a conflict rather than end one?

I know this is very dangerous ground, and could well lead me into a philosophical quagmire, but I feel these questions must be considered.

I'm confused, Tracy, and I suppose I don't really know what I'm trying to say. Perhaps what I'm proposing is that we keep a close eye on this situation, and see if at any time it might be in the best interests of humanity that we stop obeying orders. I'm writing to you because I wanted the comfort of knowing that if anything happened to me, there'd be someone who knew my mind, my doubts and fears.

And if it should ever fall to you to make a decision, I recommend that you approach Verchenko. I think he's an honorable man despite being one of the strangest son of a bitches I've ever met. Also, the fact that a Russian and an American would be willing to set aside their differences and present a unified front might make an impression on the leaders back home

I send this under personal seal. I am trusting you to open this file only upon my death.

Ingvar Saber

Chapter Eighteen

The *Apollo* had been set down on the pitted surface of Odiel. Suited figures swooped and flew about its damaged hull like exotic white birds, or manic gymnasts. Here and there blossomed the brilliant glare of a welder patching the holes in her skin. Overhead three of the asteroid's six companions crawled past like perambulating diamonds.

It was a large colony. Seventy strong. Made up predominately of Scandinavian settlers. The discovery of seven reasonably good-sized rocks all tumbling and orbiting along together had sparked the names: Odiel the Black Swan princess. The six accompanying rocks the bewitched swan princes from the Grimms' fairy tale.

Stinson, loping in long, low strides across the asteroid's surface, picked out the small figure, hands clasped rigidly behind its back, watching the repairs.

Cab, sensitive to the vibrations telegraphed through his boot soles, turned.

"Hello, how goes it?"

"I was so sure that the capture of an American ship would make the difference. But nothing. Nothing! What are they *doing* back there?"

"Good morning to *you* too, Cab."

The skin about the younger man's mouth pulled slightly, trying to raise a smile. "Sorry."

Stinson bent, and peered through the faceplate. The past weeks had not been kind to the judge. The cheekbones, always prominent, had become sharp blades. Exhaustion and worry had etched new lines about the serious gray eyes and firm mouth. Oddly enough the weeks of strain which had pared down the features had also made him look younger. Perhaps it was a trick of that too-pointed chin, or the unruly black forelock. But Stinson felt a surge of almost paternal affection for the smaller man.

"Shall we try again," he suggested softly.

"Three days ought to see it finished."

Stinson jerked his head at the *Apollo*. "And how's she armed?"

"Not too well. Unlike the two Russian ships our country-men fired off almost everything they had in an effort to avoid capture."

"Casualties?"

"Bad."

There was an awkward silence, then Stinson coughed and said, "I guess you heard about . . ."

"Oh, yes." Cabot turned back to his contemplation of the prize. Glanced back over his shoulder. "It doesn't matter. Really. I don't care."

"You're a poor liar, Cabot Huntington."

"You and Jenny. Why do you want me to be upset?"

"It would be the normal reaction."

"I can't afford the luxury."

Stinson fell into step with him as they started back for the airlock. "And just what does that mean?"

"I'm wrapped too tight, Stinson. If I let go I'm afraid I'll fly to pieces. Like a skinned golf ball. You ever do that when you were a child?"

"No."

"Oh." A too bright smile. "Then I guess you don't know what I'm talking about."

"I think I do. You've done a good job, Cab. Been a real tower for the rest of us."

"I feel like I'm playing dress up."

Stinson took a long jump to catch up. "Beg pardon?"

"I felt that way a lot last year on the EnerSun station. All dressed up in my shiny black robe, playing judge. Now I'm not a judge anymore, but I'm expected to play . . . Well, I don't know. A part that's alien to me. It's Joe's role, Joe's part. It's too big for me. I can't fill it."

"But you have—admirably."

The eyes were haunted as they lifted to meet Stinson's. "And that's what frightens me more than anything else."

And Stinson, watching him lope away, damned all nervy, introspective types. Too high-strung. Far too likely to burn themselves out. Maybe even fly to pieces.

Sigurd Nattestad leaned over Jenny's shoulder adding names to her master list. He was a tall, ruddy-faced Norwegian with bright gold hair, and bold blue eyes that seemed to rest with undue warmth on any attractive woman. When Cab entered the room he had his hand on Jenny's shoulder in a particularly proprietary way. Dull resentment climbed up the back of Cab's throat, but he was too tired to translate it into words. Coldly silent he crossed to the utilitarian bed, and stretched out.

"So how many are we waiting for?" She checked her notes. "From Last Hope?"

"Three children under the care of their uncle."

"And how long until they arrive?"

"Tomorrow possibly. The day after certainly."

"It worries me having so many evacuees waiting here."

"Why? It is only good sense. We are well situated. Better to use us for a clearinghouse rather than run about to each tiny outpost collecting women, and children, and men too cowardly to fight."

"You have no evidence these men are cowards." Jenny's tone was cool. "There's no heavenly mandate that says only women are good with children, and every man's a hero."

"*You* are a hero, Jennifer." He bent for a kiss, but cat-quick she was out of the chair, and beyond his reach.

Sigurd rolled an eye at Cab, shrugged when his daring raised no reaction from the silent figure on the bed.

His posterior was almost into the chair when Jenny said sharply, "Would you leave, please."

"Well!" Very stiff. "If you wish."

"I do. Oh, God, do I," she muttered under her breath as his broad back disappeared through the doorway.

Cab pummeled at a pillow, and stuffed it behind his back. "Well, in two days you'll be headed back to Iapetus, and won't have to deal with him again."

"Thank God." She sat on the edge of the bed, pulled off his boots, and began massaging his feet.

"What did bring you out?"

"This was a major pickup. Somebody had to oversee it,

and since I took charge of the evacuation, I thought it should be me. Also, I wanted to see you.''

"I wish those reasons had been reversed.''

She dropped his foot. "Don't pick at me, Cab, and read significance into a remark which doesn't deserve it. You could have come to Iapetus.''

"Too much to do. Actually this whole evacuation effort was probably unnecessary. They only hit that one rock with atomics.''

Jenny bit down hard on her lower lip. Reminded herself that he probably didn't mean it the way it sounded. Wasn't really trying to denigrate her work. Her tone was level when she answered.

"True, but there has been hand-to-hand action whenever they've landed to search for us. Better to have the children out of the way.''

"I'm having some trouble adjusting to you in this role. You never struck me as particularly child-oriented, Jenny.'' He smiled, and captured her hand. "After your actions on the station, and on Mars, I'd have thought you'd be out here leading the fight. I'm not sorry you aren't. It's dangerous, and it's a relief to me to know you're safe, but . . .''

"But what?''

"I'm selfish and I miss your help and support. And I suppose I'm hoping that this desertion doesn't mean more than you say.'' He slid her a sideways glance.

The mattress squeaked and rocked so quickly did she come off the bed. "Just what the hell are you driving at? And I don't appreciate that little crack about *desertion*!''

Cab swung his feet to the floor, hands balled in the blanket. "Then why do I get the feeling that this is a not so subtle way to tell me to get lost? That's the only thing that can explain your staying on Iapetus.''

"I'm pregnant.'' The words came out in a breathy rush, yanked from her by the stupidity and idiocy of his remark.

"This is the *first* time I've seen you since we left Evgeni's. *Seven weeks*. Seven goddamn weeks! Well, I'm not stupid. I can read the signals. I guess I was hoping that after all we'd been through together that you'd at least have the courtesy and the courage to *tell* me.''

"I'm pregnant.'' Stronger now. And there was also a strong sense of outrage that it had come out in this way. *Stupid! Stupid! Stupid!* She hadn't meant to tell him at all.

"I know I hurt you on Mars . . . WHAAAT?" He bounced off the bed.

"I'm pregnant."

Sank back onto it. "How?"

"The usual way."

"I didn't mean that. You know what I mean."

"No method of birth control is foolproof. Except abstinence."

"How long? I mean, how far along? Oh, my God, pregnant!"

"Four months."

"And you didn't tell me!"

"No."

"You didn't think I had any rights in all this?"

"And *that* is precisely why I didn't tell you," spat Jenny, "Rights? What rights? You slept with me. That's where your involvement ended."

"Jennifer, how can you say that?" He beat his chest with both hands. "This is *my* child."

"Children."

"WHAT!" The voice again rose and swooped across several octaves.

"Twins. Boys."

He collapsed in on himself, covered his face with his hands. "Oh, my God," he said in a muffled voice. Raised his head. "If none of this." A wide-sweeping gesture. "Had happened, what would you have done?"

"Gone back to Earth, had my children, gone on with life."

"Without me?"

"Why not? I managed for just a shitload of years without you."

He sprang to his feet, quivering with rage. "THAT IS NOT THE POINT! Children need a father."

"Lydia had five children by five different fathers, and never married a one of them."

"We don't do things that way."

"Ah, yes, the royal *we*, the proud and arrogant Huntington *we*. I knew if you found out I was pregnant you'd march me to the altar. Make an honest woman of me. Stake your claim on immortality." She dashed away tears with the backs of both hands. "God damn you, Cab. I wanted you to want me for me!" she cried.

"I do!"

"Then what about Amadea?"   .

"I thought that was resolved." His writhing fingers raised his hair into wild tangles. "I was an ass, I admitted it! What more do you want?"

"I wanted to know you loved me." He took an agitated turn about the room with her in close pursuit. "I wanted you to propose to me because you loved and wanted me, not because I was going to have your child."

"Oh, Jesus. And no matter what I say now you won't believe me. You'll think it's just a self-serving attempt to—"

"Why didn't you take me home with you?"

"WHAT!"

"Before we left for Mars. You never introduced me to your parents. I had been living with you for four months."

His fingers closed about her wrists. "It isn't what you're thinking. I am not ashamed of you. I didn't take you because I couldn't stand the prospect of seeing my mother pick at you. She's run down every woman I've ever been involved with. And I knew if she saw us together she would know that *this* time it was serious. And that would make it even worse. I was trying to spare you."

"How noble."

"All right. Truthfully, in January I wasn't sure. I am now."

"When did that happen? About two minutes ago?"

"My God, you can be a bitch when you want to." He flung down her hands, and she rubbed absently at her wrists where the strength of his grip had left pale bands. "Why are you even contemplating having these children if I'm such an unmitigated bastard?"

"I didn't say that." She touched her forehead as if the action could help gather her thoughts. "I thought about an abortion. Then I realized that these were our children. Part of you, and I wanted them. Then even if I never had you, I would have a piece of you. I never wanted to think that I had trapped you into a marriage you didn't want; or worse, be demoted from person and friend and be relegated to the role of wife and mother."

"I would never do that."

"I didn't know. Still don't. You're very old-fashioned."

"But not *reactionary*." She could see what it cost him to add, "I don't even mind if you stay with me now. In fact . . . I want you to stay."

"No, that's the one thing I can't do." He looked as if she'd hit him, and she hurried into an explanation. "Not because of you. I'd prefer to be here, but I have to think of more than just you or me or us. I have to consider my babies. I've committed to bear them, they deserve to be protected."

"Jenny, marry me."

"No."

A tiny inarticulate sound whistled past his clenched teeth. "You can't deny me my children just because I've been an idiot in the past. It's not fair. You know I love you. You keep harping back to that conversation we had on Mars. I was a jackass, yes. I hurt you, yes. But you're not being fair. I told you on the *Gray Goose* I had made my decision—"

Stinson erupted into the room with Sigurd hard on his heels. His too-sharp eyes darted from Cab to Jenny, and she turned away.

"What!" barked Cab.

"We've got big trouble. We've picked up the signature on *three* antimatter ships."

There was nothing conscious about the action. Suddenly Jenny found herself pressed to Cabot's side. His arm slipped about her waist.

"Are they just casting about?"

"No, they're cruising straight for us. I guess somebody didn't wipe their map."

"My God, and they've got three of us trapped like rats in a hole. Any chance to—"

Stinson was shaking his head even before Cab completed the question. "They're too close. If we bolt they'd run us down in no time. Speed's the one thing they've definitely got over us."

"Can't run," the former judge murmured to himself. "Fight or surrender?"

"We must surrender. My wife, children. All those other babies."

"So much for machismo," Jenny muttered.

Cab turned to her. Held her shoulders. Gazed deep into her eyes. "What do you want me to do?"

"Whatever is necessary."

"What have we got?" He rapped out the question to Stinson.

"Five Curvets, seven loaded pods. And one of the few places in the Belt where there really is a swarm of rocks."

Cab tugged at his lower lip, considering. "Past experience will make them skittish as hell. They'll pick a route designed to take them as far away from as many rocks as is possible." Cabot darted to the computer, and brought up a moving graphic of the Swan Cloud.

"They can't avoid them all." Stinson thrust a cigarette between his lips. Flipped it from side to side while he patted his pockets for his lighter. "Past experience also dictates that they'll send one ship in while the other stands off to give support."

"But this time they've got three, so will they stand off with one or two?"

"Who can say? But whatever the configuration we'll have to take them out."

"One Curvet or two?"

"I think one. We'll have to stay flexible. If they do hold back two ships we'll just have to regroup, and come out to help our lone hero."

Huntington glanced back over his shoulder. "It's going to be a hell of a position. Suicidal."

A shrug from Stinson. "So we draw straws."

"They're going to fight," Sigurd gobbled to Jenny.

It was a strange feeling. A tightness, a heaviness in the breast that was made up of equal parts fear and pride. She shook back her hair, chin lifting. "They're going to fight."

"It's crazy!"

Cab paused at the door, ran back, gathered her into his arms, kissed her. Deeply, passionately. A profound public display.

The door slid closed behind him and she sank into a chair, murmuring into her hands. "But, dear God, let him come back to me."

". . . crazy to fight," said Captain Pawlicki. He was a fat man whose thick neck bulged over the tight, high collar of his uniform.

Saber and Verchenko exchanged glances over the three-way link.

"Which of course means," began Verchenko.

"That they'll fight," concluded Saber. "They have to or lose at one blow three of their leaders," he explained to Pawlicki.

"Damn lucky catching that man and his children,"

hurumphed the Russian captain. Verchenko closed his eyes. He hated pompous bores who stated the obvious in an effort to impress their superiors.

The Admiral stroked at his cheeks. "I am left with the most command guided missiles."

"S-So you should s-stand off, and give us s-support," agreed Saber.

"I don't relish creeping through that nest of rocks." The folds of Pawlicki's face sagged into an expression of foreboding.

"Nobody does," snapped Saber. "But I have to close. These people are wanted by my government, and I want to s-send in my men. Huntington and McBride know me. Perhaps when they s-see it's hopeless it will help if they can s-surrender to me."

"Now you're being optimistic," murmured Verchenko. "If they have enough of those nasty little ships, they will fight. And that we can't know until we're well committed to the action."

"I keep telling you there's s-still time to run back to Moscow."

"And deprive you of my brilliant advice?"

Pawlicki looked ill at all this jocularity. He looked even less well after Verchenko ordered him on point. After he had signed off, Verchenko leaned back in his chair and eyed Saber.

"There's still time to back out."

"That's my line."

"I'm serious."

"S-So am I. I'm not ready—maybe never will be ready—to abandon my duty."

"You're a strange man, Saber."

"There you go again. S-Stealing my dialogue." He reached to disconnect.

"Go with God, Ingvar."

"Might I recommend the s-same to you."

"Oh, goody." Stinson eyed the short straw, holding it delicately between thumb and forefinger. Cab looked stricken. Stinson recovered first. Turned to a scared young woman who sat gulping at her terminal.

"You've got to keep those frequencies jammed."

"I understand, sir." Her head bobbed energetically.

"And it's going to be like riding a bronco. When they find

you on one band they'll switch to another, and you've got to
be right with them. Otherwise they're going to beat the snot
out of my friends with those C/G missiles.''

"Yes, sir. I understand." Still bobbing, she patted the top
of her console. Like a rider with a favorite mount.

"The jamming will help," piped Debbie Ultin. "But it's
kinda up to you." She popped gum, and eyed Stinson from
beneath shaggy bangs.

She was a small girl whose extreme thinness made her look
like a scrawny twelve-year-old. Actually Cab didn't know but
what she might be twelve. He hoped not.

"I've got a few tricks up my sleeve. But one of them takes
some preparation. Better get on it. Cab, if anything—"

"Don't."

"Okay." He stared down. Spent a few seconds pulling the
toe of his sticky boot off the floor. "Good luck."

"And to you." They embraced.

An elaborate thousand-mile-square video game. Seven rocks
all gamboling and tumbling along together. Another few solar
revolutions, and it would no doubt break apart. The tiny
attraction of seven pebbles offset by the giant pull of Jupiter.
Odiel, the mistress of all, enough mass to pull three of her
companions into an encircling bracelet. With one obvious
break. Directly above hung another. Numbers five and six
pointing the way sunward, resisting Odiel's attempts to pull
them into her plane.

Verchenko took up position four hundred miles out. Above
and to the right of the ships nosing cautiously into the gap. A
good position from which to offer support. Nothing to mar
his calm sense of well-being. Well, only one thing. A rock.
A very small rock. One rock to be watched with desperate
intensity. Infrared showed nothing. But that was not surprising. The mass of an asteroid would block most signatures.
There was no perfect strategy. In order to avoid the majority
of the rocks they had to nudge close to this one. A calculated
risk. Combat was full of them.

One last glance about the cramped bridge. Missile crews
huddled at their boards. Their young bodies so stiff that they
seemed likely to shatter at a touch.

Waiting.

•   •   •

It was the waiting that was the worst. He'd never intended to take part in the actual fighting. Wasn't it George the II who had been the last monarch to actually lead troops into battle? Cab gave himself a raspberry, the sound loud in the confines of the helmet.

> When kings the sword of justice first
>   lay down,
> They are no kings, though they possess
>   the crown.
> Titles are shadows, crowns are empty
>   things,
> The good of subjects is the end of
>   kings.

A little warning.

He wondered why his mind was such a lumber yard? Filled with useless bits of trivia. Courtroom practice maybe. He absorbed Shakespeare and the Bible and poetry. Always ready with the perfect quote to sway a jury.

He wished he'd never learned to pilot a Curvet. Wished he hadn't been good at it. They had never gone up against three before. The computer advanced the incoming ships, represented by white dots, in a series of tiny hops. The intruders had committed to their attack.

Red lines flowed across the screen as Debbie punched in a possible plan. Cab waited for input from Hank or Sigurd. Stinson was not linked. He had enough to worry about without taking part in war games. *Not games, real.* Nothing from the Odielites. Cab tapped in a few modifications. Another long wait while Debbie in her Curvet considered. Affirmation. They were set.

Sigurd and Hank acknowledged. But did they understand? Christ did *he* fully understand? His two previous experiences had taught him one valuable lesson—however good it looked on a computer screen it inevitably went to hell the minute you were into it.

Stay loose, maintain flexibility, keep calm.

It ran like a litany through his mind. Unfortunately it brought no sense of peace or calmness. Fear had turned his stomach to water.

The computer continued its quiet hum and tick, measuring

out the miles until . . . A furious chatter as it signaled. Optimum moment. Full burn. *Attack.*

They had to be behind some rock or rocks. What Saber hadn't expected was for three of them to pop up from behind Odiel. One blitzed right over the top almost shaving the pocked surface, two others came out from either side on an intricate skewed course that left a lot of doubt as to where they were really headed. Then a fourth appeared popping out from the asteroid which hung below and slightly ahead of the main rock.

It was rapidly becoming an extraordinarily confused picture. He swung his chair in a 360-degree arc, scanning the bridge screens, listening to the tense whispers in his headset, returned to his master screen. Seven ships and seven stones . . . and now the missiles. (*Ruined the poetry.*) The long-range C/Gs arcing in from Verchenko's flagship. The short-range heat seekers raging from his and Pawlicki's ship like angry bees.

And as he watched the intersecting lines and blips he saw their strategy. One Curvet would cut between Pawlicki and the asteroid. The second, approaching from the other direction to cut their line. The two ringers, bracketing them from top and bottom. Laying down a cloud of rocks. It left them only one safe direction for evasive maneuvers. A direction which put them directly in the path of Verchenko's missiles. Thank God they were command guided. But that computer jockey on Odiel was one hell of an operator. He was following every dodge and skip with the tenacity of a rattler. Surely the missile controllers would have the good sense to send them harmlessly into one of these damnable rocks rather than endanger the *Victory* or the *Kiev*?

A heat seeker found a target. Plowed through the fat teardrop section of the Curvet. Obviously missed anything vital for the little ship kept coming.

Of course it would keep coming no matter what, Saber thought. One of the great drawbacks of space combat. An object in motion will continue . . .

Stinson, with a barge pod hitched fore and aft, crept from the sheltering lee of his asteroid. He figured most of the attention would be focused on the dust up around Odiel. He should have a few minutes, maybe even as many as four to begin an undetected approach. Which was good because with the double load the Curvet was responding like a sea gull who'd been dropped in an oil slick.

He didn't have much hope of coming out of this. When he'd first seen that short straw he'd wanted to cry. *Musenda,* hadn't he given enough—his eye, his health—must he give his life as well? It seemed so. But he was by God going to give himself a chance. Hence the double load. Hence this cheese-brained plan. Which would instantly be transformed into something brilliant if it worked.

The computer began to sing out its warning—incoming object. He'd been given three minutes.

He had to fuck that ship. Force it to dodge, force it to run. Ruin their targeting solution. Give his friends a chance.

A *fifth* ship. Gods and little fishes. Casimir pounded on a console. He had known it, known it, known it! The thing looked like a drop of water with a barbell suspended on each end. What in the hell?

He ordered the heat seekers fired. Ignored the frantic glance from his navigator. *Do we dodge? Please, Admiral, say we dodge.* No. No by God. They needed a steady platform from which to control the command guided missiles.

Suddenly the barbell on the front revealed its purpose. It yawned open, dropped its load of rocks. A detonation, and away they flew, a merry little cloud, a rocky strainer all ready to clarify his missiles. Only one of the heat seekers survived to the other side. It was not feeling well. It locked onto God alone knew what, and wandered away.

The flagship and the rocks and the Curvet all continued on their intersect course. And he had another goddamn load hooked on behind. Perhaps it was time to . . .
DODGE!

The big Russian ship panicked. A long sustained burn from her maneuvering rockets, and she went hightailing it for the safety of the three princes which braceletted Odiel. Cab beat a fist on his thigh, for by *running* the moron had missed all their carefully laid traps.

"Failed his moral check," Debbie's high voice screeched in his ear.

"And if he manages to control his bowels, and comes back?" The words erupted in sharp pants, a symptom of fear and tension. "There's one loaded pod remaining. Go back for it."

"And you?"

"I'll—"

"SHIIIT!"

His head jerked to the screen. He was a little slower at this than the killer kid. He had to study the picture for several seconds before it fully sunk in.

The Russian by running had forced the American ship to evade through one of the rock swarms, and *directly into the path of a Curvet.*

Space became an incandescent white glare. The faceplate darkened, but a millisecond too late. *Jesus, Mary, and Joseph. He was blind!* And there were too many rocks floating around out here for anyone's health.

"I'm blind. I'M FLYING BLIND!"

But no one replied, and he wasn't flying for the Curvet had gone mad. The burst of radiation which had accompanied the destruction of the big ship had fried his instruments. Maybe fried him as well.

Don't suppose a sunscreen would have been much help. Would have to have a protection factor of ten—twenty thousand.

Dumb thought for your last thought. Wondered if it might have drawn a chuckle from Jenny.

Minutes passed. He blinked and strained, and decided that those funny green outlines might someday, if he were lucky, resolve into the instrument panel.

Without warning his radio cut back in. A voice, shrill with panic, and with an accent so thick as to be almost unintelligible cried out, "We surrender. We surrender."

It helped to steady him. Took his mind off how much radiation he'd probably absorbed. Pushed aside his worry over the swarms of rocks just waiting to slice him open. Postponed for the moment the question of how he was going to pilot his crippled craft home. Cab opened the com.

"Acknowledged. Put down on Odiel. And if you try anything so help me God we'll pound you into jelly."

"There will be no tricks. Please. . . ."

"What?"

"What did you use on the General's ship?"

Cab gaped.

"Wouldn't you like to know, asshole," squeaked Debbie. "We've got a secret weapon."

Yeah, it's so secret we don't even know what it is.

"I'm alive! I'm alive!" Stinson crowed. "Jesus God, I'm alive!"

He fell back in his chair. Watched the rapidly receding ship. They were running the fuck away!

And he hadn't even used the second pod. Awesome, that's what it was, just awesome.

And he had been right. His plan hadn't been cheese-brained; it had been fucking brilliant.

A gentle touch to the shoulder. He looked up, and the young ensign stepped back. Casimir touched his fingertips lightly to his wet lashes. The silence continued, and finally the baby-faced boy managed to waver, "Orders, sir?"

"Just get us the hell away from here."

"Sir."

"Yes?"

"What happened, sir?"

"A stupid, senseless, useless series of events culminating in an equally senseless death."

He fell silent, stared down at his beautifully manicured hands. Watched the long fingers tighten into claws. Hoped that the colonists cut off Pawlicki's balls. But of course that was a foolish wish. Pawlicki had no balls. A funny little sound out of the ensign. The Admiral looked up, a small, weary smile curving his lips.

"And you still don't understand, do you? My guess, Avramovich, is that a random and very lucky rock, or perhaps that small ship, managed to violate the integrity of the magnetic bottle containing the antimatter. It only takes a very tiny break. I would submit that better shielding is in order—" his voice broke, and he plunged out of the command chair.

Stumbled for his quarters. Paused in the narrow corridor. Howled aloud.

"GOD DAMN YOU ALL!"

Realized he meant it less for the colonists than he did for certain parties sitting smugly, safely on Earth.

Chapter Nineteen

"Ah, Mr. President." Purple shadows ringed the Russian Premier's deep-set eyes, and the wan smile seemed to hold more weariness than greeting.

"Mr. Premier." Long fidgeted, fingers running nervously across the edge of his desk like a man playing scales. "I don't suppose you've—"

"Heard anything? No nothing."

They regarded each other. The two most powerful men in the world. Unease, confusion, and helplessness seemed to radiate through the comlink.

"What the devil do you think is going on out there?"

"I don't know."

"Wish I had never been pushed into this! I should have backed off the minute those Kenyans were—" Long broke off, realizing it was perhaps not politic to reveal his doubts to Yuri Tupolev.

"I am becoming positively superstitious about the System." The tight little smile flickered briefly across the heavy-jowled face. "I wonder if there is something about that canned air they breathe or the water they drink, or perhaps it is cosmic rays? Something that makes these people so difficult."

"This silence," broke in the President, finding nothing amusing in the Russian's remark. "What can they be doing?"

"I have a feeling that sooner or later we are going to find out. I also have an equally strong feeling that we may not like it much."

•   •   •

"... is not by any to be enterprised, nor taken in hand, unadvisedly, lightly, or wantonly, to satisfy men's carnal lusts and appetites, like brute beasts that have no understanding; but reverently, discreetly, advisedly, soberly, and in the fear of God: duly considering the causes for which Matrimony was ordained.

"First. It was ordained for the procreation of children . . ."

Well, we got that part right.

Jenny glanced to Cab's solemn profile. He looked ragged, having lost great handfuls of hair from the blast of radiation which had atomized Saber and the *Victory*. Fortunately he and Debbie had been on the outer edge of that spreading wave. No serious or permanent damage had been done on either the surface or the cell level. P.J. had not been so lucky. Cassie was making every effort, but in all likelihood he would not live. His fingers were icy bands about hers. Could he possibly be nervous? Oddly enough she wasn't.

Odiel was seething like a disturbed hive. People rushing out to take possession of the Kiev. *A woman's keening cry; Sigurd's wife discovering her loss. Stinson capering and babbling, "I'm alive! I'm alive" Finally spotting Cab fending off the hugs and pats of well wishers. Hair plastered flat with sweat, eyes haunted with death. Coming into her arms.*

And for the second time in their relationship his tears dampened her shoulder. There was again blood on his hands. This time for the most honorable of reasons. But was he capable of making that distinction? If he couldn't, the guilt might consume him. So he needed her, had reached for her. The hard, cold knot that had taken up residence in the center of her breast softened under the onslaught of his tears. Like little Kay in the Snow Queen a sliver of ice had pierced her breast, and like Kay it was the tears of a lover which melted it.

"Wilt thou, Cabot, have this woman to thy wedded wife, to live together after God's ordinance in the holy estate of Matrimony? Wilt thou love her, comfort her, honor and keep her in sickness and in health; and forsaking all others keep thee only unto her, so long as ye both shall live?"

"I will."

No fan-vaulted ceiling arching overhead, bouquets of flowers, white tie and tails, veils and lace. Just this cramped room, the gamey odor of too many people who had a minimum amount of water at their disposal. No family—

For which you should be eternally grateful, Cabot my man. Not to mention thanking God every day for the rest of your life that she finally agreed.

But, oh God, Cecilia was going to have kittens. So probably better to let his mother have kittens after the fact rather than spoiling this moment. For she would have been neither supportive nor approving.

It was traditional and proper for captains to perform marriages, but was it also proper for them to read the Anglican service? He wondered what Verchenko made of the elaborate language. Most marriages in the Soviet Union were solemnized in a civil ceremony.

Jenny's voice, sweet and firm. "I will."

Andy punctuating his heavy breaths with a sniffle.

Strange to have Andy as his best man. He had many closer friends on Earth, and failing that he would have wished to have Joe. But Joe was again remaining behind.

It's in your hands now, Cabot. Yours and Jenny's and Verchenko's and young Belmanor's.

That endless thirteen-hour meeting. It began with suspicion, and accusations and recriminations. Only the quiet serenity of Doctor Nanak Singh combined with judicious use of his bull-like roar kept order, and carried the meeting past those first bitter hours.

Verchenko and Belmanor had called for the meeting. Belmanor, pale and grim, reading Saber's letter to prove it was no trick. Cab wanted to avoid any involvement. It did no good to tell himself that it hadn't been his fault that the Victory had blown. Just a tragic, ironic accident. Easier to kill people you didn't know. He had known Saber. Even been jealous of him. Because the General had admired Jenny, and she had responded.

On Odiel Jenny had been warm, loving, comforting. Then had come the call for a parley. Nanak had offered neutral Iapetus for the meeting. And once back on the Saturnian moon Jenny had slipped away.

It had been Dita. Brusque, abrasive Dita whom he didn't even like who had offered him advice. And it was a measure of his misery that he actually listened.

"Stop talking about your rights, and interests, and stop acting like a tight-assed hero in a Victorian novel. Show her

a little passion, a little anguish. Tell her that you love her and need her, and that the baby . . . babies are secondary to her!"

"I, Jennifer, take thee, Cabot, to my wedded husband, to have and to hold from this day forward, for better for worse, for richer for poorer, in sickness and in health, to love and cherish till death us do part, according to God's holy ordinance; and thereto I give thee my troth."

It's in your hands down, Jennifer. Yours and Cabot's and Verchenko's and young Belmanor's.

She had said some things to Joe of which she was now ashamed.

"Jennifer, you're being an unbelievable witch. Why won't you marry Cab?"

"In the first place that's none of your damn business, and in the second place, how dare you!"

"Because I'm old enough to say precisely what I think, and get away with it. Jenny, the next few weeks are going to be critical. Starting with tomorrow's meeting. This senseless war must be stopped." And Joe then made the remark about it being in her hands.

"It wouldn't be on us if you hadn't fallen apart!" she accused. The brown eyes remained locked on hers. *"Besides, he doesn't love me. He screwed around with Amadea, and only now, when I'm carrying his children, does he suddenly want to marry me."*

"Cabot loves you, Jenny. And needs you. He's hurting, and because you've got him so balled up in your own private soap opera he can't function. I don't care whether you marry him or not. It's an old-fashioned institution." He looked gray and suddenly very old. *"But don't run so hard in the other direction that you end up alone."* He gave himself a shake. *"He's the vital element, Jenny. He's going to need your strength. At least be kind."*

Verchenko glanced to Andy who with portly grace bowed, and stepped forward with the rings. Beautiful rings ordered and made on Ceres. They represented Cab's hope, but at the time of their fashioning that was all that he had. No certainty for she still hadn't agreed. The star stone blazed as it lay upon the open pages of the prayer book. Cab had had to borrow money from Joe to pay for it. His own accounts Earthside were frozen. The clean circle of the gold wedding band, and finally a guard formed of two tiny clasped hands. Very romantic. Very old-fashioned. She hadn't balked at it.

The discussion had at last centered on the essential; ultimately Earth could not win. But how much death and devastation would it take to prove that simple fact? Was there some way to avoid it all?

Yes, the obvious one. The soldiers refuse to fight. Responsibility set ahead of duty. Without the seven remaining antimatter ships Earth could not carry her war into the outer System. They might hold near Earth, but a stand-off was no solution. Someone had to open the dialogue with Earth. Go there. Run the gauntlet of the orbiting military platforms.

Verchenko had suggested using the remaining nukes to drive home their point. Cab had refused vehemently. Peace obtained by threat was no peace at all. Reason and example had to prevail. History didn't give him a lot of confidence in their power. Still, they had to try.

Who was to go? They were all exhausted after so many hours of intense debate. Running on coffee and nerves. He had sat slumped in his chair, slowly become aware of the eyes settling upon him. Jerked up, the negative hard on his tongue.

"It has to be you, Cabot." Joe sucked his pipe back to life.

He searched for support, found none. Evgeni nodding solemnly. Andy grim, but agreeing. Stinson. Jenny, suddenly raising from her chair and walking to him. Placing her hands firmly on his shoulders.

"You're the only one with the stature and the contacts to bridge the gap between Earth and System. Respected by birth and position on Earth, respected by actions out here."

"Don't ask this of me. I'm too tired. And I can't do it alone."

He watched her breast rise slowly as she drew in a deep breath. "You won't have to. I'll be with you."

Now they were three days out from Earth. Ready to open the dialogue. Their answer might be a flight of missiles.

"Jennifer, we're almost home. It may end in either death or prison. I'd like to face either of those alternatives with you at my side."

"I'm there."

"Not completely."

He had shown her the rings.

For the first time since the ceremony had begun she seemed

nervous. Her hand trembled as he placed the rings on her fourth finger. Held them there.

"With this ring I thee wed, with my body I thee worship, and with all my worldly goods I thee endow: In the Name of the Father, and of the Son, and of the Holy Ghost. Amen."

They were talking. News services interrupted regular programming. Broadcasters speculated in fruity, portentous tones. People grumbled, and slipped on discs of more interesting events. And who could blame them? The destruction of the EnerSun station and the *Victory* was shocking, horrible, but shock fades, and fear is a difficult emotion to maintain. Fighting in the Belt? It was an unreal concept to most of Earth's population. It was so far away.

Some people understood the terrible stakes that were being played. President Carmella Alvalena Rodriquez, sitting tensely in her office in Managua, prayed for a peaceful resolution. Nicaragua was a player—albeit a minor one—in the Earth to System trade. So it mattered on a national level. It also mattered on a personal one. Joe Reichart was her brother-in-law. Amparo might be thirty years in the grave, but the relationship held. So she sat, and wondered at his absence. Thinking she perhaps knew the reason. Hoping he would someday recover.

Neville Huntington prowled the confines of his senate office. The next few hours would be very critical to his future. Cabot was taking an awful risk, but such a ballsy act could make him a hero. Which could make him a threat, but Neville believed that Cab truly lacked political ambition. So being the uncle of a hero might rub off.

On the other hand he might end up a common felon, and then Neville could just kiss it all good-bye. Presidency, Senate, everything. He remembered Meredith declaring after listening to Cabot's ultimatum to the U.S. government—Three, four months ago? Had it really been so long?—"He should have been drowned at birth, or at least not be permitted to breed."

Cecilia had been furious. But who was receiving the brunt of that anger was the next question. Meredith for daring to criticize her son? Or Cabot for turning out to be an idealist? She had no patience with fuzzy-headed dreamers. Power, the acquisition of, and subsequent exercise thereof, was her consuming passion. It was certain that poor old Gerard was coming in for some pretty heavy going as they too sat and waited.

Gerard sat watching his wife's energetic perambulations about the sitting room of their English mansion. The muted voice of a news anchor provided a rumbling background for her complaints.

"We should have stayed in Washington."

"There was no way of knowing how long this thing was going to last. No one could have foreseen the fortuitous destruction of the *Victory*."

"Fortuitous? Fortuitous!"

"Unfortunate choice of words." A quick mumble.

"I should say it was!"

The head lifting in an act of unprecedented bravery. "Cecilia, just whose side are you on, anyway?"

"How dare you!"

The quick hunch and droop of the stooped shoulders.

"You've got no ships in the field—"

"Oh, please," murmured Verchenko at the mixed metaphor. Cab shot him an angry glance.

Jenny shushed the Russian, leaning in to whisper. "You've had your say, let Cab do the summation."

"We've," a broad gesture to include Verchenko and Belmanor. "All recognized the senselessness of this fight. I'm pointing out to you that without ships you can't reach us. You can neither punish us for this challenge to your authority, nor indeed even maintain that authority. Only the consent of the colonists made that possible, and you've lost that consent and loyalty. Whether it can ever be regained is problematical, and not something for me to worry about. All I want is for the fighting to stop.

"Finally—and although I've tried hard to avoid even a hint of threat this has to be addressed—if you keep pushing, the System will retaliate, and the destruction groundside will be unimaginable. We fought because you sent an invasion force against us, but we also fought to teach you the reality of the System/Earth relationship. Which, very simply, is *that you can't win*."

"So what is it you want—"

"Richie! You can't! You can't negotiate . . . I won't permit—"

"LIS, JUST SHUT THE FUCK—" The President slammed down the hold button, cutting off sound to both the Kremlin and the *Kiev*.

Tupolev tugged at his upper lip. "Do you suppose our gentle President is about to shut that bitch up once and for all?" He smirked at Cabot. "I've always thought that women on the highest levels is a recipe for disaster. Everything is placed on the personal level. While we men—"

"Mr. Premier, I'm not about to become your 'chum,' so you can spare yourself the effort. I've had my problems with Lis Varllis. I've also had my problems with *you*."

Long was back. "Justice Huntington—"

"Mister."

"Beg pardon?"

"Mister, not Justice. I've been impeached and removed from the bench, remember? I no longer have the right to that title."

"Oh . . . ah." He cleared his throat, and tried again. "What is it you want?"

"An end to the fighting. We've said that. Repeatedly."

"And I agree." Long threw out the familiar smile, but it had lost much of its glitter. "And I presume that the Premier concurred?"

"Absolutely. We were only offering support in the face of a dangerous crisis. And though some of the results of this unfortunate misunderstanding may have been regrettable, I think we have set one laudable precedent. Our two great nations have worked in concert for a common cause."

Verchenko's brows climbed for his hairline, and he scribbled a note to Cab.

Now what do you suppose the old badger is up to?

A shrug, and a tiny shake of the head. Cab quickly returned his attention to the com for Long was speaking. "Funny how you find yourself immersed in these . . . situations. All of us fighting, and not knowing for what or why."

Jenny stiffened. "Forgive me, Mr. President, but *we* knew."

"Ah . . . yes. Well." Another clearing of the throat. "If we all concur I suggest we formalize our agreement."

"Mr. President," said Cab. "I'm not a diplomat. I would rather leave the actual language of any agreement to the experts drawn from both Earth and the System. I frankly want to go home. But I will suggest that merely agreeing to suspend hostilities is not enough. Some fundamental decisions must be reached concerning the relationship of Earth and System."

"Aaaah, yes, you people in the Belt did declare independence."

"Yes." Cab's tone matched the President's for arid flatness.

"Well, I'm confident that all these matters can be resolved in the proper forum."

Tupolev's forefinger shot into the air. "We would naturally expect to be included in any negotiations, Mr. President. We too have stations, and bases and settlements within the System. In fact many nations have such holdings, though they are small compared with the U.S. presence. So I propose that we hold these talks under the auspices of the United Nations."

Long's eyes focused on some distant picture. "An excellent suggestion, Mr. Premier."

"A final point." The Soviet leader's gaze leveled on his admiral. "When can I expect you in Moscow, Casimir Dimitriov Verchenko?"

"Wellll, I can't exactly say, Comrade Yuri Tupolev. You see, I've accepted an invitation to visit with Justice . . . ah Cabot and Jennifer. Look for me sometime in the spring . . . oh, but I had planned on Paris in May—"

Cab laid a restraining hand on Verchenko's arm, casting him a reproachful glance.

"Huntington."

"Yes, Mr. President?"

"I assume you'll represent the System at these talks?"

"No, Mr. President. I expect each community will decide upon their own spokesperson. My power, such as it was, extended only to the resolution of this conflict. You've agreed to that. My involvement is at an end."

"Huntington—"

"Mr. President, our press secretary, Andy Throckmorton, has finished drafting an official statement for the press, and is preparing to release it."

That was all it took. The bifurcated screen wavered, and went blank. All of them—Cab, Jenny, Verchenko, Andy, and Belmanor—exchanged glances.

"Well." Andy heaved his bulk out of the chair. "I wouldn't want to make a liar out of you. Better go release this piece of journalistic brilliance."

"And I want to get back to the *Intrepid*. Hard to believe it's all over."

Throckmorton and Belmanor left.

Cab groped for Jenny's hand, and gripped it hard.

"Pick a feeling," she said softly.

"Let down. So much senseless suffering and death and loss, and it's all summed up in a minute as an 'unfortunate misunderstanding.' " He analyzed it for a moment, then gave a confused shake of the head. "After a bit more reflection I suppose I'd have to add anger to my collection of feelings. And you? Pick your feeling?"

"Frightened and upset."

"Why?"

"Because I'm not sure we learned anything. Oh, some of us opted for intelligence and sanity, but so much of what's occurred over the past months had its roots in fear and violence and pride, and this damnable need that people have to control other people. And I don't know if those can ever be rooted from the human spirit."

"Jennifer, now you're make *me* upset and afraid," wailed Verchenko. "We've *won*! Let's be happy. Let us drink champagne and celebrate."

"So you don't think it's over?" Cab asked, ignoring the Russian.

"Of course it's not over. Life's not a novel or a vid play. *Hey, we won. Hooray for our side! Now everything's going to be wonderful.* Life goes on. Problems continue, or metamorphosize, and new ones crop up."

He took a tighter grip on her hand. "So what do you say to us just living our own life?"

"Fine. But as Andy pointed out the world has an uncouth habit of intruding on people's gardens."

"That may be, but I for one am taking myself firmly *off* center stage, and back to my garden, and if anyone . . ." He struggled for a moment, then gave up, and uttered the profanity. "Fucks with me, I'm going to brain them with a hoe."

Jenny leaned in, and touched his lips with hers. "That's lovely, dear, just so long as I get to handle the shovel and bury them."

Chapter Twenty ─────────

Ice storms and snowstorms had transformed the chestnut trees lining the palace boulevard into fantastic crystal shapes. Another terrible winter, but the citizens of Versailles were enduring with stoicism, and even some enjoyment. Their little village, eleven miles southwest of Paris, was once again the site of a great international congress. As for the snow? Well, it could be forgiven for it lacked only three days until Christmas.

Cab and Jenny, heartily sick of the palace where they had endured so many hours of unrelieved talk, gave it wide berth, and went strolling through the Trianon Park. Their boots crunching in the snow, they stepped from the borders of the forest, and came upon Marie-Antoinette's tiny bucolic village. Thatched roof houses, looking almost sleepy beneath their load of snow, ringed the central pond and nestled at the feet of giant trees. Cab brushed the snow from a flat-topped boulder, and eased Jenny onto this rustic seat. She was at the end of her seventh month, and the pregnancy was making itself felt. The sable coat, a wedding gift from Gerard and Cecilia, fell open revealing the great swell of her belly.

"Comfortable?"

She sighed, and pressed a hand to the small of her back, then seeing his worried frown gave a quick smile. "Perfectly. Now go do something entertaining."

"Like what?"

"I don't know. Build me a snowman, make snow angels, pelt me with snowballs—God knows I'm as big as a house.

Remind me never to have twins again," she added after a brief pause.

He gathered up one mittened hand. "Do you mind so much?"

"Of course not, don't be stupid." She tenderly brushed back his falling forelock. "I'm just sick of meetings and speeches and motions and votes. And let me tell you those eighteenth-century reproduction chairs are hell on a pregnant woman."

"You could go back to California."

"And leave you here to face boredom alone? Not a chance."

"I should never have gotten sucked into this!" he exploded. "The whole thing is a damn media extravaganza, the biggest piece of jiggery-pokery imaginable. Nobody's interested in discussing the real problems which exist between Earth and System. They're all too busy cutting deals, and giving press conferences, and talking about the brotherhood of man, and the sisterhood of woman, and about how we're all Earthmen together." He drew in a sharp breath. "And on top of all that I have to put up with Lucius Renfrew babbling about Christ knows what. But since he's a delegate I have to be polite when all I really want to do is to punch him in the nose—"

She caught one flailing hand. "So it's probably a good thing I'm staying to keep you from an assault and battery charge."

He rubbed at her cold-reddened cheek with the back of his hand. "And I promised I wouldn't start in on this, and here I am boring you senseless."

"Not senseless, just to the yawning stage." He jammed his hands into the pockets of his heavy overcoat, and stamped a pattern in the snow. His brows were pulled down in a ferocious frown. "There's obviously something else sticking in your craw so go ahead and say it."

"You won't get mad?"

"I won't get mad."

"Well, it's some of the System people. I'm getting a little tired of Tad Bevel agitating to be made king of the world, or at least of space. Official spokesperson for the System, indeed! He's a power-hungry, money-grubbing little monster and—"

"Don't you think we need an official representative?"

He paced away and back again. "I don't know. We obviously need a dialogue, open communication to Earth, but no one person can speak for the entire System. It's too diverse, the distances are too vast, and the interests of each community are too varied. *Blah, blah, blah!*'' He suddenly broke into a run, went skittering down the incline to the pond, and sliding out across the ice.

''You better hope the ice is more than an inch thick,'' called Jenny, laughter filling her voice. ''Because I'm damned if I'm going to fish you out of a hole.''

''Why not?'' he yelled as he took another long skid. ''You've been pulling me out of holes for the past year and a half.'' The word ended on an oscillating note as he lost his footing and went sprawling.

Jenny supported herself with a hand, and laughed until the tears came. Cabot inspected the tear in the knee of his trousers, then fell back on his elbows, and added his laughter to hers.

''Home please,'' she called, holding out her arms to him.

''Don't I wish.''

''Must you be so literal? All right, hotel then.''

Cab dusted the powdery snow from his camel-hair coat. ''Cold?''

''No, Junior One is kicking me in the bladder again.''

They had almost reached the edge of the park when Jenny said suddenly, ''Speaking of the System.''

''Were we? Must we?''

She cuffed him lightly. ''Rumor has it that Joe is on Earth.''

''That's a hell of a rumor. Where did you hear it?''

''From the Nicaraguan delegate.''

He scratched his nose. ''Hmmm, then it just might be true.''

''I hope it is. I need to know that Joe is going to be all right.''

The first thing they saw upon entering their bedroom suite at the Tianon Palace hotel was Neville seriously considering a dusty bottle of wine.

''Oh, dear God!''

Jenny choked back a laugh, and Neville frowned.

''Hardly polite, Cabot.''

''I'm not feeling terribly polite.'' Cab stepped into the room. ''Dear Lord, did you bring the entire menagerie?'' he asked as his gaze fell upon Meredith slouched in an armchair, Anthony inspecting the room-service menu, and Cecilia sitting with military erectness on a fragile settee.

"There are important matters to be discussed," his mother replied tartly.

"You couldn't have used the com?"

Neville's blue eyes slid about the room finally coming to rest on the bottle in his hands.

"There are reasons for being present at this time."

"Which implies that something important or at least imagined to be important is about to occur. Wonder why we've heard nothing of it?" he asked of Jenny.

"Possibly because you have no political sense," came Cecilia's tart reply. "You don't build up a network, and so are isolated from the real action."

One slim brow arched miscroscopically. "Oh, you mean there *is* something occurring here other than a great deal of sound and fury signifying absolutely nothing?"

"Did Gerard . . . come?" Jenny broke in, sensing that Cabot really was working himself into a rage.

Her formidable mother-in-law pinned her with a glance. "Yes." A dismissive gesture but whether meant for her or for Gerard Jenny couldn't tell. "He's off and about somewhere."

The cork slipped free with a muted *pop.* "But to get down to business." Neville gestured inquiringly with the bottle. Cab nodded curtly. "Sentiment on the Hill is not conducive to an overturning of your removal. It sets a dangerous precedent, and it also reflects badly on the integrity of the Congress and the President."

"I would say with some justification," said Jenny icily.

Neville ignored her, handed Cab a brimming wine glass. "On the other hand the President is fully conscious of the great service you rendered both your country and the world, and he wants to see you rewarded."

"Neville, I've frankly had my fill of political rewards."

Cecilia's hand slapped the coffee table. "Stop being so damned pure, and hear us out!"

"On the President's instructions Michele Abramson has felt out various delegates of both Earth and System, and everything is in place to have you named as the Minister for Earth/System Affairs. It's an overarching position—"

"No."

"I beg your pardon?" Cecilia enunciated in frigid accents.

"It's a damn patronage position. A sop, a way to pay me off, and shut me up—"

"And just what do you propose to do otherwise?" his mother flared.

"Go back into private practice."

Anthony spoke up. "It's not so easy to rebuild a lucrative practice after almost two years away. And you have a certain notoriety. The kind of clients you represented don't care for notoriety."

"Actually." Jenny lifted the glass from Cabot's nerveless fingers, and took a small sip. "Cab and I are thinking of relocating in the System. Probably on Mars."

"WHAT!" It was a chorus.

"You can't."

"You have a duty."

"To your country."

"Your world."

"The family."

Cab's eyes were glittering dangerously in his thin face, but his tone was quiet when he said, "So many high-sounding words to cover your real meaning." He leveled a gray-eyed stare on Neville. "Your only interest is in the Presidency, and how I can be useful in that pursuit. Meredith collects family achievement the way some men collect coins. Anthony, I've never figured out what your interest is in all this Huntington hoopla. Just echoing the rest of the crowd? And as for you, Mother—" He sucked in a sharp breath. "It's taken me forty years to understand your game. Like most converts you've had to out-Huntington the Huntingtons, but it goes deeper than that. You've been playing tug of war with Father using me as the rope. I had to be *your* child, and every time I rejected the path that had been so obligingly laid our for me by all of my managing relatives, you, Mother, saw it as some kind of win for Father. Well, I'm sick of it! *Sick of it!* SICK OF IT!"

"Are you quite finished?"

"Yes!" The explosiveness of his reply seemed to shatter her icy delivery, and everyone tensed, waiting for the fight to begin again.

Neville stepped in quickly. "All right, Cabot, even assuming that all this frankly rather sickening display of armchair psychology is correct . . . so what? Does it obviate the fact that the world will always need men and women of integrity to, yes—as old-fashioned as it sounds—do their duty?''

"Someone has got to bridge the gap between Earth and System," began Meredith in his best lecture-hall manner.

Jenny cut across the elegant periods like a saw. "And he *did*. He stopped a goddamn war! And now we want to get on with our lives, so just leave us the hell alone!''

"Jennifer, go to bed," ordered Cecilia.

The younger woman stiffened with outrage. "I am *not* a child to be ordered off to—"

Cab gently took her by the arm, drew her into the bedroom. "Jenny, it's all right."

She dashed away tears. This damn pregnancy had her on a razor's edge emotionally. "No, it's not. They'll pick at you and pick at you."

"I think I'm strong enough to take it."

"I want to be there. For you."

"You always have been, you always will be."

"But—"

"Jenny, forgive me, but this really is my decision." The quiet seriousness of his tone drew a sniff from her. "There's a good girl. You have some dinner and relax. I'll be in to you later."

The door closed softly behind him, and the tears came. Running down her cheeks in hot streams. Arms wrapped tightly about herself she rocked in agony. Because she didn't trust him, and she hated herself for that lack of trust.

A shower of sparks swallowed by the black waters of the Seine. Cab fished another cigarette from the pack, and lit it with hands that trembled from cold and nerves. The harsh smoke seemed to explode somewhere in the back of his throat. With the cigarette dangling slackly from his lower lip he brought up his watch, and squinted down at the luminous numbers. *2:45*. In a little over six hours the conference would be called back into session.

Minister for Earth/System Affairs.

Revolving slowly he propped his elbows on the snow-covered balustrade of the Pont Alexandre III, and gazed back at the Eiffel Tower. The snow swirled in brilliantly lit clouds about its lacy pinnacle.

He took two more deep agitated pulls at the cigarette, and flipped it over the edge. Watched its trail. Brightness falling from the air. Watched it die.

A darker shadow among the shadows swept by beneath him. A pleasure boat running only on the current. In the stern a single light silhouetting the figure which stood looking back along his journey.

Lydia: *"Any man who can admit he's made a mistake, and try to correct it is worth a second chance."*

Amadea: *"As is always the case with great movers and shakers, they move and shake, and the rest of us wait on their pleasure."*

Tomas: *"Get the job done."*

Himself: *"With luck I'll never devolve all the way back to running for public office."*

Trying to remain aloof from all sides, and in the end being manipulated by all.

There sits a judge that no king can corrupt.

He shook out the last cigarette, thrust it between his lips, guarded the lighter's flame against the sudden howl of wind spinning off the river.

Minister for Earth/System Affairs.

But if I take this position I'll lose the respect I've fought so hard to gain.

Neville: *"You are a unique individual, Cabot, worthy of command."*

I can't, I find the power too alluring.

Anthony: *Such sentiments do you credit, but it's vital for both Earth and System that there be a spokesman.*

But no one person can speak for all.

Meredith: *Someone must set themselves above the cacophony of competing voices.*

The greatest good for the greatest number. But I've always had a nagging sense of guilt over the few. Is it really just for the few to suffer? Is the well-being of the many enough of a comfort?

Cecilia: *You can lead wisely and well.*

I demonstrated that in the Belt.

Neville: *The position will be created.*

Created by the Earthside powers. How much say had the System really had in its creation?

Cecilia: *If not you then some other man will hold it.*

Anthony: *A man perhaps not as uniquely placed to understand all sides.*

Meredith: *If you abnegate responsibility who will protect your colonists?*

Neville: *Tupolev and Long would love to see you refuse. Then having made the gesture toward you they can fill the position with one of their own.*

NO.

Mirrors. And crystal glittering brighter than their own reflections. And Cab a reflection in glass, a creature of ice and crystal.

Tad Bevel, looking peevish, gripping the edge of the podium. It must have been hard after all his politicking to find the nod going to Cab. Nonetheless his speech up till now had been gracious.

"The creation of this position represents the very real interest that the Earth has in resolving her differences with her colonies. And we welcome it. We also pray that never again in the history of mankind will the home world be threatened by her own children. God grant to the man who will fill this august position the wisdom of Solomon, the patience of Job, the strength of David. He will need them all in the coming years."

Huntington let his eyes slide away from Bevel's bitter gaze. Scanned the room noting the sour expressions on the faces of the Earth delegates. *Not very politic, Tad, to remind them of their subjugation by the System.*

Lucius Renfrew rose and spoke with his usual dentist-drill intensity.

"We welcome the creation of this first extra-national position. Our recent difficulties with the System have taught us that national boundaries are mere lines on a map. They should not exist within the hearts and minds of people. Think what we've done! After ten thousand years of useless warfare, both among ourselves and against the planet which nurtured us, we have created a global mandate. We have a man who will speak for us all as *Earthmen.* It is time that we set aside regional, racial, national, and cultural differences. To form one world, one race, one nation, if you will, of humankind."

The speech was receiving sage nods in some sections of the room, frowns and murmurs from others. The African and

Asian delegates with their ethnic pride were none too happy with this tack. One glorious world, but what was to be the color of that world? They feared it might be white. Who could blame them? Look how quickly Wairegi wa Thondu had been forgotten in the rush of events.

In the roped-off spectators' gallery Jenny sat rigid and white-faced beside Cab's father. She and Joe had debated a world government one night on Ceres while he had sat by sated and drowsy with good brandy and a fine meal. While Jenny had leaned toward the concept of a world without race and class differences, Joe had taken a different tack. The industrialist had pointed out the mischief which only a national bureaucracy had created. Begged her to imagine the potential for a bureaucracy on a global scale.

Now Cab in his leadership of the Belt resistance had demonstrated the power of the System. What was to stop the System, working solo or with the entrenched powers groundside, from forcing just such a world government?

But if the man at the top were honorable?

Dedicated to justice. Willing to guide, not coerce. Huntington looked back at Lucius Renfrew's white, intense face. A dangerous lunatic? *But he believes in his brand of ethics as fervently as I believe in mine.* Dangerous for him to lead, but not me?

Cab had a strange sense of not truly being present. His body occupied a desk, went through the motions, but his soul was floating somewhere off over his left shoulder. Watching, disconnected, uninvolved. Michele Abramson had taken the podium, and was halfway through the motion creating the position of Minister for Earth/System Affairs.

The Secretary General of the United Nations, a thin, austere Chinese woman, called the roll. The votes flashing over comlinks to be tallied by computer.

There were a few nays. Primarily from Africa and Asia, and two from the System. Ceres and the Reichart station went on record as opposed. Mars abstained, being badly split between the Jared Colony and the various state-supported settlements.

Now Abramsom, with a tight little smile, was once more on his feet. "I would now like to propose a candidate to fill this newly created position. A man who at great personal risk to himself brought a message of peace to the Earth. A man who bridges the gap between Earth and System. A man whose family has served both their nation and the world." A gracious nod to Cecilia and Neville seated at the far end of the great hall. "I am proud to nominate Cabot Huntington for the position of Minister for Earth/System affairs."

"Seconded," cried Tad Bevel, and Cab wondered what price to buy him.

Again the roll call. The flash of pain as again Ceres and Reichart voted against him. The Secretary General raised her gavel, but at the apex of its arc Cab rose to his feet. His image seemed to be reflecting back at him from a thousand directions. He watched the dream Cab walk to the podium. A rush of sound as a hundred voices sighed and tensed.

"Ladies and gentlemen, while I'm deeply appreciative of the honor you have done me this day . . . I must decline."

Abramsom, jaw drooping ludicrously, the dumbfounded expression quickly replaced by one of naked fury. A lilting cry of joy from Jenny. Then a cacophony of sound as the hall erupted into frenzied conversation.

He forced his way through the milling delegates, the banging of Xing Tao's gavel forming a counterpoint to his thundering heartbeats. Tiny, powerful hands closed about his lapels holding him in place.

His mother's face staring furiously up into his. "WHY! WHY?"

"How could you?" Neville's demand following hard on the heels of Cecilia's bitter cry.

"I was going to do it, but . . ." His eyes roamed blindly about the room searching for the ghost Cab. "I couldn't. I guess I have learned . . ." He kissed his mother on the forehead, then gently set her aside. The press boiled about him shrieking their questions. A tentative touch on the sleeve. He whirled, and grasped his father by the forearm.

"I'm proud of you."

Tears pricked at Cab's eyelids. He tried to speak, couldn't, settled for a desperate embrace. He reached the War Drawing Room. Looked briefly up at the marble relief of Louis XIV as an equestrian figure triumphing over his enemies. Felt a tangled surge of emotion. Then with a sigh released the last tiny flicker of regret. Walked to Jenny waiting silent and proud at the head of the stairs. Their eyes met in a long glance.

• • •

The snow fell silently onto the already buried garden. A Rachmaninoff concerto wept sound across the darkened room. Cabot, seated, twisted his wedding band about his finger. Jenny frozen by the window. They had been silent for a long time.

The knock brought them up and around, facing the door like wary deer.

"Who is it?"

"Joe."

"JOE!"

They tumbled to the door, threw it open, Jenny's arms clasping the older man about the neck to the imminent danger of the champagne bottle and three glasses which he held in either hand.

"We didn't know you were on Earth."

"Well, we heard but we didn't know."

"Why didn't you tell us?"

Reichart slid a glance at Cabot, that strange, secret half smile hovering about his lips. "Didn't want to put any pressure on you. I figured you had quite enough to cope with."

Joe arranged the bottle and glasses on the table, and settled himself into a chair.

"We're not going to crack that extremely expensive bottle of bubbly?" asked Jenny.

"Not just yet." Joe paused for the ritual of pipe filling. Once the old briar was burning to his satisfaction he grinned at the couple, and asked, "So what now?"

"We're thinking about settling on Mars. There are a few things to arrange, naturally. Selling the house and furniture." Cab sighed. "Which really hurts, but . . ."

"We don't feel precisely comfortable here. The only people speaking to us are our respective fathers."

"Oh, don't worry about Neville. He'll somehow twist your refusal around until it's an aid to his presidential aspirations. Your mother will immerse herself in his pursuit of that high office. And the others will follow their lead."

"We're still settling on Mars."

"And doing what, Cabot?"

"Practicing law."

"I think you should remain a judge."

"That's nice, but the Congress of the United States didn't agree." Irritation clipped off the ends of his words.

A silence fell over the room. Joe wreathed himself in smoke, and Cab played nervously with Jenny's fingers. The creak of the chair as Reichart shifted his weight was loud in the leaden quiet.

"Did you know I'm worth somewhere in the vicinity of seven billion dollars?"

Jenny chuckled. "That's of course fascinating, but isn't it rather a non sequitur?"

"Not at all. You're contemplating what to do with your lives, and I'm contemplating what to do with my money. Which since I've spent most of my life accumulating it can double for my life."

Cab eyed the older man dubiously. "You've got that look. The one you get when you're about to spring something unpleasant or outrageous on me."

"Now, Cab, would I do that?"

"Yes." And he frowned when Jenny and Reichart laughed.

"No, no, I promise you this isn't anything nasty. Crack-brained maybe, but not nasty." He again fell silent.

"Out with it, Joe," demanded Jenny.

He sucked in a slow breath, and began. "Would you consider me completely mad if I suggested that sooner or later, probably sooner, we are going to see a world government?"

"No, I'd have to agree with you."

Joe was on his feet and pacing. "For more than forty years I've pursued a dream of a just and free society dedicated to the fundamental liberties, and a free market. I thought we'd won a major battle in the Belt, but now we seem likely to lose the war. It's strange, governments are able to endure any amount of vice and corruption on the part of their citizens, but there is one thing they can't abide, and that's to be ignored. People who ask merely to be left alone are viewed as the most dangerous radicals."

"So what are you suggesting?"

"Let's put our money where our mouths are. We have a decently reliable antimatter drive. There's no reason in the world why we can't launch a colony ship. Let's see if we can create a society based on Jeffersonian tenets of freedom and individual liberty."

"But it might take years to find a suitable world."

"Centuries," amended Jenny.

"But with the time dilation factor it won't seem so long to us. Months of voyaging will translate into years in real time, but it will still be only months for us. No need for a generation ship, the worry of having our children grow up within the confines of a ship."

"Stellar maps from the Big Eye telescope in the Belt have shown substantial evidence of planetary systems," Cab said slowly.

Jenny laid a hand over her belly. "Oh, God. This is scary."

"The game's not big enough if it doesn't scare you." Joe lifted her hand, and held it to his chest.

"We'd have to design an entire society."

"Need judges for that."

Cab gave him a shaky smile. "Are we the first people you've approached about this?"

"I have to confess, no. You were balled up with this dog and pony show, and I didn't want to barge in until things were resolved. I've spoken to Verchenko, he's offered to captain for us."

"Modest of him," laughed Jenny.

"Yes, but we couldn't hope for a better one."

"And you would finance this?"

"Yes."

Gray eyes met green, held for a long searching moment. Cab finally gave a crooked grin, and asked, "Want to be hearty pioneers on Alpha Centauri?"

"A year ago that was my line."

"Have we switched? Are you now going to take my position? That our children will be raised on Earth?"

"Stupid. Of course not."

Joe grinned, and opened the champagne. Golden liquid fountained over his hands, and Jenny pressed her lips to the rim of the bottle. Came up laughing, her face drenched. Cab grabbed the glasses, and Joe dashed liquid into each.

"To the *Lydia*. Long may she fly."

Huntington sobered. "They'll try to stop us. They'll say that an undertaking of this magnitude shouldn't be left in the hands of private individuals. That there must be state control."

Jenny slipped an arm through his. "Then they're doomed to disappointment. Nothing can stop us."

"So, a toast . . . to us," proposed Joe.

"To the future," offered Jenny.

Cab walked to the window, considered the million million suns burning beyond the snow-filled sky. Turned back, and raised his glass.

"To freedom."

SCIENCE FICTION AT ITS BEST!

____ **THE CAT WHO WALKS THROUGH WALLS**
Robert A. Heinlein   0-425-09932-8 — $3.95

____ **TITAN**
John Varley   0-441-81304-6 — $3.95

____ **DUNE**
Frank Herbert   0-441-17266-0 — $4.50

____ **HERETICS OF DUNE**
Frank Herbert   0-425-08732-8 — $4.50

____ **GODS OF RIVERWORLD**
Philip José Farmer   0-425-09170-8 — $3.50

____ **THE MAN IN THE HIGH CASTLE**
Philip K. Dick   0-425-10143-6 — $2.95

____ **HELLICONIA SUMMER**
Brian W. Aldiss   0-425-08650-X — $3.95

____ **THE GREEN PEARL**
Jack Vance   0-441-30316-1 — $3.95

____ **DOLPHIN ISLAND**
Arthur C. Clarke   0-441-15220-1 — $2.95

Please send the titles I've checked above. Mail orders to:

BERKLEY PUBLISHING GROUP
390 Murray Hill Pkwy., Dept. B
East Rutherford, NJ 07073

NAME_____

ADDRESS_____

CITY_____

STATE_____ZIP_____

Please allow 6 weeks for delivery.
Prices are subject to change without notice.

POSTAGE & HANDLING:
$1.00 for one book, $.25 for each additional. Do not exceed $3.50.

BOOK TOTAL	$_____
SHIPPING & HANDLING	$_____
APPLICABLE SALES TAX (CA, NJ, NY, PA)	$_____
TOTAL AMOUNT DUE	$_____

PAYABLE IN US FUNDS.
(No cash orders accepted.)

THE NEW SHARED WORLD ANTHOLOGY!

THE FLEET

EDITED BY DAVID DRAKE AND BILL FAWCETT

Featuring a who's who of science fiction, including
Poul Anderson, Piers Anthony, Gary Gygax, Anne McCaffrey,
Margaret Weis, and an unprecedented host of others, the Fleet is
military science fiction at its best. Join the Fleet as they take on
the Khalians—vicious carnivores who take no prisoners. Ever.

THE FLEET—*Pledged to protect us all,
they're mankind's last line of defense.*

AND BE SURE TO LOOK FOR THE NEXT
ADVENTURE OF THE FLEET, COUNTERATTACK,
AVAILABLE IN DECEMBER!

_____ 0-441-24086-0/$3.50   THE FLEET
David Drake and Bill Fawcett, eds.

MORE SCIENCE FICTION ADVENTURE!

AWARD-WINNING
Science Fiction!

The following works are winners of the prestigious Nebula or Hugo Award for excellence in Science Fiction. A must for lovers of good science fiction everywhere!

☐ 0-441-77422-9	**SOLDIER ASK NOT,** Gordon R. Dickson	$3.95
☐ 0-441-47812-3	**THE LEFT HAND OF DARKNESS,** Ursula K. Le Guin	$3.95
☐ 0-441-16708-3	**THE DREAM MASTER,** Roger Zelazny	$2.95
☐ 0-441-56959-5	**NEUROMANCER,** William Gibson	$2.95
☐ 0-441-23777-0	**THE FINAL ENCYCLOPEDIA,** Gordon R. Dickson	$4.95
☐ 0-441-06797-2	**BLOOD MUSIC,** Greg Bear	$2.95
☐ 0-441-79034-8	**STRANGER IN A STRANGE LAND,** Robert A. Heinlein	$3.95

Please send the titles I've checked above. Mail orders to:

BERKLEY PUBLISHING GROUP
390 Murray Hill Pkwy., Dept. B
East Rutherford, NJ 07073

POSTAGE & HANDLING:
$1.00 for one book, $.25 for each additional. Do not exceed $3.50.

NAME _____

ADDRESS _____

CITY _____

STATE _____ ZIP _____

Please allow 6 weeks for delivery.
Prices are subject to change without notice.

BOOK TOTAL	$_____
SHIPPING & HANDLING	$_____
APPLICABLE SALES TAX (CA, NJ, NY, PA)	$_____
TOTAL AMOUNT DUE	$_____

PAYABLE IN US FUNDS.
(No cash orders accepted.)